WHEN YOU GIVE A ROGUE A *Rebel*

JANE ASHFORD

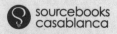

sourcebooks
casablanca

Published by Sourcebooks Casablanca, an imprint of Sourcebooks
P.O. Box 4410, Naperville, Illinois 60567-4410
(630) 961-3900
sourcebooks.com

The Repentant Rebel was originally published in 1984 in the United States
of America by Signet, an imprint of New American Library, Inc.

Meddlesome Miranda was originally published in 1988 in the United States
of America by Signet, an imprint of New American Library, Inc.

Printed and bound in Canada.
MBP 10 9 8 7 6 5 4 3 2 1

Praise for Jane Ashford

"Filled with wit and charm...highly recommend."
—*Fresh Fiction* for *Nothing Like a Duke*

"Absolutely delightful...a must-read."
—*Night Owl Reviews* for *Brave New Earl*

"This was such a great book...humor, drama, mystery, romance, intrigue, and a surprising ending."
—*Harlequin Junkie* Top Pick for *How to Cross a Marquess*

"Sweet and incredibly refined, this is a historical romance that proves second chances at love are always possible."
—*The Romance Reviews* for *Once Again a Bride*

"A story that lets the reader sigh with pleasure at the end."
—*Long and Short Reviews* for *Nothing Like a Duke*

"Jane Ashford's characters are true to their times, yet they radiate the freshness of today."
—*Historical Novel Review* for *Once Again a Bride*

"Complex characters, subtle romance, and all the sparkling wit and flirtatious banter of a Georgette Heyer novel."
—*Publishers Weekly* for *A Duke Too Far*

"A refreshingly different, sweetly romantic love story [readers] will long remember."
—*Booklist* for *Brave New Earl*

Also by Jane Ashford

THE DUKE'S SONS
Heir to the Duke
What the Duke Doesn't Know
Lord Sebastian's Secret
Nothing Like a Duke
The Duke Knows Best
A Favor for the Prince

THE WAY TO A LORD'S HEART
Brave New Earl
A Lord Apart
How to Cross a Marquess
A Duke Too Far
Earl's Well That Ends Well

Once Again a Bride
Man of Honour
The Three Graces
The Marriage Wager
The Bride Insists
The Bargain
The Marchington Scandal
The Headstrong Ward
Married to a Perfect Stranger
Charmed and Dangerous
A Radical Arrangement
First Season / Bride to Be
Rivals of Fortune / The Impetuous Heiress
Last Gentleman Standing
Earl to the Rescue
The Reluctant Rake

CONTENTS

The Repentant Rebel   1

Meddlesome Miranda   193

THE REPENTANT REBEL

ONE

DIANA GRESHAM HUGGED THE THIN COTTON OF HER NIGHT-dress to her chest and snuggled deeper into the pillows of the posting-house bed. She had never been so happy in her life, she told herself, and today was just the beginning of a glorious future. This afternoon, she and Gerald would reach Gretna Green and be married, and then no one could part them or spoil their wonderful plans—not even her father.

Of course, Papa was unlikely to protest *now*. Diana's lovely face clouded as she considered the terrible step she had been forced to by her father's harshness. If he had only *listened* this once, it wouldn't have been necessary to defy him. But almost eighteen years as Mr. Gresham's sole companion had repeatedly—and painfully—defeated any such hopes. Papa was implacable; he had never shown the least interest in her ideas or opinions, except to condemn them. Diana felt only a small admixture of guilt in her relief at having escaped her rigid, penurious home.

A tap on the door made her expression lighten. Sitting up and smiling expectantly, she called, "Come in." The panels swung back to reveal first a loaded tray, then an extremely handsome young man.

"*Voilà*," he said, returning her smile possessively. "Tea. And hot toast." He swept a napkin from the tray to display it. "I play servant to you."

Diana clapped her hands. "Thank you! I am so hungry."

"The unaccustomed exertions of the night, no doubt," he replied, placing the tray across her knees and resting a hand on her half-bare shoulder.

Diana flushed fiery red and gazed fixedly at the white teapot. She would get used to such frankness concerning the somewhat discomfiting intimacies of marriage, she thought. Her first experience last night had not been at all like the stolen kisses she and Gerald had exchanged in the weeks since they met. Yet Gerald had obviously seen nothing wrong, so Diana dismissed her reaction as naïveté. She knew she was less sophisticated than other girls, even those not yet eighteen. Because her father had never allowed her to attend any party or assembly, nor meet any of the young men who visited her friends' families, Diana was deeply humble about her ignorance, while passionately eager to be rid of it. Until Gerald's miraculous appearance during one of her solitary country walks—an event she still could not help but compare to the illustration of the Archangel Michael in her Bible—she had never spoken to a man of her own age. That her sole opportunity should bring a veritable pink of the ton (a term Gerald had taught her) had been overwhelming. From the first, she had joyfully referred every question to him, and taken his answers as gospel.

Diana raised her eyes, found her promised husband gazing appreciatively at her scantily clad form, and promptly lowered them again.

For his part, Gerald Carshin was congratulating himself on his astuteness. He had been hanging out for a rich wife for nearly ten years, and his golden youth was beginning, however slightly, to tarnish. Even he saw that. His sunny hair remained thick—automatically he touched its fashionable perfection—and his blue eyes had lost none of their dancing charm, but he had started to notice alarming signs of thickness in his slim waist and a hint of sag in his smooth cheeks. At thirty, it was high time he wed, and he had cleverly unearthed an absolute peach of an heiress in the nick of time.

Carshin's eyes passed admiringly over Diana's slender rounded form, which was more revealed than hidden by the thin nightdress and coverlet. Her curves were his now; he breathed a little faster thinking of last night. And her face was equally exquisite. Like him, she was blond, but her hair was a deep rich gold, almost bronze, and her eyes were the color of aged sherry, with glints of the same gold in their depths. She wasn't the least fashionable, of course. Her tartar of a father had never allowed her to crop her hair or buy modish gowns. Yet the waves of shining curls that fell nearly to Diana's waist convinced Gerald that there was some substance in the old man's strictures. It had taken his breath away last night when Diana had unpinned her fusty knot and shaken her hair loose.

"Your tea is getting cold," Carshin said indulgently. "I thought you were hungry."

Self-consciously Diana began to eat. She had never breakfasted with a man sitting on her bed—or, indeed, in bed at all until today. But of course, having Gerald there was wonderful, she told herself quickly. Everything about her life would be different and splendid now. "Are they getting the carriage ready?" she asked, needing to break the charged silence. "I can dress in a minute."

"There's no hurry." His hand smoothed her fall of hair, then moved to cup a breast and fondle it. "We needn't leave at once." But as he bent to kiss Diana's bare neck, he felt her stiffen. She won't really relax till the knot's tied, he thought, drawing back. A pity she's so young. "Still, when you've finished your tea, you should get up," he added.

Diana nodded, relieved, yet puzzled by her hesitant reaction to Gerald's touch. This was the happiest day of her life, she repeated to herself.

Gerald moved to an armchair by the window. "Once we're married, we'll go straight to London. The season will be starting soon, and I...*we* must find a suitable house and furnish it." Gerald pictured himself set up in his own house, giving card parties and taking a box at the opera. How the ton would stare! He would finally have his revenge on the damned high sticklers who cut him.

"Oh, yes," agreed Diana, her breakfast forgotten. "I can hardly wait to see all the fashionable people and go to balls."

Gerald scrutinized her, the visions he had conjured up altering slightly. Diana would, of necessity, accompany him. "We must get you some clothes first, and do something about your hair." She put a stricken hand to it. "It's lovely, but not quite the thing, you know."

"No." Diana looked worried. "You will tell me how I should go on, and what I am to wear, won't you?"

"Naturally." Gerald seemed to expand in the chair. "We shall be all the crack, you and I. Everyone will invite us."

Diana sighed with pleasure at the thought. All her life she had longed for gaiety and crowds of chattering friends rather than the bleak, dingy walls of her father's house. Now, because of Gerald, she would have them.

"You must write at once to your trustees and tell them you are married," he added, still lost in a happy dream. "We shall have to draw quite a large sum to get settled in town."

"My trustees?" Diana's brown eyes grew puzzled.

"Yes. You told me their names, but I've forgotten. The banker and the solicitor in charge of your mother's fortune—yours, I should say, now. You come into it when you marry, remember."

"Not unless I am of age," she corrected him.

Gerald went very still. "What?"

"Papa made her put that in. Mr. Merton at the bank told me so. Mama would have left me her money outright, but Papa insisted upon conditions. It is just like him. The money was to be mine when I married, unless I should do so before I came of age. Otherwise, I must wait until I am five-and-twenty. Isn't that infamous?"

Carshin's pale face had gone ashen. "But you are not eighteen for…"

"Four months," she finished. Sensing his consternation, she added, "Is something wrong?"

His expression was intent, but he was not looking at her. "We must simply wait to be married," he murmured. "We cannot go to

London, of course. We shall have to live very quietly in the country, and—"

"Wait!" Diana was aghast. "Gerald, you promised me we should be married at once. Indeed, I never could have"—she choked on the word "eloped"—"left home otherwise."

Meeting her eyes, Gerald saw unshakable determination, and the collapse of all his careful plans. One thing his rather unconventional life had taught him was to read others' intentions. Diana would not be swayed by argument, however logical.

Why had she withheld this crucial piece of information? he wondered. This was all her fault. In fact, she had neatly trapped him into compromising her. But if she thought that the proprieties weighed with him, she was mistaken. The chit deserved whatever she got.

He looked up, and met her worried gaze. The naked appeal in her dark eyes stopped the flood of recrimination on his tongue, but it did not change his mind. Hunching a shoulder defensively, he rose. "I should see about the horses. You had better get dressed."

"Yes, I will," replied Diana eagerly, relief making her weak. "I won't be a minute."

Gerald nodded curtly, and went out.

But when Diana descended the narrow stair a half hour later, her small valise in her hand, there was no sign of Gerald Carshin. There were only a truculent innkeeper proffering a bill, two sniggering postboys, and a round-eyed chambermaid wiping her hands in her apron.

Diana refused to believe Gerald was gone. Even when it was pointed out that a horse was missing from the stable, along with the gentleman's valise from the hired chaise, Diana shook her head stubbornly. She sat down in the private parlor to await Gerald's return, concentrating all her faculties on appearing unconcerned. But as the minutes ticked past, her certainty slowly ebbed, and after a while she was trembling under the realization that she had been abandoned far from her home.

Papa had been right. He had said that Gerald wanted nothing but her money. She had thought that his willingness to marry her at seventeen proved otherwise, but she saw now that this wasn't so. Gerald had simply not understood. Hadn't she *told* him all the terms of her mother's will? She thought she had, but her memory of their early meetings was blurred by a romantically golden haze.

It hardly mattered now, in any case. Gerald was gone, and she must think what to do. With shaking fingers Diana opened her reticule and counted the money she had managed to scrape together. Four pounds and seven shillings. It would never be enough to pay the postboys and the inn. She could give them what she had, but where would she go afterward, penniless?

Tears started then, for her present plight and for the ruin of all her hopes and plans. Diana put her face in her hands and sobbed.

It was thus that the innkeeper found her sometime later. He strode into the parlor with an impatient frown, but it faded when he saw Diana's misery. "Here, now," he said, "don't take on so." His words had no discernible effect, and he began to look uneasy. "Wait here a moment until I fetch my wife," he added, backing quickly to the door. Diana paid no heed. She scarcely heard.

A short time later a small plump woman bustled into the room and stood before Diana with her hands on her hips. Her husband peered around the door, but the older woman motioned brusquely for him to shut it, leaving them alone. "Now, miss," she said then, "crying will do you no good, though I can't say as I blame you for it. An elopement, was it?"

Diana cried harder.

The woman nodded. "And your young man has changed his mind seemingly. Well, you've made a bad mistake, no denying that."

Still, the only response was sobs.

"Have you any money at all?"

Diana struggled to control herself. She must make an effort to honor her obligations, however she felt. "F-four pounds," she managed finally, holding out the reticule.

The innkeeper's wife took it and examined the contents. "Tch. The blackguard! He might have left you something more."

"He only cared about getting *my* money," murmured Diana brokenly.

The other's eyes sharpened. "Indeed? Well, miss, my advice is to put him right out of your mind. He's no good."

Diana gazed at the carpet.

"You should go back to your family," added the woman. "They'll stand by you and help scotch the scandal. You haven't been away so very long, I wager."

Diana shuddered at the thought of her father. She couldn't go back to face his contempt. Yet where else could she go?

"Tom and me could advance you some money. Not for a private chaise, mind, but for the stage. You could send it back when you're home again."

"W-would you?" She was amazed.

Something in the girl's tear-drenched brown eyes made the landlady reach out and pat her shoulder. "You'll be all right once you're among your own people again," she said. "But you'd best get ready. The stage comes at ten."

In an unthinking daze, Diana paid the postboys and dismissed them, gathered her meager luggage, and mounted the stage when it arrived. A young man sitting opposite tried to get up a conversation, but Diana didn't even hear him. Her mind was spinning with the events of the past few days. As the miles went by, she recounted them again and again. Why had she not seen Gerald's true colors sooner? Why had she allowed him to cajole her into an elopement? What was to become of her now? She was surely ruined forever through her own foolishness. How could she look anyone in the eye again after what she had done?

Wrapped in these gloomy reflections, Diana was oblivious

until the stage set her down at an inn near her home in Yorkshire. And once there, she stood outside the inn's door, her small valise beside her, afraid to reveal her presence.

"Yes, miss, may I help you?" asked a voice, and the innkeeper appeared in the doorway.

Diana tried to speak, and failed.

"Did you want dinner?" he added impatiently. She could hear sounds from the taproom beyond. "Are you waiting for someone to fetch you? Will you come in?"

"No," she answered, her voice very low. "I...I am all right. Thank you." She would walk home, she decided. The house was four miles away, but all other alternatives seemed worse.

"Wait a moment. Aren't you the Gresham girl?" The man came out to survey her, and Diana flinched. "I've seen you with your father. They managed to get word to you, then, did they? There was some talk that Mrs. Samuels didn't know where you'd gone."

Diana frowned. Mrs. Samuels was their housekeeper. What did she have to do with anything?

"You'll just be in time for the funeral. It's tomorrow morning. Was you wanting a gig to take you home?"

"Funeral?" she echoed, her lips stiff.

"Well, yes, miss. Your father..." Suddenly the innkeeper clapped a hand to his mouth. "You ain't been told! My tongue's run away with me, as usual. Beg your pardon, miss, I'm sure."

"But what has happened? Is my father...?"

The man shook his head. "Passed away late yesterday, miss. And I'm that sorry to tell you. I reckon Mrs. Samuels meant to do it face to face."

"But how?" Diana was dazed by this new disaster.

"Carried off by an apoplexy, they say. A rare temper, Mr. Gresham had...er, that is, I've heard folk say so."

He had died of rage at her flight, thought Diana. Not only had she ruined herself, she had killed her father. With a small moan, she sank to the earth in a heap.

The furor that followed did not reach her. Diana was bundled into a gig like a parcel and escorted home by a chambermaid and an ostler. Delivered to Mrs. Samuels and somewhat revived with hot tea, Diana merely stared.

Finally Mrs. Samuels said, "I told them you had gone to visit friends."

Diana choked, then replied, "But you knew… I left the note."

"I burned it."

"Why?"

"It was none of their affair, prying busybodies."

The girl gazed at the spare, austere figure of the only mother she had ever known. Her own mother had died when Diana was two, but she had never felt that Mrs. Samuels cared for her. She did not even know her first name. "You lied to protect me?"

The housekeeper's face did not soften, and she continued to stare straight ahead. "'Twas none of their affair," she repeated. "I don't hold with gossip."

"So no one knows where I went?"

Mrs. Samuels shook her head. "No one asked, save the doctor. The neighbors haven't taken the trouble to call."

And why should they? Diana's father had had nothing but harsh words for them during his life. Part of the burden lifted from her soul. She still felt ashamed, but at least her shame was private.

"Are you home to stay?" asked Mrs. Samuels, her expression stony.

"I…yes."

"And will you be wanting me to remain?"

Diana stared at her, mystified. The woman had saved her, yet she seemed as devoid of warmth and emotion as ever. If she felt nothing, why had she bothered? What was she thinking? "Of course."

Mrs. Samuels nodded and turned away. "Mr. Gresham is in the front parlor. The funeral is at eleven tomorrow." She left the room with Diana's valise.

Diana hesitated, biting her lower lip. She walked slowly to the closed door of the front parlor, stepped back, then forward. She could not imagine her father dead; his presence had always pervaded this house. Her whole life had been turned upside down in a matter of days, and she was far from assimilating the change. She could not even imagine what it would be like now. Slowly her hand reached out and grasped the doorknob. She took a deep breath and opened the door.

TWO

On the day after her twenty-fifth birthday, Diana Gresham followed a second coffin to the churchyard. Mrs. Samuels had been ill all that winter, and, late in February, she died, leaving Diana wholly alone. Diana had nursed the old housekeeper faithfully, and she tried to feel some sadness as she stood beside her grave and listened to the rector intone the ritual words, but she could not muster much emotion. She and Mrs. Samuels had never been true companions. The closeness that Diana had imagined might come from their shared adversity had never emerged. Indeed, the older woman had merely become more dour and reclusive as the years passed, and Diana had felt increasingly isolated.

When the rector and the few mourners were ready to depart after the brief service, Diana resisted their urgings to come away and wrapped her black cloak more closely around her shoulders as the sexton and his helpers began to fill in the grave. It was a dreary morning, with low gray clouds and a damp bitter chill. Warm weather earlier in the week had turned the winter earth to mud, but there was as yet no hint of green to reconcile one to the dirt. The moors rolling away beyond the stone church were bleak. Yet Diana did not move even when the wind made her cloak billow out around her, bringing the cold to her skin. She did not want to return to her family house, whose cramped rooms were unchanged since her father's death.

For some time, Diana had been feeling restless and dissatisfied. The shocked immobility that had followed her disastrous rebellion seven years before had modulated through remorse and self-loathing into withdrawal, contemplation, and finally, understanding. She had forgiven her younger self a long while ago. Her faults had been great, but they sprang from warmth of feeling and lack of family love rather than weakness. Her mistakes had been almost inevitable, given her naïveté and susceptibility.

But with greater wisdom had also come a loss of the eager openness that younger Diana had possessed. The habit of solitude had become strong; Diana seldom exchanged more than a few sentences with her scattered neighbors. I am like Mrs. Samuels myself now, she thought, gazing over the moors. I have no friends.

Her restlessness reached a kind of irritated crescendo, and she felt she must do something dramatic, or else she would scream. But she did not know what to do. Some change was inevitable. Even had she not been inexpressibly weary of living alone, she could not remain completely solitary. Yet she had no family to take her in. Mr. Merton, the banker, had called yesterday to congratulate her and solemnly explain that she was now in full possession of her fortune. She was a wealthy woman. But she felt resourceless. Money was useless, she realized, if one did not know what to do with it.

Shivering as the wind whipped her cloak again, Diana felt she must come to some conclusion before she returned to the house. If she did not, some part of her suggested, she would slip back into her routine of isolation and never break free. She would indeed become a Mrs. Samuels, reluctant to venture beyond her own front door.

I must leave here, she thought, looking from the small churchyard to the narrow village street with its facing rows of stone cottages. All was brown and gray and black; there was no color anywhere. She had never learned to love the harsh landscapes of Yorkshire, a failing, no doubt. But where could she go?

Diana felt a sudden sharp longing for laughter and the sounds of a room full of people. Wistfully she remembered her short time at school. Her father had kept her there less than a year, concluding that she was being corrupted by association with fifty empty-headed girls. Diana recalled their chatter and jokes as part of the happiest time in her life. If only she could return to that time! But her new financial independence would not give her this, however pleasant it might be.

Briefly she was filled with bitterness. It seemed a cruel joke that she should get her fortune now, when events had rendered her incapable of enjoying it. She could buy a different house, hire a companion, enliven her wardrobe, but she could not regain her old lightheartedness or her girlhood friends. If only her father had been kinder, or Gerald... But with this thought, Diana shook her head. She could not honestly blame them for her present plight. Her father had been harsh and distant; Gerald had treated her shamefully. But she herself had repulsed the world in her first remorseful reaction, for no reason that the world could see. Naturally, those she rejected had withdrawn, and it seemed to her now that she had been foolish in this as well as in her rash elopement.

Gathering her cloak, Diana turned and walked through the churchyard gate and along the street toward home. Her father's house, hers now, was beyond the edge of the village, surrounded by high stone walls. As she approached it, Diana walked more slowly, a horror of retreating behind those barriers again growing in her. Was she fated to spoil her life? Had some dark destiny hovered over her birth?

"Diana. Diana Gresham," called a high, light voice behind her. "Wait, Diana!"

She turned. A small slender woman in a gray cloak and a modish hat was waving from a carriage in the center of the village. Her face was in shadow, and Diana did not recognize her as she got out and hurried forward.

"Oh, lud," the newcomer gasped as she came up. "This wind takes my breath away. And I had forgotten the dreadful cold here. But how fortunate to meet you, Diana! Cynthia Addison said you had left Yorkshire, and so I might not even have called! Are you back for a visit, as we are?"

When the woman spoke, Diana recognized Amanda Trent, a friend she had not seen for eight years. Amanda, two years older, had married young and followed her soldier husband to Spain. They had exchanged one or two letters at the beginning, but Amanda was an unreliable correspondent, and Diana had ceased to write after her elopement, as she had ceased to see acquaintances like Cynthia Addison, who could not be blamed for thinking her gone. "Hello, Amanda," she answered, the commonplace words feeling odd on her tongue.

Amanda peered up into her face, sensing some strangeness. She looked just the same, Diana thought—tiny and brunette, with huge, almost black, eyes. Those eyes had been the downfall of a number of young men before Captain Trent won her hand. "Diana?" Amanda said, a question in her voice.

Making a great effort, Diana replied, "I am not visiting. I never left. After Papa died…" She didn't finish her sentence because the story seemed far too complicated to review; none of the important things could be told. And she didn't want pity.

Amanda held out both hands. "Yes, they told me about Mr. Gresham. I am sorry, of course, though…" She shrugged. Long ago, Diana had confided some of her trials.

Awkwardly Diana took her hands. Amanda squeezed her fingers and smiled. "Come back with me, and we shall have a cozy talk. I want to hear everything!"

Diana wondered what she would say if she did. Amanda seemed the same gay creature she had been at nineteen; Diana felt ancient beside her. Yet the chance to put off going home was irresistible, and shortly they were sitting side by side in Amanda's carriage riding toward her parents' house a few miles from the village.

"George is invalided out," Amanda told her. "He never recovered properly from the fever he took after Toulouse, so we decided to come here for a good long visit. I am so happy to be in England again! You cannot imagine how inconvenient it sometimes was in Spain, Diana."

Thinking that "inconvenient" was an odd characterization of the Peninsular War, Diana watched her old friend's face. Now that they were closer, she could see small signs of age and strain there. Amanda was no less pretty, but it was obvious now that she was nearly a decade past nineteen. Her friend's chatter seemed less carefree, more forced. Diana felt relieved; it had been daunting to think that only she was altered. "You have been in Spain all this time?"

"Oh, lud, no! That I *could* not have borne. I spent two seasons in London, and I was here for the summer a year ago. I am sorry I did not call, Diana, but I was...ill." She turned her head away. "Here we are. Mama will be so pleased to see you."

Wondering uneasily if this was true, Diana followed Amanda into the house. Mrs. Durham was one of the acquaintances she had ceased to see years ago.

As it happened, none of the family was at home. George Trent was riding with Amanda's father, and Mrs. Durham had gone to visit an ailing tenant rather than share Amanda's drive. The two women settled in the drawing room with a pot of tea and a plate of the spice cakes Diana remembered from childhood visits.

"Are you still in mourning?" asked Amanda then, her expression adding what politeness made her suppress. Diana's clothes and hair were even more unfashionable than before her father's death.

Diana put a hand to the great knot of deep golden hair at the back of her neck as she explained about Mrs. Samuels. Amanda's dark cropped ringlets and elegant blue morning gown brought back concerns she hadn't felt for years. The black dress she wore was the last she had bought, for her father's mourning.

Amanda looked puzzled. "But, Diana, what have you been

doing all this time? Did you have a London season? Or at least go to York for the winter assemblies?" When Diana shook her head, she opened her eyes very wide. "Do you mean you have just stayed here? But *why*?"

It must indeed seem eccentric, Diana thought, and she could not give her only plausible reason. Her neighbors had probably judged her mad.

Amanda was gazing at her with an unremembered shrewdness. "Is something wrong, Diana? You…you seem different. You were always the first to talk of getting away."

Miserably Diana prepared to rise. She could not explain, and Amanda would no doubt take that inability for coldness. Their long-ago friendship was dead.

But Amanda had lapsed into meditative silence. "I suppose we are all changed," she added. "It has been quite a time, after all. What else could we expect?"

Surprised, Diana said nothing, and in the next moment their tête-à-tête was interrupted by the entrance of Amanda's family.

The Durhams were familiar, though Diana had not seen them recently, and their greetings were more cordial than she had expected. They did not mention her strange behavior or seem to see anything odd in her sudden visit to their house. But as they spoke, Diana gradually received the impression that they were too preoccupied with more personal concerns to think of her.

One cause, at least, was obvious. Diana had never seen a greater alteration in a person than in George Trent, Amanda's husband. She remembered him as a smiling blond giant, looking fully able to toss his tiny bride high in the air and catch her again without the least strain. Now, after seven years in the Peninsula, he retained only his height. His once-muscular frame was painfully thin; his bright hair and ruddy complexion were dulled, and he wore a black patch over one blue eye. Diana's presence appeared to startle and displease him, though he said nothing, merely retreating to the other side of the room and pretending interest in an album that lay on a table. His family watched him anxiously but covertly.

"George," said Amanda finally, when his conduct was becoming rude, "you remember Diana Gresham. She was at our wedding, and I have spoken to you of her."

George was very still for a moment. Then he turned, squaring his shoulders as if to face an ordeal. "Miss Gresham," he said, bowing his head slightly.

"Doesn't George look dashing and romantic?" Amanda continued, her tone rather high and brittle. "I tell him he is positively piratical and he must take care not to set too many hearts aflutter, or I shall be dreadfully jealous. Don't I, George?"

"Me and everyone else," he replied, and strode abruptly out of the room.

Amanda made a small sound, and when Diana turned she saw that her old friend's eyes were filled with tears. She felt sharp pity and feared that she intruded.

"It was only a tiny wound," said Amanda shakily. "But they could not save his eye. And then he took the fever as well. I had hoped that being home again would be good for George, but he doesn't seem to want to recover."

"You've been here only a week, Amanda," answered Mr. Durham. "Give him time."

"Yes, darling." Amanda's mother looked as if she might cry too. "I'm sure it is very hard for him, but he will come round."

Diana rose. "Perhaps I should take my leave."

The Durhams exchanged a glance.

"Please don't," cried Amanda. Then, realizing that she had spoken too fervently, added, "I beg your pardon. Why should you wish to stay, after all? It is just that I have been so…" She broke off and dropped her head in her hands.

Diana moved without thinking to sit beside her friend and put an arm around her shoulders. "Of course I will stay if you wish it. I feared I was prying into private matters."

"George does not allow it to be private." Amanda's voice was muffled. "I am selfish to keep you, Diana. It was just so splendid to see someone from the old days." She raised her head. "The things we remember of each other are so…simple."

It was true, Diana thought, and the idea appealed to her as much as it did Amanda. Whatever worries each might have, between them there was nothing but pleasant recollections. Here was an opportunity to end her loneliness without explanations or the great effort of finding and cultivating new acquaintances. At long last, fate seemed to be coming to her aid. "I should like to stay," she said. "I should like it very much."

Amanda met her eyes, and for a moment they gazed at each another as two women, a little buffeted by the world and sadder and wiser than the girls they had been when they last met. A flash of wordless communication passed between them. Then Amanda smiled and clasped her hands. "I'm so glad. We will have another cup of tea and talk of all our old friends. Do you know what has become of Sophie Jenkins?"

Returning her smile, Diana shook her head.

"She married an earl!"

"But she wished to become a missionary!"

"So she always *said*," replied Amanda. "But when she got to London, she threw that idea to the winds and pursued a title until she snared one. They say her husband is a complete dunce."

Diana couldn't help but laugh, and Amanda's mischievous grin soon turned to trilling laughter as well. They both went on a bit longer than the joke warranted, savoring the sensation.

"I hope you will stay to dinner, Diana," said Mrs. Durham then. "I know you are alone now."

Diana had nearly forgotten the older couple. Turning quickly, she saw encouraging smiles on both their faces. "I should like that. Thank you." Did they really want her?

"That's right!" Amanda's dark eyes widened as she thought of something. "Diana! You must come and stay here. You cannot live alone, and I should adore having you. Wouldn't we, Mama?"

"Of course."

Mrs. Durham did not sound as enthusiastic as her daughter. But neither did she seem insincere. Suddenly the idea was very attractive. Diana would not have to go back to that dreary house for a while; she could put off the decision about what to do. Yet the habit of years was strong. "I don't know…" she began.

"You must come," urged Amanda. "We shall have such fun." Tension was in her voice, and Diana could not resist her plea. She nodded, and Amanda embraced her exuberantly.

"For a few days," murmured Diana, her eyes on the Durhams.

But the older couple was watching their daughter with pleased relief.

And so it was that Diana closed up her father's house on the day after Mrs. Samuels' funeral and settled into a pleasant rose-papered bedchamber at the Durhams'. The room was much more comfortable than her own, attended to by a large staff of servants. Diana had dismissed all the servants but Mrs. Samuels after her father's death, taking on household chores herself as a kind of penance. She had never learned to enjoy the work, however, and she decided now that there was no further need to punish herself.

As the days passed, it became more and more obvious that Diana's presence was good for Amanda, and Diana took this as reason enough for the Durhams' kindness. That the opposite was also true, she did not consider for some time. Yet at the end of the first week, Diana realized that she was happier than she had been for months, perhaps years. Amanda's companionship filled a great void in her life, and a more luxurious style of living suited her completely.

At the beginning of the second week, as she and Amanda walked together on a balmy March afternoon, Amanda said, "We are the only two of our friends who have stayed the same, or nearly the same, anyway. I have seen Sophie and Jane and Caroline in town, and they are all vastly changed. They talk of people I don't know, and they seem wrapped up in town life. I suppose it is because you and I were cut off from society."

"Did you see no one in Spain?" Diana was curious about her friend's experiences abroad, though she did not wish to call up any painful memories.

"Some other officers' wives, but they were often posted away just as we became friendly. And I never got on with the Spanish and Portuguese ladies." She sighed. "George was most often with the army, of course. I spent a great deal of time alone."

"You came back for visits." Diana wondered why she had not stayed in England, as most army wives did.

"Yes. But then I missed George so dreadfully." Amanda's smile was wry. "We were...*are* so fond of one another. It is very unfashionable."

"I remember when you met him. One day you were perfectly normal, then you went to an assembly in York and came back transformed. We could hardly force a sentence from you. It took days to discover what was the matter."

Amanda laughed. "We were both bowled over. We married six weeks later."

"And the rest of us nearly died of jealousy."

They laughed. But Amanda's expression soon sobered again. "And now we are all scattered—Sophie in Kent, Jane in Dorset, and Caroline flitting from London to Brighton to house parties. It all seems so long ago." She paused. "Of course, they all have children, too. It makes them seem older."

Diana sensed constraint. "When you and George are settled..." she began.

Amanda shook her head as if goaded. "I have lost three. I...I don't hope...that is..." She bit her lower lip and struggled for composure. "But what am I about, discussing such things with you? An unmarried girl! Mama would be scandalized." She paused again, taking a deep breath. "You know what we must do, Diana? We must find you a husband. You are...what? Five-and-twenty now? Nearly on the shelf. How careless of you!" Abruptly her eyes widened. "I did not mean... Oh, I haven't offended you, have I? My tongue runs away with me sometimes."

"Of course you have not." But Diana did feel uneasy. "I have never had the opportunity to marry. I don't suppose I shall." Even if she did have the chance, it was impossible. No man would wish to marry her once he learned of her past. Diana knew she could never keep such a secret from a husband.

"Nonsense." Amanda examined her friend with a more critical eye than she had used so far. Diana had been very pretty at seventeen. Now, her color was not so good, admittedly, but her deep golden hair had lost none of its vibrancy, and the unfashionable way she dressed it was somehow very attractive. Her face was thinner, but her brown eyes with those striking gold flecks remained entrancing. Her form was slender and pleasing, even in the poorly cut black gown. Amanda's own dark eyes began to sparkle. It was unthinkable that Diana should not marry, and this was just the sort of problem that appealed to her. A keen interest that Amanda had not felt for some time rose in her, temporarily banishing worry. How could her plan be best accomplished? Slowly an idea started to form, which, she reasoned, might work for George as well.

THREE

"I THINK," DECLARED AMANDA TRENT AT DINNER THAT evening, "that we should go to Bath for a long visit." Four pairs of eyes focused on her face. Her parents were obviously surprised, and not overpleased. Diana looked dismayed, and George antagonistic. Amanda's pointed chin rose. "I don't know why I did not think of it before," she continued. "It would be a perfect holiday for us. We don't want the hurly-burly of London, yet the country is a bit flat at this season. So…"

"I am *not* an invalid," interrupted George through clenched teeth.

A flicker of pain, instantly suppressed, clouded Amanda's dark eyes. "An invalid?" she repeated, as if mystified. "But of course you are not. What has that to do with anything?"

Confused by his wife's bland innocence, Major Trent blinked. He was, he knew, all too likely to lose his temper these days. He tried to control his irritation, but rarely succeeded. In fact, he hadn't been himself since he had taken that damned fever. But he wasn't to be cajoled into coddling himself and drinking "medicinal" waters. Death in the field was preferable to life as a bleating invalid.

"I only thought you would enjoy seeing old friends," Amanda said, her tone reproachful. "You know that a great many of them went to Bath. You could ride with them and discuss all the news. The papers would come sooner there, you know. You would hear what Wellington is doing in Vienna almost as soon as it happens. And there would be concerts and assemblies in the evening, which I should enjoy." Without seeming to, she watched his face anxiously. It was vital to convince George. The others presented no obstacle if he could be brought to agree. And once in Bath, among friends in some cases more seriously wounded than he, surely

George could be brought to take more care of himself, and mend the faster.

Major Trent gazed at his still-full plate, a wave of guilt sweeping over him. It could not be very amusing for Amanda to be saddled with a husband such as he had been these past months. She deserved some diversion. And though this thought merely irritated him the more—for his condition was not his fault—he grunted assent. "If you wish it."

Amanda asked for no more. She had not hoped for even grudging agreement so quickly. "We will go as soon as may be," she replied. "Perhaps by the end of this week. Do you care to come, Mama, Papa? We should be happy to have your company."

Mrs. Durham knew what her daughter was doing, and she approved. George would be far happier among his own friends, and the entertainments of Bath would keep him from brooding over his loss. Yet she hated to send Amanda off alone with her radically altered husband. He was so difficult now, she thought, and, despite her experiences, Amanda was still so young. But she herself had responsibilities that could not be lightly pushed aside. As she started to speak, her husband said, "I do not see how I can go away just now, Amanda. We are trying a new method of draining the Huddleston fields, and I don't trust Bains to oversee repair of the tenant cottages. He is too likely to use inferior materials. But you might go, Celia." He exchanged a concerned look with his wife.

"I suppose I could," answered Mrs. Durham slowly.

Amanda laughed, knowing their thoughts. "There is not the least need, if you do not wish to go. I know you are both happiest here. We shall be very well entertained in Bath."

"I do not like to send you off alone," murmured her mother, hoping this would not provoke one of George's outbursts.

"But I shall not be alone," exclaimed Amanda. "Diana will be there." Seeing everyone's surprise, she spread her hands. "But of course Diana must come. I always meant her to. What would she do here in Yorkshire, without anyone?"

Diana, who had been listening with increasing unhappiness to Amanda's plans, felt a great flood of relief. The prospect of returning to her empty house had been even more distressing after her pleasant interlude with the Durhams. But she felt obliged to say, "I shall be quite all right. You needn't invite me because…"

"Oh, Diana, you will not desert me now, surely?" wailed her friend. "We have had such fun together. And think how lovely it will be in Bath."

Diana did think. The idea was immensely attractive. "I don't wish to be in the way," she said reluctantly, glancing at George.

"Don't be silly. George will disappear with his friends to discuss politics, and I shall be left alone for hours. You must bear me company."

"Good thought," grunted George.

Though his tone was sullen, this was the greatest approval Diana had heard him express during her visit. Gratefully she capitulated. "I should love to come with you."

"Splendid!" Amanda smiled and clasped her hands. "We need only pack our things, then, and we can be off. I daresay we can start in two days' time."

In the event, it took them a week to make ready. George discovered some business matters concerning his nearby estate which needed his attention. Mr. Durham managed the property for him, but there were decisions that only George could make, and he found it necessary to visit some of the tenants in order to resolve all the problems. Diana decided to put her father's house, and nearly everything it contained, up for sale. Whatever the future brought, she never wished to return there. Perhaps she would settle in Bath. And so she sorted through all her possessions and packed them up, arranging for an agent to watch over the place and handle its sale. She also called at the bank. She and Mr. Merton determined a reasonable income, to be paid to her quarterly, and the firm gladly agreed to watch over the principal for the time being.

On the day Diana left her family home for the last time, her clothes and personal items tied up and ready to be delivered to the Durhams' home, she walked through the rooms and tried to discover some scraps of regret among her feelings. She could not. As a child here, she had felt her natural exuberance repressed. As a young girl, she had longed only to leave. And in the last few years, she had labored under the oppression of her own mistakes and misfortunes. She would miss nothing in these now dusty and forlorn apartments.

Her certainty was both liberating and frightening. She could start afresh without guilt, but to have so little past—no one and no place to come back to—shook her to the depths. Her life was truly hers alone. What could she make of it? Her early efforts had been disastrous. Was she any more prepared to go forth now than she had been at seventeen?

Of course she was, Diana told herself, holding her head high. She had to be; the years she had spent pondering must have given her some wisdom. However, as she followed the carters carrying the last of her trunks and locked the oaken front door behind them, she felt a quiver of apprehension. Perhaps she should have retreated to her old home after all, where all was familiar, if unexciting. At least here she had known who she was. Diana stood still, one hand flat against the wood, then shook her head decisively and turned away.

On her return to the Durhams', Diana found the whole household in an uproar. The contrast to her own silent home was dizzying, and for a moment she could only stand amazed in the front hall, and listen to Mr. Durham and George Trent debating loudly in the library, Mrs. Durham calling to her daughter upstairs, and excited talk floating up from the servants' quarters below. Then she recovered and hurried up to Amanda.

"Oh, Diana!" Amanda exclaimed when she entered. "Did you hear the news? Napoleon has escaped from Elba and is marching through France gathering a new army. Wellington is recalled from the Congress. It will be war again."

Diana struggled to take this in.

"George is frantic to leave. Thank heaven we are nearly ready. I had to argue for an hour against going straight to London. He hates it there, and he will get the papers nearly as quickly in Bath."

"Is he… Will he go back into the army?"

"Oh, no. He is not completely recovered. And he is mustered out." Amanda grimaced. "Do not tell him, but I am glad."

Diana nodded, understanding.

"Have you finished packing?"

"Yes. I have shut up the house."

"Good. I expect we shall go tomorrow. Lud, I thought we were finished with this war."

Diana, feeling very ignorant, nodded again. She had never paid proper attention to such important matters, she thought.

They set off for Bath on a fine day in late March, Diana and Amanda in a post chaise, and George Trent riding beside, having gruffly refused his wife's plea to join them and help relieve the tedium of the journey. Diana, knowing that her friend wished to lessen her husband's exertions, had added her arguments, but to no avail. The roads were still deep in mud, but the weather was much warmer, and they made slow but steady progress southward, driven onward by George's impatience. Aside from frequent anxious glances out the window, Amanda was content, and Diana found herself more and more attached to her old friend as they endured the vicissitudes of travel together. For the first time, she began to understand how Amanda had borne years abroad and the numberless inconveniences inevitable in military lodgings. No setback seemed to worry or discourage Amanda Trent. If a horse went lame or a posting house had nothing to offer but bread, cheese, and ale for their dinner, she accepted it with cheerful optimism, insisting that things would soon be better and raising everyone else's spirits with some anecdote of far more harrowing conditions in Spain. Only her husband's moods and misfortunes could depress her, Diana saw now. She had not realized this until they were on the road and other difficulties arose. She marveled at the depth of love Amanda must feel, to be so solicitous. She herself more than once stifled a sharp retort when George Trent was particularly gruff or truculent.

March was ending by the time they reached Bath, and daffodils were showing by the side of the road. Diana was very glad when they reached the final stage, and the postboys informed them that they would arrive in the city by midafternoon. She was heartily sick of the bouncing chaise, ill-aired inn sheets, and the effort to appear good-humored for every minute of the day. She was deeply accustomed to a certain amount of solitude, she found, and though she was fonder than ever of Amanda, she nevertheless wished they might escape each other for some part of the day—as they would, of course, in Bath.

They drove into the town at three on a cloudless afternoon and went directly to the Royal Crescent, where Amanda had engaged a set of apartments. As they passed through the streets, the ladies commented on the beauties of the place. Diana had never seen Bath, and Amanda had not visited for some years.

"How lovely," exclaimed Diana as they pulled up before their lodgings. The pale buildings of the Crescent curved before them, overlooking a wide, sloping lawn with the garden below.

"You won't mind the hill, will you?" Amanda asked as both women descended from the post chaise. "I tried to find rooms farther down, but there was nothing suitable. We can always hire a chair."

"Why, it's nothing at all," replied Diana, looking back at the steep slant they had ascended. "I can walk that easily. How beautiful it all is. I can never thank you properly for asking me to come, Amanda."

"Nonsense. I should have been sadly flat without you. And here is the building, number five. I do hope they had my last letter."

All was well within, the rooms ready and quite satisfactory. As the servants carried their things inside and began to unpack, Diana and Amanda went through the apartments together and exclaimed at the elegance of the furnishings. Amanda repeatedly called her husband's attention to some particularly fine detail. "If only we could have found such lodgings in Spain, George," she laughed finally, when they had gathered in the drawing room and she no longer had to shout down the stairs to capture his attention. "Do you remember our first place in Madrid? I should have thought I was in heaven if I had walked in here then."

Diana was surprised at George Trent's reminiscent smile. "Still, we had some fine times there. Remember the night Johnny Eagleton came to dinner?" George asked.

Amanda laughed. "Do I not!" She turned to Diana. "He brought his own goose, alive, and expected me to cook it for him. I had only a Spanish girl of fourteen to help me—we could scarcely speak four words to each other—and here was this great bird flapping and hissing about the drawing room. Terrifying! And George would do nothing but laugh!"

He laughed now, for the first time since Diana had met him again. "I wonder where Johnny is now? I suppose he is with the army in America." At this thought, his smile faded again, and he turned away.

"Are you going out to gather news?" asked Amanda, keeping her tone resolutely gay. "If you pass the assembly rooms, you must put our names down. I daresay you will see a dozen acquaintances in the street. Or in the Pump Room. We must ask what is the fashionable hour there."

Major Trent did not reply, but his attention seemed caught, and in a few minutes he did indeed go out.

"Oh, I do hope he encounters some old friends," said Amanda, watching him from the drawing-room window. "It will make such a difference."

"I'm sure he will," replied Diana. "I saw uniforms everywhere as we drove in."

"Yes, a great many men are still in the army," Amanda said, though she was distracted, her eyes still on her departing husband. "He will never have a chair," she murmured. "I hope the hill does not exhaust him."

Diana wished to offer Amanda some diversion, but her mind held only envy of the major. She longed to go exploring herself.

At last Amanda turned from the panes. "I believe I will go upstairs and lie down. I am tired out from the journey."

Diana had rather hoped they could go out together, but she merely said, "Of course. Can I do anything for you?"

"No." Amanda smiled. "If you would like to see the town, you can take Fanny with you."

Diana's answering smile was sheepish, and her friend laughed. "Go on. I can see you are longing to get out."

"It is just that I have never visited such a place before," apologized Diana. "You are a jaded traveler."

As always, Amanda remembered her friend's sheltered history with a start. When one talked with Diana, it was so easy to forget that she had never been anywhere or done anything, because she seemed so knowledgeable. "Go, by all means," Amanda urged, "only keep Fanny with you and do not get lost." Fanny was the Yorkshire girl they had hired as Diana's personal maid.

"Yes, Mama," laughed Diana. "And I shall be home in time for tea."

"See that you are," responded the other with mock severity. They walked up the stairs arm in arm, laughing together, so that Diana could fetch her hat.

Diana found Bath fascinating. Never in her life had she been able to stroll through bustling streets and observe such a variety of people. Though she stopped nowhere, she paused before the exclusive shops on Milsom Street, the desire for a new wardrobe rising in her breast, and she gazed at the Pump Room and the assembly rooms with eager eyes. Despite her good looks, she herself was not much marked because of her unfashionable black gown and outmoded bonnet, but this suited Diana perfectly. She would not have known how to turn away excessive interest. As it was, she could revel in the novel sights and sounds of Bath secure under the meager protection of Fanny, whose eyes and mouth were so wide she continually tripped over her own feet.

The afternoon waned, and Diana reluctantly concluded that it was time to turn toward their lodgings. She consoled herself with the knowledge that she was actually staying in town, and that she might take such a walk every day if she chose, as well as attend the public concerts and assemblies. The prospect sent her into a happy daze of anticipation.

Thus, neither Diana nor Fanny was watching very carefully as they made their way along the pavement in the general direction of the Royal Crescent. Town dwellers might have warned them that the street was no place for pleasant imaginings, particularly in early spring when the dirt was greatest, but they were not acquainted with any Bath resident, and none was likely to accost a stranger with unsolicited advice.

They turned into one of the major thoroughfares and, skirting a wide puddle, went on toward home. Diana did not even turn her head at the clatter of hooves and wheels behind. The approach of a carriage had already become commonplace, though she would have run to the window in excitement just a week before, at home.

The noise intensified, and someone shouted, "Look out,

there!" With a sudden rush, a hired chaise swept around the corner and cut through the broad puddle in the road, throwing up a spray of mud and water nearly six feet high. Diana and Fanny were directly in its path; in an instant, they were coated from head to foot with mud. There was not even time to throw up an arm to protect their faces.

Diana was so startled that she did not move for a moment. Then she raised a hand to her face and wiped ineffectually at the stiffening mask. She heard a male voice shout, "Pull up, you fool!" She blinked her eyes rapidly, a speck of mud making them water, and tried to focus as a tall figure in uniform rapidly approached. "I *beg* your pardon," said the same voice. "That idiot of a driver didn't see you, I suppose. Are you all right? Apart from this confounded mud, of course."

Diana peered up at him, her vision still clouded. He wore the dark-blue jacket and gray trousers of the Royal Horse Guards, the red and gold trim seeming painfully bright in her present condition. But though his uniform was smart, he looked thin for his height, his broad shoulders a little too wide for his girth, and his face showed signs of hardship and suffering. He couldn't be more than thirty, she thought, but he had certainly seen a good deal of action.

The man smiled, and his thin face was abruptly transformed. He was by no means unhandsome, but his brown hair and light-blue eyes were not really striking until he smiled. His gaze seemed to take light from the air, and the planes of his high cheekbones shifted to reveal a character and temperament more attractive than mere good looks. He laughed, and this impression intensified. Diana felt an odd fluttering near the base of her throat. "I *am* sorry," he added. "I am not laughing at you, you know. It is just…"

"…that I look so very ridiculous," finished Diana, imagining her eyes looking out of a mud-covered face. Her tone was sharp, though she did not precisely blame him for the incident. He had not been driving, after all, and he had apologized. Yet she could not help but be irritated.

"Not at all." But his blue eyes danced. "Allow me to make amends by driving you home. It is the least I can do."

"We will muddy your carriage," answered Diana, who nonetheless had no intention of refusing his offer.

"It is hired, and no more than the driver deserves, for his carelessness." He started to offer his arm, then thought better of it, his smile widening.

"I ought to insist upon support," responded Diana, ruthlessly suppressing an answering smile at the thought of how his smart uniform sleeve would look covered with mud.

At once, he extended his arm again. "You are welcome to it."

She shook her head and stepped toward the chaise. "I could not spoil your uniform."

"It has seen worse than mud." His expression was wry as he turned to follow her. He had a cane and walked with one stiff knee, Diana noticed. "And I shall be putting it off for a time here in Bath, worse luck."

"You are on leave?"

He nodded as he put a hand under her elbow to help her into the carriage. "At the worst possible time, naturally." He ushered Fanny into the forward seat and climbed in after her, his stiff left leg making his movement awkward. "My name is Robert Wilton, by the by. Which way?"

Diana gave her direction and sat back. Her initial anger at the accident was fading, only to be replaced by a far more intense chagrin at the manner of their meeting. She found Robert Wilton extremely engaging. Why could she not have encountered him in the assembly rooms, or the concert hall, when she had acquired a new gown and perhaps a modicum of assurance? Diana knew she would never match the London misses who had had the benefit of a season and constant practice in the art of conversation, but she might have made a better impression than *this*. She fingered her mud-stiffened black gown. He could not even have a proper idea of what she looked like, and he must think her a perfect fool for being caught so.

Yet it should not matter what he thought. She knew nothing of him. Was she so susceptible that she swooned over the first male she met after years of solitude? Diana flushed crimson at the thought. She had made that mistake before. Had she learned nothing since then? Setting her jaw, she gazed out the window at the passing scene.

"Are you *very* angry?" asked Wilton. "I cannot blame you, of course, but I do hope you will forgive me eventually." He paused, as if waiting for something, then added, "Will you tell me your name, though I do not deserve it?"

Realizing that she could have done so when he gave his, she said, "Diana Gresham," in a stiff voice. It was an unconventional introduction.

"You are staying in Bath?"

"Yes." Why did he insist on talking?

"I, too. Perhaps we shall meet again." Again he waited, a bit puzzled. She had seemed so open at first, and he had been impressed by her reaction to the accident. Most women, he imagined, would have collapsed in a fit of the vapors and screeched at him like a fishwife. Miss Gresham had not only remained calm; she had traded a mild joke with him. What had he done to turn her so cold?

Robert Wilton was the first to admit that he knew very little of women. For the six years since he came of age, he had been fighting with Wellington's army. He had not spent more than a score of evenings in a drawing room in his life, and he was always deucedly awkward with the girls his mother put in his way on those occasions. His eldest brother, Lord Faring, rallied him about it whenever they met. Yet, with this woman, Wilton had felt no constraint at first. Probably he had put his foot in it somehow, without even knowing it. He would drop her at her lodgings and fade away as quickly as possible. But this thought brought an immediate protest from some part of him, and he found himself asking, "You are here with your parents?" At least he would know what name to seek, he thought.

"No, with friends." Diana's tone was discouraging. She would not make an even greater fool of herself, she thought. But when silence descended upon the carriage, she felt a pang of regret. They were nearly at the Crescent In a moment, she would climb down, and the incident would be closed forever. She might never see him again. "Major and Mrs. Trent," she heard herself add.

"*George* Trent?"

"Yes."

"But we are old friends. Has he recovered from the fever he took at Toulouse?"

"Not…not completely," faltered Diana.

"I must call at once." They pulled up before the house, and he jumped out to help Diana, wincing as his stiff knee jarred against the cobblestones. It seemed he might actually come inside with her. Diana searched her mind for a deterrent, but it turned out to be unnecessary. "Please convey my compliments and say I shall come soon, perhaps tomorrow."

Diana nodded.

"And, again, my deepest apologies." He bowed slightly.

She nodded again and turned toward the door.

"George will tell you that mud is my natural element," added Wilton, laughter in his voice.

When she looked over her shoulder, he was getting back into the carriage. Inexplicably, Diana felt a pang of misery. Why must she botch everything? She resolved to be a paragon of polish and elegance when Robert Wilton called on the Trents.

FOUR

WILTON DID NOT CALL THE FOLLOWING DAY, A FACT WHICH filled Diana with profound gratitude. The slight pique she felt at his omission was overwhelmed by the memory of Amanda's peals of laughter when she had entered the house covered in mud. Despite valiant efforts to control herself, Amanda had been helpless with mirth for quite five minutes, and this measure of her appearance had made Diana all the more determined to smarten it.

Thus, the two of them had set out early the next morning on a lengthy shopping expedition, returning with two gowns that Diana could wear with only small alterations and the satisfaction of having ordered a great many more. She had also equipped herself with new gloves, hats, and other necessities, to the immense gratification of numerous Milsom Street shopkeepers. There remained only one great question in the matter of toilette.

"I suppose I must cut my hair," said Diana, critically evaluating her image in her dressing-table mirror. The great knot of deep gold low on her neck seemed incongruous with the new blue muslin dress she was wearing.

Amanda, who had accompanied her to her bedchamber, got up and walked all around Diana, her dark eyes narrow with speculation. "I don't know. Your hair is not the latest thing, of course, but it is somehow right on you."

Diana laughed. "I am a hopeless dowd, you mean."

"Not at all! You are just…yourself."

"And how am I to take that?" Her expression was wry. "Is not everyone? And is 'myself' an outmoded country miss?"

"I am not saying it properly." Amanda surveyed her friend's tall willowy figure, lovely in the draped muslin. It was so lucky that the dressmaker had had this model made up. The deep, vibrant blue, against Diana's bronze hair and pale skin, transformed her from a commonplace pretty girl into a beauty who drew one's eyes and fixed it. Her sherry-colored glance seemed brighter, and even her smile was now dazzling rather than merely pleasant. The unusual knot of hair seemed to confirm her compelling individuality, emphasizing the intelligence and discernment visible in her face and warning observers that here was no milk-and-water miss such as they might meet twenty times a day. Amanda felt it would be wrong to change that, but she did not know how to convey her intuition.

"I admit I am reluctant to cut it," added Diana, turning her head to look at her hair. She too felt some intimation of lightness.

"How long is it now?"

"Nearly to my knees!" She laughed. "Horridly old-fashioned."

"Let us leave it for now," decided Amanda. "You can always have it cut off, but once it is gone…" She shrugged.

Diana gave a small involuntary shiver. "Yes." She held out the skirt of her gown and turned to look at the back in the mirror. "How splendid it is to have a new dress. Perhaps I shall become utterly improvident and order a dozen more tomorrow."

Amanda laughed. "Do. And you must wear that one to the concert tonight. You look beautiful!"

Diana threw back her head and drew in a breath. The image her mirror showed her *was* gratifying and far removed from the mud-plastered apparition of yesterday. Captain Wilton—as Amanda had labeled him—was in for a surprise.

"Robert Wilton will never know you again," said Amanda, uncannily echoing this thought.

"If he is there," replied Diana with airy unconcern.

Amanda eyed her. She had been very interested to hear of Diana's encounter. Though not, of course, precisely what she'd had in mind when she suggested the stay in Bath (she suppressed a smile), the meeting was nonetheless a beginning. And Captain

Wilton was just the sort of man she would have Diana meet. She had been careful to drop only a few scraps of information about him, and she was gratified to see Diana transparently disguising a strong interest. She decided to make another test. "Oh, I daresay he will be. Robert will be very bored on leave and eager for diversion."

Diana studiously examined the line of her hem. "Is he so jaded?"

"Oh, no. Quite the opposite. He has been in the army since he was very young, and had few opportunities for entertainment."

"He was in the Peninsula with George?"

"Yes. That is, not *with* him, exactly. Robert was attached to the headquarters staff. He visited all the regiments at one time or another, carrying messages or observing. Which is not to say that he did not see a good deal of action, for he did. I believe he received a special commendation at Salamanca."

"Ah." Diana turned, gown forgotten. "He looked ill. Or, not ill precisely, but worn down."

"He was wounded at Bordeaux, I think, after we had come home. Does he seem very bad?"

Flushing a little, Diana retreated again. "I know nothing of him, of course. I thought he was a little thin and pale, and his leg is stiff."

Amanda nodded wisely. "That does not sound too serious. But if he is still on leave, it must have been. I suppose he is as wild to rejoin Wellington as they all are."

"Has he no…family?" asked Diana haltingly.

"Oh, lud, yes. He is the brother of Lord Faring and has several sisters. His father is dead, but Lady Faring, his mother, is quite a figure in London—one of the leading hostesses."

"I wonder he does not stay with her."

"Perhaps Faring puts him off. He is a dreadful dandy." She giggled. "You should see him, Diana. He cannot turn his head, his collar is so high and starched, and his waist is cinched so small he is shaped like an hourglass."

"Ridiculous," she agreed. "But hardly enough to put one off London, I should think."

"Oh, but he is—they are, I mean. Most of the military men can't abide dandies, or the haut ton, because they were all so stupid about the war, you see. They acted as if it were unimportant. George calls them—what is the word—fribbles." She giggled again. "When he is in a *kind* mood, that is."

Diana smiled. "It is lucky we came to Bath, then. The town seems full of soldiers."

"Luck had nothing to do with it."

Amanda's smug tone made Diana look more closely. Amanda had schemes in mind, she saw, and she suddenly wondered if some of them might not involve herself. The idea startled her, for the Amanda Diana remembered would have had little time for or interest in maneuvering others. Diana could see how George's state might alter this, but what else was Amanda plotting? This question, presently unanswerable, was unsettling.

That evening, they attended a concert in the lower rooms. Diana had thought that George Trent would refuse to come, but he said nothing and seemed content when they met him in the drawing room and walked downstairs together. He had been much less prickly since they arrived in Bath, Diana realized. He still looked like a ghost of his former self, his massive frame barely covered by his flesh and his face thin and lined behind the black eyepatch. But his temper was improved, and, when they entered the concert room, she understood at least part of the reason. George was greeted from all sides by men like himself—soldiers discharged from Wellington's army. He fell immediately into intent conversation about recent developments, leaving Diana and Amanda to find their own seats among the rows of gilt chairs. Neither had the slightest objection, however. Indeed, Diana could see that Amanda was overjoyed at her husband's rekindled animation, and she felt happy for both of them.

Diana looked about the room with interest, sitting very straight, conscious for almost the first time in her life that she looked well-dressed and elegant. Amanda had lent her a string of pearls to wear with her new blue gown; a fringed shawl was draped across her elbows, and she carried a pair of gloves she had purchased that day. As the hall filled and the murmur of talk grew louder, Diana felt her heartbeat quicken. Society was what she had longed for so ardently years ago. Her chance had come when she had almost given up hope, and she was terribly excited.

Amanda had been nodding to the left and right, smiling and occasionally raising her hand in greeting. "I had no notion we would find so many acquaintances here," she said. "Half the army seems to be in Bath. I had supposed most were in America. Why, there is Anthony Linton!"

"I don't see nearly as many uniforms as on the street," commented Diana.

"Those must be the new arrivals. They don't wear uniforms once on leave, of course."

Diana assimilated this information. She had, she realized, been covertly on the lookout for a blue coat trimmed with red and gold.

"George knows everyone much better than I, naturally," continued Amanda. "But it is very pleasant to have even a nodding acquaintance with so many. It makes one feel at home."

Diana, who had begun to feel just the opposite, scanned the room again. It was filled with strangers—far more men than women—talking in small, earnest groups.

At the signal, the audience settled into chairs, and, after a short interval, the music began.

Diana, who had never been musical, found the performance merely pleasant, and, from the looks of the other listeners, she thought that many would concur. The rush to resume conversation or visit the refreshment room at the first pause was marked. She and Amanda were swept along irresistibly and had some difficulty in procuring glasses of lemonade and chairs at one of the small tables. Her unconcern at George's desertion wavered a bit, as did her elation at being out. Then, at that inauspicious moment, Diana saw Robert Wilton making his way through the crowd around the entrance to the refreshment room. At once, her interest revived. He wore a plain blue coat tonight and buff pantaloons, and he carried an ebony cane upon which he occasionally leaned when someone accidentally jostled him and threw him onto his stiff knee. He was gazing at the various groups of people, and Diana sat a little straighter, waiting for his eyes to encounter hers.

They did so, and passed on without a flicker. She frowned, then realized that he could not be expected to recognize her without the mud. Her lips curved upward at the absurdity of it. How were they to meet? Forgetting her earlier scruples, she turned to Amanda. "There is Captain Wilton."

"Where?" Diana indicated him. "So it is." Amanda raised a hand and, when she managed to catch his eye, nodded and smiled. Robert Wilton immediately started toward them, though his progress was slow because of the crush.

"Mrs. Trent," he said when he finally reached them. "I was hoping to see you here this evening. I meant to call, but I have been fully occupied correcting a mix-up about my rooms here in Bath. My letter reserving them seems to have gone astray."

"How annoying. I hope you have accommodations."

"Now, yes." He turned toward Diana with an expectant smile. He had been too occupied maneuvering through the crowd to look at her before. What he saw struck him dumb with dismay.

"You have met my dear friend Diana Gresham, I believe," said Amanda, a laugh in her voice.

Wilton nodded, swallowing nervously.

Diana, who had observed the change in his expression with surprise and chagrin, merely bowed her head. She had imagined a very different scene when she anticipated this meeting. Why was he so patently disappointed? Was it her face, her gown? Something in her appearance had clearly put him off, and this daunting knowledge made her incapable of speech. She had lost whatever assurance she had once possessed, she saw, in the years of solitude.

"A *very* odd meeting," added Amanda in the silence that followed, puzzlement replacing humor in her tone. "Is it your habit to strike up acquaintance with unknown ladies so, Captain Wilton?"

"No. No." He was too uncomfortable to acknowledge her joke. Robert Wilton had come to this concert solely to meet Diana again. His memory of the girl who had been so sporting about an embarrassing accident had grown rosier with each passing hour. He imagined that he would talk with her as easily as he did with any of his numerous male friends. Her features having been a mystery, he thought of her simply as an attractive personality.

But this hopeful vision had been shattered with his first sight of her gleaming hair, her elegant attire and delicately lovely face. She was even *more* beautiful than the women his mother pushed upon him, and she would no doubt find him as clumsy and tiresome as did they. Wilton cringed at the memory of a succession of awkward encounters. He knew nothing of London gossip or the current news of close-knit society families, and every girl he had danced with or taken to dinner in town had made it clear she found him dull and unamusing. His looks were not such as to dazzle, and his long absences from England left his wardrobe outmoded. His wide knowledge of the war and sound views upon it failed to arouse a spark of interest. Thus, he had long ago concluded that he was hopelessly out of place in the drawing room. And now, faced with a Diana no longer covered with mud but resplendent as any society miss, he felt only that he must escape before he saw bored contempt in her eyes too.

Amanda, seeing that, inexplicably, the whole responsibility for conversation seemed to rest with her, said, "When did you return to England, Captain Wilton?" Her mystification was plain. Why, she might have been asking, are two people whom I know to be intelligent and interesting standing still and silent as stones?

The implication did nothing to put Wilton at ease. "In July," he replied.

"Just after we did. And have you been staying with your family?"

He nodded quickly and started to make some excuse to take his leave.

"Oh, there is George." Mrs. Trent summoned her husband with a gesture. "George, we have found Robert Wilton."

The two men greeted one another cordially and at once fell into a discussion about Wellington's plans for meeting Napoleon in pitched battle in Flanders.

Diana watched as Captain Wilton's constraint vanished and his blue eyes lit with enthusiasm. He smiled over some remark of George's, and she drew in a breath. She had almost forgotten that smile; it made him seem a different person.

Resentment welled up in her. Why should he be so eager and talkative with George and so sullen and silent with her? What about her offended him? She had done nothing except get in the way of his carriage. But perhaps now that he had seen her, he found she could not compare with the London girls he knew. Diana nodded to herself. Yes, that must be it. He was accustomed to the daughters of the haut ton, and she had none of their polish.

Diana glanced again at Wilton's face, so alive now. That was what he had expected, undoubtedly, and she could not manage it. A sharp pang of disappointment went through her. She had hoped for something from him, she realized, despite her stern resolutions, and she had behaved stupidly, charmed by a man of whom she knew nothing. She must fight this susceptibility in herself. She would seek an introduction to every gentleman known to the Trents, she decided, and she would treat each of them with equal consideration and interest. That would soon cure her of the lamentable tendency to idealize anyone

And so, as the evening went on, Diana actively encouraged a willing Amanda to present her to officer friends, and she exerted herself mightily to chat and laugh at their sallies. Making conversation was not as difficult as she had feared it might be after her encounter with Robert Wilton. Others appeared flatteringly eager to speak to her, and even reluctant to relinquish places at her side. Diana began to enjoy herself very much indeed, and, by the end of the outing, had not a glance to spare for Captain Wilton, who stood alone in a corner and watched her with a bitter expression.

FIVE

By the beginning of their fourth day in Bath, Amanda Trent was feeling very pleased indeed with the success of her plans. Diana had been introduced to a great many eligible gentlemen, nearly all soldiers like her own dear husband, and she had made a favorable impression. George himself was far happier, and he was eating better than he had in months. His fellow officers thought nothing of the patch over his eye, for they had seen much worse, and this put him at ease. The opportunity to talk of the war with those whose experience and knowledge matched his own was also important. Indeed, George's spirits were vastly improved; he rarely indulged in fits of melancholy or flashes of temper now. As she tied the strings of her bonnet in preparation for another visit to Milsom Street with Diana, Amanda smiled at her reflection in the mirror.

Diana, in her own bedchamber, was feeling far less content. She had had an unrealistically rosy vision of life in society, she saw. It was not uniformly delightful. The elation she had felt on occasion as she was talking and laughing with a group was offset by moments like the present one, when she was definitely downcast. Living alone, she had experienced neither extreme; each day had been much like the last after her first remorseful months. Now she felt overstimulated and unsure of her reactions, as she had not in years.

Amanda tapped at the door and looked in. "Are you ready?"

"Yes." Diana picked up her gloves and came forward, smiling in a determined effort to convince Amanda that all was well. The Trents had been so kind to her, and it was obvious that Amanda was happy. She would not spoil that.

Passing the drawing room on their way out, they saw Major

Trent on the sofa reading a newspaper. "We are going shopping," Amanda told him. "We will be back in time for luncheon if you are staying."

"More new dresses?" answered the major in a joking tone, actually putting aside his paper.

Amanda colored slightly and laughed. "For Diana. She has so few."

George smiled back, reminding Diana for an instant of the young man she had met at their wedding. "Not so much as a ribbon for yourself?"

"Perhaps a ribbon," agreed his wife in the same teasing tone.

"You should get yourself something pretty; you have bought nothing since we came home, I think. Perhaps I will come with you to see that you do."

Amanda drew in her breath and clasped her hands before her. "Really, George?" She turned to Diana. "He has often shopped with me, and found some of my loveliest things. You should see how the shopgirls fawn on him."

This seemed an unfortunate reminiscence, for George's face clouded, making Amanda look as if she wished to bite her tongue. "I should be very glad of your advice," said Diana quickly. "I never had a brother to tell me when I looked truly hideous, and I believe Amanda is rather easy with me."

"I am not!"

"You allowed me to purchase that primrose muslin," retorted Diana, "and, when it arrived and I put it on, we both saw that it would not do."

Amanda frowned. "The cloth seemed so different before it was made up. I was sure it would become you."

"You see?" said Diana to George. "Your discriminating opinion is sorely needed." Silently she was wondering how it would be to have a man she scarcely knew help choose her clothes, but she could endure a little embarrassment for Amanda's sake.

"Very well," replied George, rising. He sounded half-eager, half-reluctant.

"Do you remember when we bought that pink silk dress in Lisbon?" asked Amanda. "The dressmaker was scandalized that you came. I'm sure she will always believe Englishmen are mad." She turned to Diana, gratitude for her aid shining in her dark eyes. "She wouldn't even *look* at George. She spoke only to me, as if he weren't there, and, if he spoke, she answered *me*. It was too ridiculous."

Major Trent laughed. "I don't see why a man shouldn't take an interest in his wife's clothes. I am the one who has to look at them, after all."

"You make it sound such a penance," said Amanda, wrinkling her nose at him.

"Well, when it's a case of black silk with jet beads…"

"That wasn't my fault! We lost our way one night in Spain," she informed Diana. "There was a dreadful storm, and we somehow got separated from our escort and luggage. We had to take shelter in a village, the mayor's house. His wife lent me a dress."

"A tent, you mean," said George.

"She *was* rather large."

"Rather? Might as well call Bath 'rather' hilly." The Trents' eyes met, and they laughed together. Diana suddenly understood why Amanda was so fond of him, and she felt thrust outside a charmed circle whose warmth and delight had room for only two. "Which brings up the question of transport," added George, breaking the spell. "Do you mean to walk down to town?"

"Oh, yes," said Amanda. "It is not so far, and all downhill." She caught herself. "Would you prefer to ride? Perhaps we should, after all, Diana. I—"

"I am quite up to the walk," interrupted George, and the slip threatened to spoil their new rapprochement.

"The two of you will utterly wear *me* down, I can see," put in

Diana. "And I thought I was a redoubtable walker. But let us start out, while I still have the strength."

This elicited another laugh, though less spontaneous than before, and they set out together for the shops. At first, Diana kept up a determined flow of comment on the views from the Crescent the beauty of the Bath streets, and the nature of the crowds they began to encounter lower down. Finally Major Trent put aside his pique, and by the time they reached Milsom Street, they were talking easily together again.

"Here is Madame Riboud's," said Amanda, stopping before an immaculate doorway. "We must go up and see how the rest of Diana's dresses are getting on."

"Why don't you leave me here," suggested Diana. "We could meet in an hour and go on together." She was to have a fitting, and the thought of Major Trent waiting impatiently through it was daunting.

"We might go look at hats," agreed Amanda.

Her husband's face showed that this was a fortunate thought.

"We will come back in an hour to fetch you," she added, "and then we can all go on and buy those artificial flowers you wanted, Diana."

"Ah, I'm just the man to judge *those*," said George. "If you really wish to know what looks hideous…"

"Perhaps I don't," laughed Diana, and waved them on their way.

Her new gowns were nearly finished, and she was happy with all of them. Along with her pleasure at George and Amanda's budding reconciliation, this put Diana in a very buoyant mood, and, when she descended the stairs from Madame Riboud's a little more than an hour later to find no one awaiting her, she did not care a whit. Bath was a very safe town, she knew, and the Trents would no doubt appear soon.

She gazed at the goods offered in nearby shop windows, strolling a little way along the pavement and then back in the opposite direction. She wondered whether she should go in search of her friends, but concluded that they would only miss each other.

Peering up and down the street again, hoping to see the Trents, she abruptly encountered the hugely magnified eye of a man across the way, who was examining her through a kind of lens on a gilded stick. His appearance was so astonishing that she did not immediately turn away. Diana had never seen anyone in pale lavender pantaloons, a primrose coat so tight she could not imagine how its wearer got it on, a blinding brocade waistcoat, and a neckcloth so high and starched and intricate she wondered if it were linen or carved of wood and painted. Simultaneously raising one pale eyebrow and one corner of his mouth, the man sauntered toward her, his quizzing glass now dangling negligently from his white hand.

"How d'ye do?" he said when he had picked his way delicately across the cobbles. "Lost your way?"

"Why, no." Diana was too fascinated by his grotesque appearance to snub him. And she had never learned to administer a setdown in any case.

"Couldn't help noticin' you wanderin' about the street." The man smirked. He had a drawling, lisping way of speaking that Diana found as bizarre as his apparel.

"I'm waiting for my friends," she replied, her voice cool.

"Ah. Beg pardon for intrudin.'" He looked her over with a connoisseur's eye. "Ronald Boynton," he added hopefully.

This was too much. Diana did not give her name to total strangers in the street. Robert Wilton had been a definite exception. And she found Boynton ridiculous. She merely inclined her head and pointedly searched again for the Trents.

He took her lead without protest. "Must be goin.' Perhaps we'll meet in the Pump Room? Visitin' my aunt here, you know. Deuced flat, but…" He shrugged elaborately and, when she did not reply, bowed, sweeping the pavement with the brim of his hat, and turned away. Diana watched him go. He minced, she thought with an incredulous smile; one couldn't call it anything else.

"Whoever was *that*?" said Amanda Trent behind her, and Diana swung around. They had come up when she was looking the other way.

"A Mr. Ronald Boynton," she answered, still smiling. "He thought I was lost."

"He accosted you in the street! Oh, Diana, I am so sorry we are late. We lost track of the time, and…"

"It doesn't matter, Amanda. He wasn't the least offensive. Just…odd. Have you ever seen such an outfit!"

"Often," said her friend, her worried expression easing. "That, Diana, is a dandy."

George muttered.

"Indeed?" Diana looked again, but Mr. Boynton was gone. "Is that what they look like? Amazing."

"You were taken with him, I see." Amanda grinned mischievously.

"Oh, of course." She essayed an imitation of Boynton's speech. "He was so very charmin', you know."

Amanda burst out laughing, and George, who had begun to glower, saw the joke and smiled slightly. "Well, he must have been taken with you," Amanda crowed. "I daresay he will dog your footsteps."

"He had better not," exclaimed her husband.

"I don't suppose we shall ever see him again," replied Diana. "Did you buy a hat?"

Diverted, the Trents launched into an antiphonal description of their shopping expedition, which had clearly been both successful and enjoyable. Diana watched their happy faces, Boynton forgotten, recovering her pleasant mood in their pleasure.

They visited one or two more shops before returning home in great charity with one another to a cold luncheon. Diana could not recall a jollier occasion with the Trents, or perhaps with anyone. Her despondency of the morning had been silly, she told herself. It would simply take her a little time to become accustomed to a new way of living.

"Diana," said Amanda, in a tone that implied it was not the first time she had spoken.

"What?"

"You were far away. I merely asked if you are looking forward to your first assembly ball this evening."

"Oh. Yes."

"I admit I am, too. How long is it since we danced, George?"

"Before I was wounded," he answered curtly, but his tone was not as bitter as it had once been.

"So it was. You will stand up with me tonight, will you not? We met at just such an occasion, remember?"

He nodded slowly, turning to watch her face. After a moment, he put a hand over hers on the table, and Amanda smiled up at him.

"I must see about my dress," said Diana, rising. The Trents would not always want her about, she thought. She must be careful not to intrude on their first real respite after years abroad. Neither answered, and as she left the room Diana felt wistful. It must be wonderful to have a close companion who shared one's interests and confidences, she thought. This was a side to love she had not observed before, and for that reason it seemed more attractive than the violent ups and downs of her youth. Was such a closeness possible for her, even yet? The idea was so thrilling, and at the same time so improbable that she thrust it from her mind and turned resolutely to the question of a ball gown.

In this, at least, her choice was easy. Her first ball dress had been waiting for her at the dressmaker's that morning. Diana had instructed her to finish it before the others, for she had no suitable garment for the Bath assemblies, and she was more than pleased with the results. Made of a bronze satin just the shade of her hair and trimmed with knots of silver ribbon, Diana's dress was stunning. When Amanda had suggested the combination, Diana had at first been doubtful, but she was now very glad that she had allowed herself to be persuaded. The gown was striking and distinctive, the two burnished colors a happy change from the usual white or pink, and not at all garish. As Amanda had promised, the dress accentuated Diana's unique look, and Diana anticipated wearing it with a thrill of pleasure.

George and Amanda concurred when they all met in the hall before leaving. Amanda could not stop exclaiming at how well the gown had turned out, and, with a smile, George complimented Diana on her appearance. His mellow mood had lasted through the day.

"Oh, isn't this splendid?" said Amanda as they ate. "A true assembly. And Diana is going to make such a hit."

"I shall be satisfied if I am not left standing too often during the dancing," laughed Diana. "Do not set your hopes too high."

"Nonsense. You will be mobbed; wait and see."

Diana merely shook her head.

The assembly rooms were very near their lodgings, and they decided to walk, as the night was fine. They had left their wraps and were moving through the octagon room toward the main ballroom when Major Trent was stopped by a group of friends. As they paused to allow him to exchange greetings, Diana looked around the anteroom. Men and women in evening dress stood about, flirting and laughing. The dresses surpassed any Diana had seen before this visit. Strains of music could be heard above the buzz of talk, and the air was heady with the scents of perfumes and pomades. Her heart began to beat a little faster, and she drew in her breath. One of the Trents' friends whom she had met caught her eye and came forward to request a dance. Diana looked to Amanda, received a smiling dismissal, and went off on his arm.

The first part of the evening was even better than Diana had expected. Due to the Trents' wide acquaintance and her own attractions, she was never without a partner, and her hasty practice the night before had brought suitable proficiency in the various steps. She went in to supper with a very charming young lieutenant and a party of his friends, and then she danced the first set after the interval with a dashing cavalry officer. The gentlemen seemed to judge her conversation engrossing, another hurdle that had worried her after years alone, and all in all, Diana felt her first assembly ball a great success until she spied Robert Wilton lounging against the far wall near the end of the cotillion.

His arms were crossed on his chest, and he watched the dancers with a curled lip. He thinks us all contemptible, Diana thought. Though the thought made her angry—for what right had he to sneer?—she was also conscious of a sharp disappointment. She had been hoping to see him, she realized, and perhaps even to dance with him, wiping out the memory of their last awkward encounter. But now this seemed unlikely. Wilton turned his head, and their eyes met, then dropped immediately. Diana, cursing her clumsiness, raised hers again at once, but he was no longer looking in her direction. Her poise left her where Captain Wilton was concerned. Her years of solitude had left their mark to this degree. Diana bit her lower lip in vexation and returned her attention to her partner.

Captain Wilton clenched his jaw and stared at the floor rather than the whirling couples. Why had he come here? It was just the sort of occasion he most hated and was most likely to bring off poorly. His mother could not drag him to a ball in London, and yet he had rigged himself out and appeared here with no urging, only to be as miserable as he would have been there. He had *not* come because of a girl with bronze hair and gold-flecked eyes. Yet his gaze strayed toward Diana again.

"Hello, Captain Wilton," said Amanda Trent. She was floating by on her husband's arm, nearly bursting with happiness because the evening was going so well. The gentlemen acknowledged each other cordially as the music ended. "Are you enjoying the assembly?" added Amanda, in a tone which suggested that everyone must be as pleased as she.

He shrugged, not wishing to appear surly, but unable to give the expected reply.

Amanda noticed his unease fleetingly—she was too engrossed in her own far different feelings to linger over his—and with some surprise. But, as Diana's partner just then delivered her back to her party, Amanda had an inspiration. "Diana, here is your old acquaintance Captain Wilton. You must not refuse him a dance."

Diana, startled, replied that she had no such intention, and raised surprised, but not displeased, eyes to his face.

Wilton, taken unawares, allowed his chagrin to show.

"Oh, it is a waltz, too," continued Amanda blithely. "George, we must dance. And, Diana, you needn't hesitate. There are no fusty Almack's patronesses in Bath." The Trents joined the dancers.

The captain hung back.

Diana flushed. "You needn't dance with me if you don't wish to," she said bluntly. "I shall be quite all right alone here." Diana's chin was high. "I daresay someone else may even ask me. You needn't feel *obliged*." His response to Amanda's ploy had hurt her, and she didn't care if she made him feel boorish.

"I beg your pardon," he answered stiffly. "I cannot yet dance." With a gesture, he indicated the ebony cane leaning beside him.

Overcome with mortification, Diana blushed a deeper crimson. She had forgotten all about his wound. She had been thinking only of herself, and had behaved heedlessly and callously. "I...I'm sorry," she stammered. "I—"

"It doesn't signify," he interrupted, but his tone belied his words. Clearly, he felt his inability irksome. He stood very straight and gazed out over her head at the ballroom.

She must do something to make amends, Diana thought. "Would you…that is, we could sit down and talk, if you like," she stammered, feeling awkward.

Wilton looked down, surprised. He had expected her to go in search of a partner who could dance. "I'm no good at pretty speeches and fulsome compliments," he said and waited for the inevitable withdrawal.

But Diana's reaction was immediate sympathy and understanding. She knew only too well what it was to feel out of place. Could this assured-looking man really experience some of the same embarrassments? "No, only at covering people with mud," she replied, with a smile to show that she was rallying him.

He stared, then laughed. "Indeed. And, like most of my skills, scarcely sought after in society."

"But you *can* sit? When you wish to?" Diana's dark eyes sparkled up at him.

He was amazed and delighted. He had never met such a girl in London. "I can."

"And…?"

Wilton frowned in puzzlement.

"*Do* you wish to?" If he said no, Diana thought, she would never attempt such a joking exchange again.

But his smile reappeared. "I do indeed." They moved together to two gilt chairs against the wall and sat side by side.

"I must say I wonder why you came to a ball," said Diana.

Once again Captain Wilton found himself at a loss, but the feeling was far different from that he customarily experienced in London. Diana Gresham did not appear bored with him or contemptuous of his dress and manners, nor did her eyes wander to more fashionable gentlemen nearby. Her attention was squarely on him, though its focus was wholly unexpected. Drawing on a nimble wit and flexibility that had gotten him out of some of the nastiest spots in the Peninsula, Wilton set himself to match her. "I suppose I can't give up the habit of reconnoitering when in hostile territory."

Pleased in her turn, Diana thought about this. "Would you call us hostile?"

"Not so much as in London, perhaps."

The corners of her mouth turned up. "Where you received your training in...social maneuvers?"

He nodded feelingly.

"Some would envy you such a school. It is, after all, the center for these arts."

"And it may keep them!"

Seeing that he really felt strongly on this subject, Diana modulated her tone. "You really do not enjoy—?" she began.

"No, I cannot. Put me on a battlefield, or carrying a message fifty miles across Spain, and I am content. I should far rather face the French batteries than a line of simpering chits at Almack's. There are a thousand more important questions in life than the Duchess of Rutland's rout party or Prinny's new mistress." He flushed. "I beg your pardon. I should not have mentioned—"

"Of course there are," she agreed, ignoring his slip. "But must one worry over them all the time? Do you grudge a moment's frivolity?"

"In times such as these, this"—he indicated the room with a glance—"is a waste of time and irritation to any true Englishman."

"Thank you, sir," Diana could not help replying, though she was not really angry. His vehemence was irresistible.

For a moment he did not understand her. Then he grimaced. "I did not mean you."

"I know what you meant. You are right, I'm sure. It is just that I know so little about the war. And I admit I am enjoying my first taste of gaiety, despite it."

"First?" he asked, intrigued, for she was not a child fresh from the schoolroom.

Immediately Diana wished she had held her tongue. "I...I have lived at home until now."

"Far from Bath?"

"Yes, in Yorkshire." And now he would inquire why she had not been to the York assemblies, or to London, Diana thought wearily, and she would have no satisfactory answer, and he would believe that she was administering a setdown when she turned his questions aside.

But Robert Wilton had heard the reluctance in her voice, and no one knew better than he the agonies of awkward inquiries. Without seeking reasons, he shifted the subject. "You are fortunate. The Bath assemblies are much jollier than those in London."

Diana gazed at him with relief and amazement and met blue eyes that communicated an acknowledgment of her constraint, and of her right to avoid its source if she chose. She had to swallow a sudden lump in her throat. "But less brilliant," she managed to respond.

Wilton shrugged as if to say this was a matter of definition.

Surprising both of them, the music ended. The set had seemed very short. They drew apart—for they had been leaning rather markedly toward one another, they discovered—and looked around for the Trents.

Amanda and George were on the far side of the room. Wilton reached for his ebony cane. "Don't get up," said Diana.

"I am perfectly able to walk," he replied, with some impatience but none of the bitterness she had heard in George Trent. "My knee is only a bit stiff. The doctors say I shall be completely restored in a month or so."

"Does it pain you?" asked Diana hesitantly as they started across the room.

"Very little. And it requires exercise." He smiled down at her. "So, you see, you are doing me a good turn."

Once again Diana was struck by the force of his smile. "Perhaps I should insist upon a turn about the room."

"Perhaps you should."

Their eyes held for a long moment, and each felt that there was some special quality in this new acquaintance that demanded further exploration.

"Wilton!" exclaimed a drawling voice behind them. "No idea you were in Bath, old man. How d'ye do?"

They turned to confront a vision in fawn pantaloons and a dark-blue coat hung with a profusion of fobs and so starched and cinched and padded that he could scarcely move. Diana, astounded, looked from Captain Wilton to Ronald Boynton and back again. Was it possible that these two were acquainted?

"Left Faring in fine form," continued Boynton. "Took a hand with him at White's just before I left town. His usual damnable luck." He stopped, turned to Diana, and shook his head. "Beg pardon. No wish to offend. Feelings got the better of me." He then gave Wilton such a speaking look that the latter was forced to make introductions, though he was obviously reluctant to do so.

Diana, as she acknowledged him, wondered if Boynton would refer to their earlier encounter. But he merely raised one pale eyebrow meaningfully and went on talking of himself.

"Toddled up to visit my Aunt Miranda, you know. Ill. No good neglectin' the family fortune."

"Is your aunt very wealthy?" inquired Diana, unable to resist. She glanced at the captain, to share her amusement with him, but he was scowling at the floor.

"Rich as Croesus," replied Boynton promptly. "Refuses to make a final will, too. Have to keep in her good books." He smiled ingratiatingly. "Care to dance?"

Diana hesitated only a moment. Wilton had been about to leave her in any case, and her sense of the ridiculous was aroused. Also, she realized suddenly, Boynton reminded her of her long-ago, supposed love Gerald Carshin. It was not that the two men were really alike, she thought, it was merely the style of dress and something in Boynton's manner which piqued her curiosity. How would she respond to such a man now, when she felt so much changed? Her initial reaction suggested that she had matured in ways that pleased her, but she was not averse to a further test. She agreed.

Wilton, watching her go off on the dandy's arm, felt a surge of fury. That the woman he had found it possible to talk with so easily, and had begun to admire, should so blithely accept Boynton reignited all his former doubts. Wilton thoroughly despised his brother Faring's set. They were lazy, affected, and disgracefully unmoved by the important issues of the day. They cared for nothing but gaming, gossip, and... Here he paused in horror, recalling some of his brother's more unsavory romantic entanglements.

Miss Gresham could have no idea of the sort of man she had consented to partner. An innocent such as she, never having gone into society, would not know how to take his extravagant compliments and false praise. She must be warned, he thought. Yet what right had he to be concerned about such things? She had friends in Bath. Looking over his shoulder at the Trents did not reassure him, however. They knew almost as little as Diana of the "smart set." He would have to do something. With this determination, he returned to his chair, wholly unaware that his charitable impulse had its roots in a fierce jealousy. Had anyone inquired, he would have staunchly maintained that he felt only concern for Miss Gresham's welfare, and, perhaps, a mild disappointment that she should be taken in by such a contemptible specimen. The reality was far deeper.

The captain would have been astonished and relieved had he seen Diana's amused disbelief listening to her elegant companion. He *was* very like Gerald, she was concluding. Gerald had said just the same sort of things to her, and gazed at her in the same soulful way. How incredibly silly she had been at seventeen, to have been taken in by this nonsense. Yet this consciousness of past mistakes also reassured her. Certainly she had learned her lesson. She was not the naïve, impressionable child who had gotten into such a scrape. This also meant, she concluded happily, that her judgment was now trustworthy. She need not be worried if she found recent acquaintances very attractive. Smiling, she looked around the ballroom. Captain Wilton had taken up his station against the wall once more, arms crossed. How mulish he looked.

Diana laughed for sheer joy, causing her partner to smirk complacently, sure that he had made a conquest, and making a certain young soldier not far away grit his teeth so violently his jaw ached.

SIX

DIANA AND AMANDA WERE ALONE AT THE BREAKFAST TABLE the following morning. George had gone out for an early ride, as the day was unusually fine, and the two women took advantage of their solitude to indulge in a thorough discussion of the assembly. When they had reviewed the recent history of all the Trents' old friends, the particularly striking toilettes each had noticed, and the pleasure each had felt in dancing, Amanda fixed her friend with twinkling eyes. "Now, Diana, you must say which of your partners you liked best. That is the obligation of an unmarried girl, and the prerogative of a married woman is to interrogate."

"You are scarcely two years older than I," she laughed.

"Do not try to divert me. Which?"

The gold flecks in Diana's eyes sparkled. "Mr. Boynton asked me to stand up with him. Did you see?"

"Boynton! You cannot mean that ridiculous man who accosted you in the street! Did he actually force himself upon you? Diana, you should have—"

"No, no. I was properly introduced. Captain Wilton presented me."

Amanda's mouth dropped open, and her dark eyes grew round.

Diana could not help but laugh again. "It seems Mr. Boynton is a friend of his brother's."

"Ah. That explains it. I daresay Captain Wilton was not over-pleased to meet him here."

"No, I don't think he was."

"I was so mortified when I realized that I had placed Robert in an awkward position. I should have realized that he cannot dance yet. I hope he was not offended."

Diana shook her head.

"And you are not telling me that Mr. Boynton was your favorite partner, Diana."

"Why not?" But she smiled.

Amanda did not even acknowledge this. "No. But perhaps… Robert Wilton?" She raised her eyebrows.

"I like him," admitted Diana, never having been schooled in dissimulation.

"He is a fine fellow. Yet not so handsome as Major Beresford. Or so polished as Colonel Ellmann. If it weren't for George, I should develop a tendre for him myself." She watched Diana closely as she spoke these names, and gathered more information than Diana dreamed from her expression.

"They are charming," she agreed. "But what of you, Amanda? You enjoyed the ball?"

"You are trying to turn the subject!"

"I?" Diana was all mock astonishment.

Her friend laughed and let it go. She had found out what she wanted to know in any case. "I had a splendid time."

"George seemed to enjoy himself, too."

"Yes." This word was spoken softly and gratefully. "Oh, Diana, I truly believe he is getting over his melancholy, and his weakness. This visit was an inspiration. Things are so much better between us."

"I am glad," Diana replied, sincerely, but with some reticence. She did not know how to treat confidences about marital difficulties. She wished to lend her aid without prying, and this line seemed appropriate.

Amanda appeared to understand. "What shall we do today?" she asked with a warm smile. "More shopping?"

"Not yet. I have had enough of dressmakers and milliners for a while. I have begun to feel like some sort of doll, pinned and prodded and spoken of as if I were not present, or perhaps merely half-witted."

"What then?" laughed her friend.

"A walk? Or perhaps a drive in the countryside?" Diana had been feeling the need for space and air. She was accustomed to daily tramps on the moors in all weathers. "You needn't come if you don't wish to."

"I should like a drive. I have never seen the country about here. Shall we go this afternoon? George may come with us."

Diana nodded. "Perhaps you would prefer to go together. You needn't feel that I—"

"You are the soul of discretion," interrupted Amanda, and they exchanged a look which said all that was necessary on this subject. Diana was relieved to see that she had not been a burden. "I shall write some letters this morning, then," she went on.

"I will begin my new novel."

The two ladies thus settled happily in the drawing room after breakfast, and for some time the comfortable silence was broken only by the scratching of Amanda's pen and the rustle of pages as Diana turned them. Occasionally, looking up from her novel, the latter felt a marvelous contentment. She had never imagined, living in isolation these past years, that she would come to this.

Around midmorning the bell rang, and the maid came up to announce a caller. Amanda gave her friend a speaking glance as Captain Robert Wilton was announced and gave orders that he should be admitted at once. Diana closed her book, started to rise, then simply sat straighter in her chair.

Wilton appeared, leaning slightly on his cane, and greeted them both.

"George should be back at any moment," said Amanda. "Do sit down." She moved from the writing desk to the sofa.

He hesitated, then joined her, taking the end nearest Diana's chair. There was a short silence.

"A fine day," said Amanda. The others agreed. "I hope you enjoyed the assembly last night, Captain Wilton?"

"As much as a sensible person can, in these days. I am not one of those who enjoy fripperies while important events are afoot abroad." He had meant this to open the way to a discreet warning about Boynton. All night, he had been absorbed with the necessity to guard Diana, and he had called with this single desire. But, as soon as he spoke and took in their response, he saw that he had blundered. "I did not mean that you..." he began. "That is, I was referring to those who never consider serious matters. An evening's entertainment is certainly harmless, but there are those..." He ran down, miserably aware of his lack of finesse.

"Of course," agreed Amanda, wondering a little what her friend so admired in this man. He was well enough, but she herself was drawn to rather a different type. With a smile, she remembered a younger George and the way he had swept into her life.

"I understood that the regimental officers grasped every opportunity to arrange amusements during the pauses in the fighting," said Diana, both to end the constrained silence and to make a point. It was all very well to complain that those at home ignored the war, and she understood his feelings, but it was not universally true, and she thought Captain Wilton a little single-minded. Diana had heard a great deal about soldiers' lighter moments last night. "Not only dancing, but racing and all manner of other things."

"Oh, yes," said Amanda. "Wellington loves balls. And I remember once a young lieutenant in George's regiment organized a donkey race. The riders had to sit backward. It was the funniest thing I ever saw." She grinned impishly. "George won. You must ask him about it."

Diana had seen Captain Wilton's lips twitch. "But you did nothing so frivolous, I suppose," she said.

"Compensation for hardship is somewhat different," he responded, a reminiscent gleam in his blue eyes.

"Indeed, I have suddenly remembered," put in Amanda. "Were

66

JANE ASHFORD

you not one of those responsible for the 'fox' hunt before Vitoria?" She turned to Diana, her eyes dancing again. "They flushed a weasel, and pursued it six miles."

Wilton burst out laughing. "Pluck up to the backbone, that weasel. Led us a merry dance, and got away in the end. Of course, our pack wasn't quite up to snuff."

"Three young hounds, a poodle, and a cocker spaniel," giggled Amanda. Diana laughed with them, happy for the turn the conversation had taken.

"The poodle had some natural talent," the captain informed her seriously, "but the cocker kept losing her nerve and turning for home. Our master of the hounds had a dev…deuced time keeping them to the scent."

"Of the *weasel*," added Amanda.

"Exactly."

His smile made his eyes crinkle at the outer corners, Diana thought, and they held an entrancing mixture of warm humor, mischievousness, and generosity.

Meeting Diana's interested gaze, he added, "I do not mean that everyone should be gloomy and think of nothing but the progress of the fighting. Far from it. But those who pretend that Napoleon does not exist, or that the war is simply a great spectacle put on for their entertainment, rouse my fury. Like your friend Boynton. He has a dubious reputation, you know."

Amanda's dark eyes lit with amusement, seeing why the captain had come. Diana was merely surprised. She opened her mouth to say that he was no friend of hers, just as the maid announced, "Mr. Ronald Boynton, ma'am."

Amanda had to bite her lower lip as she rose to greet the new arrival. It was too ridiculous, she thought, that the man should come in at just the instant to cause such chagrin, of different sorts, in her two companions. It was almost like a play.

Mr. Boynton rose from bowing over her hand and turned to

favor Diana with the same attention. "Miss Gresham," he murmured. "Lovelier than ever."

Captain Wilton returned his cordial nod with a glower, but this did not seem to strike Boynton as unusual. "I called to see how you did after the fatigues of the assembly," he added as he sat down.

"It ended at eleven," Diana pointed out. Bath hours were not London's.

Boynton acknowledged the difference with a grimace. "Indeed. I was speakin' of the fatigue engendered by tedium. I have never in my life encountered such a set of dowds and bores. I declare, some old poker face bent my ear for more than an hour about some rubbishin' sea battle. Can you credit it?"

"Admiral Riley, perhaps," answered Wilton, his voice filled with contempt.

"I shouldn't be surprised. I don't know why I come to Bath. It's always so."

"Well, why not go home, then," said Amanda, polite but hardly warm.

Boynton grinned, leaning back in his chair and twirling his quizzing glass in one negligent hand. "Must dance attendance on my aunt, actually. Holds the purse strings. Been dippin' a trifle deep at White's, too." He looked around as if to gather their admiration for this fashionable admission. "A spell of rustication was called for."

With a small smile, Diana wondered what he would think of her home if he called Bath rustication. She imagined Mr. Boynton forced to spend even a month in her lonely house, and her smile widened.

Captain Wilton saw her expression with annoyance. How could she be amused by this lisping coxcomb? No sensible woman would endure him for a moment. Oddly, it did not occur to the captain that he and his mother and sisters had often found his brother Faring and his friends hilarious, and that they often rallied him unmercifully about his dandified dress and mannerisms. Diana's response seemed something quite different, and ominous.

"Are you drinking the waters?" asked Amanda, angling for further amusement.

Boynton looked horrified. "I? No, no. Leave that to my aunt."

"She is ill?"

"So she says. For my part, I think she enjoys playin' the invalid and keepin' her family dancin' attendance round her bedside. Not a bad life, lyin' about, eatin' chocolates and readin' novels, and gettin' up whenever there is anything interestin' on."

"You are speaking of Lady Overton?" asked Wilton. Diana was struck by the change in his voice. Before, he had sounded so accessible and charming. Now his tone might have frozen the most impervious intruder.

Boynton did not seem to notice. He nodded. "That's it."

"I understood that she has been seriously ill all year. My mother mentioned that she nearly died recently."

The other man shrugged "So she says. Myself, I think it's just another excuse to change her will." He turned to Diana. "She alters the deuced thing every month. One never knows where one stands."

Wilton threw Diana a speaking look, as if to say: You see how callous and selfish this man is? Diana, who had reached a similar conclusion long ago, merely smiled slightly at him and lowered her eyes.

"So how is the knee?" Boynton added. "Faring mentioned you'd been hit. How long will your leave last? Perhaps you can muster out at last?"

"I shall return to my regiment as soon as the stiffness goes." Wilton's face was like stone.

Boynton shook his head. "You military fellows. Fire-breathers, eh? Can't see it myself." He turned to Diana. "I mean, the regimentals are all very well. Dashin', some of them. But you're bound to be posted abroad, and then where are you?"

"Just now, Belgium," snapped Wilton, goaded.

"Exactly." Boynton beamed on them all as if he had scored a hit.

Captain Wilton started to rise. He had had enough. "I must go," he began, only to be interrupted by the entrance of George Trent.

"Some damn fool has left a high-perch phaeton in our stable yard he said without preamble. "I could hardly get Thunderer past to the door." He surveyed the unwelcome crowd in his drawing room, looking quite daunting with his black eyepatch and impatient expression.

"Oh, dear," answered Amanda. "I wonder whose…?"

"It's mine," said Boynton. "Bought it only three weeks ago, and couldn't resist bringin' it along to Bath. Slap up to the echo, what?" Belatedly, under George's furious gaze, he added, "Sorry if it was blockin' you. Stupid groom ought to have moved it."

"Who," growled Trent, "are you?"

At once Boynton was on his feet and bowing. "Beg your pardon. Forgot we hadn't been introduced. Ronald Boynton. Friend of Miss Gresham's, you know."

This shifted George's outraged attention to Diana, who nearly gasped at the unfairness of it. Friend, indeed!

Amanda made a gurgling noise, and Robert Wilton could not restrain a smile. Diana's face had been so transparently readable.

"A new acquaintance, rather," Diana said.

Boynton bowed again. "Alas. But with great hopes."

"Fribble!" exploded George.

Everyone was still for a moment. Wilton was obviously struggling with a strong urge to laugh. Amanda looked amused but concerned at her husband's rudeness. Diana was merely taken aback, and Boynton did not believe his ears. "Beg pardon?" he replied finally.

"Idiotic sort of carriage anyway," added George. "Impractical, and deuced dangerous. Wouldn't have one on a wager."

Boynton's shock deepened. "But my dear sir. Phaeton. Absolutely all the crack, y'know. Why, Prinny himself—"

"Bonehead," muttered George, much more quietly than before. He was recovering his manners, slowly.

"Prinny!" exclaimed Boynton, aghast. "You really mustn't say such things. Not aloud, at least. No, really, he's dashed sensitive. Why, ever since Brummell remarked on his girth—"

"I'll say what I like in my own house!" roared Major Trent. "And I was speaking of you, you jingling fop."

Ronald Boynton was for a rare instant struck completely dumb. He did not entirely object to the epithet "fop," but the tone of the major's voice had made his contempt obvious, and Boynton was so accustomed to thinking of himself as the height of fashion— absolutely top of the trees—that it took him a moment to assimilate. When he had, he first gaped at the man, then shook his head. Clearly his host was as crude and ignorant as he looked. Years in benighted outposts far from London had blighted his taste beyond rescue. Boynton felt sincere pity for the ladies forced to live with such a barbarian. He threw them a commiserating glance. "Perhaps I should take my leave," he suggested gently.

"Splendid idea," replied Trent.

Boynton made a moue at Diana, shrugged slightly to show Amanda that he fully understood her plight, and made his way out of the room.

"Coxcomb," said George, dropping into a chair. "Why did you let him in, Amanda?"

"Susan brought him up without asking. We did have another caller, after all." She indicated Wilton with a nod.

"Yes. Hallo, Wilton. Well, you must tell the girl not to admit him after this. I can't stand the creature. Diana, you should not be making such friends."

This was too much. Diana hadn't a particle of interest in Boynton, beyond mild amusement, but to be continually taxed with his friendship and blamed for his faults, and then forbidden something she had never desired, annoyed her into answering,

"He is perfectly harmless, after all. I do not see what all the fuss is about."

"I shouldn't be too sure of that," said Captain Wilton.

"Oh, you are all just as bad as the Londoners!" Diana stood. "They close their minds to the war, but you think of nothing else. Must everyone be so earnest and solemn that he cannot even laugh at the affectations of a man like Boynton? *I* shall not become so!" And with this, she gathered her skirts and swept out of the room. Robert Wilton's censorious looks were simply beyond bearing. Why could he not be as before? Why must their growing understanding be spoiled by this idiocy?

In the drawing room, the three remaining exchanged an uneasy glance.

"I didn't mean…" began George.

"I was only trying…" said Wilton at the same time.

"Never mind," replied Amanda. "She will be all right in a bit."

SEVEN

A HALF HOUR LATER, WHEN WILTON HAD GONE AND GEORGE was immersed in the newspaper, Amanda went upstairs to find Diana. When her knock had been acknowledged, she put her head around the door of Diana's bedchamber and said, "Are you all right?"

Diana sat in an armchair next to the window, chin in hand, looking out. "Yes, of course. I'm sorry I lost my temper. I beg your pardon. It was silly."

Amanda came in. "No, it wasn't. Why *should* you think of nothing but the war? You were quite right. One must strike a balance. George and his friends have done nothing but fight for so long—many of them since they were little more than boys, actually—that it is difficult for them to shift their thoughts. And it is particularly hard for them now, since the outcome of their long war is about to be decided all over again, and they are not allowed to be there. And when it is a question of gossip or assemblies, which would not interest George, at least, even in the calmest times...well..." She shrugged.

Diana grimaced. "I know. I was stupid. It was just that they both seemed to hold me responsible for Boynton's presence, and"—she spread her hands, searching for a phrase strong enough and failing to find one—"I am *not*."

"Of course you are not." Amanda smiled. "They know that. They were simply making pronouncements, as men will do. They are almost always sorry afterward."

"What do you mean?"

Amanda colored slightly. "Well, it is a thing I have noticed. Men are fond of sweeping declarations, don't you think? They like to tie everything up in a phrase, which is often quite outrageously untrue, and throw it out like an edict. Later, when they are cooler, they grow more reasonable." She hesitated, considering. "Actually, they usually forget the matter entirely, and you can quietly do as you like. I remember we had a cook once…" She paused. "But you don't care for that."

"On the contrary," answered Diana. "I am fascinated." She was also impressed, as she had been several times before, with the changes in Amanda since they had known one another as girls. Diana had had no opportunity to observe the male sex or learn its quirks. Amanda had, and Diana sensed that her friend had made the most of her chance. "Do you not sometimes feel deceitful?" she asked.

"When I do as I please despite George's…hasty decrees?" Amanda shrugged. "He doesn't really *mean* it, you see. That is, sometimes he does, and I can tell. In *those* cases, I either obey or tell him my opinion, and we discuss the matter." She smiled. "'Discuss' is a mild word for some of those occasions. But mostly he just needs to explode. Often it is about something quite different from our conversation—an orderly's stupidity perhaps, or poor forage for his men. Afterward he is all right again. He does not *really* care where I purchase my chickens or"—she smiled again at Diana—"whether I enjoy a ball and forget about the war. He is merely…fulminating."

Diana laughed. "What a word."

Her friend's eyes danced. "I learned it from a lieutenant of artillery."

"But do you really think that they will forget all about Boynton and all of that"—she made a helpless gesture—"this morning?"

"Oh, George will. He will scarcely remember Mr. Boynton's existence tomorrow." She dimpled. "Unless he should happen to leave his phaeton in George's path again, and I doubt he will."

Diana frowned, taking this in.

"With Captain Wilton, the case is rather different, I think," Amanda added slowly, watching her friend's face.

"Why?"

"Well, I'm not certain, mind, but I believe that he was jealous."

"Jealous?" Diana was incredulous. "Of Mr. Boynton? But what reason could he possibly have...?"

"Boynton is very elegant. Many women are dazzled by such... ensembles. And he *does* seem to be taken with you."

"But do you mean Captain Wilton would be bothered because I danced with Mr. Boynton? Do you think he would care...?" Diana broke off, confused and thrilled by this new idea. The possibility that Robert Wilton resented her acknowledgment of another man, even such a pallid one as she had given Boynton, was not unpleasing. Indeed, the thought made her smile slightly and gaze out the window from under lowered eyelids. Seen in this light, the morning's events looked quite different. Her resentment toward Wilton dissolved, though she still believed she had been right to speak as she had.

Amanda had no trouble interpreting her look. "Why do you like him so?" she asked. "I mean, he is well enough, but... I don't mean to offend you."

Diana shook her head. "It is the way he *is*. That is a poor explanation, I know, but I am not certain I can better it. He is...oh, aware of one's hesitations and willing to let them be. He understands that others may feel what he does not, and just as deeply. He is intelligent and amusing." Diana shrugged. "And, of course, he has the most wonderful smile. I think him handsome."

"I never said he wasn't," began Amanda, then paused as she saw the other's teasing look. She shook her head. "Incorrigible. Your reasons are very sound. I am impressed. I was not half so sensible when I first met George."

This made Diana look up quickly, then down. Amanda was not mocking her, but the comparison somehow saddened Diana and dissipated the warm glow she had been feeling. She was being sensible, just as she had been so entirely the opposite seven years

ago. Yet "sensible," when spoken aloud, sounded so drearily practical and dull. In a sudden flash, she remembered her trembling
excitement when she had gone to meet Gerald Carshin as a girl.
Had that feeling gone forever? Yet it had brought her only disaster.
Raising her chin, Diana took herself firmly in hand. She was wiser
as well as older now, and she would be guided by her "sensible"
mind.

In the afternoon, postponing their drive, Amanda and Diana
walked down into the town to visit the Pump Room. It was not
the fashionable hour, but Amanda had been feeling a trifle unwell
the past few days, and she had decided to try the waters. They
kept a leisurely pace, gazing into shop windows and stopping
once to speak to an acquaintance. When they reached the rooms,
they found them sparsely populated. Amanda went at once to the
gleaming pumps and procured a glass, drawn for her by one of the
attendants. "It smells nasty," she said when she returned, sniffing
doubtfully at the contents.

"Throw it away," suggested Diana, who wholeheartedly agreed.

"Oh, no. They were so kind in getting it for me, and they would
see."

"We can walk into another room and find a discreet place to
dispose of it."

Amanda shook her head. "I mean to drink it. I haven't been
feeling the thing at all. It is just…" She eyed the glass.

Diana laughed. "Well, you decide. I would chuck it out the
window. But I will support you while you drink. Shall we sit
down?"

They did, and Amanda took a small sip. "Ugh."

Diana couldn't help but laugh again, though she pressed her
lips together when Amanda shot her an indignant look.

"It is all very well for you. You never complain of so much as a
headache. I suppose you have no idea how uncomfortable it is to
feel your whole insides heaving about like the sea."

"I fear not." Diana's eyes sparkled.

Amanda took another tiny sip. "Well, perhaps I shall slip something into your dinner one night, to show you. It is the most dreadful sensation."

"I'm sure it must be," replied her friend, truly sympathetic.

"Oh, look, there is Mr. Boynton. Do you suppose that is his aunt?"

Diana turned to see Ronald Boynton escorting a very large older woman into the Pump Room. They moved slowly, less, it appeared, because of the lady's vast bulk than due to her health. It was obvious that she had been seriously ill. Diana watched as they made their way to the nearest chair. Boynton settled his companion, then fetched a glass of the waters.

Not until he was seated did he notice the two women. Then, with a hurried word to his aunt, he rose and came across to them. "An unexpected pleasure, to see you so soon again," he said. He saw Amanda's glass. "You're not drinkin' that awful stuff?"

Amanda nodded without enthusiasm.

"You'll be sick," was his blunt reply. "Seen it a hundred times. It only helps if you're already half-dead."

Seeing that Amanda did not appreciate this information, Diana said, "Is that your aunt?"

Boynton indicated that it was.

"And have the waters helped her?"

"She's forever coddling her insides with some nostrum or other. The waters are no worse. And no better, far as I can see."

His uncaring tone made both women gaze at him with disdain. "She looks as if she has been very ill indeed," said Amanda, who looked rather green herself.

"She always appears on her last legs, yet never is," answered Boynton. He seemed unconscious of both his callousness and their contempt. "By the by, I have had some good news from London." He did not wait for them to ask what it might be, which was lucky, for neither was about to do so. They were directing pitying glances toward his unfortunate relative. "A few of my friends may toddle down here soon," he told them. "Seems London's dashed dull." He paused. "Of course, Bath is worse, but I shan't tell them that because it won't be once they arrive. Most sportin' set of fellows you could meet." He looked at them as if conferring a particular favor. "Lord Faring, you know. And five or six others. Quite a party."

But Amanda and Diana had been diverted. Awed, they had watched Lady Overton struggle up from the chair where her nephew had left her and progress slowly but majestically toward them. She looked, thought Diana, like a massive ship under full sail.

"Ronald," she said now, in a tone that made all three of them straighten and Boynton start visibly.

He turned at once and sprang up. "Oh, Aunt Sybil. Have you finished your dose? Care for another?"

Diana and Amanda exchanged an amazed glance. The change in Boynton's voice was complete. His air of slightly weary superiority had vanished. He sounded like a schoolboy who abjectly hopes he will not be caned, but expects that, in fact, he will be.

Lady Overton merely surveyed the group. Her eyes were very keen in her broad face, Diana saw, and she began to revise her opinion of the lady's state.

Apparently the older woman found them acceptable, for her next words were, "Do you intend to present your friends to me, Ronald?"

Boynton actually flushed. "Oh. Of course. Aunt Sybil, Mrs. Trent and Miss Gresham."

Lady Overton nodded. Amanda and Diana had already risen, and they murmured greetings. "Will you take my chair?" offered Diana.

"No, thank you. We must be going. My doctor says I must walk as much as possible." Lady Overton's expression suggested that she found this advice unpalatable. "Come, Ronald."

"Yes, aunt," said the dandy in a cowed voice. Diana suppressed a smile.

Lady Overton took his arm, leaning on it rather more heavily than she really needed to, Diana thought, and they started to turn away. At the last moment, her ladyship looked back over her shoulder. "You should lie down, young woman," she told Amanda. Then, gripping so tightly that Boynton showed a distinct list to the side, she moved away.

"Well." Diana laughed. "There is some justice after all. She is precisely the sort of aunt Mr. Boynton deserves. How George will enjoy it when we tell him! And I had imagined her as such a despised, neglected creature. We must invite her the next time Boynton wishes to come visit, Amanda."

"Yes." But Amanda did not laugh. "Diana, I think, perhaps, I should go home now. I…don't feel well."

Diana turned at once. Indeed, her friend was terribly pale and seemed unsteady. "My dear, of course! Here is your shawl. Take my arm."

Though she would normally have rejected any such suggestion, Amanda did so. She was trembling, Diana found, and her hands were icy cold. Frightfully concerned, Diana led her toward the door.

"It must be the waters," said Amanda. "Mr. Boynton was right, it seems. They've disagreed with me."

"We will get you a chair," promised Diana. "You'll be home in a trice."

"It is so ridiculous, but I think I would like to ride."

"There is no question about it." Arriving at the street, Diana looked around for an empty chair. Seeing one not far away, she signaled to the chairmen, and, in another moment, Amanda was settled inside. Diana walked beside the window, keeping an anxious eye on her friend. Amanda had leaned back, rested her head on the plush, and closed her eyes. She was still alarmingly white.

Privately hoping it was nothing serious, Diana said, "Those waters would make anyone sick. You must not take any more, Amanda."

"I shan't! How can they call them medicinal?"

"Some people believe anything nasty is medicine. Only think of the dreadful messes we were given when we had the whooping cough."

Amanda laughed weakly, as Diana had hoped she would. They had been ill together as children, and Amanda had stayed at the Greshams' house in order to keep her sisters from infection.

"Here is the hill," she added. "We are nearly there."

The chairmen labored a bit going up toward the Royal Crescent. Diana slowed her pace to match theirs and wished they were home.

A tall, thin figure emerged from George Street and turned toward them. Diana felt a flood of relief. "Captain Wilton!"

He looked up at once, and smiled, then frowned as he saw Diana's expression. "Is something wrong?" he asked, approaching.

"Yes, Amanda is ill. I am taking her home, but could you go ahead and warn them? A doctor should be sent for, I think, and... Oh, I don't know what else."

"Of course," he replied, concerned, and turned to go.

Only then did Diana notice his cane and remembered his injury. "Oh, perhaps I should go and you stay with Amanda," she blurted.

"Nonsense," was his only reply, and he set off at a rapid pace, swinging his wounded leg a little with each step but clearly quite able to hurry.

Diana breathed a sigh of relief, certain that she had put the problem in good hands.

"'Op it, Jem," said the leading chairman. "The lady's sick like."

The men went faster. Diana wasn't certain whether they were truly sympathetic or worried about Amanda regurgitating the horrid waters in their chair. A bit of both, she concluded. In ten minutes they reached the house and found its entire population waiting on the pavement for their arrival. George Trent looked nearly as pale as his wife as he hurried forward to help her up. "Amanda! What is it? Are you all right?"

"Only a trifle queasy," she replied, trying to stand straight without swaying. "I foolishly drank some of the waters, and they have disagreed with me. I shall be fine in a little while, when I have lain down."

"I'll take you up."

"I can walk," she protested.

"Nonsense." And he swept her into his arms and carried her inside.

"I'll pay off the chair," said Captain Wilton. "You go ahead."

Diana walked in with the maids. "Has someone gone for a doctor?" she asked.

"Yes, miss. Billy went. He said one of the grooms next door knew a good one, since his mistress is sickly." The girl wrung her hands. "Will she be all right, miss?"

"Of course! Send the doctor up as soon as he arrives."

"I will, miss."

Diana ran up the stairs. She found Amanda lying on her bed and George sitting beside it holding her hand. "The doctor should be here soon," she told them.

Amanda started up. "Oh, I don't need a doctor. It is passing already."

"Nonetheless," replied George.

His wife sank back. "This is all so silly. It is my own fault for drinking those dreadful waters. They are such a cheat, George."

"Undoubtedly. Yet you weren't feeling quite the thing before, either." He grimaced. "I sometimes fear that living abroad has ruined your constitution, Amanda. And it is all my doing. I—"

"It has not! I never heard anything so ridiculous." Amanda struggled to a sitting position. "Look, I am much better already."

George gently pushed her down again. "If you move before the doctor comes, I shall tell him you are a dreadful invalid."

She wrinkled her nose at him. "He would only recommend the waters, and then I *should* be."

They heard the bell below, and, in the next moment the maid was ushering a kindly looking older gentleman into the room. "Dr. Clark," he announced. "Your groom said I was wanted."

"My wife is ill," said George. "She took a glass of the waters at the Pump Room, and they have disagreed with her."

Dr. Clark raised his bushy gray brows. "Indeed?"

"She is delicate," added George.

"I am not!" Amanda sat up again, defiant. "I feel much better already. I daresay—"

"Perhaps *I* should be the one to do that," the doctor interrupted, though so jovially that it could not offend. "I shall just examine you, since I am here, eh? And then we shall see."

"But—"

"If you will leave me with my patient." Dr. Clark indicated the door.

Diana went out. She left her shawl in her own bedchamber, then walked downstairs again. She would catch the doctor as he left, she thought, and find out his opinion.

"How is she?" asked Robert Wilton, coming out of the drawing room and into the hall.

"Oh, you startled me! I thought you had gone."

"With Mrs. Trent so ill? How could I? But I am sorry I surprised you."

Diana waved this aside. "The doctor is examining her. He doesn't seem too concerned."

"I daresay it is nothing."

"I hope so."

They fell silent, Diana too worried to chat and Wilton watching her face with compassion and admiration. The minutes passed. After a while, Diana looked up and said, "Oh, I'm sorry. I was thinking."

"It is not of the least consequence."

Grateful to him for refraining from meaningless chatter, Diana smiled. He responded, and their eyes held for a long moment, mutually appreciative. The exchange was broken only by footsteps on the stairs.

Turning, Diana saw the doctor. "How is she?"

"Quite all right," he replied. "A passing queasiness. She must stay away from our waters. They are not for everyone, you know. But there is nothing whatever *wrong*." He seemed to emphasize this word unduly, and his eyes were bright under the bushy brows, but Diana was too relieved to notice anything else.

"Oh, I am so glad!"

"Thank you for coming so promptly, doctor," said George Trent, who had followed him down the stairs. Major Trent was grinning.

"Happy to oblige." Dr. Clark took his hat from the maid, bowed slightly, and departed.

"I must go back to Amanda." George disappeared upstairs.

Diana let out a great sigh.

"You were very concerned about your friend," said Wilton.

"Of course."

He smiled. "I was about to send this. I may as well leave it." He held out an envelope addressed to both the Trents and Diana.

"What is it?"

"An invitation. I thought it wrong to call again on the same day, but the idea occurred to me, and I hoped to secure your consent."

"My..."

"All of you, that is," he added hastily.

"But for what?"

"An excursion to Beechen Cliff. A picnic, perhaps." Seeing her inquiring look, he said, "Have you heard of it? It is on the other side of the river, and the views are splendid."

"Ah."

"One can see the whole town, and beyond to the hills opposite."

"It sounds lovely."

"Will you come, then? Next week?" He leaned a little forward.

"I shall have to ask Amanda. And be certain she is recovered."

"Yes. Of course." But his face fell.

"I should like to, very much," Diana added, and she felt her heart beating faster.

Wilton smiled, blue eyes lighting. "Would you? Good."

"I'll speak to Amanda later on."

"Yes." There was a pause. "I should be going."

"Thank you for helping earlier."

He brushed this aside.

"And for the invitation." Diana felt elated but weary. The events of the previous hour had taken a toll.

Captain Wilton seemed to sense her fatigue. He simply bowed and said goodbye. When the door shut behind him, Diana moved automatically to the narrow window beside it and watched him walk away, his gait only a touch awkward from his wound. The set of his shoulders and the small curls of brown hair at the back of his neck touched her somehow, and she went back up to Amanda clutching his invitation to her breast.

EIGHT

AMANDA WAS FULLY RECOVERED THE NEXT DAY. INDEED, SHE seemed in better frame than before. Captain Wilton's expedition was duly agreed upon for the following Wednesday, and that day dawned clear and unusually warm, to the host's great relief. Wilton fetched his party in a rented open barouche at midmorning.

Diana wore a new gown of white muslin sprigged with tiny dark-blue flowers and trimmed with ribbons of the same hue. Ruffles at neck, wrist, and hem adorned the rather plain cut. She had threaded her straw hat with a matching length of ribbon, and rejoiced that she might leave off a pelisse in the mild spring weather, though George insisted that Amanda don one over her rose-pink gown. As they climbed into the carriage, the ladies gallantly awarded the forward-facing seats, Diana saw admiration in Wilton's eyes. A warm glow suffused her; she looked forward to spending an entire afternoon in Captain Wilton's company.

They drove down into the center of Bath, across the Avon, and up again on the opposite bank. The road soon became steep, and the horses strained in their harness. "Shall we walk, Wilton?" asked George Trent.

"We're nearly there."

And, indeed, in a short time they turned sharply and came out onto Beechen Cliff, a parklike area above the town. "Oh my," said Amanda. "You can see all of Bath spread out like a map. Look, there is the Abbey Church tower."

"And there is Royal Crescent," responded Diana, pointing. "I believe I can see our very windows. What a splendid place!"

Captain Wilton looked gratified. He climbed from the barouche and offered a hand to Amanda. "Shall we walk about a little?"

The four of them strolled together for a while, exclaiming

over various landmarks and praising Wilton's ingenuity in finding such a pleasant spot. But, gradually, the Trents dropped behind, Amanda leaning a little on her husband's arm. Diana did not even notice her friend's absence until they were a good distance off. Then she hesitated, suddenly very aware of her companion's muscular arm under her hand and his shoulder occasionally brushing hers.

"Aren't these fine old trees?" said Wilton, apparently feeling no constraint. "The prospect is particularly striking when framed by two branches, isn't it? Look there." He indicated a vista between two of the great oaks.

Diana agreed, at the same time telling herself that she was being silly. George and Amanda were still in sight. The proprieties were fully satisfied. Yet she had not been alone with Wilton since their first encounter, when her feelings had been far different.

"Ah, it is good to stroll again," continued Wilton. "There was a time when I feared I never would."

Diana's preoccupation with herself evaporated. "You are not using your cane! I did not notice until just now."

He smiled down at her. "No. I left it behind for the first time today. My knee is improving rapidly now." He stopped and flexed it slightly to demonstrate. The movement was stiff, and his face showed some discomfort, but it was mixed with elation.

"So this outing marks an epoch," laughed Diana. "We should celebrate it somehow."

"It does indeed." His blue eyes were serious as they met hers, and Diana had the feeling that he was speaking of something other than his leg. She drew a slightly shaky breath at the message he seemed to convey. "For the first time, I am nearly reconciled to my wound. I cannot help but regret being absent from the army, yet, if I had not been hit, I would never have come to Bath. That would have been a tragedy indeed."

"It is a lovely place," agreed Diana, feeling the response banal but unable to think of a better one under his intense gaze. Her heart was beating very fast.

"Far more so than I had ever imagined," he replied.

He seemed to wait for some sign from her, and Diana was anxious to give it. But her tongue was suddenly clumsy. Once again she felt her inexperience, and the unfortunate effects of years of solitude. A young woman of five-and-twenty should not be so awkward, she told herself miserably. Captain Wilton would certainly expect more assurance than her blush. She made a great effort. "I had high hopes for this visit when we left Yorkshire. But they have been far surpassed."

"Ah." His face shifted slightly, the intensity a little eased by relief. "It appears we feel the same, then."

Diana raised her chin and met his gaze squarely. "Yes."

Their steps had slowed, and now they stopped altogether as the two of them looked at one another. A current of understanding passed between them, establishing many things without words. Diana knew at that moment that she loved, and was loved in return, and she felt that a wonderful future was opening up before her, requiring only a little more time to blossom.

Wilton seemed to feel the same, for he said nothing more just then. He merely tucked her hand a bit more securely into his elbow and walked on, his expression content.

"You were wounded at Bordeaux?" asked Diana after a while, eager to learn everything about him.

"Yes." He laughed a little. "I survived the whole of the Peninsular War without a scratch, only to be hit at the fag end of the thing, when we had crossed into France. A ricochet, too, they tell me. Bounced off one of the big guns."

"I wonder what it's like," mused Diana, almost to herself.

"Stopping a musket ball?" He was surprised.

She smiled at her own foolishness. "I mean the whole thing, really. The battle, and afterward. How idiotic I must sound to you."

"No. But it is not a pleasant memory."

"I beg your pardon. I should not have—"

"What I mean is, I don't think you would thank me for recounting my 'adventures,'" he interrupted.

Diana shook her head. "On the contrary. I should like to know, if you do not mind talking about it."

He shrugged, as if uncertain about this himself, and paused. "The actual battle," he said slowly then, "is all right. Mine is a cavalry regiment, you know, and, when with Wellington, I also fought with the cavalry. It goes so fast one's memory is a blur, with vivid flashes, like tableaux. I remember a mount rearing and falling, an infantryman lunging with his bayonet, a friend standing in his stirrups and brandishing his saber for a charge. The rest of the time, you simply labor. It becomes automatic; your arm moves, you direct your horse to the thick of it." He shook his head. "The waiting beforehand is far worse to me because you have time then to imagine all the horrors that might befall you and your men, you see. And of course, after, being wounded..." He shuddered.

"Was it very dreadful?" asked Diana softly, though she knew the answer from his face.

"It was the worst thing I have ever endured," he replied, seeming hardly aware of his listener any longer. "My sergeant picked me up and got me away from the fighting to a wagon. From there it was as I imagine hell must be. We rode for hours in that infernal, jolting cart, the sun burning us up and the motion making wounds gape for the flies. We thought ourselves saved when we reached the hospital, but that was the worst of all. It was rank with fevers, and the room where the surgeon examined my knee was ankle-deep in blood; a pile of severed limbs higher than my head stood in the corner. I thought he would take my leg. The stench and the sights were so vile that I fainted as I tried to plead with him to leave it." He drew a long, shaky breath. Diana pressed his arm, her gold-flecked eyes wide with horror and sympathy.

He looked down at her for a long moment, his expression quite blank. Then, suddenly, he came to himself and realized what he had said. "Good God! I...I beg your pardon. I forgot myself. I have never repeated these things to anyone, not even Trent, who no doubt saw worse. I don't know what possessed me to say them to *you*. I haven't the brains of a—"

"I'm honored that you did so," Diana broke in. "It is flattering to receive such confidences."

"*Such* confidences," he echoed bitterly. "You should not be subjected to scenes so terrible."

"You were," she pointed out.

"Yes, but I am a soldier, trained to hardship and bitter necessities. When it is necessary to fight for one's country—"

"You are always saying that no one should ignore the war," Diana interrupted. "If more people heard such stories, they could not."

"You are right." But he looked uneasy. "Yet, despite my arguments, I cannot wish it. It is enough that soldiers bear these things. Those who can should remain..." He hesitated, looking down at her. "...unburdened."

"Yet burdens are often lighter when shared."

Wilton shook his head as if to dismiss her statement, yet he silently admired her compassionate heart.

"And if one is cut off from great chunks of a person's history, one can never really know him, or..." Diana broke off. She had been about to add "love him."

Captain Wilton smiled a little. "So each must tell his direst experiences? I am not convinced. But, since I have inadvertently done so, is it not your turn now?" His smile widened, as if this were a good joke and a welcome change of topic.

Diana froze. For an endless moment it felt as if her heart had stopped. Though he thought he was jesting, she *did* have a history, one that might shock him more than his had her. She had pushed the past from her thoughts, blithely plunging into love with this man and looking forward to an idyllic future without considering its implications. What if he found out? Gerald Carshin was presumably still alive. There was no reason to think otherwise. He lived in London, or had lived there. Her secret was not safe here, as it had been in the wilds of Yorkshire. She was, perhaps, even obliged to reveal it. What would he do if she told him? Diana looked up. His feelings would change, she thought. He might understand, sympathize, but she knew the world's reaction to those women who had made such a mistake.

"What is it?" asked Captain Wilton. "You're white as a sheet. Are you ill?"

"I...I fear I am, a little," she murmured, feeling herself a coward.

"It is my fault! Why did I not mind my wretched tongue? Come, we will find the Trents, and go home, if you like."

Diana protested, but feebly, allowing him to believe that his stories of the war had made her faint. Under any other circumstances she would have scorned such an accusation, but now she was only too grateful for the diversion from questions about her past. What was she to do? Visions of a rosy future were crumbling in her mind.

They found George and Amanda under a great oak tree not too far from where they had left their carriage. But another vehicle now stood behind it, and two young men were adding the finishing touches to a linen-covered table beneath the branches. "Captain Wilton, this is magical," exclaimed Amanda. "What have you done?"

"Simply engaged the kitchen of one of the hotels to provide our picnic," he replied with a brief smile. "My landlady did not feel her staff up to it. But I fear Miss Gresham is not feeling well."

Amanda stepped forward. "Really? Diana, what is it? Headache?" One of the waiters so far forgot himself as to look openly dismayed as he set a platter bearing an entire cold roast chicken on the table.

"No, no. It is nothing," she protested. "I merely felt a little tired for a moment. I am quite all right now."

"It is my doing," added Wilton ruefully. "I have been telling Miss Gresham stories about the war." Seeing George Trent's surprised look, he said, "You cannot think me any more foolish than I do myself, George. I don't know what possessed me."

Amanda looked from one to the other of her companions as if uncertain what she should do.

"I tell you it is nothing," repeated Diana, anxious to dismiss this subject. She moved forward. "The table is lovely. It *is* like magic."

And certainly the scene Wilton's servitors had created was entrancing. Shaded by the oak tree was a square table covered with a snowy cloth that dropped almost to the grass. Four chairs were pulled up to it, and it was set with cutlery and china adorned with varicolored spring flowers. Flanking the roast chicken, which made a splendid show, were a round of yellow cheese, a brown loaf with a dish of butter, half a sliced ham, pickles and relishes, and, the crowning touch, a carefully arranged pyramid of glowing fresh peaches, their delicate hues seeming sunlit even under the tree.

"Where did you procure peaches?" wondered Amanda as they all gathered around the feast. "It is so early in the year."

Wilton looked at the other waiter, who answered, "From southern Spain, madam," causing Amanda to let out an ecstatic sigh.

"If you are sure you are all right," said Wilton to Diana.

"Of course."

"Then?" He held a chair for her.

Diana sat down, as did Amanda opposite her. The gentlemen took the remaining seats. Wilton signaled, and the younger waiter came forward with a bottle wrapped in a white cloth and four crystal goblets. Deftly he set the latter before them and poured.

"Champagne!" cried Amanda, clapping her hands with delight. "Captain Wilton!"

"I thought we might dare a little," he answered, then held his glass aloft, its facets and pale effervescent contents sparkling. "A toast to the future," he added, "to victory in Belgium and to our happiness when the war is at last definitively won."

They all raised their goblets, George cordially approving, Amanda almost tremulous with happiness, and Diana smiling but sick at heart. This was all so beautiful, she thought—the exquisite prospect of Bath spread out at her left, the perfect nearer scene, and the spring air so soft and mellow. But she no longer felt she belonged. The moment with Wilton had called up a host of old feelings and memories, those she had resolutely suppressed when she left home. And she saw now that she was here on false pretenses. Even Amanda thought her one thing when she was really another. It had been wrong of her to hide her past. She ought to have given her friend some hint at least before accepting her generous hospitality. Now it seemed too late, and the issue was further complicated by Robert Wilton, whom she had not foreseen. Had she imagined she would fall in love, she might have considered the implications, but she had unthinkingly grasped at escape without considering the effect on others. Selfish, she accused herself, but this did no good now. She must think how to undo the tangle she had made in the way least hurtful to those she loved.

"Diana?" said Amanda softly.

Diana started. She was still holding her goblet high, while the others had drunk and set theirs down. She made a dismissive gesture and followed suit, turning to watch Captain Wilton and George, who were conferring over the chicken.

"No, no," Major Trent was declaring. "You're the host, Robert. It's your job. I shan't lift a finger."

"But I'm no hand at carving," the other replied, holding the long knife as if it were some alien instrument. "I've mangled a bird or two in Spain, but no more."

George crossed his arms on his chest and shook his head, adamant.

"Well, you'll advise me, at least?" asked Wilton.

Major Trent allowed that he would do that much, and the captain bent to his task. "I suppose I can start here." He inserted the blade between the chicken leg and body.

Trent gave a tiny cough.

"No?" Wilton looked up.

"I'd, er, start at the…er, front," murmured George.

"The front?" He turned the platter, trying to remain unaware of the amused scrutiny of the waiters, who had withdrawn somewhat until they should be needed again, but were well within hearing. He angled the knife against the breast.

The major nodded. "Slices, you know. The ladies will like those."

"Ah." Captain Wilton attempted to thinly slice the chicken. The result was rather more chunk-like, and he contemplated the bits ruefully.

Amanda burst out laughing, throwing her dark head back, then guiltily bowing it and covering her mouth. "I'm sorry," she said with a gurgle. "I truly am. It is just so…"

"Ridiculous," finished Wilton, torn between complete agreement, a desire to join her laughter, and a wish to appear poised and knowledgeable before Diana. "The last time I carved a chicken, I used a saber," he added pensively.

"If I'd only thought, I might have brought George's," Amanda replied unsteadily. "It is sitting in plain sight in the dressing room."

The four exchanged a glance, the vision of Wilton attacking the chicken with his sword clearly in all their minds, and then they began to laugh. Even Diana could not resist the picture, and she found that the shared levity lightened her mood as well. She would find some solution, she decided, and, until she did, she would not brood.

"Come, George," said Wilton, holding out the knife. "You must do it after mocking me in this callous way."

"Nonsense. You are going on splendidly," retorted the major with a grin.

Shaking his head, Wilton began again, and, eventually, the bird was acceptably dismembered, and they ate their meal.

"Have you ever known anything so pleasant?" sighed Amanda after a while. "It is like the best of Portugal and England rolled into one. We are al fresco, and the food is wonderful, and there is not the least chance a troop of bandits or ruffians will appear over the crest of the hill and send us running."

"Not unless the starched-up dowagers of Bath discover what we are up to and charge en masse to disperse us," agreed Wilton.

"You think they would not approve of dining outdoors?" inquired Diana with a smile.

"I'm certain of it. When I was arranging this party, one elderly woman stepped over to assure me that we would all take our deaths of cold, if not worse. Never saw her before in my life." He tucked his chin back and spoke in a fruity but stern voice. "'Nothing is more deleterious to one's health than sitting still out-of-doors, young man. I thought everyone knew *that*.'"

They all laughed again.

"She was wide as a house and looked sick as a dog herself," finished Wilton. "I nearly asked her if she had personal experience with the dangers, but it seemed too unkind."

"She sounds like Lady Overton," said Amanda to Diana.

"Someone remarkably like her," Wilton replied.

"Who is that?" asked George.

"She is Mr. Boynton's invalid aunt," Diana added.

George looked surprised and slightly displeased at the mention of Boynton. "Not how I pictured her, really."

"She is not at all!" said Amanda, and told them the story of their encounter with Lady Overton. Before she was half-finished, they were laughing, and both men seemed very gratified by the end.

"Serves him right," said Wilton. "Puppy!"

"I just wish she kept him on a tighter leash," agreed Major Trent. The ladies groaned at his pun.

The captain turned to Diana. "When you next see—"

"If you call him my friend again, I shall throw this peach at you," she threatened, brandishing the fruit she had been peeling. Wilton drew up an arm in mock fear. "I know him no better than the rest of you."

The captain found this so gratifying that he forgot what he had been about to say, and even George Trent seemed pleased.

"I am going to put my peach in my champagne," declared Amanda. "Have them fill my glass, George." She held it out imperiously.

He instead took it from her. "No more for you. You're rowing with half an oar as it is."

"I am not!" Amanda was indignant. "I am only happy." She threw out her arms and leaned back in her chair.

"Umm. Time to be packing up, I think, Wilton."

Amanda straightened and frowned, making it apparent that her high spirits were not due to overindulgence. "George!"

He gave her a significant glance. "I'm merely being cautious, my dear."

Amanda seemed to recall something, hesitated, then agreed. "I suppose you're right. But surely we can finish our peaches."

They did so, then lingered a little while as the sun moved down the western sky. It was nearly four before they rose and reluctantly moved toward the barouche again. "What luxury," said Amanda, watching the waiters move forward. "We needn't even think of what to do with the three peaches remaining. It will all be whisked out of sight for someone else to worry over. I think we should always dine so."

"It might be less pleasant in the rain," suggested her husband. "Or in the winter months."

"Fustian!" she retorted, but she pulled him down beside her in the forward seat when they had climbed up and rode homeward with her hand tucked into his arm and her head on his shoulder.

Diana, sitting beside Captain Wilton and very conscious of his proximity, watched the Trents with wistful indulgence. How lucky they were, she thought, despite their misfortunes. If she could be half so happy... She glanced sidelong and found Wilton smiling down at her. A warm glow enveloped her, and she promised herself that she would find a way to secure such happiness for both herself and Captain Wilton.

NINE

A SERIES OF DAYS PASSED QUICKLY BUT HAPPILY FOR THE Trent party. As May unfolded, it became apparent that they would remain in Bath for an unspecified, but substantial, length of time. George was content making the rounds of military friends visiting the town, which was a constantly changing roster, always full of the latest war news, or at least fresh opinions. Amanda was obviously and luminously happy, though less strong than Diana remembered. Often she would not emerge from her bedchamber until noon, and then only to establish herself on the drawing-room sofa to read and write letters until George should come in and suggest a sedate drive in their hired carriage. Diana was thrown more on her own resources as the visit lengthened, and her long walks were usually solitary, with one of the maids trailing behind.

And yet she was not unhappy. Her fears of the picnic day gradually receded, as nothing came of them. She and Captain Wilton seemed to have reached a tacit understanding. Though nothing was *officially* settled between them, everyone appeared to take it for granted that it soon would be. He would make an offer, and Diana would accept, and all would be well. Wilton seemed content to leave it thus for now, and Diana certainly was. This situation allowed her to reap the benefits of an assured future without facing the responsibilities an actual offer would entail. She needed to decide what to tell him of her past. Indeed, on one occasion Diana turned aside the beginning of a proposal, and Wilton, after a moment's puzzlement, allowed her to do so. For he, too, had his concerns. His knee was nearly healed, and the war was by no means ended.

But though Diana thought she was the same as ever, in fact she was far quieter and less apt to chatter to Amanda about things seen on her walks or laugh over some eccentric observed in their infrequent visits to the Pump Room. Robert Wilton, absorbed in his own plans and only newly acquainted with Diana, despite his deep feelings, did not see it, but Amanda did. At first, she put it down to love. Diana was no doubt concentrating her liveliness and laughter on the captain, she thought, and it was only natural that she should see less of her friend. Diana should be serious, pondering the approaching change in her state. But as time passed and Amanda watched the two lovers together, her puzzlement returned, redoubled. They were a subdued pair, she could not help but think. She remembered so vividly the culmination of George's courtship of her. When they had become officially engaged, and even just before, they had been nothing like this. Every moment together was a dazzle of sensation and confidences exchanged. She had felt she lived only in his presence then.

She told herself that their more sedate behavior was a consequence of age. She and George had been only nineteen and twenty, and these two were five or six years older. But this explanation merely made her sad, without convincing her in the least. She had seen love bloom at fifty in precisely the same breathless way. Amanda determined that she must talk with Diana and try to discover what was wrong.

But this was more difficult than she had imagined. Diana was so often out that it was not easy to catch her at a time when they might talk privately. Her walks grew longer and longer, until the maids began to protest and, as Amanda feared, Diana began to leave them at home and slip out alone. Too, Amanda did not always feel up to pursuing her active friend. She had been overtaken by a delicious lassitude in these days, and often a morning would pass without a thought of anything but her own rosy future. At last, however, she forced herself to rise particularly early one morning, and caught Diana at the breakfast table.

Diana seemed amused by her heavy eyes and sleep-puffed face. "You are up betimes," she said with a smile when Amanda entered. "And you do not look as if the morning pleases you."

"Is there tea?" was Amanda's only response. She was finding it impossible to gather her thoughts.

"There is." Diana poured, and Amanda added a generous dollop of milk and drank, both hands curled around the cup. She finished it quickly and gestured for more.

Laughing, Diana complied. "Why did you leave your bed, if you are so tired still?"

Amanda sipped her second cup more slowly, and even felt able to nibble some buttered toast. "I wished to speak to you," she answered, "and I never find you home when I rise late."

"But you should have simply asked me to stay. Is it something important?"

Realizing that she had made a mistake in her half-dazed condition, Amanda pursed her lips and tried to rally. "No, no. I meant only that I wanted some talk with you. We scarcely seem to see one another lately."

"Oh." Diana smiled again. "Well, you have grown so lazy, Amanda. I cannot sit about the house all day. I am surprised you can."

"Perhaps I have a reason." She saw a way to explain her uncharacteristic appearance. She had meant to tell Diana her news for some time anyway, but had postponed doing so, reveling in her secret happiness.

Diana looked contrite. "I know. You have not been feeling quite the thing. I am the greatest beast in nature to have forgotten. Why do you not have the doctor again? Perhaps he can help."

"It is not a case of illness, Diana." Amanda flushed a little and looked down at her hands. "I...I am in an interesting condition."

"An...?" For a moment Diana was mystified, then light burst upon her. "You mean...?"

"Yes. I am going to present George with an heir. Or, at least, so he insists. I shall be happy with a girl. *This* time." She smiled tremulously, awaiting congratulations.

But Diana was remembering an earlier confidence. Amanda had told her of previous tragedies in this area. No wonder her friend was being so careful. This new knowledge explained many things that had puzzled and sometimes irritated Diana. She felt relief mixed with guilt for her incomprehension. "That is wonderful!" she exclaimed, trying to put all her affection for Amanda into the phrase.

"So you see why I must not exert myself." A shadow passed across Amanda's pretty face. "I must be more careful than some."

"Of course you must!" Diana reached out and grasped her hand across the table. "And I shall help you. You must let me."

Amanda laughed at her vehemence. "How?"

"I can take over some of your household duties, and allow you to rest more."

"I have hardly any duties as it is, and you would hate talking to the cook, Diana. You needn't worry. I know what to do, and we are not abroad this time, so I need not ride when I am feeling ill, or eat odd messes." The shadow appeared again, then vanished. "I feel splendid." She looked at the piece of toast in her hand, swallowed, and put it down. "Most of the time," she amended. Her face paled.

"Are you ill?" cried Diana. "What may I get you?"

"It is nothing. It often happens. No need to worry." Amanda pushed back her chair and rose. "Excuse me."

Diana jumped up also. "I will help you upstairs!"

"No, no." She managed a laugh. "If I had known you would be worse than George, I would not have told you."

"Is there nothing I can do?"

"Wait for me," replied Amanda, and rushed from the room.

Diana found this a very difficult task. She went to the drawing room and paced back and forth, anxious about her friend's condition. More than once she started toward the stairs, but Amanda had insisted she wait, so she came back each time. Diana was even less experienced than most girls with such matters. Indeed, if Amanda had not been such a good friend, and if they had not been sharing lodgings, she would probably not have been told until the situation was obvious. She was gratified to be included, but also slightly uneasy. How could Amanda endure this illness, and how did she maintain her spirits with the losses of the past hanging over her? Diana's admiration for her friend rose another notch. She vowed to do everything she could to help her.

"There," said Amanda, coming into the drawing room barely three-quarters of an hour later. "That is over. Now I shall have some Madeira and biscuits." She went to the bell pull and rang.

Diana stared at her. She showed no signs of sickness; indeed, she was positively blooming.

Amanda turned from speaking to the maid and laughed at Diana's expression. "It passes off quickly. And it only comes in the morning—just at first. There is no need to look like I have risen from my deathbed."

"You are amazing."

"Nonsense." The maid returned with a tray, and Amanda poured out a small glass of Madeira and bit into a biscuit with appetite. "Now, is everything all right with you, Diana?"

"What?" She was still staring.

"We have hardly spoken alone in a week. Tell me what you have been doing."

Gradually recovering from her surprise, Diana recounted her walks and other activities.

"Captain Wilton has called nearly every day, I believe?"

"Yes. He came walking with me twice. His knee is hardly stiff now."

"You are glad to see him?" Amanda watched her face from under lowered lashes.

"Yes, of course."

Her tone was so unforthcoming that Amanda hesitated, but she could not leave the subject yet. "Has he...spoken?"

Diana turned her head away. "Of marriage, you mean? No."

"But—"

"It is really such a trivial question, is it not?" she burst out, rising and walking toward the front window. "I mean, there is the war, and your news. I don't see why we must hurry."

"But do you not want to have your future settled?" asked Amanda gently.

Diana shrugged without turning, gripping her elbows in her hands.

"What is it, Diana? Do you find you do not care for Captain Wilton, after all? There is no need for you to think of him if—"

"No!" It was a heartfelt cry, and silenced Amanda for a full minute.

"What, then?" she said finally.

Diana came very close to telling her. They had shared so much in the past weeks, and now, this morning, the most intimate information of all. But the thought of Amanda's reaction stopped her. She had no doubt her friend would be sympathetic. She would say all the proper things about youth and naïveté and the impossibility of guarding against plausible villains when one has no family support. But she would still think Diana had been a fool, or worse, and she would regretfully conclude that such a mistake could not be simply erased. Probably she would say that Robert Wilton must be told before they were engaged. And her high opinion of Diana would be forever altered. She would not despise or revile her, of course, as others might have, but she would never admire or respect her quite so wholeheartedly, Diana felt. And this she could not bear to contemplate. "Nothing," she replied, attempting a light tone. "Except perhaps that I have been used to living alone, and it is sometimes hard to have so many people around me."

This wounded Amanda a little. "I thought you were happy with us."

Diana winced, but thought a slight hurt was better than the alternative. "I am. Very happy. But I require more solitude than most people, I suppose. It is all so different here, and with Captain Wilton..." She trailed off, leaving Amanda to draw her own conclusions.

"Of course, it is a great change, though you seemed happier at first. And to think of marriage after being alone so long..." Diana bowed her head as if agreeing, and felt dreadfully guilty. "You do care for him?" added Amanda. "Because you know you are welcome to stay with us as long as you like. You needn't rush into any...other arrangement."

Diana swallowed a lump in her throat and blinked back tears. She felt wholly undeserving of such kindness. "I do," she managed in a choked voice.

"Well, then... I suppose everything is all right." But Amanda sounded unconvinced.

Diana longed to pour out everything then, but she still held back. The risk was too great. Silence fell and stretched as both women thought over what had passed between them, each wondering if something else did not need to be said.

But their tête-à-tête was over. The bell rang, and the maid came in to announce Captain Wilton. Diana moved from the window back to the sofa, and Amanda sat up straighter. Their smiles were a little stiff.

But Wilton was too excited to notice as he came striding in. "Letters from Belgium," he cried, waving a packet in the air. "I've had a number all at once. They went to London, and my idiot of a brother waited to send them on until there was a pile." He looked around. "Where is George?"

"Out riding, I think," said Amanda. "He usually is at this time of day."

"But he must hear." The captain gazed about again, as if his wish could summon Trent from thin air.

"He should be back soon," offered his hostess. Wilton nodded, disappointed. "Will you sit down?"

"No." He went to the window and looked out.

"Is there some great news?" asked Diana, exchanging a smile with Amanda at his restlessness. "The newspapers had nothing to say this morning."

The captain turned, and seemed to decide not to wait. "Nothing that we did not know," he said. "Except that the battle, the decisive battle, must be soon." He laughed a little, to himself. "It can't be much longer now. God, what I would give..."

The ladies watched him. He seemed far away, even though they sat not ten feet from him. Wilton's blue eyes clearly looked on a wholly different scene, and the animated lines of his body were ready for action. Unconscious of their scrutiny, he flexed his bad knee several times. Then, still looking out the window, he cried, "There is George!" and turned to go to him.

In the doorway he paused, a trifle shamefaced at his rude desertion. "My friend Buffer says the Belgian foxes are too stupid to live. Won't run." And, with this, he was gone.

Diana and Amanda laughed, but only for a moment. Wilton's excitement had had an adverse effect on them, somehow, and they sat in silence, straining their ears as he met George in the lower hall and began an eager recitation of his war news.

TEN

GEORGE TRENT WAS ABOUT THE HOUSE LESS THAN USUAL IN the next few days, and Captain Wilton called seldom and seemed distracted when he did visit. They were easily found, however, in the Pump Room, or the concert rooms, or on a street corner, huddled with other military gentlemen discussing the progress of Wellington's and Blucher's joint effort in Belgium. As May passed, the excitement grew almost palpable among this circle. The mere idea of talking of anything else was ridiculous, and, when Amanda or Diana tried a different subject, the gentlemen grew abstracted and took refuge in random nods and grunts. But if they were asked about the coming confrontation, their eyes lit and the conversation became almost overanimated.

"I wish it were over," sighed Amanda one day as she and Diana sat alone in the drawing room. "Of course, I have wished that many times these eight years, and that George could think of something besides fighting." She sighed again. "That is unfair of me to say. He often does—did—think of other matters. Only just now…"

Diana nodded, fully in accord with her.

"Ah, well, they say it can't be much longer. I should be grateful we are awaiting it here instead of in the field."

"Amanda!" Diana feigned deep shock.

She put a hand over her mouth. "If George heard me! All he wants is to take ship for Brussels. Do not tell him I said that."

"As if I should. Don't be a goose."

"I know it seems cowardly, but we were with the army so long, you see, and it is so hard to wait and wonder whether one's husband—"

"Amanda! I was roasting you. I am completely on your side. George has fought long and well. He should leave it to others now, and be thankful he got through it with only…" She hesitated.

"Only losing his eye, yes," Amanda agreed. "I have thought a great deal about that, and I do think it is better than losing a leg or an arm. George does not always believe it, but look at Colonel Peterson. He will always use a crutch, and…" She frowned and shook her head. "How did we begin such a dismal subject? You are right. George has done enough. So has Captain Wilton—nearly eight years at war. I wish they could see it so."

"It is unlikely to matter how they see it," replied Diana. "They are settled in Bath."

"Yes." Amanda sounded unconvinced. "But does it not seem to you that they are plotting something lately?"

"Plotting?"

"Since Captain Wilton received those letters from Belgium, whenever I come upon the two of them suddenly, George starts and looks guilty."

"I haven't noticed anything."

"Perhaps it is only my fancy. I hope so." But her expression remained concerned.

The sounds of hooves in the street and the front door opening heralded the arrival of the major. He nearly ran up the stairs and strode into the drawing room with shining eyes. Diana was abruptly struck with the improvement of his appearance during these last weeks. She had somehow overlooked it until now, perhaps because he had lacked the present air of eager elation. George Trent's color was normal again, and his great frame had filled out. Now the black patch over his eye was indeed rakish rather than merely pitiful, and he might have sat for a portrait of the pirate hero of romance.

"Amanda, I must speak to you," he said.

Diana rose to go.

"No, no, Diana. Stay. This concerns you as well."

Surprised, she sank down again.

But, having gained their full attention, the major seemed

reluctant. "Well, the thing is, Amanda," he began at last, then stopped again, shifting from foot to foot.

"George! Is it bad news?" his wife exclaimed.

"No, no. That is, I don't think so." He seemed to gather courage. "Wilton and I, and a few others, are going up to London tomorrow to see about returning to duty."

Amanda went very still, dismay plain in her face.

Seeing it, the major hurried on. "It's intolerable sitting here while the war is finished, Amanda. Most of us have devoted our lives to this fight. We thought we had seen it through. We deserve to be in at the end."

Diana saw that Amanda could not speak. "Do you not rather deserve a rest?" she asked, trying to give her friend time to regain control.

"Rest?" George seemed astounded.

"You have done so much," she added, less confident in the face of his obvious incomprehension.

"Do you abandon an important task when you decide you have done 'enough'? Whether or not your job is completed? No." He shook his head and turned back to Amanda. "Can you understand?"

"You mustered out," she murmured.

"When I thought it was over. And with this eye." He grimaced, then recovered. "But that is changed now. And Wellington needs men. Wilton thinks there's a chance."

"Does he?" Amanda sounded forlorn.

"Yes. He is slated for duty in London, you know. But he is applying to Wellington himself. Friend of his family."

"But, George, I cannot go abroad," she answered with a catch in her voice. "You know I must be careful just now. Before, when I rode or…" She paused and cleared her throat.

"Of course you cannot," he said. "You will stay home this time, Amanda, and take care of yourself." Seeing her chagrin, he added,

"I know it is said to be very gay in Brussels, but the army could move at any time. And I consider the balls and parties quite out of place, anyway. I daresay I shan't be away long. And when I come back, the war will be over, and we can truly plan what we shall do and where we shall settle for good."

"You will leave me alone, in my situation?" Amanda could not help but say.

"No, no," he responded eagerly. "That's the beauty of it, you see. Diana is with you now. You needn't go back to Yorkshire. I know you get lonely there. And it won't be as it was when you stayed in London. You are settled here. You have friends. You might even have your parents for a visit. You will scarcely know I am gone."

"Oh, George!"

He had the grace to look ashamed, like a small boy who knows he has gone too far in arguing for a special treat. "Well, no, of course we shall miss each other. But they say the war cannot last the summer, Amanda. I'll be back long before you are brought to bed." He glanced at Diana, flushed a bit, and hurried on. "I *must* do this, love."

Amanda had risen and moved toward him. Now she scanned his face. "Must you?" she asked wistfully.

George nodded, a little guilty, but determined.

"Very well."

He strode forward and swept her into his arms. "Darling! I knew you would understand."

"You won't leave from London, though? You will come back and say goodbye?"

"Of course."

Diana left them then, to discuss the matter more intimately, and went up to her bedchamber. Only now did she have leisure to consider that Captain Wilton was also leaving Bath, perhaps forever. Surely he would come to her first, she thought. But what would he say? The various alternatives that occurred to her were all unsettling.

Perhaps, fortunately for her peace of mind, Diana did not have long to ponder the possibilities. Wilton called about an hour later, and asked for her. She received him alone in the drawing room.

"I wanted to be certain George had broken the news," he said. "I came as soon after him as I dared."

"Letting him absorb the heavy fire?" asked Diana with a smile. She had picked up a number of military terms in the last few weeks.

"From Mrs. Trent, yes. You may let fly at me when ready."

His smile was so engaging that Diana felt her throat tighten. She didn't want him to go. Yet she dreaded the approaching exchange.

Her face seemed to encourage the captain, and he moved closer. "I wanted to say goodbye, of course. But, even more, there is something to be settled between us."

"Settled?" She did not even recognize the high squeak as her own voice.

Wilton hesitated, a bit puzzled. He had often found Diana puzzling recently. Though he was certain she cared for him, she seemed to draw back whenever he made a move to deepen or confirm their relationship. He had not touched her, though he had wanted to, because of this, trying to give her time and room to adjust. But now, circumstances forbade waiting. "You must know what I mean," he went on. "Indeed, I am sure you do. We have understood one another since the picnic, though we have said nothing. Have we not?"

Diana looked at the floor, biting her lower lip.

"I love you," he finished simply. "And I hope you will consent to become my wife."

This was the moment she had dreaded. It was the proper time to tell him her secret and allow him to withdraw if he chose. Diana wanted nothing more than to say yes, but she felt it unfair to do so without revealing the truth. She could not so deceive him. Yet to be honest was very likely to lose all chance of happiness. The conflict made her tremble with anxiety.

"What is it?" said Wilton, seeing her distress but unable to guess its source. He tried a lighter tone. "You must say *something*, you know. It is extremely impolite to ignore a proposal of marriage."

Diana gazed up at him, the love she felt mingled with pain in her dark eyes. Her throat seemed frozen. She could not speak.

Still not understanding, but responding to the appeal in her gaze, Wilton stepped forward and slid his arms around her, pulling her close so that she might rest her head against his shoulder. His hand rose automatically to stroke her deep-gold hair, and the embrace seemed exquisitely right to him. "It's all right," he murmured, though he did not know what "it" might be.

Gradually Diana's trembling stopped. She felt a vast sense of safety and comfort descend upon her, and the question of her past receded slightly. What if she never told him? It might not matter. His caresses lulled her into optimism, and she raised her head to meet his eyes. Her mouth shaped the word "yes," though no sound emerged.

Wilton gave no sign of hearing, but he bent and kissed her very gently, his lips merely brushing hers. Diana curved her arms around his neck, and he pulled her closer, molding her body against his and kissing her more urgently—once, then again.

Diana felt a passionate response rising within her, and she wanted nothing more than to hold Wilton tightly to her forever. Yet this new and charged sensation was confused by her dilemma, and, she was disgusted to find, by memories of the only other occasion in her life when she had been similarly embraced. Unbidden, the image of Gerald Carshin formed in her mind, enacting scenes of the foolish, illusory love she had felt for him. Her tepid, uneasy reaction to Carshin's touch interfered with this very different feeling. She strove to push the memory down, but the mocking recollection would not be banished, and, finally pulling herself away from Robert Wilton, she began to tremble once again.

"Yes," said the captain in a shaken voice. "I beg your pardon. I...I rather forgot myself." He was breathing rapidly.

Diana made a dismissive gesture.

He straightened his shoulders and smiled. "I can take that as my answer, with pleasure, but I should like to hear you say it as well."

"I…" She still could not speak.

"Isn't it odd how an offer of marriage ties one's tongue?" he said. "I thought I should never get it out. And yet we talk together easily about all sorts of other things." He took her hand and bent a little to look in her face. "Diana?"

"Couldn't we…just leave it until you come back?" she choked out.

He stared at her for a long moment, then murmured, "I am the most selfish beast in nature."

Diana was startled. "What?"

"To ask you to make this decision when I am about to go off to battle, where anything may happen. I suppose I didn't think of it because I have been so lucky in the past. But there is no telling whether I shall come out of it as I am, or…" He paused. "You are right, of course. We will not speak of this again until I return."

"That is not what I meant!" she cried, appalled that he should think this.

"There is nothing wrong—"

"It isn't!"

He met her eyes, and nodded. "Well, I'm glad *I* thought of it, then, for the idea is sound." He grinned. "I warn you I *mean* to return unscathed, however, and *soon*. So you must be ready to give me your answer then." He raised his free hand and very lightly stroked her hair again. "I was just so eager, you see."

"Oh, don't!" Diana threw her arms around his neck and buried her face in his coat. She had been so absorbed in her own worries that she had not even thought of his being hurt, perhaps even killed, in Belgium. The possibility tore at her heart, and she held him fiercely, as if to prevent his going.

He returned the embrace gently, then put a hand under her chin and raised it to kiss her lightly before stepping back. "You really needn't worry. My friends insist I lead a charmed life. And now I should go, for I have several things to do before leaving Bath."

"You will come back before you go abroad?" asked Diana, hearing herself echo Amanda.

"Yes."

She reached out to him again, and he took both hands. "I've handled this badly, and I'm sorry..."

"You haven't! It is I who—"

He laughed, putting two fingers over her mouth. "In any case, we will settle everything properly when I return. And I shall see you again soon, after London."

"I didn't..."

But Robert Wilton shook his head and turned to go, and Diana could not bring herself to voice her one wish: that she would marry him today, if he liked, and follow him to Brussels or to the ends of the earth. Her desires were not in question, but Wilton's possible revulsion upon finding out her secret sealed her lips.

ELEVEN

MAJOR TRENT AND CAPTAIN WILTON DEPARTED WITH THEIR friends the following morning, high-spirited as boys going adventuring. Amanda was quite cast down when they had gone. She remained by the window for some time after they had disappeared toward the London road, chin in hand, close to tears. And Diana was, at first, too preoccupied to cheer her. She could not decide if she was more glad or sorry that Wilton had gone. Diana knew she would miss him, but his absence conveniently postponed difficult decisions, for which she still had no resolution. She welcomed the chance to push the questions aside. This was cowardly, she felt, but better than forcing confrontation. She would have a little more of the enjoyment and frivolity, which had been so rare in her life thus far, before she had to withdraw once again.

For this now seemed the most likely outcome to Diana. She would go back to Yorkshire. No one had bought her father's gloomy house; it awaited her there, its contents as yet intact. After her brief taste of gaiety, it would receive her again as if nothing had happened. In her more despondent moments Diana felt that, perhaps, Yorkshire was where she belonged. Each time she had ventured out, she had botched things. Probably her father's teaching had made her unfit for society and the sort of loving home Amanda had established.

Part of her recoiled in horror from this prospect, and urged her to dare all to grasp happiness. But it had to combat a fatalistic voice that had been nourished by years of solitude and contemplation of her mistakes. It was far easier for Diana to convince herself that she had made a mull of things again than to rouse the energy to fight.

It was scarcely a question of battle, in any case, she reasoned. If she, like Wilton, had been riding off to face an enemy with saber and pistol, she might have managed. The prospect was daunting, but conceivable. But Diana had no weapon with which to fight the disgrace that would engulf her should Wilton learn of her past. Rather than a snarling adversary, she would confront a lover and watch him turn, not into an enemy, but something distant and disapproving. The thought made her shudder.

And so she made a great effort not to think of it. She turned her attention resolutely to Amanda and exerted herself to keep her friend amused and comfortable. Since Amanda's physical condition was as delicate as her emotional state—she was still often ill in the morning and tired during the rest of the day—the task was engrossing, and Diana found she could forget her own troubles for hours at a time.

"We should go out today," Diana insisted on the third morning after George's departure. "You cannot mope about the house this way. You always took a drive before, remember? You need fresh air."

"With George," was the melancholy reply.

"Yes, well, you will have to make do with me now. And he will be back before you know it. Indeed, he is to return in two days' time, if all goes well. You do not want to greet him all pale and languid, do you?"

This had some effect. But Amanda was not easily rallied. "He will be going away again almost at once."

"Perhaps. However, there is one thing we have not considered, Amanda."

"What?"

"The army may refuse to take him back. He did fight long and hard, and he has lost an eye."

Amanda, who had been reclining laxly on the sofa, sat up. "Oh, do you think there is a chance?"

"I do, though never tell George I said so."

"He would be furious," she agreed, sitting straighter still. "I suppose I am a horrid selfish cat, but I hope you are right. Particularly if the fighting is not to last long this time. It seems so silly for him to go."

Diana nodded, thinking that it really was very likely the major would be refused. Captain Wilton was another matter. "Why don't we go to the concert tonight?" she suggested then. "You enjoy the music, and it would not be strenuous. You can keep to your chair the whole time, if you like."

Amanda considered. "All right," she answered slowly, as if unable to find a suitable excuse for refusing.

"Good. And this afternoon, we will go for a short drive. You really are looking wan, Amanda."

This also was allowed, and, after dinner that evening, the two women set off to the concert rooms—if not exuberantly, then at least with a calm contentment. Amanda wore a gown of primrose muslin and really looked much better for her drive. Diana had chosen an amber sarcenet that was nearly the same hue as her hair, worn with some amber beads that were her mother's only legacy. They arrived just as the musicians were striking up and slipped into seats near the back.

Diana was pleased to see the tight lines in Amanda's face relax a little as the music began. Her friend was fonder of music than she, a fact that had influenced Diana's choice of activity for tonight. Gradually Amanda leaned back in her chair, bowed her head, and half-closed her eyes.

Amanda's enjoyment ensured, Diana was free to look about her. The room was fairly full, as there was no assembly this evening, and she saw a number of Trents' acquaintances dotted about it. She also glimpsed Ronald Boynton and his aunt near the front, evidently part of a large party. As she watched, Boynton leaned across his massive relative and spoke, quite loudly, to a brownhaired man. A dowager in purple just behind him glared through her lorgnette. With a slight smile, Diana composed herself to listen.

At the interval, Amanda was almost cheerful. "This was a splendid idea, Diana," she said. "You were very right to insist."

"Would you like something? Tea? I'll go and get it."

"I'll come with you," said Amanda, half-rising.

"No, no. There will be a great crush in the refreshment room. You wait here."

"But you should not go alone."

Diana was amused. "What could happen to me here? I'll just be a moment." And she moved off before Amanda could protest again.

It was indeed very crowded, and Diana was subjected to several quizzical glances as she made her way through the press. It was customary for the gentlemen of a party to fetch refreshment for the ladies. She ignored the stares, however, and slowly moved closer to the viands. When at last she had procured tea and cakes and was picking her way back with a small tray, she heard her name called. But, as she recognized the voice as Ronald Boynton's, she did not even pause. Let him think she hadn't heard.

Mr. Boynton was not easily discouraged. He repeated his call and, in the next moment, had hurried forward to confront Diana. "Miss Gresham!"

"Oh, how do you do? You must excuse me, I am just taking this tray back to Mrs. Trent."

"My friends have arrived from London," he replied, oblivious of her excuse and not offering to take the tray. "Nearly the whole group. Is it not splendid?"

Nodding without enthusiasm, Diana tried to make her way around him.

"You must come and meet them. They are prodigious fashionable, you know."

His pleased excitement might have amused Diana under other circumstances, but just now she was simply annoyed. "I cannot. I must deliver this tea. If you wouldn't mind stepping out of the way?"

"What?" He became aware of Diana's burden for the first time, and this awareness brought with it the knowledge that he should come to her aid, though he clearly did not wish to.

The succession of emotions visible in his face made Diana smile, but she was weary of waiting. "Let me pass, please."

"Er, certainly. I, er, I must..."

She didn't linger to hear his excuses. Slipping between two chatting groups, Diana left the refreshment room.

"I'll bring them round to meet you when the concert is done," she heard Boynton call after her, but she paid no heed.

The interval was nearly over by the time she reached Amanda, and they drank their tepid tea in silence. Amanda seemed to enjoy the second part of the concert as much as the first. She was smiling and humming softly when they rose to go. Diana, on the other hand, was preoccupied by the thought that she must get someone to fetch their carriage, though all available servitors were besieged by others with similar desires. It was much more comfortable, she realized, to go out with a gentleman who took responsibility for such details.

"I am afraid we may have to wait a little," she told Amanda. "Everyone is trying to leave at once."

Amanda nodded, and they withdrew a little from the crowd at the doors.

"There you are, Miss Gresham," exclaimed Ronald Boynton, bearing down upon them from the concert rooms. "Did you forget that I promised to present my friends to you?"

In fact, she had, and she found herself wishing that he had been equally forgetful.

"Some of the most elegant folk now in Bath," he was telling her confidingly. "You won't wish to miss the chance. Nor will Mrs. Trent, I vow." He nodded to Amanda, who looked amused. "Lord Faring is among them," finished Boynton, as if offering them a great prize.

This did pique Diana's curiosity a little. She would not object to meeting Robert Wilton's older brother, she thought. She would be interested to see what he was like, though she already knew that he did not much resemble the captain.

Boynton took her hesitation for eagerness. "Just come along this way," he instructed. "We're waitin' within until the crush eases."

Diana glanced at Amanda, who shrugged, and they allowed Boynton to usher them through an archway and back into the concert rooms. "He reminds me of a cat we once had," whispered Amanda very softly. "She was forever bringing me the mice she caught, and dropping them at my feet."

Diana stifled a laugh. The comparison was perfect, and the treat Boynton promised seemed nearly as distasteful.

"Faring," Mr. Boynton cried, and a slender brown-haired man ahead of them turned. "Like you to meet some of my Bath acquaintances." He gestured.

"You are wrong, Amanda," murmured Diana. "*We* are the mice." And indeed Boynton seemed pleased to be presenting such a pretty girl to his noble crony. He performed the introductions with a complacent smirk.

"Enchanted," said Lord Faring, bowing over Diana's hand. She would never have known him for Wilton's brother, she thought. Their coloring was the same, and an informed observer could trace certain similarities in the lines of Faring's face. But, in every other respect, the brothers were clearly opposites. Faring's dress was the height of dandyism, and his countenance showed evidence of years of excess in its pouchy eyes, premature lines, and lack of color. He surveyed Diana with an appreciative insolence that made her wish to turn her back.

"Miss Gresham is a friend of your brother's," added Boynton.

"Indeed?" Faring seemed to find this amusing. He spoke in the same drawl as Boynton, but more languidly. "You must not judge our whole family by the gauche Robert. His years abroad have left him ignorant of everything except shooting, I believe."

"On the contrary," answered Diana coldly. "I found him remarkably well-informed. And he is a valued friend of Mrs. Trent's husband, Major Trent."

"Ah." Again Lord Faring seemed amused.

Boynton was not yet done with introductions, however. He reeled off the names of several other gentlemen and, finally, hailing another who came up just then, said, "And last of all, but by no means least amusin', Miss Gresham, my friend Gerald Carshin."

Diana had already begun to turn, and Amanda was facing the newcomer. The latter was a fortunate circumstance, for Amanda's polite response covered Diana's frozen immobility and allowed her the necessary instant to force herself to resume movement. She did not, however, recover her composure, and she faced Gerald Carshin in wide-eyed silence.

He, too, was patently startled. But his self-possession, or perhaps effrontery, was greater. "Miss Gresham and I have met before," he murmured and bent to kiss her limp hand.

"I might have known," joked Boynton. "You always know the pretty girls, Carshin. Where did you meet?"

Carshin did not answer, but this was evidently not unusual. "How are you?" he asked Diana.

She tried to speak, and failed, the implications of this encounter boiling up in her mind.

Amanda sensed some strangeness in her friend. She looked sidelong at Diana, then at Carshin, and said, "We must be going, I'm afraid. We were waiting for our carriage."

"We will escort you," offered the newcomer. "Boynton here can send for your vehicle." Adroitly he slipped Diana's hand into his arm and started off, leaving the group a bit nonplussed.

"If he is not the most complete hand," Boynton was heard to murmur.

"Do you call it that?" responded Faring, who was obviously used to more deference.

One of the other men, recalling his manners, offered his arm to Amanda, and the rest of the party followed toward the exit.

"You are as lovely as ever," said Gerald Carshin to Diana. He could feel her trembling on his arm, and he rather enjoyed the sensation.

Diana was silent. She was gradually recovering from the shock, but she was not yet up to conversation.

"You seem unchanged, in fact, though it has been…what, seven years?" Carshin had not thought of her in nearly that long, but now details were coming back to him. Had it not been seven years until Diana came into her fortune? "I see no ring on your finger?" he ventured. "You have not married?"

"No," she managed.

"Ah." Carshin's brain began to work. His financial position was no better now than it had been seven years ago. If anything, it was worse. The charity of men such as Lord Faring, who was by no means a leader of fashion, kept him afloat. And he had had no luck in attaching another heiress whom he could imagine as his wife. The reappearance of Diana Gresham, obviously not in disgrace with society, seemed providential. *And I objected to coming to Bath,* he thought with a shake of his head. "Nor I," he said in a melancholy tone that sought to imply he had never gotten over her.

Diana understood it, and the audacity of the man made her stare up at him in amazement. He tried to look soulful, and succeeded merely in impressing her with the change in him since they had parted. Diana remembered Carshin as a blond Adonis. He had, indeed, been handsome. Moreover, such a memory partially explained her foolishness in her own eyes. She had been dazzled. But the man she saw now was scarcely dazzling. His pale hair was thin, and an incipient paunch strained his waistcoat. The weight of years of hard living stamped his features. A hint of jowl marred his clean jaw, and his blue eyes gazed out from a network of tiny wrinkles.

"Perhaps it was fated thus," he went on, throwing her another intense look.

"Fated?" Diana was nearly herself again.

"That neither of us should be attached, and that we should meet again after all this time."

"I can't believe the fates so stupid," she replied tartly, not really believing him serious.

"To keep us apart so long?" Carshin realized that she still resented the past. Only to be expected, he supposed, though she seemed to have retained her position in society. But he had his work cut out for him. It was fortunate that he enjoyed a challenge and that the prize was so worth the effort.

"To bring us together at all."

He bent a little toward her, not enough to cause comment, but so that he could whisper in her ear. "Too hard! You cannot have forgotten those golden days when we first met. The tulips I brought you? Our walks over the moors?"

A luminous haze did lie over those recollections, Diana realized. Though she had bitterly deplored her own stupidity at seventeen, she had concentrated on the elopement itself. The preceding time retained some of its magical aura.

"I was a fool," murmured Carshin. "Worse! But I have been sorry for it ever since. If you knew how I regretted—"

"So much that you could not even write," she interrupted.

"Exactly. I was afraid to write to you. I knew how you must despise me. A thousand times I began a letter, only to tear it up in despair."

For a fleeting moment Diana almost believed him. Her active imagination pictured the scene he described. She had known enough despair herself to be reluctant to judge others. But then she met Carshin's eyes, and the illusion dissolved. At seventeen she had been blind to the calculation and self-love mirrored there. At five-and-twenty, she was not. There had been no letters, and no regrets. Gerald Carshin had probably not thought of her from that day to this unless—Diana's heart froze with her next thought—he had told their story to his cronies, to amuse them. Briefly, she couldn't breathe. Then she realized that none of the other men had seemed to recognize her name.

"But now I have been given the opportunity to make amends," Carshin was saying. "I can scarcely believe my good fortune. I will show you how—"

"No." She looked at him, coolly appraising. "I don't wish to see you again. Please do not speak to me."

He paused, weighing various replies. "Surely you would not be so unforgiving as to—"

"It has nothing to do with forgiveness. I simply don't like you, and I don't wish to associate with you." This bluntness felt amazingly good. Diana drew in a breath, pleased.

"Do you not?"

"No." She withdrew her arm. "If you will excuse me, I must see about the carriage and join Mrs. Trent."

"I wonder what your friend Mrs. Trent would think if she knew the story of our…association? Apparently you kept it secret somehow, but that need not go on."

Diana stared at him, appalled.

"Ah, that catches you up, does it? Perhaps there are others who would be interested in the story." Seeing her expression, he added, "Perhaps some whose good opinion you value even more highly, eh?"

"You—"

"Now, now, don't say anything you'll be sorry for later." He stepped close again. "You will see me, and speak to me, and do as I tell you. For, if you don't, all of Bath will hear our romantic history." He grinned unpleasantly. "And your friends shall hear all the most intimate details." He looked her up and down in a way that brought back that night they had spent at the inn. Diana flushed crimson.

"You horrible—"

He held up a warning finger. "What did I tell you about name-calling?"

She turned away, moving toward Amanda, and Carshin added, "So good to see you again, Miss Gresham. I shall certainly call tomorrow," in a voice that all could hear.

Once Diana and Amanda were safely in their carriage, Amanda, though weary, turned to her friend and asked, "Wherever did you meet that man Carshin, Diana?"

Diana looked away so that her friend couldn't see her expression. "He visited Yorkshire several years ago."

"Indeed? That must have been one occasion when you were grateful for your father's reclusiveness. The man's manner is quite unpleasantly insinuating. I hope he does not actually call."

Gazing out the carriage window, Diana thought despairingly that Amanda would never understand her ill-fated elopement of years ago.

TWELVE

DIANA PASSED A DREADFUL NIGHT. PERHAPS SHE HAD KNOWN, somewhere deep down, that Gerald Carshin could turn up. But she had never really believed he would. That episode of her life was so remote it seemed to Diana as if Gerald must have faded away as well.

Faced with his indisputable presence, and his threats of exposure, she was, at first, devastated. She saw no way to fight him, and the precarious happiness she had begun to embrace crumbled silently into nothing. Diana was not even certain that flight would save her, for Carshin knew her home, and he might follow her there should she retreat to Yorkshire for a while. He was determined to have her fortune this time. She had seen that in his eyes. Nothing else she could offer him would slake that greed.

For a wild moment, as she tossed and turned in her bed, Diana considered trying to sign her money over to Carshin, on the condition that he never come near her again. But the idea died almost at once. The scandal would be nearly as great, and she did not really wish to lose all her wealth to such a cause. Carshin would probably not consent, in any case.

When the maid came in with early tea, Diana was awake; indeed, she had scarcely slept at all. Yet no plan of escape had come to her. She washed and dressed in a cloud of despair and went down to sit at the breakfast table alone and drink two more cups of strong tea. Amanda would not be down for some time, but Diana had no desire to take her usual walk. In fact, she had no desires whatever. She sat gazing blankly at the wall until the servants silently signaled that they must clear up.

She removed to the drawing room and resumed her pose, her mind utterly empty. Only the sound of carriage wheels below at midmorning roused her, and then not quickly enough to allow her to escape. As she reached the drawing-room doorway, she heard footsteps on the stairs and knew that she would be seen leaving. Diana stood very still, trying to tell from the sound if it was Gerald Carshin. But would not the maid have announced him? On this reassuring thought, George Trent and Robert Wilton strode in.

"You're back!" she cried, her relief making her almost exuberant.

They nodded, unsmiling.

Diana gazed from one glum face to the other.

"It was no good," responded Wilton. "They turned us all down flat. Said there wasn't time to get us to Brussels even if we were completely fit, which we weren't."

"Damned paper-pushers!" exploded George. "What do they know about it? Where's Amanda?"

"In her room," said Diana.

Trent turned on his heel and went out without another word.

"I'm sorry," added Diana. "I know how much you wanted to go."

Captain Wilton nodded again, then shrugged. "I considered simply getting on a ship, but Wellington would more than likely send me back."

Diana couldn't think of anything really comforting to say. And her own new dilemma dwarfed Wilton's problems in her mind.

"At least...I shan't be leaving Bath after all," he said after a while, with a valiant smile. "I hope you are glad of that."

"Yes. Yes, of course." But Diana's voice lacked conviction. How much better it would have been if he had been posted abroad, she thought. Perhaps, somehow, in his absence, she might have found a solution to her problem and freed herself to accept his proposal when he returned.

"You don't sound so," he countered, half-amused, half-concerned. "Is something wrong?"

"No." Her tone was too vehement, she thought. Why could she not control her voice?

"Mrs. Trent is not ill?"

"No. She is quite stout. We went to a concert last night. Amanda enjoyed the music very much."

Wilton eyed her. Diana searched her brain for some remark that was both sensible and safe. But before she could think of one the recurring sound of carriage wheels froze her tongue.

"We returned as soon as we heard the army's judgment," said the captain, trying to put her more at ease. "There was no reason to stay, and we were both eager to be back. The journey went quickly."

Diana heard only the bell, the front door opening, and more footsteps. The maid knew that Captain Wilton was here. She would see no reason to turn away other callers. And Diana could hardly rush out and give those instructions now.

"Mr. Gerald Carshin, miss," said the servant, and Carshin strolled into the room, resplendent in yellow pantaloons and a pale blue coat.

"How d'you do." The newcomer was blandly cordial. "Miss Gresham. And Captain Wilton, is it now? I believe we've met at your brother's."

Wilton was clearly annoyed at the interruption, and by one whose posing he despised. But his emotions were nothing to Diana's. She thought, at first, that she might actually faint, though she would have scorned such a suggestion only days before. As she gathered her scattered sensibilities, and the two men surveyed one another, the contrast between them was graphic. Robert Wilton stood so tall and slender, his face cleanly etched and open, while Carshin was battling corpulence and irredeemably sly. The thought of the one telling the story of her past to the other made Diana feel ill.

"I dropped in to see if you would care to go for a drive, Miss Gresham," Carshin went on. "Pleasant day."

"As you see, Miss Gresham is occupied," answered Wilton.

"Indeed?" The other man looked about the room as if seeking the nature of this occupation.

Diana saw Wilton tense, and she cringed. "Perhaps another day," she offered, hoping to placate Carshin. The captain stared in amazement.

"But another day it may rain," insinuated the caller. "I think you would do much better to come now."

The command, and the threat, were patent. Diana did not dare refuse, especially with Robert Wilton standing by. Conscious of his outraged, incredulous gaze, she stammered, "Well, perhaps...I have not been out today, and...we will be meeting again soon, Captain Wilton."

"Do you mean to say you are going?" he demanded.

"That seems to be the gist of it," replied Carshin, an amused sneer on his face.

Wilton continued to look at Diana.

"I...I... It is a pleasant day."

Stiff with astonished anger, the captain merely bowed and turned away. He could not imagine what Diana was about. To put him aside for this coxcomb! It was beyond bearing, particularly after his defeat in London.

Diana, desperate, opened her mouth to recall him, but she did not know what to say. She was trapped, she thought, and she could no more loose herself than could the rabbit or the quail. The worst unhappiness she had left in Yorkshire was nothing compared to this.

Wilton was gone. Gerald Carshin smiled complacently and gestured toward the door. "Shouldn't you fetch your hat?"

Whirling abruptly, Diana almost ran to her bedchamber.

It was some time before she returned to the drawing room, but, when she did, she was once again in control of her feelings. Something must be done, she had decided, and at once. She could not endure more scenes like this morning.

Carshin was chatting with George Trent when she came in. The major looked thunderous. "Not a very pleasant fellow," said Carshin as they climbed into his hired carriage. "Deuced surly, in fact. You'd have thought I was a dunning tradesman or one of his wife's family putting the squeeze on." He laughed. "The eyepatch is a bit thick."

"Major Trent was wounded in the war," answered Diana coldly. "And he is not fond of dandies."

"Well, if he thinks me one, he's sadly out." Carshin seemed genuinely offended. "Even a soldier should be able to see that I don't indulge in their freaks."

It was true, she conceded to herself. His dress was not as exaggerated as, for example, Mr. Boynton's. But George would not see any difference.

"But we shouldn't be talking of him." He turned the carriage in the direction of the Sydney Gardens. "We have much to settle between us." He looked over at her, then turned back to the road. "You really are more beautiful than ever, you know."

"I don't want your compliments. Indeed—"

"Don't take that line." His tone was conciliatory. "Why be angry? I have apologized for my mistakes. Can we not be friends again? I really am sorry, you know." And he realized that he was indeed sorry. It had been foolish of him to abandon this lucky find—a beauty and an heiress. He must repair his slip and get her for his own.

"I'm not angry," responded Diana. "What passed between us was over long ago. That is the end of the matter."

They had entered the gardens, and now he pulled up. "Shall we stroll a little?"

"No."

"Come, come. It is a beautiful day. What harm is there in a walk?"

Frustrated, Diana tried to think of some objection, but she

had more important concerns. "Oh, very well!" She jumped down without waiting for him to help her and refused to take the arm he offered.

Carshin left his groom to walk the horses and followed her. "Would it really be so bad?" he asked as they walked along one of the paths. "To be married to me? I would be an exemplary husband, you know. I swear I should never give you cause for complaint. We would have our town house as we planned, remember?" He leaned a little toward her.

"I remember that you planned to set yourself up in town with my money."

"To set both of us up," he corrected. "I wasn't going to rob you."

"Were you not?"

"I can understand your annoyance. It is true, I was young and stupid. But I have learned better since then." He stopped and faced her. "Money is important. It is far easier to be happy in comfortable circumstances. You cannot deny that. But other things are equally important. That is what I did not see seven years ago." Before she realized what he meant to do, he had stepped forward and slipped his arms around her waist. "Seeing you again, all my old feelings have returned. There is no one else I wish to spend my life with. Dare you claim it is not the same for you?" And pulling her close, he kissed her passionately.

Diana's few wisps of golden memory dissolved. Her calf love for Gerald Carshin had been wholly fantasy and foolishness, she saw now. Not only the elopement but even the first meetings had been empty and vain, the intensity of feeling purely a product of her own loneliness and longing. Had she had the usual opportunities to meet young men, she would never have idealized Carshin. She didn't even like him, nor had she really then. She had been swept away, not by a man, but by her own airy dream. His kiss left her unmoved, except for distaste, and she realized that it had always been so. At seventeen she had had no standard of comparison.

Having met and loved Robert Wilton, she could judge the true value of Carshin's vows and caresses. With all her strength she pushed him away.

Startled, Carshin staggered back. He had been certain he was about to win her over. He was rather vain of his success with women, though it had been mostly among those for whom money was a prime motive, and he did not put much stock in Diana's protestations. She had believed his avowals once. Why should she not again? And, when he held her, his intellect was overwhelmed by a rush of desire. She was so lovely!

Diana turned back toward the carriage. "I don't want to see you again," she said. "If you call at the Trents', you will be refused. And if you dare to touch me again—"

"Just a moment." He strode after her, enraged by thwarted desire, and grasped her upper arm, pulling her around. "You are forgetting one small matter, are you not?"

"Your threat to expose me?" In her anger, she nearly had. And she had determined to argue with him so coolly. "You would not tell a story so detrimental to yourself. The ruin and abandonment of a girl of seventeen would make you look despicable."

"You think so? There are many ways of telling a tale. And in any case, *I* should not come out the worse. You would be far more affected."

Diana pulled her arm free, but she did not turn again. "You could not be so…" Biting her lower lip, she tried to think of arguments to sway him.

"Alas, one is forced to distasteful actions sometimes." He eyed her. "I daresay Captain Wilton would find the story interesting, at the least. I have the impression you would not care for him to hear it."

She could not help but wince.

"I thought so. Perhaps he is the reason you will not listen to me, as you once did. A pity. But there it is. Can't say I think much of your new tastes."

"Stop it!" Diana clenched her fists. "I will give you money, if you will just leave me alone."

Carshin laughed. "It is not only your money I want, my dear Diana. I think you know that very well. Besides..." His smile broadened. "I shall get it all when we are married."

"I shall never marry you!"

He gazed admiringly at her blazing eyes and rigid figure. She really was a beauty. Even that outmoded way of dressing her hair seemed to contribute to her appeal. He was filled with greedy desire. "You shall marry no one else. I'll see to that. What other man would take you? Shopworn goods are not much in demand, m'love."

Burning with rage, Diana slapped him as hard as she could, then drew back, her palm stinging from the impact.

Carshin, an angry red mark rising on his cheek, grasped her shoulders and shook her a little. "Spitfire! You have changed, haven't you? But I know how to deal with such as you." Crushing her against him so that her arms were pinned between them, Carshin kissed her savagely again.

Diana kicked at his legs and tried to jerk her head from side to side, but he was too strong, and she was trapped until he released her.

"There!" Carshin at last allowed her to move away. He was breathing quickly, and his blue eyes burned with determination and desire. "We shall not be bored, lovely Diana. What a life it will be."

Diana could not speak. She was awash with conflicting emotions: revulsion, rage, a desperate calculation.

"I see no reason why we should not announce our engagement at once. We can put it about that we are old friends meeting again after a time and confirming our long-standing attachment."

"I shall do no such thing!" Diana started toward the carriage again, walking swiftly.

In three strides he caught up with her. "I don't see that you have a choice."

Diana's hands itched to strike him again. If she had had a weapon, she realized, she could have killed him easily. This certainty further unsettled her. "Do your worst," she answered through gritted teeth. "I would rather be ruined than married to you. I lived alone in Yorkshire for seven years. I can do so again!"

Carshin, who would not have contemplated living in the wilds of Yorkshire for even seven days, had not counted on this, for he judged others' reactions by his own. "Here, now, no need to be so violent. Perhaps I have gone too fast. I see that I have. We will talk of this again."

"If you come near me again, I shall leave Bath and go home," she declared, though her heart sank at the prospect.

"You are overwrought. When you have had time to consider, you will see…" Carshin's voice trailed off as they reached the carriage. Diana quickly climbed up, pushing aside his assistance.

When they sat side by side in the vehicle, she replied, "Understand that I shall never marry you, whatever you do. If you choose to spread stories in spite of this, you will. But it will gain you nothing except my deeper contempt."

"And the satisfaction of seeing you prevented from marrying any other," he snapped, his temper overriding his common sense.

Diana merely turned her head away from him, her face like stone.

Regretting his words immediately, Carshin sought to make amends. "I beg your pardon. I did not mean that, of course. It is just that you have provoked me to—"

"There is nothing more to be said between us. Ever." Gazing at her exquisite profile, Carshin experienced a deep pang of regret and anger. He refused to lose this prize when he held such a strong hand. She was angry now, and ready to say anything, but when she was cooler, the prospect of ruin would seem less bearable, and then he would try again. Pondering his next approach, he urged the horses forward.

THIRTEEN

DIANA DID NOT SPEAK A WORD ON THE DRIVE BACK, AND SHE evaded Carshin's aid when she climbed down from the carriage and entered the Trents' house. She went straight to her room and flung off her hat and shawl, then curled up in the armchair before the fireplace and burst into violent tears.

Her confused emotions demanded such release, and it was some time before her sobs changed to sniffs and then silence. When she finally raised her head, breathing deeply, she felt better, though nothing had changed.

Diana stared at the floor and considered her situation. Though she would never marry Gerald Carshin, she dreaded the consequences. Despite her brave words to him, the thought of disgrace and her friends' shock and disapproval made her shiver. She had only just become accustomed to the warmth and small gaieties of society, and now they were to be taken from her. She could retreat and live alone. She did not doubt that. The years in Yorkshire had taught her much about her limits and possibilities, and she knew that books and daily chores would provide a bare minimum for existence. The breath of scandal could not harm a solitary who asked nothing from society.

But she wanted more. Now that she had seen something of life, and been offered love, she resisted losing it with all her strength. The thought that she would never see Robert Wilton again made her throat ache anew. Yet, once he was told of her past... Diana clenched her hands in her lap and tensed as if preparing for a blow. There seemed no way out.

Diana's helplessness brought back memories of that earlier time when she had been abandoned by Carshin. Then, too, it had seemed that the world was against her, that she was wholly alone. Yet help had materialized, she reminded herself, and luck had swung her way after misfortune. Straightening, Diana allowed herself a small grain of hope. She could not see a solution just now, but all was by no means lost. She would not give up, as Carshin no doubt wished she would.

With this tenuous optimism she rose and washed her face. As she dealt with the wisps of deep gold hair that had escaped from the knot on her neck, she realized that she was extremely hungry. She had eaten hardly any breakfast this morning in her worry.

Diana found the Trents just sitting down to a buffet luncheon in the dining room. Amanda looked radiant, and George seemed to have recovered somewhat from his disappointment.

"There you are," said Amanda. "We were just about to send someone. What have you been doing this morning?"

"I went out driving."

"With that fellow Carshin," said George. It was not a question nor, quite, a criticism, but the major's opinion was obvious.

"The man from the concert?" Amanda was surprised.

"Wilton seems to have left in a hurry," added George, and Diana raised her eyes to find that he was watching her closely. This was so unlike him that she at once concluded Captain Wilton had confided his intentions. She flushed slightly and dropped her eyes.

"Was he here?" exclaimed Amanda. "And he did not even say hello."

"You were not yet downstairs," replied her husband. "Though I thought he meant to stay awhile."

He was looking at her again, Diana knew. Misery descended on her once more. "I suppose he wished to get settled in his rooms after your journey," Diana offered.

The major merely grunted, and Amanda looked from one to the other of them in puzzlement.

"Will you go for a drive this afternoon?" asked Diana quickly.

"Oh, yes." Amanda smiled up at the major, who responded in

kind. "To Sydney Gardens, I think. To see the flowers. You have walked there, haven't you, Diana?"

Struck dumb by mention of the scene of her morning's humiliation, Diana merely nodded. But she watched the Trents with a mixture of envy and sadness. They were so happy together. They'd experienced tragedies, but no dark secret hung over them. Despite the major's infirmity and his recent disappointment, he gazed at Amanda with love and contentment. And Amanda seemed a different woman from the languid, dismal creature of yesterday. They would never truly understand, Diana thought, if they were told her story. They would feel pity and regret, but she would become an embarrassment for them. "Excuse me." She pushed back her chair. "I believe I will go for a walk."

"So soon after luncheon?" Amanda looked startled. "Won't you sit with us a little first?"

Unable to form a polite excuse, Diana simply shook her head and hurried out. Amanda turned to her husband, frowning. "I wonder if something is wrong. Should I go after her?"

"No." He hesitated. "Wilton loves her, you know."

"I thought he did." Amanda smiled happily.

"Told me on the way home that they were practically engaged."

"Oh, George, that's…"

But he held up a hand. "Think something's gone wrong. Wilton didn't say so, but I'm fairly certain he meant to settle things between them this morning. No reason to wait now. I expected to find them when I came down, and to hear the good news. Instead, Wilton's gone off, and Diana sets out with this Carshin popinjay. Know anything about him?"

"Not really. He is a friend of Mr. Boynton's. We met him at the concert. Lord Faring was there as well."

"Wilton's brother? Ha." Major Trent fell into a brown study, his brow furrowed. "Can't make it out," he added after a while. "Wilton thought the thing was certain."

"Perhaps he made a mistake? He may have taken something Diana said..."

"Not Wilton. He's not that sort. Not one for the ladies, you know." Trent shook his head again. "No, something's amiss."

Amanda looked distressed. "I must talk to Diana."

"Do that. She won't do much better than Wilton, you know."

She nodded absently.

George stood. "Believe I'll just stroll down to the Pump Room. See if there's any news. I'll be back soon."

"In time for our drive."

"Of course."

Amanda saw him out with a smile, then walked slowly into the drawing room and sat down. She could not imagine that Diana admired Gerald Carshin. Indeed, she knew that Diana cared for Captain Wilton. What, then, was happening? She hoped that Diana's walk would not be as lengthy as usual.

Diana, striding briskly along the high common, was no longer thinking of the Trents. She was trying not to think at all, in fact, for every line of thought led to unpleasant conclusions. She concentrated on the beauties of the budding June landscape and the pleasures of brisk movement. As always, walking was a relief.

It was impossible to keep her mind blank, however she strove to suppress its spinning. Recent events, and her dilemma, would surface, and then she would go round and round again, ending up at the same impasse. Carshin had the upper hand.

Diana paused to watch a group of children playing hide-and-seek among the trees. Then she moved on, walking in a great circle that brought her back to the Royal Crescent at midafternoon. The Trents were out, as she had calculated they would be, and she had the place to herself.

But she had no sooner entered the drawing room than she heard the front bell, then hurried steps on the stairs. She turned, to meet Robert Wilton in the doorway.

"I had to come back today," he said. "I must talk to you."

Diana's heart turned over. He looked so handsome in his dark-blue coat, his thin face worried and intent. As for Wilton, he was more than worried. He had walked off his anger during the hours since he left the Trents' house, and, as it faded, fear had risen to take its place. He had thought Diana his. Now it seemed he might be losing her, and the idea was unbearable. Old insecurities arose when he considered his apparent rival, for Carshin was a town beau, his dress and manners those of the haut ton. Captain Wilton was accustomed to being thrust aside for such men. It had happened repeatedly in London. And, though he had thought Diana different, her behavior this morning had shaken his opinion as well as his certainty of her affection for him. His first impulse—to throttle Gerald Carshin—was clearly unacceptable, but he had little faith in talk, his only recourse.

Now that he faced Diana again, no words came. He simply gazed at her, his blue eyes questioning.

"I...I am sorry about this morning," she murmured, looking down. What explanation could she possibly give him?

"It did seem...odd," he replied. "I very much wanted to talk to you."

"I know. I..." She searched for words.

"When we spoke before I left Bath, I thought..." He retreated a bit. "But I have been too precipitate. I have assumed things I had no right to assume. You must put it down to my deep feelings for you. And I hope you will forgive any—"

This was too much. "There is nothing to forgive!"

"No?" He bent to try to see her face. "Well, I am glad of that." Wilton paused, hoping she would volunteer some explanation of her actions. When she did not, he added, "This Carshin, you have known him for some time?"

Diana looked swiftly up, then down again. "Amanda told you?"

"No, my brother. Carshin is one of his friends, you know, and

I inquired when I saw Faring in the Pump Room today. It...was important to me."

"We met years ago. We have not seen each other since," she replied. Her heart was pounding, and she felt again like a trapped animal, beating on the doors of her cage, desperate for a way out. Diana wanted nothing more than to tell Wilton everything and throw herself into his arms. But she did not dare. She searched for a way to reassure him of her love without revealing the truth.

"Ah. He is very elegant, I suppose. Faring says the ton finds him charming." How his brother had enjoyed giving him this information, Wilton thought. His own fears must have been obvious, and Faring had always reveled in a superior position.

"Really?" Diana strove to sound blandly surprised. "That seems a bit strong."

"You do not?"

"No."

"Yet you were very eager to drive out with him this morning."

"I wasn't. I...I had said I would, and..."

"It appeared that he only then asked you."

Near tears, Diana turned away.

"Miss Gresham. Diana!" He put his hand on her shoulder and turned her back again. "You will say I have no right to interrogate you so, but—"

She shook her head. "It is not that. It is that I cannot answer you." And she began to cry.

At once he pulled her into his arms, cradling her head against his shoulder, a hand in her gold hair. "I'm sorry," he murmured.

Diana had never felt so comforted. His arms around her, his voice in her ear, were an exquisite relief. For a few moments it was as if all her cares were lifted from her shoulders. But, as her tears lessened, the necessity to explain once again arose, and she pulled back.

Wilton offered his handkerchief, and she took it to wipe her eyes.

"Let us forget the whole matter," he said then. "I care less than nothing for Carshin, unless you do."

Diana shook her head again, miserably.

He smiled, his face lighting. "Well, then." He reached for her again, putting his hands on her upper arms. "You know how I feel. I have told you that I love you and want you for my wife. Now that my future is more settled, will you not give me your answer?"

She gazed up at him through tear-filled eyes.

"I should tell you that I have some little income besides my army pay. I had thought to retain my commission, but, if you would prefer another sort of life, I am not averse. My war service is ended, in any case. I have a small estate in—"

"Stop!" Diana could not bear to hear him reciting his prospects, as if she were to judge him by such standards.

He waited, then added, "Will you not say something?"

She must, Diana thought, but she could not think what. She could neither accept nor refuse him—the first because of Carshin, and the second because she loved him dearly. The only proper course was to tell him her history, and that she was afraid to do. "I *want* to marry you," she stammered, and, before she could go on, she was in his arms again.

For Wilton, all doubts and fears were swept away by that phrase. The terrible worry that she was lost to him dissolved, leaving in its wake such happiness as he had never known. His life opened out before him in myriad scenes of bliss: Diana in his arms, their children, their home together. He kissed her with a mixture of exuberance and passion.

Diana resisted halfheartedly for a moment. She had meant to go on. But her love for him soon won out, and she gave herself to the embrace. Her whole self seemed to rise up to meet his, and her arms slid automatically around his neck. It was some time before she even realized that the obstacles she had felt before were gone. The reappearance of Gerald Carshin, and his despicable behavior, had expunged him from her happy memories. No longer did his image intrude as Diana responded more and more eagerly to her love's caresses. She was free of the past at last.

But this very realization made her draw away, for she was not, in fact, truly free.

Wilton let her move only a little. His arms stayed about her waist as he laughed down at her, his eyes warm with love and desire. "We can announce our engagement at once. You must come to London to meet my mother. And there is no reason to delay the wedding beyond a month or so, is there? Oh, Diana, we shall be so—"

"No!"

He stood very still, looking down at her. "What?"

"I cannot marry you. That is…I…"

"Did you not say that you wished to?"

"Yes, but…there are things which prevent…"

This was the moment to tell him, Diana thought. Perhaps she was mistaken; perhaps he would pass it off as unimportant now and feel just the same about her. But, as she met his pained, puzzled eyes, she felt a shiver of fear. If the love there should change to withdrawal, she could not bear it.

"Has this something to do with Carshin?" he asked very quietly, his face growing hard.

Seeing it, Diana quailed. "Why do you…?"

"There is nothing else it could be. Our situation remains the same, save for him." Captain Wilton's expression became almost grim, and Diana concluded that she had been right to hold back her story. But he was thinking only of the man who appeared to be preventing their happiness. Diana had never seen this side of Robert Wilton's character, for she had never seen him at war. Though she knew, of course, that he was a soldier and had fought for most of his adult life, this conveyed little to one who had no experience of battle. Her own fears led her to misinterpret his determination as disapproval, and she moved farther away.

Wilton let her. Indeed, he seemed withdrawn, his gaze inward. Diana almost cried out to him, terrified that she had lost him. In fact, he was merely shifting to another mode of thought, one he had never used in a drawing room before. He was sizing up Gerald Carshin as he would have a French army camped before his lines, examining his apparent weaknesses and planning a campaign. There was no question in the captain's mind that he would win, but, since he was a first-rate soldier, he left nothing to chance.

"It…it is not exactly Carshin," blurted Diana. "It is me. Or, at least, both, in a way." She would tell him, she decided. Nothing could be worse than the way he looked through her now. She had to.

But Wilton brushed her efforts aside, engrossed in his plans. He needed more information, he thought, and at once. He could not move without better intelligence. And Diana was not the best source at this stage. Wilton straightened. "I must go."

"Now? I want to tell you…"

He smiled at her, and ran a finger down her cheek. "Everything will be all right. You needn't worry."

"No, I need to tell you."

"I shall take care of it."

She could not imagine what he meant, or what he planned to do. "You don't understand," she answered.

"I understand enough."

He didn't. He couldn't.

Abruptly he pulled her close again and kissed her, thoroughly but quickly. Then he stepped away and smiled again, almost jaunty. "Don't worry," he repeated, and, with a sketch of a salute, he went out.

Diana, mystified, ran to the window and watched him move away along the street. Where was he going? To Carshin? She shivered and wrapped her arms around herself. Surely not, for he had looked almost happy. She should run after him, but he was going very fast. He passed around the corner and was gone. Diana went to the sofa and sank down, head in hands.

FOURTEEN

SEVERAL QUIET DAYS FOLLOWED, AND DIANA GRADUALLY overcame her conviction that something terrible was going to happen. She had written Captain Wilton a note on the evening after their encounter, asking what he meant to do, but he had put her off with a soothing, and uninformative, reply. Dispirited, she allowed time to pass without acting. Indeed, a kind of lethargy seemed to have descended upon her. She could think of no solution, so she left developments to fate.

Wilton, meanwhile, was very busy. He talked to a number of his acquaintances in Bath, wrote letters to London, and even questioned his brother about Carshin, so subtly that Lord Faring got no inkling of the focus of his interest. He found this campaign almost as satisfying as a true military action. By the beginning of the following week, he felt he had gathered all the intelligence he needed. Though he still did not understand precisely what lay between Gerald Carshin and Diana, his greater knowledge of the man's character fostered theories, none of which made him more kindly disposed to his rival. He was nearly ready to act.

On a balmy afternoon in mid-June, Amanda Trent came into the drawing room in search of Diana. "A huge basket of flowers has arrived for you," she said. "It is beautiful. Come and see."

They went into the hall together, and Diana gazed at the tall bunch of roses and daisies.

"Aren't you going to look at the card?" wondered Amanda. She was watching her friend's face closely. Despite the Trents' growing preoccupation with the coming addition to their family, Amanda had noted Diana's low spirits and loss of vivacity. She and George had repeatedly puzzled over the apparent rift between Diana and Robert Wilton, but neither Amanda's inquiries at home nor George's outside it had yielded any substantial information. Amanda was determined now to discover the cause. "Is it from Captain Wilton, do you think?" she added.

Diana slowly reached for the small envelope thrust between the stems. If it was, she thought, she would only feel more guilty. Pressing her lips together, she tore it open. Then, with a disgusted sound, she dropped the card on the hall table and turned away. Amanda hesitated only an instant before picking it up. "Gerald Carshin," she read, frowning. "What can he mean by 'Will you not reconsider?' Reconsider what?" She replaced the card and followed Diana into the drawing room. She was standing at one of the front windows gazing out into the street. "Diana, what is the matter?"

"Nothing."

"Nonsense! You *will* tell me."

Diana turned, startled by the command in her friend's voice. She had never heard Amanda speak so sharply.

"It is obvious that something is wrong. And this Mr. Carshin is the cause, isn't he? Is he the reason for your quarrel with Captain Wilton?"

"We haven't quarreled."

"Call it what you will. Diana, he told George his plans. What happened?"

"I suppose half Bath knows by this time," Diana murmured, turning to lean her forehead dejectedly against the window glass. This was a foretaste of what her life would be like when the secret was out, she thought.

"Oh, lud!" cried Amanda. "I could just *shake* you!"

Again Diana turned, surprised.

"You have been mooning about in the most irritating way. You act as if it is too much even to say good morning. But, when I try to help, you insist there is nothing the matter, or you moan that everyone knows. Knows *what*, Diana?"

Acknowledging the justice of Amanda's complaints, Diana

came out of the window embrasure and stood straighter. "I cannot tell you."

"Indeed? And whom can you tell?"

"No one."

"Not Captain Wilton? Or Mr. Carshin?"

"He...I..."

"Diana, I cannot bear your moping much longer. It is driving me distracted!" Amanda Trent, though capable of similar behavior, was unskilled at standing idle while her friends suffered. She was much happier taking them in hand and doing something. Indeed, this impulse had been partly behind her original invitation to Diana.

Diana nodded. "I know. I have been a poor sort of guest these last weeks."

"You have!" Amanda smiled a little, but Diana did not look up.

"I think I should go home. That would be best for everyone."

"Home! To Yorkshire? You shall do nothing of the kind. I did not mean—"

"I know, but I have been thinking of it for a while. I can't see any better solution."

"To what? Oh, why won't you tell me?" Amanda's tone was pleading. "I have told you so many things. Are we not good friends?"

Diana felt torn. She wanted to confide, but she was still afraid.

"How can you simply shut me out?" added Amanda, her face showing real pain.

Bowing her head, Diana gave in. She could not stand against such pleas, particularly not when they urged her own inclination. Amanda would guard her secret, whatever her reaction, and her response would tell Diana something about how others would react. "I told you I met Mr. Carshin in Yorkshire years ago," she began.

"Yes."

It was very difficult to go on, but Diana forced the words out. "We were not mere acquaintances." And with gathering speed, the whole history of her elopement poured out.

When she finished, there was a long pause. Diana, who had kept her eyes on the floor through her recital, looked up to find Amanda frowning and biting her lower lip. Diana trembled a little as she waited to hear what she thought.

"You were foolish," said Amanda after a while.

"Yes."

"But you were very young, and you had no one to guide you. Your father was… Pardon me, but he was horrid, really."

Diana made no reply. She was trying to discover Amanda's feelings from her tone, without much success. Her friend sounded more puzzled than condemning.

"And I suppose Carshin seemed charming," she went on doubtfully.

"I had been allowed to meet no young men, and he was practiced at seduction." She hadn't meant to excuse herself, but she couldn't help it. "Oh, Amanda, do you despise me now?"

"What?" Amanda looked up, surprised. "Of course I do not. I have just been trying to decide why I am not more shocked. I could never despise you. I feel I *should* be shocked, but I am not, really. It seems the most natural thing."

Diana stared at her.

"That you should have made such a mistake," Amanda explained. "If I had had such a father… But of course there was George, and we… Yet I should never have met him if I had not been allowed to go to the assemblies… And in any case—"

She was cut off by a joyful embrace from Diana. "I was so afraid you would think me sunk below reproach!"

Amanda returned her hug. "You should not have done it, of course," she said when they separated.

Diana laughed, weak with relief. "You need not tell me. I have thought of little else during the last seven years."

"That is why you were living alone in Yorkshire?"

She nodded.

"But did no one else know?"

"Only our housekeeper, and she kept the secret. More from taciturnity than love for me, I think."

"Ah."

"I really am deeply sorry for my mistake. I have repented it bitterly since that day. If I could make amends…"

"You have, I think. Seven years alone! You might as well have been in prison."

I was, Diana thought, but she said nothing.

"Besides, it is for Mr. Carshin to make amends. He behaved despicably. You were merely foolish."

Diana laughed again, without humor. "He wishes to. He wants to marry me, now that I have my fortune safe and sound."

Amanda opened her dark eyes wide.

"He is so eager; he threatens to drive off any other suitors by telling them the truth."

"He did *not*?" gasped Amanda. "Then that is why you and Captain Wilton…?"

"Yes. You see the tangle I am in. And I am afraid to tell him."

Amanda did not have to ask whom she meant by "him." "Umm. Gentlemen feel rather differently about these matters," she murmured, imagining George's response to such a revelation.

"Yes," replied Diana miserably.

"Yet you cannot marry that…blackguard."

"I shan't. I shall go home first, and live as I did before."

"Oh, Diana! You love Robert Wilton, do you not?"

"Yes." Her face was bleak.

"You and he are such a good match. You would be happy, I know it."

There was no reply to this.

"We must think of something, make some plan!"

"I have thought until my brain whirled. I can see no way out. Carshin is implacable."

"But there must be a way." Amanda stamped her foot. "I won't see you made unhappy now, after all this. I will think of something."

Diana smiled a little, amused and touched by her vehemence, though not optimistic.

"Just give me a little time," added Amanda "I often have quite good ideas."

"Of course you do."

"You think I don't, but you did not see me in Portugal. I had to contrive the most astonishing things at times. And I shall do so with this."

Despite her doubts, Diana was heartened. It was wonderful just to have someone on her side, and Amanda's certainty was contagious. Could there be some way out, after all?

"Come and change for dinner," Amanda went on, linking her arm with Diana's. "And do not so much as think of the problem until tomorrow, after the assembly. Leave it all to me."

Diana started. This was an unsettling echo of Robert Wilton's words, and it made her uneasy once again. But Amanda, in her exuberance, would not allow Diana to brood. She swept her friend upstairs and commanded her to dress in a tone that elicited automatic, if laughing, obedience.

Diana chose her gown carefully, for she knew the assembly that evening would be an ordeal. Carshin was sure to be there, as was Captain Wilton, and they would be surrounded by a host of curious eyes. She settled on a dress of deep gold satin, trimmed with knots of gold-shot brown ribbon that had charmed her when she discovered it in the dressmaker's shop. It was a bit overformal for a Bath assembly, but the trim echoed the hues of her eyes. She fastened an extra knot of ribbon in her coif and, surveying the result, was satisfied that she looked well, at least. The cut of the gown, with a deep, square neck and full, puffed sleeves, complimented her unusual hairdressing, and her eyes seemed to sparkle with the glints of the ribbon. Fastening her string of amber beads around her neck, she took a last look, then went down to dinner.

The meal was dominated by military talk. George had gathered news in town after their drive, and he could think of nothing else. Napoleon's forces were advancing into Belgium, he told them, and a battle was imminent. All other concerns were driven from his mind by this one great issue, and he dominated the conversation with his speculations as to where the armies would meet, how Wellington would fare in his first real confrontation with Boney, and what Blucher's troops would do under the guns of the French. Amanda seconded him as best she could, and Diana joined in for the first part of dinner. But with the second course, her thoughts drifted back to her own dilemma. The war was, she thought guiltily, more important, of course, but she could not seem to keep her mind off personal matters.

The dancing had already begun when they arrived at the assembly rooms, and they found chairs at the side as a quadrille was finishing. Major Trent deserted them almost immediately, saying, "There is Randolph. I must speak to him."

Amanda was philosophical. "I didn't really expect him to dance tonight. The news is too exciting. Let us move over there beside Mrs. Brown and her sister so that I will have someone to talk with when you dance."

"I'll stay with you," protested Diana. "I don't want to dance."

"Nonsense," declared Amanda, rising.

"But, Amanda..."

The diminutive Mrs. Trent looked back and up. "You must forget your troubles and have a splendid time. I insist upon it. Come." But her expression as they crossed the room was far from carefree, and, when Gerald Carshin approached a few moments later to solicit Diana's hand, Amanda had to hide a grimace.

"I don't think I shall dance tonight," Diana replied to him.

"Not dance? But you *must*." His emphasis on the last word made both Diana and Amanda raise their chins defiantly. Carshin would not be denied, and, at last, Diana followed him out onto the floor. As the music began, her heart sank. She had not realized it was a waltz.

Smiling as if he knew her thoughts, Carshin encircled her waist with his arm and swung her into the set. Diana, glancing up at him, then down, wondered miserably how she could ever have thought she liked this man. How different this assembly was from her first in Bath. Then she had been so excited and happy, thinking a new world was opening before her. Now things were even worse than before her escape from Yorkshire.

"You are very lovely tonight," ventured Carshin in his most ingratiating tones.

"I don't want your compliments," replied Diana coldly. "You forced me to dance with you, but you cannot make me talk."

Carshin cursed inwardly, though his smile did not waver. Since his last encounter with Diana, he had been racking his brain for a plan to captivate her. Despite his threats, he did not really want to reveal their history to the world. For he wanted not only her person and fortune; he longed for the social position her money could bring. Those of the haut ton who now despised him as a mere hanger-on would come round quickly enough when he had a town house and carriage and an irreproachably suitable wife. Carshin wanted to sit in the bow window at White's, and be greeted with deference when he entered a drawing room. Diana could provide the necessary element—money—but it would be worthless if she were disgraced. Though he was careful not to let her suspect the truth, he was nearly as eager as she to keep their secret. He was determined to capture her as she was. At this point, he looked down, savoring Diana's curve of cheek, her glowing hair and skin, the rounded contours of her shoulders and neck. She was everything he desired, a damnably lucky chance at this point in his career. He would win her!

They turned in the dance, and Carshin's gaze encountered Captain Robert Wilton leaning against the far wall, arms crossed over his chest. The captain watched the dandy steadily, as a hunter does his prey, and, for a moment, Carshin was shaken. Wilton's eyes were so coldly calculating. Then his brief uneasiness was swept away by rage. The thought of any other man getting Diana made Carshin nearly sick with fury. He had unearthed this prize. It was his by right! And before he allowed anyone else near it, he would spread the tale of their elopement, and damn the consequences.

Wilton's mood was far different. Any anger or jealousy he might have felt at seeing Diana in the arms of his rival was submerged in his meticulous plotting of tactics. Tonight was to be his final observation. He wanted to see Diana and Carshin together once more before he decided what to do. And what he had seen so far merely reinforced his view of the situation. Diana had not wanted to stand up with the man. That had been evident to one who knew her well. He had somehow compelled her to do so, and this confirmed Wilton's conviction that Carshin had some power over the woman he loved. At that moment, his soldierly control nearly broke, but he quelled the desire to go after the interloper with his fists by recalling his training. No sortie succeeded without planning and discipline, he told himself, and returned to observation.

Carshin was a devious opponent, Wilton decided as the waltz continued. Such a man would never attack openly. He would try to manipulate or maneuver. Indeed, in his world, this was the rule. But that made him all the more vulnerable to a frontal assault, Wilton thought, a daunting smile curving his lips.

Diana, unaware of this scrutiny, was praying for the music to end. Being so close to Carshin, his arm about her, was intolerable, and she was conscious only of a frantic wish that he would vanish from her life.

"Have you forgotten all the plans we made for our life together?" Carshin said abruptly. Before she could answer, he hurried on. "We were to have one of the most elegant houses in London, and fill it with the haut ton. You would have all the dresses and jewels and carriages you pleased, and I can assure you that you would be a great hit—a reigning toast. I have a wide acquaintance, and I know just where we should find the best house and whom to invite. It would be splendid." By this time he was entranced by his own vision. "How lovely you would be, clothed in the height of fashion, and rubies—no, emeralds. We would go to Brighton in the summer. The Prince would receive us, without doubt. You would be presented at court, of course. I could guide you as to just how—"

"No," interrupted Diana.

"What?" He looked down, his delightful dream broken.

"I don't want any of that, particularly not with you."

"You do not want to be a leader of fashion?" Carshin did not really believe this. He could not imagine another ambition than his own dearest wish.

"No."

"But…but…to live in town."

"I may someday visit London, but I do not need you for that—or for anything."

"On the contrary," he retorted, his temper flaring again. "You will never mingle with the haut ton without me. You will not be accepted in any society if I speak out."

She shrugged. "Then I shall have to do without it." Something in his tone tonight had gradually heartened her. He seemed nearly desperate. And then, with a jubilant flash, she realized Carshin's dilemma. The life he wanted was impossible without her consent. He could ruin her, yes, but, by doing so, he would also spoil his own prospects. They were at a stalemate. She laughed aloud.

"You find our discussion amusing?" He sneered.

"Yes. For I have just now realized that you can never have what you want."

Meeting her eyes, Carshin saw that she had understood his predicament. The knowledge infuriated him. He felt an almost irresistible impulse to choke capitulation from her lips.

"If you speak," Diana added, "you will lose all chance of your house in town and great position. For you do not come out so well in that story, either, and I doubt that any wealthy lady will welcome your addresses when it is known."

"Vixen," he hissed, and Diana laughed again. "You needn't gloat just yet," he went on. "I can still queer things for you. You have hopes of Wilton, do you not? Well, he won't have you. No man will. I shall see to it."

"Even though you have no chance of getting what you want?"

"Yes!"

Diana turned her head away.

"Consider," he urged. "Would you not be happier with me than disgraced and shut away in Yorkshire?" He could see only one answer to this, and his hopes revived.

But Diana shook her head, and, the music ending at last, she walked away abruptly, causing a few stares and titters among the other couples.

Wilton watched it with pleasure. Diana had achieved some sort of victory, he sensed. But the thunderous look on Carshin's face as he strode out of the ballroom told the captain that it was not complete, and his plans remained unchanged.

Diana refused two offers to stand up and sat beside Amanda for the next sets, feeling both elated and distressed. She had at last bested Gerald Carshin in an encounter, and this she had enjoyed immensely. But her situation was really not much better, for he still threatened her heart's desire. Yet Diana could not remain dejected. The music and the crowd, her small triumph, inevitably raised her spirits, and, when another waltz struck up and Robert

Wilton came up to her, she accepted him with a heart-stopping smile. He responded with one as warm, and they moved onto the floor together.

It was astonishing, thought Diana as she slipped into his arms, how the same steps and posture could be so utterly different. She was intensely aware of Wilton's arm about her waist, his hand holding hers, and of his shoulder under her fingers, but the sensation was pleasurable and exciting. With Carshin she had wished only to throw off an intrusive touch; now she remembered closer embraces with longing. But even as she moved happily to his direction, another concern surfaced. "I am glad for this opportunity to talk to you," she said.

"Are you? That's good." He smiled down at her again, making her heart beat faster.

"I wanted to ask you about what you said at our last meeting." Though she wanted only to relax in his arms, Diana was determined to speak.

"What I said?" Wilton's tone was warm and loving. He had completed his plan and was feeling at peace with the world. In a very few days, he was certain, his future with Diana would be settled.

"I have the feeling you are plotting something," she blurted, "and it worries me because—"

"Do not allow it to," he responded. "I know what I am about."

"But what is it?"

He simply shook his head.

"Captain Wilton!"

He held her eyes. "Do you not trust me?"

Diana bit her lower lip, trying to find some clue in his face.

"Do you think I would do anything of which you would disapprove?"

"No. Not exactly, but…"

"Then do not worry." He smiled, and his blue eyes held such

love and admiration that Diana's heart seemed to turn over within her breast. This man deserved the truth, she knew then. She would have to rely on his love to make him understand. "There is something I must tell you," she answered.

But Captain Wilton shook his head. "You needn't."

"Yes. Not...not here, but..."

He understood that she was ready to reveal whatever Carshin held over her, but it did not matter, he thought. He swung her in a sudden turn, and laughed at her mild startlement. "Let's simply enjoy ourselves tonight," he said. "This is, after all, a ball."

Diana could not resist his smile. Her worry seemed to melt before it. "But, Captain Wilton," she laughed, "I thought you detested balls and all such frivolity."

"Not when I may waltz with *you*." He pulled her closer. "You have quite changed my opinion."

"But, sir, there is a war going on!" she teased.

Wilton nodded seriously, causing her smile to fade.

"In Belgium," she added, uneasy again over something in his face.

"In Belgium," he agreed, "and other places. But all is well in hand."

"Captain Wilton..."

"Someday," he said, "you will call me something other than 'Captain Wilton.' I find I look forward to that very much."

"But—"

"No more, or I will kiss you here and now." He grinned, in high spirits.

Diana could not restrain a nervous look around the ballroom, and Wilton laughed. "For a man who disdains society, you are very bold," she retorted.

"Perhaps I was a bit harsh in my judgment. Some things about society are far from distasteful, I find." He bent his head a little. "The waltz, for example."

For an instant, she almost thought he would kiss her; then he drew back, and Diana let out a sigh that was half relief, half disappointment. Wilton laughed. Diana hesitated, then joined him.

FIFTEEN

THE NEXT DAY DAWNED WARM AND CLEAR, A PERFECT EARLY summer day, and Diana went through her usual routine with almost her old cheerfulness. At breakfast with the Trents, she teased Amanda gently about her expanding girth. She took a long walk, as she had not done for some time. And, over luncheon, she joined the discussion of war news, encouraging George to repeat the small store of known facts yet again, his substitute for real information about the course of the campaign.

Amanda, noticing the change, was delighted, and, when the two women had a moment alone together and Diana explained the cause of her renewed spirits, she clapped her hands with glee. "You have forced him to a stalemate! He will do nothing now."

"Unless I do," answered Diana, thinking of Wilton.

"Well, yes, but...still, it is a step."

She could not help feeling the same herself, and Diana nodded, smiling. Major Trent was heard in the hall, calling his wife.

"Oh, the carriage is ready. I must go. But we will sit down for a real talk after our drive." And with a flutter of gloves, she went out.

Still smiling, Diana sat on the drawing-room sofa and considered what to do with her afternoon. She wished that Captain Wilton might call, but he had said nothing to indicate he would. Indeed, he seemed wrapped up in his own schemes and had not visited them as frequently as before. Diana felt a passing uneasiness, but pushed it down. It was so wonderful to feel herself again; she refused to worry.

The bell rang, and she stood, thinking that her thought had brought Wilton to her. But the maid came in with a card bearing Lord Faring's name. For a moment Diana gazed at it with astonishment. Why should Wilton's brother call on her?

"Shall I show him up, miss?"

"What? Oh, yes, I suppose so."

The girl went out, leaving Diana staring at the card, and soon Lord Faring was standing in the doorway making his bow. It was disconcerting, Diana thought as she greeted him, how little like Captain Wilton he was. The same frame, though without the musculature of a soldier; the same coloring, though washed out by indoor living and excess; the same thin face, though never lit by that entrancing smile.

"You will be surprised by my call," drawled Lord Faring, moving languidly to the chair she offered.

Diana acknowledged this by her silence.

"We are not very well acquainted, but we do have mutual friends. And I come on a mission from one of those. Perhaps two, actually." He leaned back in the armchair, looking quite bored.

Had his brother sent him? Diana wondered why.

"I speak chiefly of Gerald Carshin, of course," added the visitor, and she understood. "He has told me of your situation and asked for my help."

Diana froze. Had Carshin spoken after all? And to Wilton's brother?

"It is unconventional, of course," Lord Faring went on, showing no signs of emotion. "But I do have some connection with the case. Carshin feels that you are rejecting his suit because of my brother, and I am best fitted to speak to you about Robert."

This did not seem like exposure. Diana found her voice. "Really?"

Lord Faring nodded, not seeming to hear the sarcasm. "Had you a father or guardian, I should apply to him, naturally. But Major Trent does not seem to fall in that category, so I am forced to speak directly. Most awkward."

He did not act as if he felt awkward, Diana thought. Indeed, he seemed scarcely interested in the matter. She thought of dismissing him, but she was curious as to what he had to say.

"Carshin's a good fellow, you know. Amusing. Up to every rig and row in town. And he's taken with you. Never seen him like this. Be a good husband."

"I really don't think..." began Diana.

"That it's any of my affair. Perhaps not. But, if you're on the catch for Robert, perhaps it is, you know."

Diana gasped. "On the—"

"Beg pardon. Wrong way to put it. Not as if you're after a fortune, is it?" He smiled what Diana supposed he imagined was an ingratiating smile. Again she felt the urge to throw him out, but his next words stopped her. "Robert's nothing to boast about, you know. No address, no style, not a particle of town bronze. And his expectations ain't great, mind. He has a little money, but barely enough to set up his household."

Diana stood. She would not listen to this contemptible man criticizing his own brother. "I think you should go."

Lord Faring did not move. "In a moment. Main thing I wanted to say was this: if you're hanging out for a title, you're sadly mistaken."

"A title?" Diana was mystified.

"I shan't stick my spoon in the wall like Richard, not by a long chalk. Catch me near a battlefield! And, in time, I shall set up my own nursery, so you're fair and far out if you expect Robert to succeed."

"I have no idea what you're talking about," replied Diana. "Who is Richard?"

Lord Faring examined her with narrow eyes, and evidently decided that she was serious. "Brother. Robert is the youngest."

"You have other brothers?"

"Had. Richard was killed in the Peninsula in 1809."

She stared at him, unbelieving. Captain Wilton had never mentioned this to her.

"That's why they tried to keep Robert home in the beginning

and then had him assigned to headquarters staff," added Lord Faring. "And why they won't let him go back."

"It wasn't his knee?"

He made a derisive noise. "There's nothing wrong with Robert's knee. Not now. Wellington merely hopes I'll break my neck and Robert will step into my shoes. Old 'friend' of our family, you know. He's always coddled Robert. My father didn't want another Wilton in the thick of it."

Diana was speechless, trying to take in this information.

"So, you see, you shan't be Lady Faring. You may as well take Carshin; he's by far the better man."

"You are contemptible!" Diana blurted, and immediately regretted it.

Lord Faring blinked. "Beg pardon?"

She could not keep silent. "How can you speak of your own brothers that way? And one of them killed!" She turned half away, overcome by the thought of this sorrow that Captain Wilton had not shared with her.

Lord Faring stood, his face even more studiously bland. "My brothers never gave a rap for me. Nor did my father. If one didn't care to risk one's neck at every turn, he lost interest. I owe none of them a farthing." He took a breath. "Good day, Miss Gresham. I hope you will consider what I have said." And with a nod, he went out.

Diana sank down again, bemused. How little she really knew of Robert Wilton, she thought. And yet this new knowledge brought no doubt of her love. Indeed, if anything, it increased it. How dreadful it must have been, to lose his brother in the war. She was extremely glad they had refused to send him back, she thought with a shiver.

Leaning her head on the sofa back and gazing at the ceiling, Diana thought of Wilton with a fond smile. He was so thoroughly admirable, such a stark contrast to Gerald Carshin. Her choice this time was wise.

This brought back her problem, and made her realize that Carshin must be feeling quite desperate to have sent Lord Faring to talk to her. Did he really expect to change her mind? It seemed he did, though she could not imagine why. But, if he was uneasy, perhaps there was a chance of beating him after all.

Diana sat up and stretched her arms over her head, more optimistic than she had been in weeks. She would find a way!

Suddenly there was a great crash below as the front door was flung back on its hinges. Booted feet hammered on the stairs, and Captain Wilton ran into the room, closely followed by George Trent. The captain wore his uniform. "Diana, he's done it!" cried Wilton. "He's actually done it!"

"Wilton met us on the road with the news," added George. "It's only just come. I must get to town and find Simmons. Amanda's coming. See to her, Diana." And he ran out again.

"Who's done what?" asked Diana, bewildered. "Is Amanda all right?"

"Splendid!" Without warning, the captain pulled her close and swung her round and round until she was dizzy. "Everything is splendid!"

"Stop, stop! What do you mean? Why are you wearing your uniform?" Was he going to Belgium after all? Diana felt a sudden coldness gripping her heart.

Wilton stopped spinning, and looked a bit sheepish. "I couldn't resist putting it on. Foolish, I know."

"But what has—?"

"Wellington's done it! He's beaten Boney for good and all. There was a great battle near Brussels, I think, on the eighteenth. The news is sketchy yet. But he has definitely beaten him."

"Oh, Robert!" She flung her arms around his neck and hugged him.

He responded enthusiastically, then laughed. "I said you should call me 'Robert' someday soon, but I didn't know it would take an end to the war."

Diana drew back and smiled up at him. "It is really true?"

"You think it a ruse to get you in my arms? Trent my accomplice?"

"Idiot!"

"It is really true." He kissed her.

"Is it not wonderful news?" said Amanda from the doorway, and the lovers moved apart, startled. "Oh, do not mind me." But they were self-conscious, and Amanda laughed. "We must have a celebration tonight," she added. "With champagne and…oh, everything. You will stay, won't you, Captain Wilton?"

"Indeed I shall." He smiled at Diana again.

It was the happiest evening Diana could remember. The men went first to the Pump Room, where all the former soldiers had gathered. Diana and Amanda gave orders for a sumptuous dinner and then retired to change into properly festive gowns. When they met again in the drawing room, George, too, had donned his uniform, and, though they teased him and Wilton, both women found this impulse endearing.

They ate sturgeon and roast beef and ices from the confectioner's, and toasted Wellington and an endless list of his officers in pale champagne. By the end of the meal, all four were elevated by the wine—Diana and Amanda, who were not used to it, more so than the men. Indeed, in the drawing room afterward, Amanda insisted upon standing on a footstool and singing George's regimental anthem in a very loud voice. George laughed, but went to lift her down and, still carrying her, said, "Amanda had best go to bed. She must take care of herself. I will say good night."

"I, too," said Captain Wilton. George nodded and went out, Amanda waving over his shoulder.

But Wilton did not go at once. He stood looking at Diana and smiling. He was far from befuddled by the champagne. It had only lent a golden sheen to everything around him, most particularly this woman he loved. She seemed the most beautiful he had ever beheld.

Diana was exhilarated by the unaccustomed indulgence. She laughed and took a step toward him.

He gathered her into his arms, and they kissed, long and passionately. Diana gave herself up wholly to it, every part of her responding to his touch. And when at last they drew a little apart, she said, "It seems as if everything were all right now, doesn't it?"

He nodded, and kissed her lightly again. But her words had reminded him that one task remained. "I must go," he replied softly.

"Must you?" Lifting her hand from his shoulder, she very lightly touched his cheek.

"Yes. But I will call tomorrow with news."

"I suppose there will be more details from Belgium in the newspapers."

"No doubt."

She had a puzzling sense that war news was not what he had meant, but it was lost in regret as he took his leave.

"Tomorrow," repeated the captain.

"Yes. Will you come to dinner again? George and Amanda would be glad, I'm sure."

He hesitated. He had thought to come early. But the advantages of a whole evening together occurred to him, and he nodded.

"Till then." Diana looked wistful.

He bent and kissed her lightly again, then stepped back. With a final smile and a small salute, he went out.

Alone, Diana held her arms out at her sides and whirled, making the skirt of her evening dress bell out. But she found that her balance was imperfect and, after tripping and sinking down on the sofa to avoid falling, giggled at her own foolishness and went slowly upstairs to bed. It was not until she was beneath the covers that she remembered that she had not asked Wilton about his brother.

The captain strode jauntily down the street, hands in the pockets of his uniform breeches, buoyant and elated. Diana, the news of victory, and the champagne all combined to make him feel that this was one of the best moments of his life. And he realized then that it was also the moment to act. The hour was not so very late, and all of Bath was celebrating. He could find his adversary without trouble. His smile fading to determination, Wilton turned toward the center of the town.

He knew the inn where Gerald Carshin was staying, one of the less expensive near the river, but he did not expect to discover him there so early. He went instead to the hotel where Faring had put up. His brother's group was there, drinking champagne and brandy and toasting Wellington and his army along with the crowd. Captain Wilton settled himself in a corner, waving aside the offer of a glass from revelers who noticed his uniform. He did not intend to draw attention to his mission by dragging Carshin from among his friends. He would wait and go out with him.

It was a long vigil. Lord Faring's set rarely ended a carouse before the early hours of the morning, and this occasion had the novelty of purpose. With an actual event to commemorate, they went on and on, ordering fresh bottles until the waiters grew surly.

At last, however, with dawn only a few hours away, they broke up, Boynton and Lord Faring heading for their rooms in the hotel and the others scattering to various other lodgings. Wilton rose and followed Gerald Carshin. The hours of waiting had dissipated the effects of the champagne, and anticipation had kept the captain alert. He now felt as he most often did just before going into battle: intent and aware of everything around him.

Carshin was thinking only of his bed. He was certain that Faring had put his case persuasively to Diana, and tonight's indulgences had driven his worries from his mind. He was not befuddled—countless nights of far greater dissipation in London had given him a very hard head indeed—but he was unprepared for anything more taxing than removing his clothes and sleep. When Wilton spoke his name just outside the inn door, he started violently and whirled as if to face footpads. "Wha... Who is it?"

"Robert Wilton."

He peered at him in the dim street. "Wilton? What are you doing here?"

"I want to talk to you."

"Now? It's after three."

"Now. Shall we go in?"

Automatically Carshin rang, and, after a few minutes, the landlord came to let them in, growling about the lateness of the hour. Carshin waved him off, and he returned gratefully to bed.

"A private parlor?" suggested Wilton.

By now both curious and intrigued, Carshin indicated a door, and they went inside, Wilton shutting it behind them. The last embers of a fire remained, yielding enough light for Carshin to see to kindle a lamp. Then he turned and surveyed his visitor. "Put on your uniform for the great day, did you?" He sneered. "Touching." Now that he had had time to gather his wits, Carshin found this development very interesting. Wilton's visit must have to do with Diana. Could Lord Faring have caused such an immediate effect? Was this her response?

Carshin moved to the fireplace and stirred the coals, adding fresh wood to create a blaze. He felt only interest and anticipation, for, in his eyes, Wilton was a poor opponent. He had encountered him occasionally in town when the captain had been persuaded by his mother to join in the festivities of the season, and Carshin judged his address and manner hopeless. He had also absorbed Lord Faring's contempt for his socially inept younger brother, which did not acknowledge, of course, his accomplishments in other fields. Altogether, Carshin felt an amused superiority as he sat in an armchair before the hearth and crossed one leg over the other. "Did you want something?" he asked.

Wilton remained standing. "Yes. I came to speak to you about Miss Diana Gresham."

How ham-handedly direct he was, thought Carshin, a supercilious smile spreading across his face. This would be almost too easy. "Indeed?"

"It is clear to me that you have been annoying her. This must cease."

For a moment what he saw as Wilton's effrontery kept Carshin silent and staring. The idiot actually spoke as if he had some advantage. He was apparently too stupid to realize that he was helpless in Carshin's practiced hands. He must be even less knowing than Faring had said. Carshin hardly knew how to reply to such clumsiness. "Does Diana say that I have annoyed her?" he replied finally, using Diana's first name as a calculated barb.

It struck home, but Wilton ignored it. "She has no need to do so. It is obvious."

"I see. And did Diana send you here to me?"

"No."

"Then what, my dear captain, is your interest in this matter? Though I do not admit that I have 'annoyed' anyone."

"Miss Gresham and I am going to be married, and I forbid you to speak to her or of her ever again."

Carshin laughed. "Such high flights. You should go on the stage, Captain Wilton. Do you claim that Diana has accepted you?" He reached inside his coat and drew out a silver snuffbox, flicking it open with his thumb.

"She has," answered Wilton. And he felt this to be no more than the truth, if, perhaps, stretched a little.

Carshin was still for a moment; then he proceeded to take the snuff, making of it a prolonged and careful ritual. Finally, when he had brushed the crumbs from his waistcoat with a handkerchief and replaced the box, he said, "Impossible. Diana will marry me, or no one."

"You!" Wilton found the idea revolting.

The other merely nodded. "She is mine, Wilton. You may as well go back to your marching and maneuvers. You have no chance here."

"On the contrary, it is you who will go."

Carshin was becoming bored. He was tired and ready for sleep, and this bumpkin was too dull to provide the least amusement. Toying with him was fruitless. He did not even understand the process. Carshin must be as blunt as he. He had decided at an early moment to tell Captain Wilton the whole story—it would be so amusing to see his reaction, and would remove a rival from the field once and for all—but he had thought to prolong the enjoyment, dropping hints and letting him work it out for himself. This was clearly impossible. The man could not work out a betting sheet. "Diana belongs to me," he replied. "She eloped with me at seventeen, and spent the night in my arms before returning to her home." Seeing the shock in Wilton's face, he maliciously added, "What a beauty she is, eh? You should see that hair all down over naked shoulders and—"

"You lie!" The thought of this worm touching Diana turned Captain Wilton's stomach. He had not devoted much thought to the reasons behind her predicament, once he had satisfied himself that it existed. But, whatever thoughts he had had, none had approached this.

Enjoying his horror, Carshin shook his head. "Ask her yourself. She cannot deny it. She has no more forgotten that night than I."

"Why are you not married now, then?" Wilton forced out.

"Ah." For the first time a bit uneasy, Carshin looked away. "A small contretemps concerning the lady's fortune."

"You ruined her, then abandoned her over money?" Wilton

ruthlessly suppressed his shock and concentrated on his feelings about this man. Fury and contempt battled in his breast.

"An unfortunate necessity. But I am prepared to make amends now. We shall be wed as soon as possible."

"No." Of the few certainties left Wilton, this one was most clear. Diana did not wish to marry this blackguard.

"My dear sir, there is nothing you can do—"

"She doesn't like you. A child can see that. You will leave her alone."

Carshin began to get angry. "Her preferences are not at issue. She will have me or the world will know of our elopement." He smiled triumphantly.

This was it, then, thought Captain Wilton. This was the threat that had changed Diana from a carefree, laughing girl to a melancholy recluse. Gazing at Carshin's fat complacent face, the captain almost laughed. Did the man really believe it was so easy?

He shook his head. "If you ever come near Diana Gresham again," he said, "or so much as mention her name, I will kill you."

Carshin pulled back in his chair, aghast.

"I will discover some pretext," continued Wilton, "and I will challenge you. I am rather good with sword and pistol, and I shan't stop until you are dead. You will not escape me. I will follow you wherever you go and call you out."

"Are you mad? Dueling is forbidden. You would have to flee the country. You—"

"I have lived abroad for many years. I rather like it. And I should have the satisfaction of knowing that you were dead."

Carshin stood and backed around the chair. Why had he not noticed the terrifying implacability of Wilton's expression before? "I could speak before you reached me," he said in a quavering voice. "The girl would be ruined in any case."

Wilton smiled without humor. "True. But you would be dead. I cannot agree with those who argue the former is the worse fate."

"I... This is merely a bluff. You would not—"

"I assure you I would."

Meeting Wilton's blue eyes, hard as cold steel, Carshin was convinced. The man must be mad. His only wish now was to escape. "Very well," he said, his dreams of riches once more falling about his ears. "I shan't speak of it. But I can hardly promise never to come near the chit again. In Bath, one often encounters—"

"Yes. That is why I suggest you leave this morning, as soon as may be."

"But that is scarcely three hours..."

Captain Wilton shrugged and turned away, his purpose accomplished. He now wanted only to obliterate all memory of this man from his mind. His personality sickened him.

"How am I to explain to my friends, your brother?"

If he had thought by this to gain some measure of sympathy, he was sadly mistaken. "I don't care a damn what you say," replied Wilton, moving toward the door. "Or what you do, so long as I need never see you again." And with a sharp jerk of the oak door, he was gone.

Carshin heard the outer door of the inn bang, and sank into the armchair, running shaking hands through his hair. Never in his life had he faced the threat of physical violence, and he decided he was quite unsuited for it. He felt dizzy and sick. "Barbarian," he muttered, then wiped his mouth with the back of his hand. Wilton had to be bluffing. But, when he remembered his look, his calm threats, he didn't believe it. And he could think of no way to evade the captain's promised attack. He was convinced the man would carry out his promise.

And so this lout would get the heiress, he thought, grinding his teeth, and he was back where he had started. They could come to London and gloat over his failure, and he could do nothing. His revelation had not seemed to discourage Wilton, though Carshin was not surprised, for he would not have thrown away a fortune for such a reason. But at least he had given the man something to think of when he held his bride in his arms. The picture he had painted had shaken Wilton. He had seen that. And it would rise again and again through their marriage. That was something.

Suddenly Carshin had another thought, one which made him smile despite his disappointment. Diana had been most upset at the idea that Wilton might be told the truth. She should not be allowed to escape scot-free.

His smile widening, Carshin moved to the writing desk in the corner of the room, carrying the lamp with him. He had promised never to see Diana again, he thought as he found paper and pen. He had not sworn he would not write. That pair should have much to talk over when next they met. Laughing a little, he wrote, "My dear Miss Gresham," at the top of the sheet.

SIXTEEN

DIANA BREAKFASTED ALONE THE NEXT MORNING, AS WAS NOW usual. Thus it was not until she finished eating and went to inquire if Amanda wanted anything from town, where Diana intended to walk, that she received Carshin's missive. The letters were always taken to Amanda with her breakfast tray. Diana's correspondence was limited to the bankers in Yorkshire and an occasional bill.

She was surprised, therefore, when Amanda held out the envelope, saying, "There is a letter for you. I would have had it taken downstairs, but I knew you would be up."

"For me?" She shook it and looked at the direction. The handwriting was unfamiliar. "What can it be?"

"I know how to find out," answered Amanda.

Smiling, Diana tore it open. But her pleased expression soon faded to apprehension as she glanced at the signature, then horror as she read, "This is to inform you that I had an extremely interesting conversation with Captain Robert Wilton last night. I am leaving Bath, and you may think you have won. But the captain now knows all about you, and you may find his feelings quite altered."

"Diana, what is it?" exclaimed Amanda, sitting bolt upright in her bed. "You have gone white as chalk. Is it bad news?"

Wordlessly Diana handed her the note. Amanda read it quickly, then let the paper drop on the counterpane. "Oh, no."

Diana felt as if she had been encased in ice. Even her heart seemed to have ceased beating.

Her friend searched for comforting words, and found none. She picked up the letter again. "He says he is leaving Bath, and that you have won. Do you suppose he means to let you be? He must. He says nothing about meeting you again. But why? I wonder what Robert Wilton—?"

"What does it matter?" blurted Diana. "He has told the story. I suppose everyone in Bath is talking of it by now. And sneering behind their hands."

"He says only that he has told Robert. You do not think Captain Wilton would repeat…"

"Of course not. But Carshin would not stop there. Why should he?" Diana paused to swallow a lump in her throat. "Besides, if Captain Wilton knows…"

The two women were silent for a long moment, contemplating this disaster. Amanda longed to say that it would make no difference, but she did not believe it. No man could help but be affected by such a revelation, she thought, and the ones she knew best— George, her father—would have been outraged and repelled. She imagined herself in such a situation, before her marriage. George would have rushed from her directly to the battlefield, she thought, and played the reckless care-for-nobody hero. She would probably have pined away at home, thinking of him. There would have been no match. Tears filled her eyes at the vision. Then she shook her head at her own idiocy. This was no way to aid Diana. "You can't be certain the story is spread," she offered. "Something has happened." She concentrated. "Indeed, I think Captain Wilton has driven Carshin off. Why else would he go so suddenly?"

Thinking over the events of the last few days, Diana was forced to agree. "He has been planning something."

"Robert?"

She nodded.

"There! He has saved you. Just like a knight in a fairy tale." Diana looked at her, and she faltered. "That is…"

"And Carshin has retaliated by telling him the truth. Like a malign dragon breathing fire. And so I *am* ruined, though I may continue to live in society as long as I please."

"Diana…"

"I care more for Robert Wilton's good opinion than any other's!

Indeed, had I that, I should not mind what…" She choked, unable to go on. Amanda got out of bed and came to put her arm around her shoulders. "Oh, Amanda, what am I to do?"

"You…you can talk with him. Perhaps…" But she could not finish.

Diana imagined facing Wilton under these new circumstances. The thought made her wince. If his eyes now held contempt and revulsion instead of love—and how could it be otherwise once she had been linked with a man such as Carshin? She would not be able to bear it. And yet a small flame of hope also flickered. Amanda had understood her plight. Might he not as well? Tonight, when he came to dinner, she could judge the chances.

But at that moment there was a knock at the door and one of the maids came in. "A note, ma'am," she said, holding out a sealed missive. "It is for you and Miss Diana, the man said."

"Man?" said Diana, more sharply than she meant.

The maid gazed at her. "The man what delivered it. He didn't wait."

"Thank you, Annie," said Amanda, and she unfolded the sheet as the girl went out. A silence followed.

"What is it?" asked Diana apprehensively.

Amanda looked up, distressed.

"Amanda. What?"

"It…it is from Robert. He begs us to excuse him from dinner tonight as…as he has pressing business. He says he will call soon."

Diana did not move. She felt that, if she stirred or spoke, she would shatter in a thousand pieces on the carpet. She had hoped, she realized. She had not really given up till now.

"Perhaps he does have business," stammered Amanda. "His brother, or…"

Carefully Diana shook her head. Then she turned and moved slowly toward the door.

"Where are you going?"

"To my room." Her voice sounded alien in her own ears.

"Are you all right?" As soon as she asked it, Amanda knew the question was ridiculous.

"No."

"What can I do? Will you not stay here? I…"

"I will be better alone for a while, Amanda. But thank you." Diana went out, closing the door very quietly behind her. Amanda gazed at it with tears in her eyes, Captain Wilton's note still clutched in her hand.

———————

Robert Wilton would have been astonished and horrified had he witnessed this exchange. But having no knowledge of Carshin's letter, he sat in his lodgings secure in the thought that he had ample time to adjust.

For Carshin's story had indeed shaken him. There could be no denying that. As the Londoner had hoped, the picture he had painted—of Diana in his embrace—haunted Wilton, making him at once furious and sick. Like most men of his class and generation, Robert Wilton had been taught to value innocence in a woman above many other qualities. He had, he saw now, a certain vision of his wife, though he had not been conscious of forming it. Diana had matched all his desires, until this revelation.

Wilton understood far more than Carshin had said. He had no doubt that the blackguard had deceived and misused a naive girl. Even knowing little of Diana's history, he was certain that none of it was her fault. A man such as Carshin was heedless of propriety. Diana had done nothing. But, even as he assured himself of this, the vision rose again. He could see it damnably clearly: her golden hair streaming down, her innocent acceptance of Carshin's lying endearments.

With a wordless exclamation, Wilton leapt up and hurled his shaving mug into the grate, where it shattered against the bars. He could not bear it! How could he ever look at Diana again without seeing that picture?

Catching up his riding crop, he strode from the room and down to the stables. If he stayed inside a moment longer, he thought, he would begin to beat on the walls with his fists. A long, hard ride was the thing. If he could settle nothing in his mind, at least he would be tired out.

The conventional course of action in his situation—breaking off with Diana while keeping forever silent as to the reason—satisfied him no more than its alternative. He loved her, or had loved her, dearly. He could name her sterling qualities and enumerate her beauties. Never to see her again—the thought made him clench his teeth.

Mounting up, he headed away from the town, pushing his horse hard. The motion eased the turmoil of his brain a little, and he attempted an objective analysis. Nothing had changed in the Diana he loved, he told himself. The incident with Carshin had occurred years ago, and no doubt she had regretted it bitterly. The way she treated Carshin showed her dislike for the man and the memory. She was not even the same person, really, who had been taken in by him.

Yet his anger remained. He could not seem to ease it.

Wilton wished for a confidant. If only there were someone he could turn to for advice. If his father were alive… But no. He could not share this story and expose Diana to the chance of ruin. And his father's counsel would have been harsh, he suspected.

Spurring his horse, he galloped down a green lane, oblivious of the lush summer vegetation and the scent of roses. It almost seemed as if he could outrun his dilemma, if he went fast enough.

But when he at last pulled his mount to a shivering, blowing halt, his problem was as pressing as ever, and he was no closer to deciding what to do. Remorseful, he walked the animal for a while, and then rode on as the morning turned to afternoon, still wrestling with his desires and prejudices.

At three, Diana came downstairs wearing a bonnet and shawl. She found Amanda alone in the drawing room. The latter rose at once. "Diana, how are you? You missed luncheon. Do you want something?"

"No." Diana hesitated, looking at her. "I'm leaving, Amanda. I'm going home."

"What?"

"I know it is a cowardly thing to do, but I cannot bear to stay. My house is still there. I can hire one or two servants. I will be quite—"

"But you can't go without seeing Robert! Diana, you *must* talk with him. You do not know how he feels. Perhaps—"

"He has let me know. Do you not see that, Amanda? His message today was designed to tell me in a way that hurt less than meeting. He is gone. It was, I suppose, kind." Tears threatened, and she turned her face away briefly.

Amanda tried to think of objections, but her friend's reasoning seemed depressingly plausible. "You cannot be sure," she answered weakly.

Diana gazed at her. "I am sure."

"But…but…you needn't return to Yorkshire, to that cold bleak house." She shivered slightly. "No one else knows your story, and I do not think they will. I feel it, somehow. So you can stay with us. We could go to London if you do not like to remain in Bath. Or, since it is so late, Brighton or…"

"No," replied Diana softly.

"You would forget him after a time, with the diversion of society."

"Would you have forgotten George so?"

Amanda was silent, looking unhappy.

"Truly I care nothing for society. It has not matched my expectations. I shall be better off alone."

"You won't! How can you say so? I can't bear to think of you living solitary in that house. You have been so much happier since you left it and came to us."

Diana could not dispute this. She did not try. She knew she was reacting in her old constricted pattern, and, perhaps, wrongheadedly. To hide from the consequences of her actions might be unwise, but she did not feel able to face the alternative. She had always chosen to avoid censure and contention rather than endure the unhappiness they engendered.

"But I will miss you so!" wailed Amanda, giving up reasoned argument. "I thought you would be with me for weeks yet. Months, perhaps. You cannot go."

This was difficult to take. Diana knew she had been a great help to her friend in her current delicate state of health, and their companionship had warmed them both. But Amanda had her family, and she would before long be engrossed by an addition to it. "I'm sorry, Amanda. George will be here."

"Yes, but…" She pressed her lips together, and tears spilled over her lashes.

"I am sorry!" cried Diana. "But I cannot help it, I swear. I could not go on as usual after this. I would be of no use to you."

"Perhaps I could be useful to you."

"Oh, Amanda." She stepped forward and took both her hands. "You are truly my dearest friend, and, if you will, sometimes come to visit me at home;I will be grateful. But even you cannot make up for what I have lost."

Amanda held her hands as a lifeline. "You are not allowing enough time!"

Diana gave one last squeeze, shook her head, and moved away. "I am taking Fanny. She has no objection to returning to Yorkshire. I must go and arrange for a post chaise."

"George will be home in a moment. Let him go."

"It isn't necessary."

"Let me do *something*!"

"Amanda, I can't bear sitting still—and thinking. I beg your pardon, but I will go myself. I will say goodbye before setting out." She turned away.

"You can come back anytime you like," blurted Amanda. "Perhaps a stay at home will help, and then you can return to us."

Diana hesitated, hating to disappoint her, though she was certain she would not return. "Perhaps," she replied finally, and went out.

All the arrangements were complete within two hours. The post chaise waited outside the front door of the Trents' lodgings as Diana's things were brought down and loaded. The two women stood together in the drawing room, Amanda watching her friend's face and Diana gazing sadly at the floor. George, who had come home in the meantime, alternated between supervising the servants and joining his wife and guest. "Are you certain you will not wait until morning?" he said for the fourth time when he had seen the last valise carried down. "You have scarcely a few hours until dark, and there is no moon."

"I want to get started," answered Diana.

The major shook his head. He was utterly mystified by this sudden start, but clear signals from his wife had kept him more or less silent. "Well, the baggage is loaded."

"Thank you." Diana stepped closer and offered her hand. "I must also thank you for all your kindness to me. You have been the best of hosts, and a good friend."

He clasped her hand awkwardly, seeming even more puzzled. "Why go, then?" he could not restrain himself from saying. It was obvious to George that this parting grieved Amanda, and he would prevent it if he could. "If you hadn't been happy with us, or if there had been a quarrel…" He paused, fishing.

"How could there be?" Diana assured him warmly.

He looked from his now tearful wife to Diana, whose smile was patently forced. "I don't understand any of this."

"I'm sorry. I must go," was Diana's only reply. She did not think she could bear further goodbyes. "Fanny is waiting for me in the carriage."

"Oh, Diana!" Amanda ran forward and flung her arms about her friend. "I shall miss you so." She was crying openly.

"And I you."

They clung together briefly; then Diana gently disentangled herself, tears showing on her cheeks as well. "You will visit me."

"Of course."

With an attempt at a smile, and a nod to George, she hurried from the room. Amanda ran to the stairs to watch her go out, and, in a few moments, they heard the chaise pulling away. "For God's sake, what is going on?" said the major.

His wife shook her head and walked into his arms to be comforted.

He enfolded her. "You're not going to explain, are you?" Silence answered him, and he sighed. "Well, it is a great pity. You were so pleased to have her here." This, not unnaturally, caused Amanda to cry again, and Major Trent cursed his clumsiness and devoted himself to restoring her spirits.

The Trents' dinner that evening was not festive, and, when George suggested that they go to a concert, Amanda merely shook her head. The room seemed echoing and overlarge, and the rattle of cutlery intrusive, without Diana's additions to the conversation.

Afterward, they sat in the drawing room, and George exerted himself mightily to be amusing. But Amanda would not be jollied. Finally, in the midst of an anecdote the major thought uproarious, she said, "The world is really so unfair, George."

"Eh?"

"Nothing happens as it should, and the nicest people are made to suffer for the actions of bad ones."

"Who do you mean?" he responded, puzzled.

"Um?" She looked up as if surprised. "Oh, nothing. Go on with your story. It is very funny."

The major eyed her. "Well, Rollins had bought the chicken, but he had nowhere to cook it. Sergeant Hooker had a fine pot, but nothing to put in it. Yet they were so much at odds that..." He paused, aware that Amanda had ceased listening. "That Rollins deserted to the French rather than cook his bird in Hooker's pot," he suggested. Amanda merely nodded. "And so, of course, Hooker led his troop in an assault on the enemy position and recaptured the chicken. He carried it back across the lines in triumph. It made the most frightful row, squawking and flapping its wings. He held its feet and waved it about like a banner."

"Urn," said Amanda again.

"And so Wellington gave him a medal and put him in charge of foraging for the entire army. Amanda, what is the matter?"

She started. "What?"

"I have been talking the veriest nonsense for five minutes, and you have not heard a word."

"Yes, I have. It was about..."

The major took her hand. "Won't you tell me what's wrong?"

She hung her head. "I can't, George. It is not my secret."

"Secret?" He raised his blond brows.

They were interrupted by the sound of the bell and, just after, footsteps on the stairs. In the next instant, Captain Wilton appeared. "I told the servant you would see me," he said. "I am sorry to call so late, but I must speak to Miss Gresham. It is very important."

Amanda leapt to her feet. "Oh, no!" She put both hands to her lips.

Wilton stared at her, and George looked from one to the other. "Miss Gresham left for Yorkshire four hours ago," he said finally.

"Left...?" The captain seemed stunned.

But the major had been diverted. "Amanda, are you all right? You look ill." He went to her and put an arm around her waist. "Come and sit down. You are pale."

"I'm all right."

"Don't be ridiculous. You must take care." He led her back to the sofa and seated her. "Wilton, perhaps—"

"I must talk to Captain Wilton," declared Amanda decisively. "Would you leave us alone, please, George?"

"What?"

"It is about Diana, and I must talk with him."

The major appeared torn between hurt and outrage.

"George, please!"

Meeting her pleading eyes, and glancing at Wilton's tense white face, the major gave in. But he was clearly offended at his exclusion.

"I will explain all I can later," offered his wife. With a curt nod, he left the room.

Amanda and Captain Wilton gazed at each another, each trying to gauge the other's knowledge and state. Amanda spoke first. "She did not think you would call again. And so she went home."

"But why should she think that? In my note I said—"

"She decided it was a hint you would come no more. Because of Carshin's story."

Wilton stared. "How...do you...?"

"She told me the whole. And Carshin wrote to her about your...meeting."

"Damn him!" he exploded. "I'll pay him back for—"

"Captain Wilton. Why have you come?" Amanda leaned forward and searched his face.

"To...to see Miss Gresham."

"And?"

"What do you mean?" He avoided her eyes.

"What did you plan to say to her?"

He turned half away, frowning.

"Please. I am her friend. I know the circumstances. This is not prying."

Wilton turned back and looked at her. Here, unexpectedly, he had perhaps found the confidante he had sought. "I'm...not sure. I have spent this whole day thinking—and getting nowhere. It is... difficult. But as I was riding home, I realized I had to stop here. I could not stay away. And she has gone!" He looked toward the windows, curtained now against the dark.

"Yes." Amanda still watched him, trying to understand what he felt. "Will you sit down for a moment, please? There is something I should like to tell you."

"I don't know. Perhaps I should..."

"It is very important."

Something in her voice brought him to the sofa and made him sit beside her.

There was hope as well as hurt and confusion in his eyes, Amanda saw exultantly. "I don't believe Diana ever spoke to you about her childhood," she began. Wilton shook his head. "Well, I want to do so now."

He looked puzzled but not unreceptive. "Very well."

Amanda took a deep breath, relieved that he meant to listen. She thought for a moment, then began.

She talked for nearly half an hour, without interruption from her visitor. His expression altered with her words, but he did not speak. At last, hoping that she had proved a good advocate, she finished, "It was years ago, and Diana is much changed. I can testify to that."

There was a silence. Amanda bit her lower lip.

"I never imagined it was her fault," said Wilton quietly then. "I do not blame her, precisely. Particularly after what you have told me."

"No one could."

He raised his head and met her eyes. "But it is still very difficult to...accept. I don't know if you can understand."

She nodded, sad.

"I feel as if I were being torn in five different directions, and, frankly, I do not know where I shall end up."

"But you intend to talk to Diana," she urged, leaning forward again.

"I did. But if she does not wish to see me…"

"She went away because she believed you would not see her, and she could not bear that. You must go after her."

"You think so?" He rubbed his hands over his face. "I am tired and confused. I do not know what is right anymore."

"I'm certain of it," insisted Amanda.

He hesitated, then nodded. "Yes. Yes, you're right. I must see her."

"She meant to stop at a posting house on the road north. She can't have gone too far."

Wilton stood, suddenly determined. "I'll go at once." He glanced at the mantel clock. "It is scarcely ten, and I can travel faster than a laden chaise. I will speak to her before she sets out again tomorrow."

Amanda hadn't quite expected this. "You will ride in the darkness?"

This elicited Wilton's first smile. "I have often done so in Spain. And I shall not even have to worry about bandits here."

She rose to face him. "I wish you the best of luck, then."

"Thank you. I wonder what that may be?" With a wry salute, he turned to go.

"Oh, I wish I could go with you!"

He glanced back over his shoulder. "You have been a good friend. But the rest…" He shrugged. "Go to George. He is probably near bursting with curiosity by this time."

Amanda smiled slightly, then bit her lip again as he went out.

SEVENTEEN

DIANA HAD TRAVELED THROUGH THE LONG SUMMER EVENING and twilight and stopped at a small posting house when darkness fell. Sitting in the hired chaise, Fanny in the opposite corner, she had kept her mind carefully blank. It was no good regretting the past, she told herself, and the future held little to anticipate. It was best not to think. Diana watched the passing scenery with wide, abstracted eyes, seeing it without registering details. She answered Fanny's occasional remarks, though these grew fewer as they drove and the girl picked up Diana's mood, and she attended to whatever mundane duties the journey entailed. But Diana felt as if she was only half-alive in the carriage. A large part of her was sealed off, perhaps forever, from the joys and pains of the world.

At the inn, they bespoke a room and a late supper, but Diana could not eat, and when she was in bed, sleep did not come. In the quiet darkness, it was more difficult to ignore her situation, and, as the hours passed, Diana became more and more dejected.

Captain Wilton, riding through the night, his pace necessarily slow, was not much better off. He, too, had given up thinking. It led him round and round the same questions without a glimmer of resolution, and he had taken refuge in action. Fortunately, the way was difficult without light, and keeping to the road and avoiding obstacles required all his faculties. He had a good idea of how far Diana's chaise could have gone in the time elapsed, but it was hard to judge distances without landmarks, and he had often to pause and calculate where he might be. In this way, the night passed rapidly for him, and, when the first streaks of dawn appeared on the horizon, he was surprised.

A glance at the rising sun told Robert that he had somehow

strayed off the main north road and into a lane, but, when he turned his mount and galloped back, concerned in spite of his uncertainties that he would miss Diana, he reached the highway quickly. And another half hour's ride brought him to the posting house where she was most likely to be. Inquiring, he found he had judged correctly, and he swung down from his horse and went in to order breakfast.

Diana had meant to make a very early start. But her sleeplessness in the first part of the night had given way to exhaustion as morning approached, and she slept heavily until eight, stirring only gradually at Fanny's urging.

"You said to be sure and wake you," the maid said defensively when Diana rose on one elbow and blinked to clear her vision.

"Yes."

"I'm sure I *would* have let you sleep."

"It's all right." Diana felt as if her head were stuffed with cotton batting. "Is there tea?"

"Yes, indeed, miss." Fanny indicated a small tray on the side table, then poured out a cup.

Diana drank gratefully, returned the cup, and rubbed her eyes. Feeling a little better, she pushed back the covers. "You needn't help me dress, Fanny. Would you find the postboys and tell them we will be leaving right after breakfast?"

"They're ready now, miss."

"Oh." Feeling slightly flurried, Diana washed and put on her traveling dress. Fanny picked up her night things and toilet articles. In twenty minutes they were walking downstairs together.

"I'll put this in the chaise, miss, shall I?" said the maid, holding up the dressing case.

Diana nodded and went on toward the private parlor where her breakfast would be waiting. But, as she opened the door, she heard her name and turned back, to confront Robert Wilton approaching from the taproom.

She gasped, and turned bright red, then ashen, her hand trembling on the doorknob.

For an endless moment they merely stared at one another, each frozen by conflicting impulses. Then Wilton ushered her into the parlor with a light touch on her elbow. He felt her shaking and he wished at the same time both to soothe her and flee from this excess of emotion.

Inside, a small table was set for the morning meal. To Diana it seemed ludicrous—this very ordinary scene in such intensely extraordinary circumstances. She almost laughed, but the sound she felt rising in her throat was distinctly hysterical, and she suppressed it.

Wilton understood that it was up to him to begin. Briefly wishing that he knew what he meant to do, he said, "I called at the Trents' to speak to you, and they told me you had gone. I…I followed…to speak to you."

"Yes?" Diana did not dare hope. For an instant, when she had first seen him, a flame of possibility had blazed, but his tone and behavior had dimmed it again.

"I… Shall we sit down? I did not intend to interrupt your breakfast. Please go on."

Did he actually imagine she could sit calmly and eat as they talked? Diana shook her head and went to the armchair before the fire. Wilton took its mate opposite. Silence fell again. Captain Wilton searched for words. "I did not imagine Gerald Carshin would write to you," he said at last. "If I had, I would certainly have…" He stopped, with no idea how to end this sentence.

Diana gazed down at her clenched fists. "What passed between you and Mr. Carshin?" she found the voice to ask. "How did you…? I don't understand it."

He took up this less emotion-laden topic eagerly. "I saw that he threatened you. So I told him that, if he did not give it up, I would kill him."

"What?"

Not quite realizing how strange this sounded to Diana, he recounted the story of their confrontation, keeping his eyes focused on the hearth rug. His military life had made him familiar with violence, and he did not think of his threat as outrageous.

"Do you mean you would really have killed him?" Diana said when he had finished.

Wilton shrugged.

"But…" She couldn't find words.

"I knew it was unlikely to be necessary. The man is a coward. Only a coward would prey on women." Absorbed in his story, he met her eyes, and the gaze held as each of them learned things from the other. Diana was genuinely shocked, Wilton realized, and, seeing the episode from her perspective, he could not precisely blame her. Diana glimpsed the motives behind the captain's actions. Generosity of spirit and, yes, love had guided him, she saw, and his threat had been without malice or enjoyment. She felt a thrill at his gallantry.

"It was the only way to be sure of routing him," blurted Wilton.

"Thank you," said Diana at the same moment.

They paused, embarrassed, then fell into silence again, left with the question of the future. Neither felt able to broach it.

Finally Wilton squared his shoulders and said, "I spoke with Mrs. Trent before I started out. She told me…something about your father and the…circumstances—"

"I do not place the blame on others," Diana broke in. "Whatever my difficulties, the fault was mine. Others struggle with youth, ignorance, loneliness, harsh rules, without doing what I did."

This was brave, thought Wilton. He admired those who did not make excuses. For the first time since they had met in the corridor, he examined her. The morning sun was slanting through the window and lighting her hair to molten bronze. Her face was in shadow, its exquisite contours accentuated. But, more than her beauty, he saw her pain, and her determined control of it. He seemed to see in her expression all the years since Carshin had passed from her life. They had molded her almost as the war had him, he thought. And if she had done something to be regretted—as he had, more than once—the mistake had made her an extraordinary woman. Indeed, without it she might have become like the London misses he so disliked, or a dull, shallow countrywoman. He would not have been drawn to her, or come to love her. So, he told himself, though it was still difficult to think of that long-ago incident, he had, amazingly, reason to be grateful for it. The revolutionary nature of this thought made it slow to assimilate, and the silence in the room lengthened.

Diana, concluding that he must be condemning her, clenched her hands even tighter, until her nails dug into her palms and the skin whitened. Why had he come after her? Why could he not have simply let her go and spared them both this scene? Finally, unable to endure it any longer, she rose. "My chaise is waiting. I must go."

He stood to face her. "Diana—"

"I thank you again for helping me. It is…good to know that my…story will not be common property. And it was…kind of you to come and say goodbye. I—"

"I don't say it."

Something in his voice held Diana motionless, her heart pounding chokingly in her throat.

"Why do you think I followed you? I admit I was not sure myself for a while. But some part of me understood and brought me here." He stepped forward.

"What?"

"I love you, Diana. I have told you so before, and my feelings have not changed."

"Even after…"

"No. Or perhaps they have changed, in a way. But only because I now understand more about you and why you are so dear to me."

Diana took a shaky breath. She could not quite believe him yet. Everything she had been taught, and her limited experience, told her that he could not still love her. Her harsh father, her distant neighbors, the insinuations of Gerald Carshin, all argued the opposite. Among her acquaintances, only Amanda had taken her part, and she had seemed convinced that Captain Wilton would not. "Are...are you saying this out of pity?" she ventured. It seemed an unlikely explanation, but she could think of no other. "You needn't. I shall be quite all right. I can look after myself."

"I know. It is one of the things I admire most about you." He smiled, and Diana waited, puzzled. Was this a withdrawal? "But there is a difference between being capable of managing and being happy, you know. I learned that in Spain." Seeing her expression, he added, "I could get along very well on my own when I first joined my regiment. Indeed, I prided myself on it. Yet that satisfaction soon gave way to routine and isolation, and I feared I was not suited to military life. I nearly sold out before I discovered the value of helping out my fellows and allowing them to help me." He paused then. "I should like to look after you...sometimes."

"I don't think..."

"Diana." He stepped forward and took both her hands before she could retreat. "This is *not* pity. I love you!"

Still incredulous, she met his eyes and searched them for signs of other feelings. She found none. Slowly, tentatively, she began to believe. It felt as if the sealed part of her were gradually opening, relieving a terrible pressure and constraint.

Watching her gold-flecked eyes shift, Wilton smiled again, more naturally. After a time, Diana returned his smile—shakily, then with growing joy. He laughed and pulled her into his arms, holding her close.

They stood thus for a while, reveling in their new understanding. Then Wilton put a finger under Diana's chin and raised her lips to his. She responded eagerly, all barriers between them gone.

The release from the tension each had felt at the beginning of their interview intensified their passion now. Diana clung to him, and his hands moved tenderly over her back as the kiss went on and on.

When at last they drew apart, Diana swayed a little in his embrace. She had endured dreadful anxiety in the last day, and eaten almost nothing. Combined with this new rush of emotion, it was almost too much.

"Are you all right?" he asked.

"Yes."

"Come and sit down." With a sudden movement, he picked her up and carried her to the sofa on the other side of the room. There, he sat down with Diana across his knees. "That's better." And he bent to kiss her again.

They were wholly engrossed for some time, and each was increasingly elated as loving desire erased their previous moods. When they drew apart again, they grinned at one another delightedly.

"When shall we marry?" said Wilton. "I can get a special license in a week. My mother is very thick with a bishop."

Diana laughed. "Why not?"

"Do you mean it? I thought females required a month at least to prepare for such an event."

"Indeed? Well, I am not 'females.'" She looked haughty.

"No." His face softened with admiration. "That you are not. But are you serious?"

"If you are, certainly. I have no family and want no grand wedding."

"Family," he groaned. "I suppose my mother will have something to say about this."

Diana stiffened a little. "You think she will disapprove?"

"On the contrary, she will be so excited to have her first son wed that she will probably invite half the realm." He considered. "You must meet her, Diana."

This reminded her of something. "You have told me so little about your family. Lord Faring said that your brother…" She hesitated, fearing to wound him.

"Have you talked with Faring? Yes, Richard was killed." A shadow passed across his face, then cleared. "That was hard, but he died bravely, and we remember him so."

"By why did you never tell me?" It seemed a slight, not to have mentioned this important fact.

He seemed surprised. "The occasion did not arise."

"Indeed? Though we are to share our lives?" Diana was rather offended.

Frowning, he considered. "I see. I hadn't thought of it from your side. I would have told you, of course, eventually. I honestly did not think of it." He paused. "We avoided thinking or talking of such things, you see, in Spain. Comrades were constantly falling in battle. If one began to dwell on it…" He shrugged.

"Oh." Diana felt stupid. "I never thought of that. It would be terrible. I'm sorry."

"Why? You could not know." He caressed her deep-gold hair. "We have much to tell one another. I expect it will take years."

This was such a pleasant thought that they merely gazed at each other for a while.

"You will come to London with me, then?" he asked finally.

She nodded. "We must go back to Amanda's first, however. I cannot leave her wondering what has happened."

"Perhaps they will accompany us."

"Oh, I hope so!"

"And, afterward, we can go down to Kent. I have a house there, which I hope you will like."

"I shall love it."

He smiled, then kissed her lingeringly again, and Diana gave herself up to the embrace. They were both oblivious of all externals when the door opened and Fanny peeked into the room.

"Miss!" she gasped.

Diana raised her head dreamily, then sat straight. "Oh, Fanny." She took in the girl's bulging eyes and dropped jaw and struggled with a smile. A glance at Robert made this more difficult.

But they rose. "I have come to take Miss Gresham back to the Trents," said Wilton. "We will be starting soon. You may inform the postboys."

Fanny goggled at Diana, who nodded, then backed out of the parlor. They heard her run down the hallway toward the inn yard.

"Oh, dear." Diana was still sensitive at the idea of scandal.

"Forget her," he replied. "We answer only to each other. And you know my opinion."

Diana sighed. "I do not know why I have been so lucky."

"Do you not? Fortunately, you can also rely on my opinion there." And he pulled her close once again.

MEDDLESOME MIRANDA

ONE

OF COURSE, I HAD NO NOTION, WHEN I FIRST ARRIVED AT Clairvon Abbey, that anything was *wrong*. Indeed, I was in such a flame at Mama and Papa for fobbing me off on Rosalind instead of taking me to Rome that I scarcely noticed how pale she was.

I still think it was all unnecessary, and I might have gone. It is all very well to say that I am a young lady of seventeen and to be presented next Season, but Mama knows quite well I care nothing for such things and am *determined* to be an author. That is why I keep this journal.

At least, that *used* to be the reason. Since I have been in Northumberland—three days, for I came on Tuesday—I have decided to set down everything that occurs while I am here, for it is a perfectly shocking place, and Rosalind is *not* happy, whatever she may pretend. And so I shall establish a record in case it should be *necessary in future*. I shall try, as Papa advises, to be both logical and complete.

(Perhaps, if I am to be honest, it is not quite true that I care *nothing* for the Season. But I might have come back from Italy in time to go with my aunt to the dressmaker—I shall have *masses* of new dresses! If I can travel to Northumberland on my own, surely I can return from Rome. But none of them would listen to me. I dislike excessively being the baby of the family.)

To begin, then, Rosalind is my eldest sister. Indeed, she is the eldest of us all, nine years older than me. First comes Rosalind, then Portia, who is three-and-twenty then James. Mama adores Shakespeare. I don't actually *mind* being called Miranda. It sounds exotic and mysterious. But her next daughter was to be Titania! Papa strictly forbade her to call James, Oberon. He said she might label us girls anything she pleased, but no son of his would fight his schoolmates from dawn to dusk because he was named for a fairy king. Whenever we want to make James growl, we call him Oberon.

But that is by the by. I must keep to the facts. Papa says I must mind my tendency to stray from the subject in my writing. Rosalind has been married nearly two years. She was practically on the shelf when Papa providentially inherited the estate of his second cousin Alfred and became *Sir* Anthony Dennison, with heaps of money. (Mama says I mustn't use such vulgar expressions, but I shall do as I please in my own private diary.) Before that we were disgustingly poor. Mama comes from a long line of impoverished clergymen, and Papa's father, who died before I was born, was a famous classical scholar who spent all his inheritance on trips to Greece and Turkey and publishing his own works (which are frightfully tedious, hundreds of pages long and crammed with Greek quotations—I shall *never* show this to Mama!).

And so Rosalind got a dowry and was presented by Aunt Hattie and made a great marriage to Philip, Baron Highdene. At any rate, we all thought it a brilliant match, having no notion he would carry her off to Northumberland and *imprison* her there. Portia married a year later, and James went up to Oxford. That is why it was so unfair of them to leave me behind. It was only me, and I would not have been the least trouble in Rome. I had *nothing* to do with the monkey who pulled off the dowager Duchess's wig at Ascot. It was all James and his horrid friends.

But Rosalind became a baroness. And Philip is prodigious handsome and rich. Papa says he looks very like Lord Byron. I have never seen Lord Byron, as Mama would not let me go to the theater the night they all saw him there, and, now that his wife has actually left him because he is so wicked, I don't suppose I ever shall see him. (I have tried and tried to discover what Lord Byron has actually *done*. No one will say anything, so it must be terrible. Perhaps he made her join in some weird rites he learned in the East?)

Philip is tall and dark, with black eyes that positively *burn* with intensity under straight thick brows. His nose is straight, too, and his chin has a cleft. We all thought him the height of fashion when we first met in London, but, here at home, he dresses in riding breeches most of the time, his neckcloth knotted anyhow and no points to his shirt at all. His manners, which we thought so polished, have changed markedly. He was quite short with me at breakfast yesterday—not to say rude! I might easily put this down to living in such a lonely, *dreary* place, but Philip insists he prefers Clairvon Abbey to a hundred Londons. (Isn't this positively *sinister*?)

It is so lowering to see Rosalind in such surroundings, for I have never denied that she is the prettiest and gayest of us all. She has Mama's red-gold hair and neat figure (Portia tends to be plump) and the loveliest blue eyes. Fortunately, looks are a matter of complete indifference to *me*, since I intend to devote myself to a writing career, and so it doesn't matter a whit that I am thinnish with pale yellow hair that will not curl and dark-green eyes. Papa says I have a vast deal more imagination than Rosalind, which I can see quite well is true.

And there are times when I look well enough. The new sprig muslin gown Mama had made up in the spring before she left is very flattering. I should wear green, Aunt Hattie said, which not every girl can do, and avoid yellow, which makes me look sallow. Aunt Hattie (she is not really my aunt, but an old school fellow of Mama's who married a viscount) knows everything about fashion. Mama pays no heed (and looks splendid in the merest *rag*), and Rosalind and Portia have such different coloring. When I am in London, I intend to do whatever Aunt Hattie says about clothes.

But I must explain why I have begun to suspect that Philip's resemblance to Lord Byron goes beyond mere lineaments. He is not at all what we thought him. He is silent and dour, and he lives in a great drafty castle that looks just like the home of the wicked, kidnapping duke in *The Haunted Wood*.

The day I arrived was cold and dank, as it always is here in the north, seemingly, even in June. I had made the long journey from London with some friends of Mama's who were going to spend the summer in Scotland (fancy!) and offered to escort me. At the first sight of Clairvon, I was fascinated, I admit. It consists of mossy stone, with three turrets and masses of crenellations, and it stands on a cliff above the sea, with waves crashing on the rocks below and wind swooping down from the moorlands. One is strongly reminded of all one's favorite romances, and I would not have been surprised to see a knight ride forth in armor to greet me.

You can imagine, then, my sentiments when Forbes opened the door. Forbes is the butler, and the tallest, thinnest man I have ever seen. He makes me feel an absolute dwarf, though I am well above middle height. He has a way of looking down with his eyes half closed and his mouth pursed up as if he smelled bad drains, and saying, "Yes, miss?" in a perfectly *daunting* voice. And he looks ancient, but not old, if you see what I mean. His face is craggy like the cliff rocks, and his hands are gnarled and *gigantic*. I asked Rosalind how she can bear to have such a servant directing her household, but she just laughed. I am afraid living all shut away here has turned her brain!

I've come to thoroughly dislike the place. My room is huge and drafty, with a fireplace that smokes and a ceiling so high I feel like a bug on a plate. The corridors are drafty, too, and dark and cold. They go twisting on for miles so that I am continually getting lost. And, outside, it does nothing but rain. I sew with Rosalind when she is free, or read. It is lucky I am training to be an author, for, without my journal, I expect I should go stark mad. I suggested yesterday that I go riding with Philip, for he rides every day, whatever the weather. That is when he was so rude, saying he "can only bear to ride alone." I immediately wondered *what he does* out on the moors that he wishes to keep so secret.

And so, just this morning, I made up my mind to find out and to help Rosalind in whatever way I can. I don't yet see just what that might be, but I shall *stop at nothing* in defense of my sister's happiness.

TWO

PHILIP, BARON HIGHDENE, SAT AT THE BREAKFAST TABLE scowling over a letter that had just arrived. His thick black brows darkened his handsome face like a thundercloud, and the set of his mouth was daunting. "I suppose I shall have to do something about Alan," he muttered.

His wife Rosalind looked up from the boiled egg she had been unenthusiastically consuming. Its yellow residue was already making her queasy. "What is the matter now?"

"He is gambling again. High stakes. And drinking. He was nearly called out last week for insulting young Beresford. Darby writes that he only just managed to quash it."

"Oh, dear." Rosalind sighed and pushed her eggcup away. "Is Alan's wound better?"

"Only a little. That is the problem, of course. He can't box or hunt, and he is restless and bored. The war didn't do him any good, either."

"Five years," agreed Rosalind, "and two serious wounds. Poor man." The sympathy in her lovely oval face made it even more appealing. "It seems so unfair he was hurt at Waterloo after we all thought the war was over." She paused, the disagreeable sensations in her midsection discouraging conversation.

"I believe we shall have to invite him here." Philip eyed the letter with distaste, as if it was somehow to blame for this necessity. "I am his only living relative."

"Of course." Rosalind smiled a little at her husband's sour expression. "Write him at once."

"We shall have a regular house party," he complained.

"My sister and your cousin hardly make up a house party. Actually, it is a very good notion. Alan and Miranda will be company for one another."

"I doubt it. Alan is a man of four-and-twenty who has seen a good bit of the world. He can have very little in common with a chit of seventeen."

"Miranda is extremely intelligent. She is always reading."

"No, she is not! She is always lurking about the place and staring at me as if I were some sort of wild beast about to spring at her. And we have nothing to say to each other. I still think she might have gone to your sister instead of..."

"Philip, do be quiet. Miranda may come in at any moment."

"No, she won't. I saw her walking toward the shrubberies not ten minutes ago. Why she wants to go outside before breakfast, and in this mist, I do not pretend to understand."

"She is bored," replied Rosalind crisply. "We have been over this a dozen times, Philip, and I thought we were agreed. She could not go to Portia with Gerald's mother so ill and needing to be nursed day and night. Besides, I was *happy* to have her. It is a good opportunity for us to become better acquainted. And she is company for me, since we are so far from any neighbors."

Philip turned away and began to re-read his letter, the grimness of his face almost frightening. Rosalind watched him with anxious eyes. The friction between them on this subject was both painful and unsettling. She knew that, for him, Clairvon and the surrounding countryside were engrossing and sufficient. With his estate duties, his books, his various sporting ventures, and her companionship, he was wholly content. But up until a few months ago, he had seemed to understand her wish for more society. They had made visits, invited guests. Lately, however, he had changed, grown silent and reclusive. Rosalind was convinced he was deeply worried, but he always denied it when she asked.

Rosalind sighed. She sometimes wondered, recently, whether she would have married Philip if she had known him better. In London he had seemed the fulfillment of her dreams—handsome, witty, kind—the sort of man she had always hoped to marry. But she had not counted on Northumberland. They were miles from their neighbors, and a trip to town was a significant undertaking. She often longed for the parties and outings of which she had had so brief a taste after her father's unexpected windfall.

She looked up, meeting Philip's intense dark eyes, and knew that she would have married him whatever the circumstances. But that did not mean she could not wish for others to talk to occasionally. Her stomach protested, and she involuntarily put a hand over her bodice.

"Are you ill?" said Philip, pushing back his chair and half rising. "Shall I call Jane? Would you like a glass of water?"

The anxiety in his voice made Rosalind force a smile and sit back. "No, no, it's nothing. A touch of dyspepsia only."

"Again? You don't think the doctor…?"

"Philip, it is perfectly natural, in my condition. Please don't worry. Mama assures me it will pass in a few weeks."

"A fine time they chose to go abroad," burst out Philip savagely. "And for perhaps a year! I think your mother might have waited until the baby came, to be with you."

"She would have, if I had asked her. But I shall have either of my aunts, and Portia, if I like, and Mama and Papa have always longed to travel. Now that they have the money, and Europe is safe once more, we could not deny them, Philip."

"I have no wish to deny them. I only think they might have waited six months."

Footsteps in the corridor ended this dispute, to Rosalind's relief. "Good morning, Miranda," she said as her sister entered the breakfast room. "Did you have a walk?"

"Yes. I went to the cliffs to watch the sea. The spray is crashing up out of the mist like fireworks at Vauxhall, Rosalind. You must come and see."

"It is far too damp and chilly for Rosalind to go out," declared Philip.

"Nonsense," said his wife. "We shall walk a little later. But now you should eat something, Miranda."

Philip made a disgusted sound and said, "I must see Cramer about the tenants' new roofs." He strode out of the room. Both of the women watched him go, Rosalind with concern and Miranda with fierce suspicion. Rosalind sighed, and her sister pounced. "Are you ill, Rosalind? You look so pale. I think it would do you heaps of good to get out. Do you not ride at all anymore?"

Looking at her, Rosalind almost smiled at the militant set of her head and her aggressive pose, hands on her hips. Miranda had always been such a vehement little thing, even when she was tiny. And full of the most astonishing ideas. Rosalind honestly welcomed this opportunity to know her better. The nine years between them seemed to lessen with age. However, she did not feel quite ready to communicate her interesting state of health. Miranda seemed so far removed from babies and mundane domesticity. She was, Rosalind realized with amazement, a bit wary of her response. "I am just a little tired," she said. "Come and have tea. There are sausages on the sideboard."

As she expected, this diverted Miranda, and Rosalind smiled as her sister filled a plate. Sausages had always been one of her passions. Indeed, Miranda had a prodigious appetite for one so slender. It had always amazed the family that Portia was plump, when she seemed to eat next to nothing, and Miranda remained thin despite enormous helpings. "I have a piece of news," said Rosalind.

"What?" Miranda sat down and picked up her fork.

"We will be having a visitor."

Miranda stopped cutting sausages. "Truly? Who?"

"A cousin of Philip's. His name is Alan Creighton, and he is just out of the army. He is something of a hero, actually. He fought in the Peninsula, and right up through France. He was wounded at Waterloo, but he is nearly recovered."

"Oh." Miranda's enthusiasm had died. "I suppose he is quite old, then. Is he much like Philip?"

Rosalind stifled a smile. "He is four-and-twenty not so *very* old. As to what he is like, I cannot say. I have never met him. He was abroad with the army until last summer, and this year we have been…"

"*Stuck* here in the north," put in Miranda.

"Keeping close to home," corrected Rosalind. "And Alan has been in London. But now he is to come for a visit."

Miranda ate a sausage.

"We will organize some expeditions to show you both around the county. The weather is sure to clear soon. We do have some lovely days here in summer."

"It has rained every day since I came!"

"I know. It is abominable, isn't it? But that is only five days, and I promise you it will get better. And then we shall see the sights."

"The sheep on the moors, I suppose?" said Miranda.

"No indeed. There are a number of historical places you will adore."

"What?"

"I don't know that I shall tell you, if you continue to look so sour."

Miranda frowned, then looked down at her nearly empty plate. After a moment, she looked up again, contrite. "I beg your pardon. It's just that…" She paused, bit her lower lip, and added, "I do so hate constant rain."

"I know. Last summer we had weeks of fine weather. Really."

Miranda smiled, then speared her last sausage. "Tell me about the sights," she demanded in her usual cheerful tones.

Rosalind smiled back with a great sense of relief. There was no one more lively and amusing than Miranda when she was in good spirits, and no one more gloomy when she was not. "Well, there is Hadrian's Wall. Although it is about three hours' journey by carriage from here."

"Hadrian? The Roman emperor?" Miranda and Rosalind exchanged grins. Their father was one of the few men outside a university who could recite the names of all the Roman emperors, from first to last. And he did it in a nursery singsong that showed he had learned it early. Indeed, *his* father had taught him while he was still toddling. The recitation had made them scream with laughter when they were small.

Rosalind laughed. "Philip jokes with his mother's family about the great wall all the way across England to keep out the terrible heathen Scots. And it is still there. At least, partly."

"Oh, Philip."

Ignoring her hostile tone, Rosalind continued. "And there is Lindisfarne Island just up the coast. It is crammed with ancient ruins. And Seahouses. That is a seaside resort about ten or fifteen miles to the south. I was there last summer. It is very pleasant."

"Oh, were you allowed out then?" Miranda frowned at her, but Rosalind looked away.

"And of course, we can picnic on the moor any day. It is beautiful later on when the heather blooms and the sun is out."

Miranda started to speak, then changed her mind. She drank some tea. "It sounds like great fun," she replied.

Rosalind nodded. "Alan will enjoy being in the country again, I daresay." As she spoke, it suddenly occurred to her that a man who had been fighting Napoleon for five years, and then raking about London for another, might not be the best companion for her naive little sister. But there was nothing to be done about that now. Surely any cousin of Philip's would be safe? Then the troubles Philip had mentioned came back to her—gambling, drinking, fighting duels—and Rosalind sighed. Her stomach protested again.

"Are you all right?" asked Miranda.

"Yes. Of course."

"You look…rather *green*."

"No. It is just… I think my breakfast may have disagreed with me. I will go upstairs for a few minutes, if you will excuse me, Miranda." Rosalind stood abruptly, swallowed, and hurried out of the room. Miranda stared after her, her deep green eyes full of concern and steely determination.

THREE

I CANNOT BEAR MY MAID. INDEED, ALL THE SERVANTS IN THIS place are extremely *odd*, to put it politely. I have already written about Forbes, the butler, who I am persuaded *never* smiles! Just today I discovered that he stuffs small birds and animals for display. He has in his pantry a stuffed fox, a badger, and a weasel made with his own hands! Jane Jenkins, the lady's maid I share with Rosalind, told me so herself! It is so horrible. I can scarcely bear it now when he offers me a dish at dinner or hands me my cloak. I find myself staring at his gigantic hands and thinking of the weasel, and I *shudder* convulsively.

Jane Jenkins does not approve of him either, but she does not approve of *anything*. She is very thin and dark, with narrow little eyes and a mole on her cheek. I daresay she must be forty years old. Since I have been here, she has given me *five* tracts about the torments of hell and the certainty of eternal damnation unless I *immediately* repent. She thinks I am a hardened sinner because I will not wear my hair braided and wrapped about my head, but will have a knot on top with wisps around my face. (It is *vastly* more becoming, which she will not admit, even though they are wisps instead of curls. I don't believe Rosalind understands how very lucky she is not to have straight hair. Jane feels it is God's punishment for something I have done, but I refuse to believe God would punish me in such a *petty* way.)

Jane is married to Henry Jenkins, Philip's valet, and he is just like her. I have never seen such a sour face in my life. Yesterday, when I asked him if he knew where I might find Philip's book about Hadrian's Wall, he told me he had no knowledge of such heathen things, and that I would do better to be reading my Bible than such trash, or the devil's books I brought with me. (Jane must have told him about those, which is extremely *interesting*, for, in the novel I am reading just now, the Spanish Inquisition has captured the hero and is about to submit him to terrible tortures. I daresay Jenkins would be quite at home in the Spanish Inquisition.)

There is no footman. Indeed, they don't require one to announce visitors or carry messages in this *desolate* place. Mrs. MacCrory, the cook; Alice, the kitchenmaid; and several housemaids and gardeners make up the rest of the household staff. Mrs. MacCrory is fat and pleasant, with gray hair and twinkly blue eyes. I believe I would like her very much if I could understand one thing she says. She is from Scotland—she came here with Philip's mother long ago, Alice says—and her real language is Gaelic. She might be speaking it, for all I can tell, though Alice claims to understand her perfectly well. Mrs. MacCrory also has the Sight. Whenever I go to the kitchen, Alice pulls me aside and informs me, in a *piercing* whisper, that Mrs. MacCrory has just predicted some dire event halfway across the world. It is impossible to tell, of course, whether there has been a terrible earthquake in the North Pole or a plague in the African jungles. And I am not at all certain that Alice is not making it up. Mrs. MacCrory looks so kind and jolly! She also makes the loveliest scones and muffins I have ever tasted.

Alice is really my only friend here, aside from Rosalind, naturally, and she talks of nothing but disasters and the ghosts that *throng* Clairvon Abbey. I have not yet seen any of these phantoms myself, but last night I scarcely slept listening to the noises and silence of the place. Oh, why did Mama and Papa not take me with them? Imagine being in *Rome* instead of dreary Northumberland! I would be a paragon of virtue and good manners and help Mama in all sorts of ways. But, of course, I cannot abandon Rosalind now that I have seen what it is like here. It is odiously selfish even to think such a thing, and I shan't again. (Though Rosalind could come with me. That is it! We could both escape to Rome, where it is *warm* and sunny and crammed with people.)

Philip's cousin arrives tomorrow. I have a notion, from a conversation I overheard, that he didn't really wish to come, and so, perhaps, he is not much like Philip after all. But there is something strange about him, for, whenever I ask Rosalind what he has been doing in London or what sort of amusements he prefers, she looks very conscious and tells me nothing. Perhaps he is a *libertine*. I heard Papa call Lord Byron that once. Perhaps he and Philip share the same *vile propensities*. If Mama had allowed me to read *The Corsair*, I might have some idea what these are and be able to help my sister now that she needs me.

My investigations have not got on very well so far. I stayed awake half one night last week and looked about the abbey after everyone else was in bed, but I lost my way trying to get to the east wing and spent most of the time wandering the corridors. They are so cold! I must make a systematic plan and a map. I have tried once or twice to hint to Rosalind that she may confide in me, but she passes it off with a laugh. I can tell she is *hiding something*, but, if I even start to suggest that Philip is not a paragon, she grows quite sharp. And yet she is pale and often ill. Perhaps she is *afraid* to tell me!

———————————

Alan Creighton arrived at midday today, in a post chaise, and we have all just spent our first evening together. He does not look much like Philip. He is not so tall or so muscular, though I think he is thin because of his wound. He was shot in his left shoulder at Waterloo and is only just now recovering the full use of his left arm. I expect that is why he looks tired, too. His hair is brown, not black like Philip's, and his eyes are a really brilliant blue. I do prefer blue eyes to dark.

He is not very jolly. He and Philip spent most of the evening talking about the Duke of Wellington and Parliament. I have always found that politics is far less interesting than many people seem to think. Rosalind kept to her sewing, but after a while I gave it up and went to open the pianoforte. I must say that Alan (I am to call him Alan, it was decided, since we are cousins by marriage) seemed to realize then that I was present and came over to examine the music with me. We sang some duets (he has a good voice), and then I left them to come up to my diary. It *will* be more amusing with Alan here.

But I must not let it distract me from my *main purpose*. I shall to go to bed very early tonight, for I am worn out with worrying over Alice's silly ghosts, and then tomorrow I shall have a good look around the abbey when the rest have gone to bed. *Particularly*, I shall go through Philip's study to see what secret documents he may keep there. I have been wondering whether he may be feeding Rosalind a *slow poison*, for she was never sick before she came here.

FOUR

MIRANDA OPENED HER BEDROOM DOOR A CRACK AND LOOKED out into the corridor. All was still. She slipped through and closed the door gently behind her. She had put on her heavy flannel nightdress and a warm wrapper and slippers, and she carried a large silver candlestick in one hand. Her green eyes were very large and dark in the dimness. She stood still, listening.

There were all sorts of noises—the intermittent creaks and groans of old timbers, the slither of tapestry and drapery in the incessant drafts, the occasional scratchings she was uneasily certain were mice, or worse. There was nothing she had not heard, and partly become accustomed to, during her visit so far. Slowly, she started along the hallway to the great staircase.

Her feet were cold. They always were in this house, for a constant cold wind seemed to run along the stone floors just at the level of one's ankles. It did not do to wear fur-lined traveling boots indoors, though she rather wished she had put them on tonight, when it did not matter. But Alan Creighton had seemed to appreciate her pale kid slippers and her white muslin gown sprigged with green and trimmed with bunches of dark-green ribbon. If only one did not have to drape oneself in heavy shawls in this house, she thought. But the alternative was goosebumps and shivering visibly, which was not particularly attractive.

At the head of the great stair that swept down into the vaulted hall, Miranda paused. The lower regions seemed vast and echoing, and she found she did not at all want to descend. Anything might lurk in the corners of that huge room. Her branch of candles would light only a small circle, and she would be exposed on all sides. The thought made her shudder.

But then she remembered Rosalind and all her resolutions to

help her, and she put one foot carefully on the first stair. As she moved downward, a current of air fluttered the candle flames, and made her heart beat even faster. What would she do, she wondered, if the candles went out? She was very much afraid that she would scream and bring the whole household down on her. Miranda raised her free hand to shield her precious light.

Reaching the flagstones of the hall, she crossed it quickly, looking neither right nor left, and scurried through the door that led to the west wing. Here lay Philip's study and estate offices, below the long portrait gallery on the second floor. Miranda held her breath as she turned the knob on the study door and eased it open. All was dark within. She slipped inside.

There was a lingering odor of tobacco and the smell of fine leather. Her candles illumined most of the room; she could see the crowded bookshelves along the walls, the long blue curtains covering the French doors, and the great desk with its piles of papers. She went at once to these, setting her candlestick on the desktop and bending to read.

She found bills, a letter from Philip's solicitor about water rights, one political journal, and a monograph on animal husbandry, but nothing sinister. Telling herself that of course he would not leave such things lying about, she turned to the desk drawers.

It was a difficult thing for Miranda to open the first drawer. That act seemed different, somehow, from simply looking over papers sitting on the desk—more like stealing. Her cheeks reddened a little in the darkness as she pulled on the top drawer. She would not engage in such low snooping, she told herself, if she were not so worried about her sister.

The top drawer held crested stationery and the middle drawer pen nibs and ink and blotting paper.

The bottom drawer was locked.

Miranda sat down in the desk chair and contemplated this problem. What she wanted must be there, of course. She should have realized that Philip would keep his secrets safe from prying eyes. But how was she to see them? She could not break the lock, even had she been able. That would cause an uproar. She would have to discover the keys and "borrow" them.

This idea made Miranda even unhappier. It did not seem much like the adventures of the heroines in the novels she read. In those, the villain was most often pursuing the heroine with some deadly purpose, which was very clear to see. She, on the other hand, was plagued with a nagging doubt that she might be mistaken, and by scruples that never seemed to arise in a novel. How pleasant it would be to forget her suspicions, go back to bed, and wake tomorrow refreshed and innocent.

Miranda sighed. Perhaps if she spoke to Rosalind and explained her fears, they could be dispelled once for all. But when she remembered her sister's pale features and strained expression, she again doubted.

It was at that moment that footsteps sounded in the corridor outside.

Miranda froze, her heart pounding like a bass drum, her throat dry. She reached for the candlestick with trembling hands and listened. They were slow heavy steps, coming from the direction of the hall. Visions of Alice's ghosts rose in her mind—awful headless forms in ancient dress, sobbing women in clinging white draperies, a child holding out bloody hands and wailing like a lost soul.

The footsteps stopped outside the study door. Miranda gasped, then blew out her candles and crouched beneath the desk, her arms wrapped around her knees, her face buried in her sleeve to stifle the sound of her breathing.

The door opened, and light returned. There was a pause, and then Miranda heard, with horror, a quiet *sniffing*. She gripped her knees even tighter and curled farther under the desk. The steps approached the front of the desk and hesitated. Miranda heard the scrape of her candlestick across the leather surface. The thing, whatever it was, was taking her only source of light!

This loss gave Miranda the courage to move. As the footsteps retreated to the far side of the room, she uncurled and lifted her eyes just above the desktop. She saw Forbes, trying the French doors to make certain they were locked. He held a lighted branch of candles in one hand, and he had set her candlestick on a small table nearby. Miranda fell in a silent heap beneath the desk, relief tinged with annoyance at her own silliness and at Forbes for prowling the house at this late hour. He would take her candles and leave her in the dark, and it was all too maddening.

The butler sniffed again, clearly puzzled about the scent of fresh wax in the room. He pushed the door latch as if wanting to be doubly certain it held, then opened the curtain slightly and peered out, his craggy face set in harsh lines that would have terrified Miranda had she dared to peek. At last, still unsatisfied, he turned to go, picking up her candlestick as he went. Miranda listened to his steps cross the rug and pause at the door. It opened and closed, leaving her in blackness.

She crawled out at once and groped her way across the carpet, bruising her shin painfully on a footstool she didn't remember seeing. She listened, then crept out into the corridor. Forbes was just at the entrance to the great hall. He shut that door behind him, bringing darkness down again.

Heedless now of discovery, Miranda ran along the corridor, hands outstretched in front to cushion any impact. She hit the closed door with a thump and waited for a terrified moment to be confronted. But there was no light, no sound. The darkness seemed to press in on her from all sides, mocking and ominous.

She plunged through the door and into the great hall, where whispers of air nearly drew a scream. Then she realized that she could see a little. Her eyes were adjusting, and there was a faint dusting of moonlight through the high windows. She could make out the carved oak balusters of the stair and the long trestle table in the middle of the room. She ran, and stumbled up the stairs as fast as she could.

Once upstairs, she felt better, though there was less light. She could more easily explain her presence in this upper corridor, should anyone find her, and she was near the refuge of her own room, which, at this moment, she never wanted to leave again. Taking a deep breath, she crept on, sliding one foot forward, then the other, so as to make the least noise. She kept her right hand on the wall, for she could tell her own room, she knew, by a niche with a bust of Cicero that came just before.

She felt the first doorway, and noted it. Two more, and she would be safe. Then she heard the groaning, coming from beyond the wooden panels.

It was too much. She couldn't move. The moans rose and fell like the protests of a creature in agony. They were not loud enough to be heard except so close, but they held more fear and pain than Miranda had ever imagined. This had to be one of Alice's phantoms, the one who left its victims raving mad and gibbering when dawn came. Miranda's feet would not move. She dug her nails into the oak of the door frame and stared like a bird before a snake.

The moaning paused. There was a brief silence, and then the door was flung open and light dazzled her eyes. Miranda cringed and threw up her arm with a gurgling scream. The figure in the doorway lurched in surprise and gasped.

Miranda and Alan Creighton gazed at one another with wide eyes and open mouths, each stunned to find the other there.

After a long moment, Alan raised the single candle he held higher and contemplated her. "What the dev...deuce are you doing here?"

"I...I..." Miranda couldn't seem to make her mouth work. Alan continued to look at her, and she became very aware of her nightclothes, her blond hair falling in disarray over her shoulders, her bare ankles. Her face grew warm, and her hands even colder. "I heard you groaning," she claimed. "And I came to see what was the matter."

For an instant, he looked taken aback, then his penetrating blue eyes narrowed. "Without a light?" he asked.

Miranda looked at the carpet.

"And I expressly asked for a room well away from any others. You cannot have heard anything from your bedchamber."

"I was...I woke up, and I..."

"Yes?"

"And I came out into the corridor. It is no business of yours!"

He considered her averted eyes and guilty stance. "No, I don't suppose it is." Alan had been dreaming of the field hospital at Salamanca, where he had taken his first serious wound of the war. He had felt again the bone-jarring jolting of the cart, the burning agony in his leg. He had seen the tangle of amputated limbs outside the surgeons' workroom and felt the bitter terror of being carried there himself. It was all he could do to keep his hands from shaking, and just now he welcomed any company, even this silly girl he scarcely knew. "I am going to the kitchen, to see what may be found in the larder. Come along."

"No, thank you. I will just..."

"Unless you want me to rouse Philip and Rosalind, you will come." He couldn't bear the idea of walking about this strange house alone just now.

The threat, and the easy command in Creighton's voice, drew Miranda after him along the corridor she had just traversed, down the wide stair, and into the east wing, where the kitchen lay. He ignored her and went directly to the closed larder. "Ah, not locked. That's lucky. And we have half a game pie, bread and cheese, and most of a ham. Riches."

"I'm not hungry," said Miranda, in the coldest voice she could muster. As soon as she said it, she realized it was a lie.

"Well, *I* am," he replied. Food often helped dispel the nightmares, he had found. The only thing better was drink, which drowned them out. He came to the kitchen table laden with booty. "Do you happen to know where I might find a plate and cutlery?"

Miranda's visits here had shown her this much. "In that cupboard." She pointed.

"Splendid. Get them, will you? I'll be right back." He turned away as Miranda stiffened with outrage, then paused. "Ah, a lamp." Taking it up from the table, he lit it with the candle flame. "There. You have light. I won't be a moment."

When he was gone, Miranda stood seething in the middle of the stone floor. She would not be ordered about as if she were one of his lieutenants. He could get his own plate. She was only sorry she had told him where they were! If she did not believe he really would wake Rosalind, she would go back to her own room immediately and bolt the door.

This made her think. If she was safe in her room, innocently in bed, surely he would not rouse the house. What could he tell them? She rushed toward the kitchen door, only to have it swing open in her face revealing Alan Creighton carrying a decanter of brandy.

"Here we are. One useful thing I learned in the Peninsula—foraging."

Miranda tried to slip past him, but he stepped in front of her. "No. We are going to talk a little."

"You can't keep me here!"

"Probably not. But I can chase you up the stairs shouting, 'Stop, thief,' at the top of my lungs. The army is fine training for the voice."

"You are the most odious man I have ever met."

"And you have such a wide experience of men."

"Well, no, but…"

Alan nodded and went to fetch a plate. "You're sure you won't join me?"

"No! I mean, yes!"

He nevertheless brought two plates to the table, then added knives and forks. When he tried to slice the ham, he held his left arm stiffly along his side. "Sit down," he suggested.

"No, thank you."

He put down the knife. "Look, Miss…Miranda. This is your sister's house, and you have a right to do as you please in it. Perhaps I was in the army too long and grew over suspicious. If you want to wander about in the dark, it's all the same to me. I…suppose I was just looking for company after waking so…suddenly. Go upstairs. Take the candle. I'll find another."

Miranda picked it up and turned to go. But now that she was free to do so, perversely, she wanted to stay. "Are you in great pain from your wound?" she asked.

Alan looked up from slicing the game pie, a bit surprised at the question. "No, not particularly. It is mostly stiffness unless I try it too hard."

"I thought…you were moaning so."

"Ah." He looked down at his plate. "I was dreaming," he said crisply.

"A nightmare." Somehow, Miranda found herself sitting opposite him at the kitchen table and cutting herself some bread and cheese. "Was it dreadful? Did it have ghosts and monsters? Alice the kitchenmaid says this house is full of ghosts."

"Does she?" There was a smile in his voice, though it did not reach his features. "I wager they're quiet, well-mannered ghosts in Philip's house. He's a high stickler."

"Is he indeed?"

"Don't you care for Philip?" He poured a glass of brandy and took a sip, savoring it on his tongue. He did not offer this part of the feast to Miranda.

"I…I scarcely know him," replied Miranda.

Alan Creighton nodded. "I've only met him a few times myself, when I was home on leave. I must say he's always been civil. Though just lately..." He broke off, and a sad, strained expression passed across his face.

Miranda leaned forward. "What?" she asked.

"Nothing. Will you have some ham?"

Absentmindedly, she held out her plate. "I...I have a *reason* for asking," she said. "I am not just being odiously inquisitive."

Alan raised one dark eyebrow and waited.

"You see." Miranda hesitated, then threw caution to the winds. "I have been worried about Rosalind. She used to be so gay and lively, and now she is often ill and tired and so unlike herself. I have been wondering..."

"If it is Philip's fault?" he finished.

His skeptical tone made Miranda bridle. "He brought her to this *forsaken* place and practically imprisoned her. They never go out. And he is so brusque and rude. He rides out alone every day, for hours and hours, and he looks like Lord Byron!"

Alan Creighton's lips quivered. "Does he indeed? I have never seen Lord Byron."

"Well, neither have I, but my father says so. And you know all the wicked things *he* has been up to."

"Your father?" She glared at him, and he added, "No, Lord Byron, of course. I did hear something. What sort of wicked things are they?"

Miranda tried to look knowing and sophisticated. "He treated his wife very badly."

"Did he? Beat her, perhaps?"

"I...I don't think so." Miranda was shocked at the idea.

"And you think Philip is up to something similar?"

"Well, not...*that*, but... He is not at all the fashionable person we thought him!"

Alan watched her frown and bite her full lower lip, more amused than he had been in some time. The boredom and emptiness that he had felt since being shipped home from Belgium lightened a touch. "He does seem to have some black moods," he offered.

Miranda leaned forward. "Yes? I am not the least surprised."

"Of course, your sister looks very well to me."

"But you did not meet her when she was in London. She was so happy, so full of jokes and stories. Now she is hardly able to stay awake through an evening. I find that *very* suspicious. And I am sure she would like to go out more. She has told me so, in a way. So you must see that I have to find out what is wrong."

"That's what you were doing tonight," concluded Creighton.

Miranda sat up straight. "What if I was?"

He took in her stiff spine and raised chin, her defiant expression. He ought, he knew, to discourage her. Philip and his wife seemed no more unhappy than a dozen married couples he could name, and happier than many. If her sister felt confined at Clairvon Abbey and bored, that was scarcely persecution. And his knowledge of his cousin, though mostly secondhand, did not suggest anything sinister.

But it was a wonderful joke, and his life had been short of levity for too long. Alan Creighton succumbed to temptation. "Might not be a bad notion," he answered. "You can never tell about these things. Philip does seem a trifle grim."

Miranda nodded, clasping her hands on the table. She was at once glad not to be mocked and a bit daunted by his agreement. She hadn't *really* believed her own theories.

"I might be able to help," he added. "I have a good deal of experience in reconnaissance."

"Oh. Oh, yes."

Seeing her reluctance, Creighton felt a pang. He pushed his plate away. "I'd better put all this back in the larder. It is late."

Miranda jumped up. "I'll wash the plates."

"No need. I'm quite used to that sort of thing. You should be going upstairs."

She nodded. She felt that herself, very strongly. She was suddenly scandalized by her situation—alone, in her nightclothes, with a near stranger in the middle of the night. "Will you wipe the plates and put them away? And...and clean off the table?"

He smiled at her, and Miranda's heart speeded up. "A careful housekeeper, are you?"

"No, it is just...I'd rather no one knew that I...was here with you. It is not...proper." She gripped her hands together, feeling young and awkward.

Alan Creighton looked much struck. "I don't suppose it is. You must pardon me. I've forgotten all the proprieties I ever knew in the war."

"It doesn't matter."

"On the contrary. Take the candle. I will make sure all is tidy here."

Miranda nodded and snatched up the candlestick. She nearly ran to her own bedchamber, candle flames streaming out behind. Once there, she bolted the door and leaned on it, breathing rapidly. This was a real adventure, and, since she wasn't in the least sleepy now, she went to the bureau and got out her diary.

FIVE

IT WAS A DREADFUL SHOCK WHEN I WENT DOWN TO breakfast this morning and found Rosalind rallying Alan Creighton about his midnight raid on the larder. It seems Cook had accused Jane Jenkins of stealing (how I wish I could have seen *that*! I knew they didn't get on), and Alan confessed. Rosalind thought it a great joke, but I could not join in; I was in such a quake I might be found out, too. Rosalind is the dearest sister, but she has always been the least bit *stuffy*. She would be shocked to hear that I was a member of the party, and, at one moment, when Alan was laughing and he looked at me, I thought he might tell.

Of course, he did not. Breakfast passed off well enough with all the bantering—even Philip laughed—and then I was left with Rosalind to sit in the morning room. Very flat. I suggested a ride, but she put me off. And, when I declared she looked ill *again*, she could not deny it. If she had not looked so wretched, I would have questioned her right then. I did say it seemed odd she should be so ill in Northumberland when she never was so before. I believe she began to tell me about Alan to keep me from going on.

He is Philip's only close relative, as Philip is his, which seems *unusual*. How did all the others come to die? Well, I know, of course, that Philip's father was an invalid for years, and his mother was carried off by a fever when he was only six. But now I find that his aunt and uncle (the Creightons) were lost at sea three years ago, and there is no one else. Philip grew up alone with the servants, Rosalind said, because his father seldom ventured downstairs before his death. This made my blood run cold! Imagine having Forbes and Jenkins as your childhood companions? I could almost pity him if it weren't for Rosalind. But then when I think how *strange* he must be, and also my sister's husband, I am filled with dismay.

In the novel I am reading now, *The Black Abbot*, the heroine has no family left. But that is because the abbot has been killing them one by one to get them out of the way so that he may have her in his power. There is only her old nanny left at present, and I am fairly certain she is being poisoned. Perhaps Forbes poisoned Philip's parents? It is all very well to say it was a fever, but what if it was brought on by some unknown Oriental drug? And mayn't he have kept the old baron a virtual *prisoner* in his room? What if he wasn't an invalid at all? But I have to admit I cannot see how Forbes could have arranged for Alan Creighton's parents to be shipwrecked.

There is no denying that Forbes gives one shivers, and he has had charge of Philip all the times he was not at school. This must explain a great deal.

At any rate, Philip and Alan have never been close because Philip is six years older, and then Alan joined the army when he was nineteen and went to fight the French. They really only began to be acquainted when the Creightons were drowned, but then Alan had to go back to Spain. And he has been a year in London without visiting. I think perhaps he doesn't like Philip either.

It is rather pleasant to have him for an ally. He must know all sorts of things I do not and will be able to help me should anything dreadful happen. He is not much like Papa or James in appearance or behavior. In fact, I have just realized that this is my first opportunity to become well acquainted with any man outside my family (a cousin of my sister's husband hardly counts as family), which it is *vital* for me to do, if I am to be an author. I must know all sorts of things that most girls don't. Mama is quite wrong to say that it will come with time, for how can it if I am never allowed to go about or speak to people who have not been introduced?

I shall study Alan's character to learn what I may about soldiers, and I shall ask him about his experiences in the war. I'm sure he will be glad to have an audience.

———

Tomorrow we are to have an outing! Rosalind announced it at dinner, while Philip positively *scowled* at her. We are to drive down the coast a little and see the ruins of Dunstanburgh Castle, with a luncheon packed for us and a fire to make tea. This is something like!

———

I must record the *loathsome* thing that happened to me when I returned to my room to go to bed tonight. We had music again, and I was quite cheerful when I came up with my candle and began to undress. I had put on my night clothes and was brushing my hair (Jane Jenkins does not come to me at night, thankfully), when I noticed something odd about my bed. The coverlet was turned down, as usual, but there was a black hat or shawl on the pillow (this is what I *thought*). I went to look, and I discovered a great dead crow, its neck broken and its wings all twisted and spread, lying there. I have never been so shocked in my life. I am certain I had what one of my old governesses used to call a spasm, for my heart seemed to turn over in my chest, and my throat closed up until I thought I would choke. I wanted to scream, but I couldn't. (Of course, I was very glad later that I had not disgraced myself.) Finally, I made my legs move and ran out into the corridor.

Philip was standing just outside the door, talking to Forbes! They were huddled together, plotting. I could see that perfectly plainly. Philip was frowning, and Forbes was *distinctly* uneasy. They *jumped* when I threw open the door, and Philip said, "What the devil?" It was so interesting I nearly forgot the crow.

They *pretended* to be making the evening rounds of the house, but why should Philip do that? I thought then, and I believe now, that he was *lurking*, waiting for me to find his horrid crow and shriek. He must have told Forbes to put it there. Yesterday he scolded me soundly for looking into an old shed on the moor, claiming he was worried for my safety. But why should he be?

When I showed him the crow, he went *white* with guilt. Forbes took it by the feet and tried to hurry away. But I would not let them go without asking who might have put such a thing on my pillow. They could not answer that! "Well," I said, "if this is someone's idea of a joke, I find it disgusting. If it is intended to frighten me, it didn't!" I stared directly at Philip, and I could see he was shaken. He looked as if he would have liked to speak, but had not the courage. I was immediately glad I had put a bold face on things, even though I was quaking inside! For I shall not stop my investigations because of cowardly tricks. However, I mean to keep my bedroom door locked from now on (and I have thrown away that pillow). I wonder what Alan will make of this?

———————————

Well, Jane Jenkins thinks the crow was a Sign. I suppose everyone in the household knows of it by this morning. Alice will probably tell me a ghost left it. Jane said crows are creatures of the devil, and that I have been warned to change my ways and reform. And that, if I do not, I am doomed to endless torment and misery. It is *very* lowering to hear such things while one's hair is being arranged. First thing in the morning, too. She left me another tract.

SIX

"ARE THE HAMPERS IN THE CARRIAGE, FORBES?" ASKED Rosalind at ten that morning.

"Yes, my lady."

"And is my sister ready?"

"She came downstairs a few minutes ago, my lady, but I don't know where she may have gotten to. Perhaps she is in the attics again."

"The attics? Whyever should she be?"

"She has been seen there once or twice, my lady. Roaming about the moors, too." Forbes kept his face carefully impassive, but his tone let Rosalind know he disapproved.

"Oh, well, she is used to more company, you know, and a livelier household. I daresay she misses our brother James and is a trifle bored."

"Indeed, my lady. I only mention it because we have been worried she might be hurt, exploring odd corners."

"Hurt? How would she be hurt?"

"A fall, perhaps, my lady? In the cellars. She might not be found for some hours."

Rosalind shrugged. "I'm sure Miranda has no desire to go through the cellars. Will you see if she can be found, Forbes, and tell her the carriage is ready?"

"Certainly, my lady." But Forbes looked as if he was far from satisfied about Miranda's desires, and not at all happy about them. As he turned to go, Rosalind watched him with a puzzled frown. It was not like Forbes to complain.

At that moment, Miranda came running down the stairs. "Are you ready? I just went up for my other shawl. Can you believe the sun is shining at last? I am so glad we are going out."

Rosalind smiled. "I told you we would have some fine days. Come along, the carriage is waiting."

They walked out into the soft June morning. The sun was indeed bright. It lit the rolling moors beyond the walls in folds of brown and green, and made even the gray stone of Clairvon Abbey sparkle with tiny chips of light. There were daffodils by the doorstep, tossed in an errant breeze, and bluebells at the end of the lawn. "Isn't it a glorious day?" said Miranda.

"It is indeed. Here are Philip and Alan. Let us be on our way."

The two men reined in their mounts beside the carriage, and Rosalind and Miranda were handed in. "You're *certain* you don't wish to ride, too?" asked Miranda as they started down the gravel lane leading to the gate.

"Certain," replied her sister. "But I have said you may ride."

"I wouldn't leave you all alone." Miranda gazed out the window. "Have you been to this castle before?"

"No. But I have heard it described as a very interesting ruin. It should be just what you like."

"I *am* rather fond of ruins. When I write a book, I shall set the great final scene in a ruin, in the moonlight. And I believe the villain shall be killed by falling from the remains of a tower, as he is trying to carry off the heroine, who has fainted."

"But won't she fall, too, in that case?" asked Rosalind with a smile.

Miranda bit her lower lip. "Well, yes, I suppose, but only a short way. Her…her gown will catch on a jagged bit of rock, and she will *hang* there during the fight between the hero and the villain. She will wake in the midst of it and see where she is and be *terrified*."

Rosalind laughed out loud. "Why do you wish to write such hair-raising stories, Miranda? Nothing of the sort ever happened to you."

"I know. That is just the *point*."

Rosalind shook her head. "I don't know how you think of these things."

"It is mostly from reading," her sister admitted. "But I expect I shall soon be learning from my own adventures."

"What do you mean, soon?"

"Well, I am nearly grown up. Mama cannot keep me at home forever. *Or* leave me with you. In a year or so I shall begin to know all sorts of things. And then I can really begin to write."

Rosalind gazed at her with warm fondness and a kind of pensive regret that Miranda was too engrossed to notice.

"Look there," cried Miranda. "What is that? Philip? Alan? Is that a warship out to sea? Or maybe a trader going to the Indies?"

"It is a rock," replied Philip in a discouraging tone.

There was a pause. "It looks rather like a ship, though," added Alan Creighton. "Really a very suggestive shape."

"It is called Ship Rock," agreed Philip grudgingly. "They say a customs cutter—" He broke off.

"What?" said Rosalind, leaning forward to see.

"Nothing!" Philip glowered at her and spurred his horse to a canter. Miranda glanced quickly from one to the other, and then to Alan. He raised one eyebrow and shrugged.

"This coast looks treacherous," Alan said. "Boney can be glad he never tried an invasion. Those rocks would have given him some trouble."

"They look like teeth," agreed Rosalind.

"We are nearly there," called Philip from up ahead, and he kicked his horse again and began to leave them behind. Alan went after him, and Miranda leaned far out the window to catch her first glimpse of the ruined fortress.

When Dunstanburgh finally came into view, she gasped with pleasure. Tumbled stone and mangled battlements littered the cliffside above the now calm sea. Great rocks lay scattered as if by a giant's hand, and one could see the remains of walls and bastions, banquet hall and dungeons. "Oh, it's splendid!" she cried, throwing Rosalind a glowing look.

Her sister nodded, and Miranda was too excited to notice the discomfort in her face.

As soon as they stopped, Miranda jumped down and ran a little forward. "I want to see *everything*," she declared, spreading her arms wide.

"Come along then," answered Alan Creighton with a smile. "I can keep you from mistaking an arrow slit for a romantic peephole for hidden priests." He offered his arm, and Miranda took it with a flourish.

Still sitting in the carriage, Rosalind sighed. "I suppose I should not let them go off unchaperoned. Mama would expect me to do better. But we can see them wherever they go, after all, and Alan seems trustworthy. I must believe his behavior in London was an aberration. I am glad to have him here to amuse Miranda."

"You will stay right where you are," said Philip savagely. "And I will start a fire and make tea. You look sick as a cat."

"Thank you, sir. I always know where to come for compliments."

"Rosalind!"

"All right, perhaps I don't look well. But it is not something I wish to hear about. And I shall *not* stay in the carriage. I will sit on a rug on the grass and enjoy the sun. We can spread the cloth by that rock there." She started to step down, and Philip hurried to help her, keeping one arm around her waist as they walked to the rock. Rosalind raised her parasol and settled beside it. "I am quite comfortable," she said then. "And quite all right. But I would like tea."

Philip nodded curtly, and Rosalind gazed after him as he strode off to start gather wood.

"Can't you just *see* the knights and ladies and jesters who must have lived here?" Miranda said to Alan as they picked their way between fallen rocks. "I can picture a great tournament right here, with pennants and lances and the huge warhorses snorting through their armor plate."

"Ah, well, I think this would have been the kitchen garden," he replied. "That looks like the midden there."

"It doesn't matter." Miranda turned away. "Where do you think the hall might have been, where they sat at night and listened to the minstrels and poets and drank the health of Richard the Lionheart?"

"Let's see." He scanned the ruin. "Perhaps there?" he said, pointing.

Miranda started in that direction. "Don't you just *long* for those days? How I should have liked to be in the seats watching the tournament and giving my favor to my chosen knight."

"I don't know how many tournaments they would have held here," said Alan. "This must have been built for coastal defense. The French again, I suppose. It always is the French. Must have been a cold, lonely post in winter." His blue eyes flickered with memory.

"Well, but, still, they...they probably had a minstrel. Wandering. Minstrels wandered."

Alan smiled. "That must have been a miserable thing in winter, too. Slogging along in freezing rain half the time. And then having to *sing* when you arrived. That would have been more than I could stomach."

"They loved it!" retorted Miranda. "They chose to live in such a way, so that they could be free and write songs and poetry."

"No doubt it was better than working the fields," he agreed.

"Have you no spark of romance in your soul?" she cried. "Must you see everything in terms of...mud and work?"

He met her snapping green eyes for a moment. "I beg your pardon. I suppose there has been too much of both those things in my life so far."

Immediately, Miranda felt ashamed. "No, I'm sorry," she said at once. "You know a thousand times more than I do about knights and fighting, I'm sure. They probably were cold, especially here. I just enjoy the stories."

"And why not?" He felt a bit abashed himself. His wartime

hardships were of no interest to a gently bred girl. "I believe the dungeons must be over there. Shall we go and look?"

"Oh, yes. Do you think the prisoners may have carved on the walls? There was the most affecting verse in Walter Scott. How did it go? I can't remember."

Forbearing to tell her that most of the castle's prisoners probably could not write, Creighton took her arm once again and led her forward.

They spent the entire morning examining the ruins and then returned to the carriage to find their picnic spread on a white cloth on the grass. Rosalind looked lovely beneath her pink parasol, and Philip lay on the grass beside her, reading.

"I forgot my sunshade," said Miranda guiltily. "I shall be horridly brown."

"Not so horridly," said Rosalind. "I have some lotion you may use. Are you hungry?"

"Yes!"

"We all are," said Philip, closing his book. "Come and eat."

Cook had sent them cold ham and beef between thick slices of her fresh-baked oat bread, with pickles and mustard and hard-cooked eggs. There was cheese and fruit and biscuits, as well as a dozen cherry tarts wrapped in a checked napkin. And lemonade and ale and the tea that had been brewing over the small fire the coachman had made. All of them, even Rosalind, fell to with enthusiasm.

For some minutes, there was silence. Then Alan said, "You have a fine cook, Rosalind."

Miranda nodded, her mouth full of cherry tart.

"Don't I?" Rosalind smiled. "Even though I can scarcely hold a conversation with her. I tell her what I would like for dinner, and she nods and smiles. If she has something to say to me, the kitchenmaid has to translate."

"The cook is a foreigner?"

"Well, she's a Scot," answered Rosalind, with a teasing look at her husband.

"She is perfectly easy to understand," replied Philip. "She speaks English as well as…" He broke off.

"As well as what?" teased Rosalind. "You grew up with her. I don't think she is even speaking English, or Gaelic, either. It is some language she has made up from the two, and you must be acquainted with her for a dozen years before you can grasp it."

A reluctant smile crossed Philip's handsome face. "There's something in that, I suppose. She likes you, though."

"And I her. Particularly when she makes cherry tarts." Rosalind took a second one. "She knows they're my favorite."

"They're delicious," pronounced Miranda, taking her third. "This is the best picnic I have ever had."

"Out of such a great many?" asked Alan Creighton.

"I have gone on picnics before!" Miranda saw no need to mention that they had all been with her sisters and brother.

They sat for a while with cups of tea, while the sun started down the sky in the west. They were beginning to think of packing up the hamper when Rosalind said, "Philip, would you walk a little with me?" Her voice sounded tight and uneasy.

"Where do you wish to walk? You're comfortable where you are," was his reply.

"Please!"

Seeing her face, he sprang up and went to help her rise. She clung to his arm as they walked along the edge of the ruins toward the hill behind. "What is it?" he said.

"I am going to be sick. Get me away from them."

Setting his jaw, Philip supported her until they were hidden from the others by a screen of foliage, and then held her as she rid herself of lunch, his face a grim mask. When she was better, he wiped her brow with his handkerchief and gently lowered her onto a fallen stone. "Don't move until you feel better," he commanded.

Rosalind managed a weak smile. "Am I to sit here until winter then?"

"Your mother promised you would be better before that!"

"Yes, Philip, of course. I was joking."

"How can you when you are so ill? I cannot bear it, Rosalind. I feel…it is all my fault, and I…"

"Don't be silly. Here, help me up. We must go back before Miranda—"

"Stay where you are!" Philip's voice sounded savage. Neither he nor Rosalind noticed Miranda approach behind the bushes. "You were a fool to come out today. I told you that. You must stay at home and rest. Miranda will have to understand that you cannot be jolted about the countryside and parked in the sun whenever she wishes for some amusement. We did not want her here—the timing is abominable—and she will simply have to adjust to our way of living."

"Philip, you are exaggerating all out of…"

"Be silent! You *will* listen to me. You *will* do as I say. You are not to go out. I will lock you in your bedchamber, if necessary!"

Appalled, Miranda fled.

"Will you indeed, my lord Highdene?" responded Rosalind. "And feed me on crusts and water, I expect? And forbid me any pleasures?"

"You know what I meant," he muttered.

"I know you are talking like an idiot, my dear. Women have babies every day and are none the worse."

"Not my wife," he replied.

They looked at each other in silence for a moment, neither daring to say, or perhaps even think, that some women *were* the worse, that some even died in childbed. Rosalind, whose fears were springing to life with her constant sickness, pushed the thought resolutely from her mind. "Help me up," she said again. "We must be getting home."

The drive back to Clairvon began in silence. Miranda was in turmoil after what she had overheard, and Rosalind was both ill and worried. But at last Miranda could contain herself no longer, and she burst out, "Are you sorry I came to stay with you, Rosalind?"

"What do you mean? Of course not."

"Mama and Papa *insisted*, you know. I was longing to see Rome."

"I do know. But I thought we agreed that we were both glad of the chance to become better acquainted."

"Yes." Miranda could not admit that she had eavesdropped. But she couldn't forget what she had heard either. "Rosalind..." she began.

"Yes?" said her sister when she did not continue.

"Are...are you happy here? In Northumberland, I mean? D-don't you wish you had never come?"

"Not at all. What makes you say such a thing?"

"You are ill all the time!" cried Miranda, goaded. "You never have visitors or any parties. You love parties! And Philip...Philip is beastly to you." She shrank back against the carriage cushions, frightened by her own temerity.

"Beastly? Nonsense."

Miranda lost her head. All her concern for Rosalind, as well as her own imaginings and frustrations, burst out. "He is dreadful," she insisted. "He is not at all what we thought him. Mama and Papa would be furious if they saw the way you live, practically a prisoner. And so ill. Why don't we go away? I will go with you to London, or Rome, anywhere you like. You have to escape from this horrible place before he does something really wicked, Rosalind!"

Rosalind's pretty face had gone stern and cold. She had every intention, at the start of this conversation, of explaining to Miranda the cause of her "illness." But the remarks her sister had made about her husband went too far, especially in light of her own doubts. She could not afford to think such things, and she would not be lectured about marriage by a chit not yet out.

"You know nothing about it," she said. "How dare you come to stay in my house and then say such things! Philip is exactly what I thought him, and we are very happy together. I forbid you to mention this matter again."

"But Rosalind…"

"Miranda!"

They drove on in silence, both miserable. Miranda felt dreadfully guilty for having displeased her sister, but she could not feel she was wrong. Had she not heard it herself?

It was only then that she remembered she had meant to tell Alan Creighton about the ominous incident of the crow.

SEVEN

I DON'T BELIEVE I HAVE EVER FELT SO LOW IN MY LIFE. Rosalind is really angry with me. When we reached home again after our picnic, she went directly to her room to lie down, and she has not come out. I knocked once, but there was no reply, and the door is locked. *Perhaps* she was asleep, but I don't believe it.

I have never quarreled with Rosalind before in my life. Indeed, she was always the kindest older sister. Portia can be quite sharp, and, of course, James and I were always arguing about something. But Rosalind has the sweetest temper. It must be all my fault that we are at outs.

Yet I *heard* what Philip said to her. She cannot deny that. Except that I cannot tell her, or she will think I am an odious snoop as well as quarrelsome. What shall I do?

I went to look for Alan, but he is nowhere about. Philip has taken him off to look at some horse somewhere. It feels as if I am the only person in this great drafty pile of a castle. I never imagined that living in a castle could be so dreary. In the books I have read they do not mention the drafts and *chilling* damp that comes off stone walls. And for all their talk of flowing gowns and lace, I should like to know what the heroines wore *under* them, for they never seem to have icy hands and ankles as I do most of the time. Even my flannel petticoat does no good.

What sort of shoes did they wear? Perhaps, actually, they had high boots, rather like Hessians, but lined with fur, which kept them warm as toast right to the knee? That would be the thing for Clairvon! And I quite see now why they wrapped veils all about their necks. I thought it unattractive, but it must be cozy in winter.

I shall set my book in a hot climate. Possibly Egypt, or the Indies. I think Egypt. The heroine will be taken there by her parents, who would not dream of leaving her behind, and then she will be overtaken by an ancient curse. I shall have to find a book on Egypt to discover what sort of curse it might be. No doubt Philip has one. He has books on every sort of history.

You might think we could talk about that, since I like history so myself. But he brushed me aside when I tried to say something about Hadrian's Wall. I suppose he thinks I am silly and stupid, but I listened to Papa's classical stories, as Rosalind never did! Or even James. Papa says I have a sharp mind and a fine memory. I might even have learned Greek had not Papa been sick to death of it. He never even taught James. He left it all to schoolmasters. Philip doesn't like me. He has never even tried to. The truth is...

———————

I have been for a walk. It was too melancholy sitting in my room alone worrying about Rosalind, and it does not get dark until very late here in the summer.

I suppose I should not have gone outside the park. Clairvon is surrounded on three sides by a tall stone wall, and within it are the gardens and stables and such. But I have walked everywhere there. I have seen the roses and the pine grove and the sea cliffs. And so I went out the front gate and around the wall to explore what might be along the cliffs that way.

The landscape *exactly* suited my mood. Clouds were coming in from the sea, obscuring the brief sunshine we had this morning and making the prospect all browns and grays. The cliffs twisted on and on ahead, throwing great shadows over the water, and the seabirds made the most mournful cries.

I found a path that runs along the shore and walked for a while. I was thinking about Rosalind, and not really heeding where I went, so that I was startled to come upon a building set in a cleft or ravine where a stream flows into the sea. I thought, at first, it was someone's cottage, but then I saw that it was in very poor repair— one corner falling in and holes from missing roof slates. Philip has complained about abandoned outbuildings on the estate, and the work that is necessary to repair them all. I believe his father did not manage well, because he was so ill.

But the *odd* thing is this. When I made my way down to the place, just to look in, I found a great fierce mastiff chained in the doorway. His head was as high as my waist, I swear, and he growled and barked and threw himself against the chain in a really frightening way. I was very glad his tether was thick and sturdy, for his teeth and the look in his eye made me back away as fast as I could (James has told me never to turn my back on a hostile animal, for then they see that you are afraid).

Thinking of James made me wonder if this dog was being kept for fighting. James has seen a cock fight, in London, even though they are forbidden, and he says there are sometimes dog fights as well. Men have such peculiar tastes. The very idea of watching two animals tear at each other makes me shudder, and yet James says it was very exciting, with everyone shouting and wagering on their favorite bird. I daresay Forbes would like cock fighting. Perhaps it is his dog?

I could not see inside the building; the mastiff would not let me close enough. So I could tell no more about it. I didn't like to walk past either, in case he should somehow get loose, so I returned home and found everything just as I left it. Forbes glowered at me when I came in, and actually asked me where I had been! I told him nothing, of course. I had only time to write this before dinner. I do hope Rosalind has gotten over being angry with me by now. I shall apologize.

EIGHT

THE EVENING MEAL AT CLAIRVON ABBEY WAS EXTREMELY awkward that night. As Miranda entered the hall, Forbes was just announcing that the lady of the house was unwell and would not be down. This made Philip look thunderous, and Miranda quail before him. Only Alan Creighton maintained his composure, glancing from one to the other with bemused concern.

The roast lamb was delicious, and the chantilly cream exquisite, but there was very little conversation to accompany them. Alan made some remarks about the horse they had seen, to which Philip replied in grunts, and about the ruins they had toured, to which Miranda nodded or shook her head nervously. All three were greatly relieved when the last dishes were cleared away and Miranda could withdraw.

She fled immediately to her sister's chamber, but when she knocked, the door was opened by Jane Jenkins. "Her ladyship is resting," she was informed in a harsh whisper.

"I must speak to her, only for a moment," insisted Miranda.

"I'm sorry, miss. I can't allow it. She's only just dropped off, and in her condition I can't allow her to be disturbed." The woman's thin dark face was set in uncompromising lines.

"C-condition?"

"Yes, miss, it is a serious thing, whatever anyone may say." Jenkins looked utterly grim.

Miranda turned pale and pulled her India shawl tighter around her shoulders. "But what is wrong?"

"I don't say *wrong*, miss. But it is certainly foolish to gad about the countryside. The Lord helps those who help themselves. And He expects us to do what is right and sensible. If we don't, well..." She shrugged, as if this sort of attitude was hopeless, and shut the door.

Bewildered and frightened, Miranda debated whether to knock again and *demand* to see Rosalind. But she was rather afraid of Jane Jenkins, and she certainly had no wish to harm her sister. She turned away and walked slowly down the corridor toward the stairs.

Miranda felt completely alone. Without Rosalind, this place was desolate for her, and she feared she might have lost her sister's regard just when she was beginning to know her. Tears welled in her eyes and blurred her vision. Her throat grew tight and hot. She turned the corner and walked into Alan Creighton's arms just as her tears began in earnest.

That gentleman, finding himself suddenly embracing a weeping girl, acted with remarkable presence of mind. Keeping an arm firmly about her shoulders, he led her into the small drawing room and over to the sofa in front of the fire. He settled her there, then went to the corner cabinet and poured a thimbleful of brandy into a glass. "Here," he said when he returned. "Drink this."

Automatically, Miranda took it and drank. The brandy burned her throat and made her choke, but the coughing stopped her tears.

"That's better," said Alan encouragingly.

"No, it…isn't!" managed Miranda, still choking. "It's awful."

"Can't be. You've stopped crying," he pointed out.

"Only because…oh, never mind!" She turned away from him and contemplated the end of the room. "Where is Philip?" she asked after a while.

"He's gone to his study. Said he had work to do. My opinion is he just wanted to get away from us."

"No more than I wished to be rid of him," retorted Miranda fiercely, and at once regretted it. No matter what her feelings, she should not talk so about her brother-in-law. What if Rosalind should come down after all?

"It wasn't a convivial evening," agreed Alan. "I hope your sister is feeling better?"

Tears threatened once again. "She won't see me, and I don't know what is *wrong* with her. We…we had a disagreement on the way home today, and…"

"I'm sure you'll patch it up tomorrow," replied Alan quickly, anticipating more tears. "These things pass off with a little time."

Miranda said nothing. She didn't believe him, but she couldn't bear to talk about it anymore. Silence lengthened between them until it occurred to her that again they were without a chaperone. The thought of her mother's undoubted outrage had she known cheered her enough to bring back a memory. "I have been meaning to tell you what happened to me," she said.

Alan Creighton was all attention.

"It was the most appalling thing." And Miranda told the story of the crow on her pillow. "I believe Philip told Forbes to do it because he does not like me and wishes me to leave," she finished.

Alan glanced uneasily at the door. "That seems unlikely," he said.

"No, it is not, for I heard…" Miranda stopped. She was not yet ready to tell anyone what she had overheard.

"I believe Philip is under some sort of strain," added Creighton slowly. "I don't know what it is, for I can't get him to talk, but I can see it quite clearly." Five years of war had made Alan Creighton thoroughly familiar with the signs of strain in a man. "And there was something today." He paused, frowning.

"What?" asked Miranda, diverted from her own troubles.

He hesitated. What he had seen today had roused real concern in Alan, and he did not care to involve a young lady in it. On the other hand, from what he had observed of Miranda, he knew it would be impossible to keep her wholly out. She was likely to wander anywhere and poke into things without the least understanding of what they might imply. "I saw several men in the village," he answered slowly, "of a type I, unfortunately, recognize."

"What type?"

He thought a moment. "Not every man wishes to be a soldier," he began. "Indeed, not every man is cut out to be one, but, when you are fighting someone like Boney, you must have an army, or your country will be overrun and lost. And so, some of these... unsuitable men are taken into the forces. Pressed, some of them, against their will." He looked down, shook his head. "Many of them are never more than ruffians."

Miranda watched him with wide eyes.

"In the army, they can be controlled. War even offers some... compensations to such men. But, when they are out again, especially when they can find no work, or, perhaps, do not like the work they can find, then they become...a problem."

Miranda was fascinated, and very flattered to be talked to in such a serious way, but she did not understand his point. "Perhaps they should stay in the army?" she wondered.

Alan started, as if jolted from deep thought. "I beg your pardon. I have been prosing on in the most tedious way."

"I was interested," protested Miranda.

He shook his head. "At any rate, I only meant to say that I saw a group of these men in the village today. And that is odd, because they cannot have come from a small place like this. They were Londoners. I know their type." He frowned. "And if they *are* here..."

Miranda watched his face. He looked grimly resolute. She was impressed with his knowledge, and with an ability to command and get results that she sensed more than saw. Abruptly, she remembered something. "It must be their dog," she exclaimed. Alan turned to look at her, and she told him what she had seen on her walk. "They are probably keeping him to fight," she said. "It sounds like they are that sort of men."

Creighton nodded, thinking his own thoughts.

"We must tell Philip," added Miranda, then stopped, frowning. "But Philip must know they are here."

That was exactly the thing, thought Alan. He must know, but he had ignored them completely.

"What are you going to do?" Miranda was certain, from the look on his face, that he meant to do something.

"Eh? Oh." He contemplated her. She was an engaging little thing, actually. Those eyes were compelling despite her youth. "I'm not sure there's anything to be done."

"But of course we must find out what is going on!" Miranda was indignant. "These men are just another *sinister* element. I thought you were going to help me investigate."

"I think you should forget that idea," he replied. This joke had become a bit perilous.

"I shall do nothing of the kind!"

She wouldn't, he realized. It was no use arguing with the blaze in those eyes. A spark of admiration blossomed in him. "No, I don't suppose you will."

"Just when things are coming out," she scoffed. "What do you think me?"

He had to smile. "Very well. But I insist upon this. You will confine your explorations to the house and park, and not go wandering as you did today. I shall take the village and surroundings." Seeing her start to protest, he added, "If you do not agree, I shall go to Philip at once." He should do so in any case, Alan thought a bit guiltily. But his cousin was so closemouthed and dour. He might well just tell Alan to mind his own affairs. And the chance of a mystery had dispelled the boredom that had been plaguing him for months. He would play his own hand for a time, at least. "Well?"

"All right!" said Miranda. "You were a tyrannical officer, weren't you?"

Alan merely laughed.

NINE

I HAVE BEEN MAKING A LIST OF ALL THE PLACES IN THE HOUSE that I have not yet explored. I believe I have seen everything there is to see in the park, though I shall go round again to make sure. I have also made up my mind to force Rosalind to see me first thing tomorrow morning. No matter what the situation, it was wrong of me to say what I did. I have remembered that one of Mama's strongest rules is never to interfere between a husband and wife. Last summer, I overheard her telling Aunt Hattie about her friend Anna, who had come to her and endlessly complained about her husband, even once coming to stay with Mama for three days when they had quarreled. And Mama had tried to help with advice and a little money. Then, the woman went home again, and, the next time she saw Mama, she cut her dead! Mama was certain it was because she did not wish to associate with anyone who reminded her of unhappy times. I wish I had remembered that story yesterday!

Not that it is exactly the same. Rosalind is not complaining (when she should be!), but she is certainly cutting me and I am miserable while she is so angry. Whatever is going on will come out when Alan and I have finished our investigation, and then Rosalind must see for herself and decide what to do. I think Papa would be proud of me for behaving in such a responsible manner. (I also remembered *his* story about the Greeks killing the messenger who brought bad news.)

I must have patience, which is not a thing I am good at. Miss Lidsey, my old governess, used to make me write out lists of my virtues and faults every Saturday afternoon, at the end of our week of lessons, and contemplate them to "stimulate the desire to change." The faults always took more space (she added to that list, but never the other!), and some of them never disappeared—like impatience. Will it ever, I wonder?

It was such a triumph to cross a fault off my list. I remember when nail biting went, and forgetting to practice the pianoforte. It took me nearly a *year* to be rid of "impertinence to my governess and to Mr. Phelps, the dancing master." I don't think Miss Lidsey ever realized that I was still vastly impertinent inside my head. But then, perhaps, she did not care, as long as I kept it to myself. She once said (when she had had rather too much of Cook's special sherry) that silence was the chief virtue of a woman and also her chief defense. She was not very happy, I think. Indeed, she...

I don't wish to go on and on about my old governess in my journal. Besides, she found a new position with the five young daughters of an earl, and she was in raptures all the last weeks she was with us. I am sure they are all patient and sweet-natured and never speak unless asked a direct question, and that Miss Lidsey is utterly content now.

I must keep my mind on the reason I am writing. I shall put in a copy of my map when it is done, with all the places I have examined, marked, and annotated. (That is a fine word; I learned it from James just before he went up to Oxford.) When it is done, I shall show it to Alan as well.

I find that I think about Alan a good deal. Of course, that is only natural, since we are working together. He really has the most extraordinary eyes—such a *bright* blue and so very penetrating. He seems to miss nothing that passes. I suppose that comes of being in the army and in battle. I think he is rather handsome, too. Not so handsome as Philip, of course, which is ironic considering Philip's *unhandsome* temperament. But the shape of Alan's face is pleasing, and there is something about the way he cocks one eyebrow and smiles just slightly that makes me feel quite flustered. And then, when he *really* smiles—which is not often—well!

I do believe he likes me a little. It is unfortunate, in one way, that we did not meet in London next year, when I am out, for then I will have all sorts of fashionable new clothes and, I'm sure, a great deal more *polish*. On the other hand, we could not have become nearly so well acquainted at evening parties and such. (I *do* look forward to being out! I don't expect I shall be a belle, since I am not really beautiful, but look at Miss Sperling, who made a hit the year Portia was presented. *She* had more wit than beauty. Everyone said so. And I truly believe I can be very witty if I try. I often make Mama and Papa laugh.)

In any event, I am very glad Alan came here. I wonder, could he not be my very first *flirtation*? (I suppose this is what Miss Lidsey would call an unworthy thought.) I don't mean anything by it, but it seems to me that one should *practice* things one will be called upon to do later, like the pianoforte. During the Season, everyone flirts. Why should I not try it out a little?

That does not mean I would neglect my efforts to help Rosalind. That must, of course, be my major object. But there couldn't be any harm in the other, could there?

———

Jane Jenkins just came in with the ironing, looking so sour you would have thought she had read what I was writing. Wouldn't she be shocked? I don't suppose she has ever flirted in her life, not even when she was young. Imagine flirting with that dried-up stick Henry Jenkins? I think they must have agreed to marry like merchants striking a bargain. Or, perhaps, they were drawn together by a tract. Perhaps she gave him one of her dreary leaflets on eternal damnation, and he pulled its mate from his pocket, and their eyes met... It is too ridiculous. I must return to my map.

TEN

THE WHOLE PARTY AT CLAIRVON ABBEY MET AT BREAKFAST the following morning. Little was said as the four filled their plates and poured out tea or coffee. Rosalind looked white and strained, and Philip sullen. Miranda said nothing. This left conversation up to Alan Creighton, and he chatted manfully about the chances of rain and the fineness of Cook's kippers. There was general relief when Philip rose and abruptly asked whether Alan would care for a ride and a look at some cottages on the far side of the estate. Alan agreed, and the men went out.

In the silence that followed, Miranda gathered her courage. "Rosalind?" she said.

"What?"

Her sister's white face and unhappy expression wrung Miranda's heart. "I am so sorry! I should never have said those things to you, and I will never do so again. Please forgive me!"

Rosalind, who had spent a restless, unhappy night, and who was as miserable as Miranda over their breach, did so gladly. She had also been thinking. "I must tell you something about my 'illness,'" she added. "It is not really that. I…I am increasing. That is all."

"In…? Oh!"

"Mama says one is often sick, at first. But it will pass off in a few weeks." Rosalind had determined to be quite matter-of-fact about this revelation, but she found she was talking rapidly and nervously. She slowed down. "It is a nuisance, of course. The illness, I mean. But nothing to worry over."

"No. I mean, well, congratulations! Are you…you must be very happy." Miranda felt young and awkward. No one had ever confided such a thing to her before. Or discussed it in her presence.

Though she had always felt that to be stupid and insulting, she was nevertheless at a loss.

"Yes." For the first time this morning, Rosalind smiled. "Very." The conversation brought back her flood of happiness when she had first known about the baby. "It will be around Christmas. We are starting to clear out the old nursery."

"Christmas! Too bad," exclaimed Miranda. "How lowering, to have a birthday just then, and get only one set of presents."

Rosalind laughed. "We shall try to make it up to him, or her."

"Well, you should," agreed Miranda.

"So now will you stop worrying about me?" asked her sister. "And not mind if I am a little ill or cannot ride with you?"

"Of course! I am so sorry for being such a…"

"How could you know? Shall we go to the morning room? I have some sewing, and I'm sure you have a book."

"I'm just finishing *The Black Abbot*. I could read aloud," offered Miranda.

"I don't know whether I can tolerate more of the abbot. Is he torturing anyone just now?"

"Oh, no. That is all over with. They are chasing him through the catacombs, and they must catch him soon, for there are only twenty pages left."

Her sister laughed again. "Well, I must hear *that*."

"I'll get it," said Miranda, and ran upstairs to her room.

They spent the morning together in perfect amity and enjoyed a light luncheon of cold meat and fruit. But in the afternoon, when Rosalind went up to lie down, Miranda fetched her map and a candle and headed for the basements. These were the major unexplored territories left in the house, and she was determined to go through them at the earliest opportunity.

The door to the lower regions was just outside the kitchen, and she crept along the uncarpeted corridor listening intently. She particularly wished to avoid Forbes.

"Shall I peel these potatoes, then?" she heard Alice say. Cook answered with something that sounded to Miranda like, "Ayo-ich." Placing her feet carefully and silently, she reached the cellar door. The knob squeaked when she eased it open, and she froze for an instant, then stepped quickly through and shut it behind her. There was no sound of pursuit.

It was very dark. Her one small candle let her see three or four dusty wooden stairs and nothing else. Silence spread around her. Miranda folded up her map and put it in the pocket of her gown. She would not be able to mark it in this gloom; she would have to memorize the turns and write them in when she was back in her room. For a wistful moment, she wished she was back there now. Then she shook herself and stepped down.

The stairs ended in a large brick-walled room filled with boxes and barrels. When she lifted the lid on one of the latter, she found flour. Through an archway to the left was the root cellar. Miranda held her candle high and examined the apples, potatoes, and carrots reposing in the cool earth there. Back in the other direction, she discovered the wine cellar, racks and racks of dusty bottles marching off into the gloom. She spent only a minute there, for this was Forbes's domain, and who could tell when he might come down to get the wine for dinner?

Beyond these domestic areas, the stone floor deteriorated and became treacherously uneven, but there was at least a bit more light, from small barred windows set high in the walls. She found a huge echoing room supported by brick pillars and containing only a few moldy trunks. Opening one, she discovered a miscellany of broken crockery, worn-out tinware, and straw which looked very like a nest. She closed it again quickly.

Further on was another room, identical except that it was empty and had large damp spots on the floor and walls. After this, the walls were hewn stone, the same stone as the sea cliffs, and the cellars were exceedingly damp. Miranda began to have high hopes of finding a secret passageway down to the sea, used by pirates in times past. Perhaps one of Philip's ancestors had been a pirate? But the rooms merely went on and on, getting smaller and meaner without any sign of a hidden door. Miranda wandered here and there for almost two hours without finding anything more interesting than an ancient ax, crusted with dirt and rust, leaning in the corner of a cell-like chamber under, she thought, the west wing.

At last, discouraged and rather dusty, she gave up and started back the way she had come. She had made careful note of every turn she took and retraced them faithfully to the large room with the trunks. It was there that she began to hear the voices.

They were deep—men's voices—and low, as if they didn't wish to be overheard. Miranda crept forward to the doorway and listened. They were coming from the left, the wine cellar.

She snuffed her candle, darted into the storeroom, and crouched behind two barrels just outside the entrance to the wine cellar. The first thing she heard was Forbes, saying, "I told you never to come here."

"I come where I like," replied a gravelly, brutal voice. The mere sound of it made Miranda shiver. "I ain't no lord's lackey." She stifled a gasp. Imagine saying such a thing to *Forbes*.

But he replied only, "What do you want?"

"A word, no more."

"Say it then."

There was a pause, and a shuffling sound. Miranda longed to go and peer around the doorway, but she didn't dare.

"What's this, then?" said the stranger's voice. "Some o' his lordship's fancy wine. Red, eh?"

"A claret," answered Forbes, in a tone that would have made Miranda cringe before him.

"Aye. I've had such in France. More than you have, eh, old man?"

"No doubt. Perhaps you could give me the message? I may be missed upstairs."

"Oh, right, his lordship may be needin' you to fill his glass or hand him 'is handkerchief." His mocking tone changed. "How can you stand it, man? Come away and join us. Your nephew's made more money than you do in a year in this place."

"I'm too old to change my habits," answered Forbes, in a tired, controlled voice that made Miranda ashamed of her suspicions about him. "Please just give me the message."

There was the sound of someone spitting. "All right, then, old fool. Harley says, if those two new ones keep snooping, something bad will happen."

"I have no way of stopping guests in this house from going where they please," protested Forbes.

"You better find a way."

"I've tried with the girl. She won't listen. And his lordship's cousin is a former army officer. I am sure he…"

"Officer?" was the sharp exclamation. "What regiment?"

"The tenth cavalry."

"Ah. None o' ours, then. But we know what to do about an officer."

"You'd be mad to…"

"Never mind what we'd be. You just keep after that girl and keep your mug shut. You know what'll happen if you don't." The ugly threat in his voice made Miranda crouch still lower, and that was fortunate, for in the next moment, the two men came out and walked toward the stairs. When they were past, Miranda ventured a look. Forbes held a branch of candles, and by their light she could see his narrow, upright figure flanked by one almost as tall and far broader. The stranger wore a ragged uniform with the insignia torn off, and a battered tricorne. His hands were huge, even larger than Forbes's.

Just before the light disappeared above, Miranda hurried to the stairs, but she waited at the foot, in darkness, for some time before groping her way up. She had no wish to meet Forbes's companion in the upper corridor! At last, judging they must be gone, she slowly ascended. At the top, she paused, listened, then slipped out, only to come face to face with Mrs. MacCrory, the cook.

The older woman asked an unintelligible question.

Miranda, whose heart was pounding with the fright of meeting her, stammered, "I was just…I went to look at the cellar. I…just to see, you know, what it is like. Such an…old house."

Cook put her hands on her ample hips and regarded Miranda with fond astonishment. She said something else, shaking her head. Alice, the kitchenmaid, peered around the kitchen door. "She says you're an odd little thing," translated Alice. "What have you been doing? You're all over dust."

"I was…looking at the cellar."

"Looking at it? Whatever for?"

"Just to explore." Some of Miranda's confidence was coming back, now that it seemed certain Forbes and his visitor were gone.

"I hate going down there," said Alice with a shiver. "There's *rats*."

Miranda thought that she would rather have encountered a rat than the man with Forbes. "I didn't see any," she replied.

Mrs. MacCrory took her arm and, nodding and smiling, urged her into the kitchen. Alice backed away in front of them. "We've been making scones for tea," she confided. "It's nearly time."

The sight, and smell, of the mound of steaming scones on the kitchen table made Miranda realize that she was ravenous. "Oh, could I have one now?" she asked. Cook smiled more broadly and gave her one. Miranda bit down. The pastry was hot and flaky and filled with raisins. It seemed to her the most delicious thing she had ever tasted in her life. She finished it in four bites and gazed longingly at the platter. Laughing and making another mysterious remark, Cook passed a second. "She says she loves to watch a girl enjoy her food the way you do," said Alice.

"And so do I," added a male voice from the doorway. "Is this a private party, or may I join in?"

"Alan," cried Miranda through a mouthful of scone. "I *must* speak to you at once."

"Not until I've had one of these," he said, taking two scones and grinning at Mrs. MacCrory.

"We're just taking in the tea," objected Alice.

"I promise you I shall do it justice," said Alan. "Mrs. MacCrory makes the best scones in the north, and that means the best scones anywhere, of course."

"Alan," said Miranda.

"Ready."

They went out together, and Miranda led him to the empty morning room. "I must tell you what I heard," she began, and poured out the whole story.

When she was done, Creighton's buoyant mood had dissipated. He looked grimly thoughtful. "This is too much," he concluded. "I must speak to Philip."

"Philip!" Miranda was outraged.

"This is no longer a joke," he replied.

"It never *was* a joke. You cannot tell Philip. He may be behind... whatever it is."

"You don't truly believe that?"

"Well...he may be. Think how unpleasant he is, and how he is always snapping. He didn't want me here, either. I heard him say so to Rosalind."

"None of this means he is involved. He might well not want you looking about if he feared something illegal was afoot."

Miranda thought about this.

"And if Forbes is being threatened, it seems likely Philip is as well."

"Ye-es," answered Miranda slowly.

"We cannot let this go on. I must see him." He turned to leave, and Miranda followed close on his heels. "You stay here," he told her. "Or go and find your sister."

"No. I'm coming with you."

Alan shook his head. "This is not a game now, Miranda. It is serious business."

"I know that."

"You must keep out of it after this. Philip and I will…"

"When it was a 'game' I was welcome to play? But now that you see it isn't, I must stay clear?" Miranda's eyes had begun to snap.

"You must see that you cannot…"

"I see that I have found out nearly everything we know, and now you are pushing me out. I won't go!"

They faced one another for a long moment, eye to eye. Alan was surprised to find that he couldn't daunt her. He had faced down any number of belligerent soldiers, but Miranda Dennison stood firm. "Pluck up to the backbone, aren't you?" he finally admitted. "But that is only because you have no conception of the sort of men involved. I cannot allow you to come."

"Allow? You have no authority over *me*!"

He smiled a little, charmed by her pugnacity. "Perhaps not. But if I ask Philip to speak to me privately, I think he will." She started to reply, but he forestalled her. "And I think if you attempt to convince him otherwise, he will agree with me."

Miranda wanted to deny this, but she couldn't. She and Philip were not exactly good friends. He would undoubtedly side with his cousin. "You *can't* do this!" she said, half furious, half pleading.

"I am sorry, but…"

"You aren't! You aren't the least sorry. You are happy to have a mere girl out of your way. It is always so! But you may find you are wrong, in the end!" And picking up her skirts, she swept out of the room, followed, unknowingly, by Alan Creighton's deeply appreciative gaze.

ELEVEN

I HAVE NEVER BEEN SO ANGRY IN MY LIFE. NOT WHEN MAMA and Papa told me I was to stay in England, not when James threw my best hat out the window, not even when Sophie Franklin wore that shocking dress to the school fete and *lured* Reverend Allistair's son Robert away from me. Alan Creighton is the most arrogant, *stupidest* man I have ever heard of. It was I who discovered the house on the cliffs, and I who overheard Forbes and that man. He did not find a dead bird in his bed! Without me, he would know nothing at all. It is not fair!

He and Philip are closeted in Philip's study. They have given orders that they are not to be interrupted for tea, or anything else. The door is too thick to let any sound through, and all the windows are shut, because of course it is raining *again*. I cannot bear it!

When I think that Alan is hearing the whole story, whatever it may be, I can scarcely keep from screaming. Perhaps I was wrong about Philip. But how am I to know that if I am told nothing? I daresay Alan will not even mention my plan of investigation. I am in such a flame, I can hardly write. I am going out walking; I don't care about rain.

———————

My head is clearer now, even though my walk was quite nasty. It is a thin, cold rain and gets down one's neck and into all the crevices of one's cloak. And when I came back, Rosalind was waiting in the drawing room looking dreadfully melancholy. Philip and Alan had not come out, and I could not be found, and she had been left there with the tea tray to worry. I had to sit with her for a while, and she looked so woebegone that I could not even *hint* anything

was wrong. I told her I thought Alan was discussing some business
matter with Philip, and this reassured her at once. We had our tea,
and Rosalind chatted about the baby clothes being made by some
village women. As soon as I could get away, I came back here to
record *what I have decided to do*.

Of course I shall not give up. If Mr. Alan Creighton imagines
that I will merely fold my hands and wait to be told the story when
it is over, he has not understood my character. I intend to *show* him
his mistake, and soon, because I have had an absolutely *brilliant*
idea.

One of the trials of my childhood was Mama's penchant for
reading Shakespeare aloud. By the time I was six years old, I had
endured uncountable sessions of nervous bewilderment. Mama
reads with *great enthusiasm*, and so we were always conscious that
terribly important things must be going on in what she read, but
none of us ever understood more than one word in five. She would
have to explain events to us every few minutes, which you might
have thought would annoy her and make her wish to stop, but it
didn't. Until today, I have looked back on those afternoons as an
utter waste, and that just *shows* that Papa is right when he says you
never know what will turn out to be needed in the future. (It is his
reason for never throwing anything away, no matter how disgustingly worn.)

But, as I was walking in the dreary wet shrubbery, I suddenly
remembered one of the stories from Shakespeare. I can't recall
which play it may have been, but in it, the heroine disguises herself in order to find out the truth about something (I can't remember what), and she dresses as a *boy*. This lets her go everywhere
without being remarked and hear all sorts of things she never
would in her proper clothes. And I suddenly saw how I might do
the same, to discover what is going on in the village before Alan
has any notion whatsoever. And the really *providential* thing is that
Rosalind was showing me just the other day where all Philip's old

things are kept. The servants stored everything in his old school-room, which is just now being cleared out. I can use his clothes!

It is so perfect I almost had to jump up and down when I thought of it.

Of course, I am not so silly as to think I can just walk into a small country village and be told secrets. I shall have to have a good story. But I have thought of a splendid one. I shall tell them I am Alan's valet. Only the servants here know that he has none, and I shall take care to keep out of their way. I am certain I can find out the truth before the masquerade is revealed. And then won't Alan stare?

I am going to fetch the clothes now, while Rosalind is in her room dressing for dinner and the servants are busy below stairs. Then I shall be ready as soon as an opportunity comes along. I shall have to think what to tell Rosalind so that I may get away for several hours.

Of course, there is no question now of flirting with Alan Creighton. I would rather flirt with Forbes. I see now how easy it is to be mistaken in a man, just as Mama has so often told me. They may seem quite charming and reliable, but, when it comes to something important, they are simply not to be trusted. I hope I shall not find at each turn in my life that Mama has been right. How tiresome!

TWELVE

ALAN FOUND HIS COUSIN IN HIS STUDY, BENT OVER A CRUDELY lettered sheet of paper. "Philip," he said, "you must tell me what is happening. It is perfectly obvious that something is afoot."

Philip looked surprised and uneasy. "I don't know what you mean."

"I think you do." Alan used the voice he had found so effective with his troops. "Those ruffians we saw in the village, what are they up to?"

"Ruffians?" Philip swallowed. "You mean the villagers? I really don't think you should…"

"Miranda encountered one of them in your cellars, threatening your butler," interrupted Alan.

Philip turned white and made a strangled sound, then stood up behind the desk, his arms very rigid and his fists clenched. "What?"

Alan simply gazed at him. Philip stood there shaking for a moment, then the anger seemed to go out of him, and he sank back into his chair. "In my very house?" he murmured. "What am I going to do?"

"You are going to tell me everything," Alan answered, in a calm, commanding voice that seemed to comfort Philip. "And then we shall put our heads together and make things right."

"You make it sound easy," was his cousin's answer. "But it's a deuce of a coil, Alan."

"It must be. You've been sour as an unripe plum since I arrived. Tell me."

Philip considered him for a moment, then gestured toward the chair on the other side of his desk. "Smuggling," he replied simply.

"Ah. Fairly common on these coasts, isn't it?"

Philip shrugged. "Perhaps. A ship or two. A few kegs of good French brandy. But this is more than that. It's a systematic operation, and not just local men."

"Cashiered soldiers," said Alan.

"Yes. You spotted some of them in the village, the leaders of a gang that is terrorizing the countryside. I don't even know how many there are. They have been sending word to their fellows in London and other places. A few more arrive every week. They have just about taken over the closest village, and they are bringing in ships of contraband whenever the seas are favorable. They have partners in the Midland cities who sell the stuff and ship out their own goods illegally."

"The authorities?" asked Alan.

Philip put his head in his hands, rubbing his eyes as if they ached. "Of course my first thought was to call them. Forbes begged me not to."

"Forbes?" Alan's voice conveyed his incredulity.

Philip straightened and met his puzzled gaze squarely. "You must understand that the servants here, and the villagers, were my only companions growing up, Alan. I hated school, and made few friends there. I was always longing to come home. I love this house, and this place."

Alan nodded. "But why should Forbes…?"

"His nephew is involved. So is the kitchenmaid's brother, and two of the grooms. There was smuggling here before these men came—the odd, insignificant cargo—the kind of thing you mentioned. At first, the newcomers played on that, and on some discontent hereabouts. We aren't a wealthy region. Very few of the villagers found it easy to refuse a bit of extra cash."

"And, after they were in deep enough, things started to change," said Alan.

"Exactly. While I hesitated, reluctant to have childhood friends taken in charge, these ruffians increased their numbers and consolidated their power. They are nearly invincible now. They learned organization and intimidation in the army." Philip sounded bitter.

"Perhaps," replied Alan. "But surely you are not still hanging back?"

His cousin's face fell into grim lines. "They have threatened Rosalind. I have been told that if any revenue cutters or excise men are so much as seen in the area, she will pay for it." He bent his head again. "I live in...*terror* of a commonplace coastal patrol. I ride out every day to check the countryside. I have wondered what I would do if I actually encountered an excise man. I dreamed once that I killed him." His face, when he raised it to Alan, was stark with anguish.

"But, Philip," said Alan kindly, "why not simply send Rosalind to stay with her family? Her sister can accompany her on the journey, now that she is here with you. And then you and I will put an end to this petty tyranny."

Philip slumped. "Of course that was my first thought. But Rosalind refused to go. She has been...unwell. She is increasing. Her parents are abroad, and her married sister is fully occupied nursing her father-in-law. Rosalind wouldn't hear of visiting anyone else, and the only way I could convince her would be to reveal the truth."

"Well then." Alan was a bit impatient.

"If I tell her, she will insist on staying with me, or urge me to leave as well. And I cannot abandon my responsibilities here."

"Perhaps you misjudge Rosalind's..."

"I know her! You do not."

Alan had to concede this, and he also saw that his cousin's romantic temperament had inflamed him to something near hysteria during the weeks he had wrestled with this problem. Alan had seen similar states in battle. Philip would have to be handled carefully.

"Rosalind could be protected," began Alan.

"I refuse to take the chance!" Philip almost shouted. "You say one of the devils was seen in my own cellar. Do you think I will risk my wife and child with odds such as that?"

Alan watched him, his eyes full of sympathy and pity. "No. No, that's too much to ask."

His cousin fell back in his chair, relieved and exhausted.

"But still, Philip, something must be done."

"I have thought of little else for weeks. I have racked my brain for an idea that does not expose Rosalind. If you can assure that, I will do whatever you like."

Alan frowned at the carpet. "The villagers are no longer sympathetic to them."

"No. With a few exceptions they would like nothing better than to be rid of all the outsiders. There have been incidents—wives, daughters." Philip's lips twisted with anger and frustration.

"So, if we could manage something, they would support us?"

"*If* we can guarantee their families' safety? Yes."

Alan nodded. "I shall have to think. Would Forbes's nephew, or another of the villagers, give us information, do you think? Details of their plans?"

"Those connected with my household are under constant suspicion. Lately, they are not even permitted to visit their relatives here without witnesses. It would be difficult to manage."

"We might use a code."

"I don't want to see these people hurt, Alan."

"We would have to be careful," agreed his cousin. Alan's mind was working furiously, and his spirits were soaring. This problem brought back all the instincts and skills he had developed during years of war, and the challenge exhilarated him. He had no doubt he could find a solution and carry it out. Had he not helped beat the French? This was a handful of crude bullies. He would soon show them their mistakes. "Where is the nearest military garrison?" he asked.

"We cannot go to the army," protested Philip. "I have just told you…"

"You have. And I have understood. I shall do nothing hasty or obvious, cousin."

Philip hesitated a moment longer, then he said, "There is a small detachment in the fort at Lindisfarne, up the coast."

"Hah. And what is Lindisfarne?"

"An island. There was once a famous monastery there, in ruins now."

"Ruins?" Alan's blue eyes gleamed. "The sort that people go to visit?"

"Ye-es." Philip watched him with a frown. "It is widely known. There is bathing, too, for those hardy enough to try the North Sea."

"Perfect. I'm sure Miranda would like to see such a place. You must organize an expedition there as soon as possible."

"What do you intend?"

"Why, to view a ruin," replied Alan with a smile. "And to escort your charming sister-in-law all over it. And Rosalind, too, naturally."

"Rosalind is to know nothing of this!" said Philip sharply. "You are *not* to speak of it."

"Of course not. Not to Rosalind, or anyone."

Philip relaxed slightly. "But if you are seen contacting the army…"

"Philip, you must trust me a little. I shall put no one in danger. I give you my word."

"Not purposely, you won't. I know that."

"You have let these petty ruffians intimidate you," objected Alan. "I know their kind. Don't worry."

But, seeing the excited gleam in his eyes, and the smile playing about his lips, Philip began to sincerely regret telling his cousin the truth. He recalled Alan's reckless behavior in London and was even more uneasy. "Swear to me you will always act to protect my family and friends," he said.

"Of course," replied Alan, but his expression was not reassuring.

THIRTEEN

IT WAS MUCH MORE DIFFICULT THAN I IMAGINED, DISGUISING myself as a boy. Shakespeare makes it sound so simple. I remember distinctly that there was no trouble at all. One moment the girl in his play was wearing dresses and being called by her name (how strange that I cannot recall it, even though we all have such names). And the next moment she has on—I don't know—a doublet and hose, I imagine, and she is someone else entirely. No one suspects. Hose! There is no explanation of what she does with her hair, and I know they wore their hair quite long in those days. Longer than mine. But I have spent the last hour locked in my bedroom trying to achieve a convincing disguise with Philip's outgrown clothes, and I do not feel at all confident about it.

The first obstacle to be overcome is the sheer *impropriety* of it. I cannot remember that Shakespeare's heroine even considered this I know if I am to be a real writer I must be ready to learn all sorts of scandalous things, and I *am*. But somehow actually taking off one's gown and stays and putting one's leg into riding breeches is extremely unsettling. It was twenty minutes before I felt I *might* be able to venture out the door in such a garment, and I still have not managed any ease of movement. I know I shall be completely unconvincing.

The second thing is all the fastenings (I shouldn't think of discussing such things except in my private journal, Mama). Having no little brothers, I have never had to learn how a boy's clothes go together, and it has taken me *ages* to deduce how to keep the stockings up. And I *cannot* tie a neckcloth; I get only great bulky knots that nearly choke me. I shall have to be a very unfashionable boy and wear a kerchief.

If, that is, I can ever get my hair all up under a cap. I do *not* believe that the woman in Shakespeare did so, either. I have decided that he had no concern for verisimilitude. It took me dreadfully long even to find a cap. I was almost late for dinner. I suppose Philip didn't care for them when he was young, since he rarely wears a hat now. The one I found is an ugly shapeless thing of gray tweed with a little stiffened visor in the front, and, when I push my hair into it, it bulges and flops about on my head in the stupidest way. Not only that, but tendrils of hair *will* slip out in front. It is obvious, looking at me, that I have hidden long hair. I shall have to find another sort of hat.

The final indignity is that these clothes *itch* (I almost wish I could see Mama's face). They are made of much coarser cloth than I am used to, and I am continually driven to scratch my legs and my neck. Of course, I can resist, but it is hideously uncomfortable. How do boys *endure* it? I have heard people talk of the greater freedom of men's clothes, and perhaps I will find I can move about better in breeches (!), but I shan't envy them any longer after this. Unless perhaps pantaloons…? Oh, it would almost be worth leaving this journal about for Mama to find, to see her read *that*.

At any rate, after all my labors, when I look in the mirror, I see a slender boy with drooping stockings and clothes a bit too large for him, with a soft, girlish face and an odd cap. In fact, he has a *girl's* face; there's no denying it. The costume, I might carry off, but I must do something about the head before I let anyone see me in this guise.

It is vastly irritating. I long to resume my investigations, but in order to do so I must move freely about the village. And I can't do that in my normal dress. I will search for another sort of cap tomorrow.

No, not tomorrow. I had forgotten we are to go and see Lindisfarne tomorrow, at the command of Philip and Alan. I am so angry at them that I can scarcely write it. They came to dinner after having been shut up together for hours, and of course they said nothing about what they had discussed. But Alan looked so pleased with himself that it was all I could do not to hit him. He was *detestably* jolly all through dinner, chatting to Rosalind and laughing at his own so-called witticisms until I thought I should shriek. At least Philip did not laugh. Indeed, he seemed much as usual—*brooding* and, it now seems to me, unhappy. What can be the matter? I feel I shall *burst* if I do not find out soon.

I do not even want to visit Lindisfarne, which is what Papa would call most ironic, since only yesterday I would have been in ecstasies at the plan. But now I want only to discover the mystery, and old ruins seem much less interesting to me than before. After all, even in a novel, it is the *adventures* that take place in the ruins that are important. But I shall have to go. If I plead illness, it will just be put off, since the whole expedition is being arranged for my enjoyment. And, if I say I do not wish to go at all, everyone will suspect something. It is all vastly annoying. Why does nothing ever go as one wishes? Just look at this list:

1. I *begged* to go to Rome, and Mama and Papa refused.
2. I found out all kinds of important things to help my sister, and now I am not to be allowed to help her at all. (We shall *see* about that!)
3. I thought of a splendid disguise, and it looks merely odd.
4. I at last managed to meet a man outside my family (at least my *immediate* family) and try a little flirtation (only in anticipation of my come-out, naturally), and he turns out to be an odiously arrogant, unfeeling *beast*! If Alan asked me to stand up with him at the most *opulent* ball of the Season, I would refuse and sit by the wall. If he sent me a bouquet, I would throw it in the gutter. If he offered for my hand in marriage, I should tell Papa that I preferred a *nunnery*.

Not that he is likely to do any of those things. I could tell by the way he laughed at dinner that he thinks I am a silly, romantic schoolgirl whose head is full of ridiculous fancies. Well, I have said I was most likely wrong about Philip. And I suppose Forbes, too (though I am not so certain about *him*). Has Mr. Alan Creighton never made a mistake? I'm sure he thinks so. But I shall show him that, this time, he most certainly has.

FOURTEEN

"ARE YOU SURE YOU FEEL WELL ENOUGH TO GO?" SAID PHILIP to his wife the next morning. "This expedition might be put off a day or two, I think."

"I have told you I am quite well," responded Rosalind. "Indeed, I think the sickness is passing off just as Mama promised."

"Oh." Philip turned to gaze out the window. From Rosalind's boudoir, one could see beyond the park to the edges of the village. Nervously, he examined the road for travelers. He hated letting Rosalind step out of the house these days. He felt besieged by threats to her and all his happiness.

"Is that all you can say? 'Oh'?" When he did not answer at once, Rosalind put her hands on her hips. "Philip!"

"What?" He turned, his expression blankly inquiring.

Rosalind was hurt and confused. He seemed more distracted than ever this morning, and what should have been wonderful news had not even penetrated. "Please tell me what's wrong," she said.

"Wrong?"

"Philip, I can see that something is…"

"You imagine it," he interrupted, brushing off her concern with a gesture. "Come, we had better get ready. It will take us two hours to reach Lindisfarne. I still do not see why we need stay the night."

"Your cousin Alan particularly requested it," retorted Rosalind.

"Oh." Philip's eyebrows drew together as he remembered this, and the reasons for it. "Yes. Well, we had best be starting." And he went out.

Tears filled Rosalind's eyes and spilled over her cheeks. All her pleasure at feeling well evaporated, to be replaced by a great wave of loneliness. Philip seemed to retreat further from her every day. If he was not short-tempered and harsh, he was distracted, as if he had far more important things than Rosalind on his mind. And she was accustomed to being most important to him. Was this what marriage became, she wondered? She had seen couples in London who barely seemed to speak from one week to the next. She had scorned and pitied them, reveling in her love match. But perhaps everyone was reduced to that after a certain number of years? She couldn't bear it if that were true. She longed to fling herself onto the bed and cry like a heartbroken child, but she was not a child. She had responsibilities, guests. And she could not even ask for comfort from her sister, whose opinion of Philip was already low. Rosalind straightened and went to her dressing table to blot her reddened eyes.

"Have you been to Lindisfarne before?" Miranda asked Rosalind when they sat in the carriage half an hour later. Her tone was desultory, almost bored.

"No. We have talked of going, but never done so." Rosalind was equally bland. Both women were too occupied with their own thoughts to notice anything unusual.

There was a prolonged silence.

"A fine day," said Rosalind suddenly, as if waking up after an unintended nap.

"Yes. Wonderfully warm," replied Miranda abstractedly. "One might almost think it summer."

"It is."

"What?"

"Summer." Rosalind stared at her sister, roused at last from her own preoccupations. "It is summer."

Miranda frowned. "Well, of course it is. Everyone knows *that*."

"But you just said… Miranda, what *is* the matter?"

"Nothing." Miranda also came fully back from musings. "Nothing at all. I was just thinking…about Lindisfarne. It is a wonderfully interesting place."

Rosalind sat back. This was more like her sister. "Tell me about it. I am, as usual, woefully ignorant."

"Well..." Miranda searched her mind for scraps picked up from Philip's book, and from things he had said. She couldn't remember anything, and, for the first time during her visit, she heartily wished Philip was with them. "Well, it is in *Marmion*."

"Is it?" Rosalind was genuinely delighted. "What does Walter Scott say about it?"

Miranda racked her brain. She had read it recently, just after Philip told her. She must remember something. "'In Saxon strength that abbey frown'd,'" she quoted finally. "With something, something, something round. And there was the heathen Dane, I remember that. He, er, something 'his impious rage in vain.' And also 'moulder'd in his niche the saint.'"

Rosalind smiled. "That sounds uncomfortable."

"And there was a great battle," replied Miranda. Her enthusiasm was reviving. "If only I had thought to bring the poem, we might have read it in the ruins. Wouldn't *that* have been splendid?"

"It would indeed."

"It was something about the Vikings fighting the Saxons. Twelve hundred years ago, I know he said that. *Think* of it—twelve hundred years! I am glad we are to see it." She was, Miranda realized. One day would make no great difference to her investigations.

"So am I," said Rosalind, and almost meant it.

Miranda looked over at her guiltily. She hadn't been paying the least attention to her sister this morning. "Are you feeling well?" she asked.

"Very well, particularly now that I know about Walter Scott." Her blue eyes twinkled, and Miranda knew she was roasting her, but she didn't care. It was too wonderful to see the old Rosalind back. "I only hope there is someone other than moldering saints who can show us about," she added.

"There is a village there," Miranda assured her. "And sea bathing; I heard Philip say so."

Rosalind shivered. "I shan't try that. Imagine how cold!"

"I suppose it must be." Miranda looked wistful.

"There is absolutely no doubt of it."

Miranda sighed once for the warm seas of Italy.

They arrived at midmorning on the coast opposite the island. A horse-drawn cart was pulled up there to take passengers to Lindisfarne, and fortunately, it was full low tide, so that they could go at once. Their hampers, valises, and miscellaneous possessions were loaded immediately, and then Philip helped the ladies in. They left their carriage and horses with the coachman.

"What happens when the tide is high?" wondered Rosalind a bit nervously.

"Why, then, ma'am, we stays at home," replied the cart driver.

"We will go at low tide tomorrow morning, Rosalind."

"Yes, of course," said Rosalind. She turned to look at the island, a bit embarrassed by her unease. "Look, Miranda, there are ruins."

Miranda was clasping her hands before her and gazing up at ancient stones with rapture.

They were met on the other side of the strait by several villagers, two of whom carried their baggage to the small inn Forbes had known of. At Miranda's urging the four visitors made their way directly to the fallen walls up the hill. "It was a priory," Philip informed them, "and a small monastery. St. Cuthbert's relics were kept here for a while, I believe. It was dissolved with the rest of the religious establishments by Henry VIII almost three hundred years ago. This island is mostly fishermen now. I have heard they take fine lobsters in these waters."

"Lobsters," echoed Miranda in disgust at this prosaic information. "I shall walk up there." She pointed to the ruin of the main priory.

"And I shall be happy to escort you," responded Alan Creighton.

"I will be perfectly all right alone," she said. But he ignored her, pulling her arm through his and nearly dragging her up the hillside. "Let go," she hissed, not wanting Rosalind to overhear. But he simply walked on, and she was forced to go with him unless she wished to make a vulgar scene.

When they passed behind one of the ruined walls, however, she jerked away at once and stood facing him with blazing eyes.

"You are still angry with me," he concluded.

Miranda didn't bother to reply.

"I see that you are. You are wrong, you know."

She was absolutely determined not to speak to him. She turned to gaze at the red sandstone wall as if she were fascinated by its broken contours.

"And I am right. You should not be involved in Philip's troubles."

Miranda trembled with the effort to keep silent.

"They are not something you can remedy. And the men who are responsible are..."

Whirling on him, Miranda exploded. "You are the most... *insufferable*, self-satisfied...prig I have ever encountered. You are so certain you know what is appropriate for me, what is good for me. How dare you? If it weren't for me, you would know nothing about it. Whatever it is!" The fact that Alan now knew the whole story, and clearly had no intention of telling her, made Miranda almost incoherent with rage.

"I would have caught on soon enough," he said easily. "The clues were plain. You merely..."

The "merely" goaded Miranda beyond endurance. She clenched her fists at her sides to keep from flailing at him. "I see," she said with an attempt at icy calm.

Alan was lost in admiration of her snapping green eyes and flaming determination. She wore a dress of pale green muslin today, trimmed with darker ribbons just the shade of her eyes, and her pale hair fell in charming wisps all about her face. It seemed to Alan he had never met a girl who was both so pretty and so spirited.

"Well, you may find out everything yourself from now on," Miranda added.

"If you observe anything further, you must tell us," he objected. "This is a serious matter, Miranda. It is no time for petty revenge."

She had to swallow a choking fury before she could reply, "No? I have no way of judging, of course, since I am to be told nothing."

"You may take my word for it," he assured her.

"May I? *Thank you.*"

Alan suddenly realized that she really was angry, as he himself might be angry, or any of his friends. This was not some silly girlish pique. Alan Creighton had had very little to do with women of his own class in his life. He had spent his young manhood at war, and the women he encountered in the camps and contested cities had not attracted him. He had no experience in dealing with the gentler sex in society. His view of them came mainly from other soldiers' talk about their families and from his imagination. Confronting Miranda, he saw that this was inadequate. But he still believed that she should not come within a mile of the sort of men who were plaguing Philip. This type he did know, and the thought of Miranda having any contact with them made him shudder. "You don't understand," he began.

"I have been given no opportunity to do so," she retorted, and turned away. "I think we should rejoin Rosalind and Philip."

"Wait a moment. Let me…"

But she walked away, and she gave him no further chance to speak to her privately during their visit.

The party from Clairvon walked about the ruins until one, then went to the inn for a luncheon of cold lobster and mayonnaise. Afterward, they examined their rooms, which were as good as could be expected in such an out-of-the-way place, and then went to explore the island more thoroughly. Late in the day they reached the fort on the top of the north crag, and were greeted by the officer in charge of the small garrison there. Miranda, absorbed in the wide view of the ocean from this height, barely noticed when Alan went off with him. She supposed they were comparing army experiences.

The inn offered a passable dinner, augmented by some things brought by Rosalind, and they retired to bed early, partly from fatigue after their active day and partly because the chimney in their private parlor smoked badly.

"Did you enjoy yourself?" Rosalind asked Miranda as they undressed in the room they were to share.

"Yes," lied her sister. "It is a wonderfully picturesque place." But in fact, Miranda was feeling very low. Any pleasure she might have had in the ruins had been blasted by Alan Creighton. For some reason, his treatment of her, and his refusal to confide, no longer made her angry. She felt bereft, as if she had lost something very precious that would never be found again. Her melancholy had been building all day, and now she was close to tears. She couldn't understand it.

"It is," agreed Rosalind. "And Philip knows so much about it. Wasn't he interesting?" Her voice was full of pride. Rosalind was feeling much more in charity with Philip. He had really exerted himself to see that everyone had a pleasant day.

Miranda merely nodded.

"We will have to organize some other expeditions," her sister said. "After what Philip told us today, I quite long to see Hadrian's Wall. Shall we plan to go there next week?"

Miranda shrugged and climbed into bed. She didn't care if she never saw another ruin as long as she lived, she thought. They were nothing but piles of stones.

"Miranda, are you all right?" Rosalind got into bed beside her, but remained sitting up.

"Yes. A little tired, perhaps."

"You, tired? I don't believe I have ever heard you say such a thing before," teased Rosalind.

"Well, I am." Miranda turned so that her sister could not see her face. "And I should like to go to sleep!"

Rosalind raised her eyebrows. She started to say something more, then closed her lips and considered. Finally, she too lay down, and snuffed the candle on the little table next to the bed.

FIFTEEN

I HAVE DONE IT! LOOKING INTO THE MIRROR THIS AFTERNOON, I see not a young lady called Miranda Dennison, but a boy of fifteen or sixteen in rather loose, ill-fitting clothes. That, I have decided, is an advantage. I do not want to look too well-off, for that would attract attention in the village. I stole some pomade from Philip's room, and it holds my hair back perfectly, along with pins. The cap looks quite natural now. But the splendid thing is my face. I discovered that by simply rubbing a little dirt on my face, I change it completely. It is as if the smudges were a mask over my own features.

Of course, it is not very pleasant to be dirty. But I know I can wash it off when I return. Funnily, the most difficult part of the whole disguise was procuring the dirt! I conceived the idea and went out into the garden to fetch some, and then realized that I had nothing to put it in. I could not just grub a handful of earth and take it to my room. Aside from being thought utterly demented if anyone saw, it wasn't practical. And then when I returned to my bed chamber I could not find any suitable container. In the end I had to take a jar from the kitchen when Cook and Alice stepped out for a moment, and then Cook nearly caught me filling it! How she would have stared to see me scooping garden earth into her fine clean jar.

But it is done now. And I have hidden the jar in the very back of the wardrobe, where I keep my borrowed clothes. I really *do* think I have been exceedingly clever. And now it remains only to try out my disguise. Philip and Alan are out, and Rosalind is lying down in her room until tea. I intend to walk around the park and through the village, keeping my cap well down over my face and speaking to no one this first time. It will be merely a trial of my ingenuity, and my *nerve*. The idea of actually venturing outside my room in breeches still unsettles me considerably.

———————

What a ridiculous adventure! I shall set down everything just as it happened, for it is such an odd tale that it will be good practice for me, though it is *not* the sort of story I shall write in my own novel.

When I finally got up the courage to leave my room, I slipped on a hooded cloak in case I should encounter any of the household on the way downstairs. It is a warm day, and I knew I should get some puzzled looks for the cloak, but they would be as *nothing* to the astonishment my costume would provoke.

Fortunately, I met no one in the hall or at the door. I crept out and hurried at once to the shrubbery that lines the drive. And I have to admit I was most relieved to disappear into it; I stood there for quite five minutes waiting for my heart to stop pounding and to gather the courage to go on. How silly I must have looked, crouching under the cedar branches in my heavy cloak! It was very hot.

Finally, though, I told myself that I must either go on or go back, and the latter seemed so cowardly that I at once threw off the cloak, hung it on a branch, and stepped out into the drive. And nothing happened. There was no earthquake or bolt of lightning. Indeed, it was almost a disappointment, after all my worrying. There was no one about. Everything was just as usual. The birds sang, a squirrel leaped in the tree, one of Philip's dogs barked near the stable. It seemed there *ought* to be some marking of my venture, but there was not. Still, I was relieved, too, as I started walking down the drive toward the road.

It was then that I saw Forbes. He was walking toward me along the gravel drive, his hands clasped behind him, his eyes on the ground. He seemed far away and, perhaps, troubled. All of this was extremely *odd*, of course. In the first place, Forbes does not take *walks.* And in the second, whenever I have seen him in the house he has looked perfectly imperturbable. Except the one time when he was speaking to that man in the cellar.

And so this was an interesting circumstance, but most of these conclusions came to me only later on. At the moment when I saw Forbes, I was *paralyzed* with fear. I had not imagined any such test of my disguise this first time, and for a moment, I could not even move.

But as Forbes came closer I knew I had to do something. I could not meet him face to face. I thought of diving back into the shrubbery, but it was too thick just there. I would have attracted his attention for certain. I felt like a trapped rat!

Finally, when he was scarcely fifty feet from me, I made up my mind. I shoved my hands deep in my pockets, bent my head so that my cap hid my face, and began walking very fast down the drive, determined not to stop for anything.

I could hear Forbes's footsteps crunch on the gravel. I kept to the verge of the drive, as far from him as possible, and absolutely *plunged* along. He hesitated, then stopped. "You there," he said, and my heart seemed to flutter in my chest. "Who are you? What are you doing here?"

I was even with him, and I did not pause. Indeed, I walked even faster. "You are trespassing," he called. "Stop and explain yourself."

I ran. Down the drive toward the gates as fast as I could. (It *is* far easier to run in breeches.) Forbes followed for a little, then gave up when I easily outdistanced him. He is rather old, so I take no great credit for getting away. And I was so overset by the meeting that I had to sit down along the road and put my head on my knees for a considerable time. Dreadful pictures rose in my brain and made me tremble—what if it had been Alan or Philip I met? I should not have outrun *them*, and how would I have explained myself? I saw that I had not planned nearly well enough, and was very grateful for my luck.

After a while, though, I determined to go on. There was no

sense giving up when I had already surmounted the greatest obstacle. So I continued along the road to the village, keeping a careful watch for riders and a hiding place always in view.

I met no one else until I reached the edge of the village. There, I passed a woman who stared, it is true, but I felt certain it was mere curiosity about a stranger, not penetration of my disguise. The villagers do not know me.

It was quite exciting to walk about the streets as a boy. Few people paid any more attention than the woman had. That is, they stared, wondering who I was, but no one accosted me or spoke. One little boy, goaded by his companions, shouted, "Who are you, then?" But I merely nodded and kept walking. I began to think it was all very easy, and to feel almost comfortable in my strange garb, when I came to the little inn near the center of the town.

It is really just an alehouse. There are very few travelers here, and it is used mainly by the village men. I had no thought of going in—I am not so foolhardy—but I paused beneath a window to see if I could hear anything, and I *did*.

Several men were talking inside, their voices rough and angry. "I say we do something about 'im," said one. "I've seen 'is type. He'll be sticking 'is nose in, giving his damned orders, swanking about as if 'e owned us."

Another man snorted contemptuously. "We ain't in the army any longer, Bob. Ain't nothing 'e can do."

"Call in the bloody 'cisemen," protested the first.

"His lordship will see about that," was the answer.

There was a sound of spitting and a short silence. Then another man said, "When's the next?"

"A week," replied the second voice. "A big 'un too."

"Hah."

At that moment, I heard footsteps approaching around the corner of the building, and I knew I must not be caught listening. It was vastly frustrating, for I had not yet understood what they were talking of, but I moved away, and in the next instant came face to face with Alice the kitchenmaid!

We stared at each other, and then Alice's eyes widened and she said, "Miss Miranda!"

Well, I could see she was utterly scandalized. I had to make up some story to excuse my behavior. And it could not be the truth, for I did not know how far she was to be trusted.

I do not know how I thought of it, for my mind was whirling. Somehow, the words just came from my mouth. I told Alice it was a joke on Rosalind, that I meant to try to fool her and I needed to practice my role first. I talked all sorts of nonsense about our childhood, and how we were always arranging the most elaborate, outrageous jests on one another, and how Rosalind had caught me last and I wished to pay her back. It seemed quite unbelievable to me, but Alice appeared to be convinced. I believe she thinks the "quality" are all slightly mad anyway. When I ran out of words, she giggled and said, "I'll help you try it out on the village." She giggled again. "We'll put it about that you're a second cousin of Cook's from the North, and we can go about together. Won't that show Eddie Forbes, then?"

It occurred to me later that perhaps she didn't believe me at all, or at least didn't particularly care what I was up to since it fit in with some plan of her own. But at the time I was simply grateful that she didn't intend to tell anyone. We walked back to the house together, and she helped me slip upstairs. She has invited me to a village wedding in three days. I don't know whether I shall go. I have no time to think. I must change and wash in time for tea.

SIXTEEN

ALL OF THE CLAIRVON PARTY MET AT THE BREAKFAST TABLE the following morning, and in better spirits than had been seen there during the whole of Miranda's visit. Rosalind's sickness had almost completely passed off, and the bloom in her cheeks was soft and bright once more. This morning, in a gown of rose cambric, she looked achingly lovely.

This change in itself was perhaps enough to explain Philip's elation. Miranda knew no other cause for it, in any case, and her brother-in-law was talking and laughing as she had not seen him do since they met in London. Alan Creighton, too, seemed pleased with himself and the world. Miranda found herself in the unusual position of being the least lively person at the table.

"My bailiff will be here soon," Philip told them. "I shall be with him all morning, I'm afraid, Alan." But he did not sound particularly put out by this prospect.

"And you will thoroughly enjoy reading every word of his reports and talking on and on about what is to be done on the estate," teased Rosalind.

Philip looked sheepish, but did not contradict her. "I don't suppose you'd care to join us," he said to Alan. "You are welcome, of course…"

"No. I don't have your interest, or stamina," replied Alan. "Perhaps Miranda would ride with me along the coast?"

"Oh." Miranda was surprised. This was the first such offer he had made.

"A splendid idea," said Rosalind. "You have not ridden since you have been here Miranda, and I know how you like it. I don't care to try just now, but Fitch could go with you and Alan, couldn't he, Philip?"

Philip was frowning, his good spirits dissipated. "I don't know about that... Fitch may be busy this morning."

Rosalind stared. "What could he have to do that cannot wait?" She awaited an answer with wide innocent eyes.

Philip scowled at his empty plate. Rosalind looked from him to Miranda to Alan and back, hurt and bewildered by this sudden change.

"Who is Fitch?" wondered Miranda, also puzzled.

"Our head groom," Rosalind told her. "He has lived here all his life."

"Knows the countryside to an inch," added Alan. "A very reliable man." He looked at Philip.

Grudgingly, Philip nodded. He still looked unhappy.

"What do you say, then?" Alan asked Miranda. "Will you go?"

Though she had still not forgiven Alan Creighton, the prospect of a ride was alluring. The day had dawned clear and warm, with the scent of the sea and the moors blowing in through her bedroom window. It was a perfect morning for a gallop. She couldn't resist. Miranda nodded.

"Good. After breakfast?"

"Yes. I'm finished. I'll go and change."

"And I will order the horses. Which for Miranda, Philip?"

Lord Highdene considered. "Tell them Chara."

"I ride rather well," put in Miranda, in case he should be giving her an overplacid "lady's" mount.

Philip smiled slightly. "So I have heard. You will like Chara. She is sweet-tempered but spirited. Not Rosalind's sort of horse." Rosalind wrinkled her nose at him, but did not object.

Miranda stood. "I shall be ready in a quarter hour."

"I'll wait for you outside," said Alan with a smile that nearly made her forget what an exasperating man he was.

He was waiting on the sweep of gravel before the front door when she came out, chatting with a small, wizened man of about fifty in the livery of a groom. In buff riding breeches and a dark blue coat, with his broad shoulders and military bearing, he looked very handsome, and when he turned to Miranda and smiled, saying, "Ah, there you are. How smart you look," she found it hard to maintain the cool distance she had determined upon.

She *was* pleased with her appearance. She had a new habit of dark green cloth, with a close-fitted bodice and long sleeves above the sweep of the skirt. It buttoned up to a foam of lace at the collar, and the matching hat gave her a jaunty grace. It was the first ensemble her mother had had made in anticipation of her come-out next Season, and she knew it was the latest thing. It also brought out the green of her eyes and the creaminess of her skin.

Yet Alan Creighton was not to think he was forgiven, so she merely thanked him and went directly to the mounting block.

"This is Fitch," said Alan, following. The groom tipped his hat as Miranda nodded. "He says there's a pretty ride to the south."

"Very well," she agreed. "This is Chara?"

"Yes, miss. And a fine little goer she is."

Miranda took the reins and greeted the horse. She looked well, and there was a spark in her eye as well as obedience in her movements. Miranda led her to the block and mounted before either of the men could help her, bringing a smile to Alan Creighton's eyes. "Shall we go?" she asked.

"By all means." He swung into the saddle just ahead of Fitch and rode to her side. The groom fell in behind them. They trotted in silence down the lane and left along the road that skirted the cliffs.

Alan drew in a deep breath and let it out. "Ah, what air," he said. Miranda did not reply. "A glorious day," he added.

"Yes, indeed." She turned her head slightly. "Shall we have a gallop?" And without waiting for an answer, she spurred Chara and leaned forward as the horse gathered speed.

Briefly, Miranda enjoyed having startled the two men and

pulled away from them. But soon she was aware only of the wind on her face and the powerful stride of her mount as they hurtled along the rutted road. Her own muscles moved with the rhythm of the gallop; she both guided the horse and aided her. It was wonderfully exhilarating.

Alan's larger mount soon drew even, and then they were pounding along side by side, both grinning and bright-eyed, glancing across to see that they weren't outdistanced, at one in the joy of speed. They did not slow until the horses showed signs of tiring; then they pulled back to a walk to let them breathe. "How well you ride," exclaimed Alan. "I don't know when I've seen a woman handle the reins better."

"I used to ride with my father and brother," she replied, her own breath still coming quickly. "James and I were always trying to outdo each other." Even before her father had gained a fortune, they had somehow found the money for horses.

"I wager he was hard put to better you." Alan smiled, and Miranda found again how very engaging that smile could be.

"He would never say so. Brothers are such exasperating creatures."

"So I am told. I wish I knew first hand."

Remembering his lack of family, Miranda felt a twinge of pity.

"How are they exasperating?" he added with a smile.

"Oh, well... James has always pretended to be martyred by having three sisters. He makes a great fuss about it and plays all sorts of tricks on us."

"Tricks?"

She nodded. "Once when we were on a picnic and Portia left her hat on the grass, James filled it with cockleburs. She didn't see them and put it back on, and they stuck in her hair so badly they had to be cut out. She looked like a badly sheared sheep for months."

Alan laughed. "That does seem a bit...extreme."

"Portia was *furious*. I don't think James realized how bad it would be, but she wouldn't listen. She put itching powder in all his clothes." He laughed again. "Mama and the laundress had a dreadful time getting it out, and James…" She stopped, and giggled at the memory of her brother's frantic wrigglings.

"It sounds to me as if sisters must be quite as exasperating as brothers. Having neither, I cannot judge degrees."

"Well, James and Portia are the greatest jokesters in the family," Miranda told him. "Rosalind and I would never have done such things."

"Certainly not," he agreed with a twinkling sidelong look.

For a frozen instant, Miranda wondered if he knew something of her attempt at disguise, then she dismissed the idea with a shake of her head. Alice had sworn she wouldn't tell, and Miranda didn't believe she would speak to Alan Creighton even if she broke her promise. "Well, we wouldn't."

"You are fortunate to have such a lively family. You must miss them a good deal."

"Yes." Miranda was a little surprised that he would understand that. "I particularly miss the days when we were all still together. We had such fun. But with Rosalind and Portia married and James up at Oxford, that is all over. And next Season I shall be presented."

"And then you will be far too busy to miss anyone," he finished for her.

"Oh no." She turned to look at him. "You have been in town for a Season, have you not? Tell me what it is like."

"Your sisters could tell you better than I," he replied, not meeting her eyes.

"I have asked them, but you must have quite a different view. Did you go to a great many parties?"

"Not so very many." Creighton gazed out over the sea on the left. Now that he had been away from London for a time, he looked back on his conduct there as a regrettable lapse from the standards he strove to uphold. He had allowed self-pity and boredom to undermine his convictions, and done things of which he was now ashamed. Certainly he could not speak of them to a young lady. He found the whole subject of London uncomfortable.

"But you must have attended some? And met the girls coming out?"

"Some." He tried to discourage her with his tone.

But Miranda was not to be diverted, not even by her own annoyance at the man. This was a priceless opportunity to learn what the sophisticated London girls were like and what men thought of them. "Tell me about them."

"Them?" He had been thinking of the money he lost at the gaming tables. It was not more than he could afford. He was not a landed noble like his cousin, but he was comfortably off. It was the way he had behaved—heedless, caring for nothing and no one. He could not understand now how he had let it happen.

"Did I say something wrong?" asked Miranda.

"What?"

"Your face. You looked so…sad, and…sorry. Did I remind you of something painful?" Perhaps he had been jilted in London, Miranda thought. Rosalind had hinted at something before he came. Perhaps he had been in love with one of those polished London misses, and she had refused him. Was he even now nursing a broken heart? Perhaps she had *died*? Somehow, the idea that Alan might be pining for a lost love was not at all pleasant or romantic. On the contrary, it struck her as very stupid and annoying.

"My time in London was not entirely happy," replied Alan.

"Oh." Suddenly, Miranda had no desire to hear more. She did not wish to pry into his private affairs, she told herself. She sat very straight in the saddle.

"It was strange being back among society after so many years at war," he added. "I fear I did not…go on just as I should." Miranda's face was turned away, and Alan reddened slightly when he noticed her averted profile. Of course she was not interested in his lapses. She was very properly indicating that he should keep them to himself. "But what did you wish to know? Oh, the girls. Well, I fear I found them a rather silly, frivolous lot. Couldn't think of anything to say to them. But I have spent too long away from that world, no doubt, and grown clumsy. I'm sure they thought me the veriest oaf. I never became well acquainted with any."

"You didn't?"

"No, nor with any other London women, I fear. So I cannot give an opinion. You should ask Philip that sort of thing." For the first time with Miranda, Alan felt as he had in London—untutored and unpolished, far inferior to men younger than himself who could move easily from the drawing room to the ballroom and bow over a lady's hand with consummate grace.

"But what did you mean then?" Miranda blurted out.

"Mean?"

"About…about not going on as you should?" She was flushed with embarrassment, but too curious to hold her tongue.

"Oh." He hesitated, then found to his surprise that he wanted to tell her. "I fell in with some bad companions. Indulged a bit too freely. I don't excuse myself, but it was rather a change from barracks life."

Miranda turned to him again. This was familiar ground—the romantic hero who has committed excesses, even crimes, in the past but is now repentant. "Did you drink 'blue ruin'?" she asked in a hushed voice.

Alan stared at her, and then gave a great burst of laughter. "Where the deuce did you hear of blue ruin?"

"Well, James told me the name. A friend of his at Eton had an older brother who was not at all the thing, and that is what he did. At least, he may have done other things, too, but that is the only one James would tell me."

"I should hope so indeed. I am beginning to think this brother of yours is a bit of a loose screw."

"He isn't!" Miranda paused and eyed him. "What is a loose screw?"

"Never mind. And do not repeat it before Philip, or Rosalind either, for that matter."

"Is it so wicked?" Miranda grinned at him.

"It is slang, and I don't want them thinking I teach you unsuitable expressions."

"I won't tell them," agreed Miranda, "if you will tell me what is going on here at Clairvon."

She looked at him with wide green eyes. Alan gazed back at her with rueful appreciation. Perhaps he should tell her. She really was a sensible girl. Far more sensible than any girl he had met in London, or anywhere else since he returned from France. And her eyes were really very fine. She could not become involved in the measures he and Philip were taking, of course. She must stay right out of things, as he had told her before. But perhaps she had the sense to see that. He was beginning to think he had underestimated her. "It concerns a set of ruffians from the south," he began.

He was cut off by a sudden sound so familiar that Alan acted without thinking. He lurched for Miranda's arm and pulled her from her horse, leaping himself so that he fell with her to the ground and broke her fall. They rolled there together as the stinging whine was repeated. Alan thrust Miranda into the shelter of a large rock and crouched beside her, one arm still around her shoulders. "Fitch! Look out, man, that's gunfire," he shouted.

From his expression, it was clear the head groom knew precisely what it was. But instead of dismounting, he pulled his horse's head around and spurred it onto the moors in the direction of the shots, urging the animal to a perilous gallop over the uneven ground. "Fitch!" shouted Alan again. But the man gave no sign of hearing.

"Gunfire?" repeated Miranda in a shaken voice. "Hunters?"

"Hardly."

"But…what then?"

Alan Creighton thought he knew. This was a warning from the men he sought to stop. They had discovered something of his efforts, perhaps. Or they merely suspected that he would not let their activities continue unopposed. Possibly, they had never intended their bullets to find a mark, but only that he understand their determination. Alan didn't care. He was filled with a fury such as he had never known in his life—not on the battlefield or in the hands of the surgeons. His grip on Miranda tightened until it hurt. "You are all right?"

"Yes. But who was shooting?" Miranda felt shaky, disoriented.

His thoughts of explaining things to her had vanished. At all costs, she must be kept clear of men such as these. The mere thought of what they had attempted against her today suffused him with murderous rage. Silently, he raised his head a little way above the rock. There was nothing to be seen. Fitch had disappeared over a rise.

"The horses," said Miranda, recovering her composure a little. "How will we get back?" For their mounts had bolted in panic when they leaped off.

Alan merely waved her to silence. He was watching and listening with senses trained in just such situations. Someone was coming.

Fitch re-emerged from the bushes and rode up to them. "I'll catch the horses, sir," he said.

"What did you find?" asked Alan impatiently.

Fitch only shook his head, then wheeled to go after their runaway mounts.

"Damn the man," said Alan between his teeth.

Miranda crouched silently beside him, grateful for his arm on her shoulders. She had regained enough of her wits to understand the warning in those shots, and she was very frightened. This was no game. They might have been killed. Indeed, she supposed that they would have been, if their assailants had wished it. But they had sent a threat first, to force Alan to pull back. Miranda looked up into his face, and saw that he never would. His mouth was grim, his blue eyes hard and merciless. She was shaken suddenly by a terrible fear, and she involuntarily clutched his lapel.

Alan glanced down and, seeing her white face, partly shook off his fury. "It's all right," he said. "They've gone. That sort doesn't stay to face you. Fitch will find the horses, and we'll go home."

Miranda clutched tighter. "Perhaps you should let them be," she exclaimed. "I didn't know…the next time they come upon you they might…" She couldn't voice her fear aloud.

Alan tightened his grip for an instant. "Don't worry. I know how to deal with men like these."

Watching his eyes, Miranda knew that he wouldn't retreat an inch, and that he no longer had any intention of telling her the story. He would march proudly on, just as he had in battle, and never consider his own peril. She felt a pain in her chest, and shuddered again with fear.

"It's all right," he said. "Look, there is Fitch with the horses."

She would have to help him, Miranda concluded. She was badly frightened, but she could not give up when he meant to press on. Perhaps there was nothing she could do; it seemed likely. But she must try. Left to himself, he might be killed the next time. Miranda shuddered again.

Fitch stopped beside them. "There's no one about now, sir," he said. "We'd best be getting back."

Slowly, Alan stood. He waited, one hand holding Miranda down, and gazed all about. There were only the sounds of the sea and the small creatures of the moor. "All right." He helped her up and into the saddle, then mounted quickly himself. "Don't dawdle," he said, a command, and they started off at a canter.

The ride back to Clairvon passed in silence. Alan was lost

in thought, and anger. Miranda had nothing to say. And Fitch stayed well behind, as if he wished to avoid them. When the abbey appeared over a rise, Miranda breathed a sigh of relief and spurred Chara lightly to reach the welcome shelter of the walls. She couldn't shake off a feeling of being spied upon. And the dreadful *consciousness* of danger that seemed to reside between her shoulder blades made her long for her room. When they pulled up before the front door, she jumped down without aid and sprang up the steps. "Aren't you coming?" she asked Alan when he stayed on his horse.

"I shall go to the stables with Fitch," he replied.

"That's all right, sir," said Fitch quickly. "I'll take care of the horses."

"But I wish to speak to you," said Alan, quietly but relentlessly.

Fitch looked far from happy at the idea, but he did not protest further, merely taking Chara's rein and turning toward the stable block.

"Will you be all right?" Alan asked Miranda.

"Yes."

"I think you should not mention this incident to your sister," he added. "There is no need to worry her."

"Yes," she said again, exhausted now and numbed by the aftermath of fear. Alan nodded to her and turned away. Miranda pulled open the door and made her way slowly upstairs.

SEVENTEEN

I HAVE NOT WRITTEN HERE IN MY JOURNAL FOR A WHOLE DAY. Too much has happened, and I did not know how to set it down. Some of the things I wrote at the beginning of my visit seem so cruel and foolish now that I am almost afraid to write, lest I sound just as silly.

Adventures are not what I thought. When you read about some heroine fleeing in the night from a madman, it is quite thrilling and amusing. But, though your heart may pound, it is all sham. You know it will come out all right in the end. She will escape and find the hero and, more than likely, marry.

But real adventures are not like that. You have no idea how they will come out, and you are frightened all the time that something dreadful will happen, that you will walk downstairs for breakfast and be told that someone is hurt or...

How much I admire Alan Creighton! He is a true adventurer. He does not make silly speeches like the heroes in books, but he faces danger as coolly. I don't believe it even occurred to him to draw back after what happened on our ride. He has some plan, and he will carry it through unless he is stopped. I wonder if these men, whoever they are and whatever they are doing, understand that. And, if they do, must they not shoot more accurately next time?

It *is* infuriating that he will tell me nothing. But I begin to understand him better now. He thinks he must protect me. It is almost an instinct with him. And after today I feel some gratitude for that impulse. He is right. He knows more about this sort of thing than I. Yet I feel I could help, if he would allow me. I don't wish to leave him alone in this. The things he said about London worry me. He seems to have a kind of recklessness at times, a joy in the thought of battle that seems dangerous. His shoulder is not entirely healed. And he has no fellow officers here to aid him— only Philip, who is unaccustomed to fighting. I shall not give up my investigations.

Alice wishes me to go with her to a village wedding in my ridiculous disguise. She has some scheme in mind, I can tell, and after the shooting I am uneasy about going. But I shall. If I can find out even the smallest piece of information, it might make the difference. And so I have no choice but to try.

Smuggling. It is smuggling. I should have guessed. I managed to overhear a conversation between that man I saw in the cellar and another like him. There is a ship due in a week with a rich cargo. All the gang will be there to receive it. This must be the time for Alan's plan to go forward. I slipped a note under his door, telling him what I learned without revealing myself. I *could not* go to him, for then I would have had to reveal my disguise and my appearance at the wedding, and he would have been angry with me. Also, I fear he would laugh.

It was quite ridiculous. I had not understood before that a thing can be laughable and frightening at the same time.

I went to the wedding as Alice's beau—not a very impressive one, with my cap over my eyes and smudges on my face—but she didn't care. I found when we had been there a while that I had been brought to rouse jealousy in a certain Eddie Forbes, the nephew of Forbes the butler! I actually had to dance with Alice while he glowered on the sidelines with his arms crossed on his chest. I made a very bad job of it, too. I have never felt so ridiculous in my life, and I was in terror that he would offer to fight me for her favors! Shakespeare's characters did not have such silly misadventures, did they? It never seemed silly when Mama was reading it. It is almost impossible to dance with your head down and your hands in your pockets. Everyone thought I was extremely strange.

When Alice at last let me go, I tried to disappear in the crowd. But everyone stared, and asked all sorts of questions about where I came from and who my family was. I had to leave. It was only by chance that I encountered the two men on my way and managed to eavesdrop. I think I only managed it because they were drunk.

These men are frightening. Hearing them speak, I had no doubt they would do anything to save themselves from discovery. They are not from the village either. They talk quite differently. From things I heard a few villagers say, I believe they are greatly feared. Is this why Philip has done nothing? I suppose it must be. But Alan will not be daunted, and they will kill him if they must. It is terrible!

———————

Jane just came in to do my hair for dinner. She brought me a new tract on the importance of repentance. After all that has happened I felt quite warm toward it. It seemed so homely and familiar, so outside the world of those rough brutal voices at the wedding. I could see she was surprised when I thanked her. Now, I suppose, she will think I am softening and redouble her efforts to convert me. Well, let her.

I must go down to Rosalind. She is getting suspicious. She looked for me while I was at the wedding and came within a hair's breadth of catching me in my disguise. I think she must be feeling suspicious of Philip and Alan, too. She is not stupid, and the air is full of plotting and secrets. I wonder, should I tell her what I have discovered? It would worry her so. And she has just stopped being ill. I don't know what to do. For the present, at least, I suppose I will follow Philip's lead and say nothing to her, though I feel such a sneak keeping things from Rosalind in her own house. Everything is more difficult and complicated than I ever realized.

EIGHTEEN

"I HAVE A DELIGHTFUL PLAN FOR TOMORROW," SAID ROSALIND when the party gathered in the drawing room before dinner. "I have arranged an expedition to Hadrian's Wall. We will start out very early and drive there, stay the night, and then drive back the next day."

"Nonsense," replied Philip. "That is all of thirty miles. It is too far."

"It will take half a day," admitted Rosalind. "But it is such an interesting sight. And Miranda has had so little to do on her visit to us. I know she would like to see it. Alan, too."

"Not if it is too far," said Miranda, understanding now that Philip did not care to expose them to dangers on the roads, and heartily agreeing after her own brush with bullets.

"I'm not much interested in antiquities," admitted Alan.

Rosalind looked from one to the other, and Miranda was certain in that instant that her sister was aware of the undercurrents in the house. "*I* should like to see it," Rosalind said. "You have been telling me for two years what an amazing accomplishment it was, Philip. And yet we have never been there."

"Because it is so far. An exhausting journey, particularly now, when you are…"

"I am extraordinarily well. All the sickness has passed off. I think the outing would do me good."

Miranda wondered then if her sister had concocted this plan to force Philip to confide in her. It was not like Rosalind to be so insistent, and she had not been especially interested in Hadrian's Wall before.

"No," declared Philip. "It is not the time for such a journey." He exchanged a look with Alan.

"Why?" demanded Rosalind.

"I have just told you that…"

"You have *told* me nothing!" Rosalind gazed at each of them in turn again. Miranda hung her head, feeling very guilty. "Unless you can give me a good reason, I intend to go to Hadrian's Wall tomorrow."

Alan looked at Philip. Miranda stole a glance at him under her lashes. Clearly, he was torn. The silence lengthened.

"It is a good distance," said Alan. "Well away from the, er, daily concerns of the estate. And I believe you have no pressing business for a day or so."

Philip looked at him. "No."

"Perhaps it would be good to get away, then. We can always break the journey if it is too long."

"Yes," said Philip slowly. "To get well away. We might take…all right, Rosalind. We'll go."

His wife looked far from pleased at this acquiescence to her wishes. Indeed, she seemed quite put out. But there was nothing more she could say, having been granted her request. Rosalind frowned at her plate in frustration.

The group that set out the next day bore little resemblance to carefree holidaymakers. Rosalind was sulky and Miranda ashamed. Philip and Alan rode beside the carriage but seldom came close enough for speech. And they gave no satisfactory explanation for the three serving men who followed, saying only that they would be a help to the coachman.

The rocks of the coast gave way to forest as they drove southwest. The roads were not direct, and they twisted between rows of great trees with the sun now on the left, now behind. Inside the carriage, the only sounds were the creaking of the wheels and harness, the clop of horses' hooves, and an occasional birdcall from the woods.

At last, Rosalind turned from the window and gazed at Miranda. The younger girl's guilty expression was unmistakable.

"*You* know something, don't you?" accused Rosalind. "Have they told *you* what they are up to?"

"Up to?" echoed Miranda in a high, squeaky voice.

"Philip. And Alan. But Philip mainly." When Miranda said nothing, she added, "I have eyes and ears, Miranda. I see them plotting together and falling silent when I come near." Tears gathered in her blue eyes. "Philip used to tell me everything he was doing. On the estate. Books he read. Now, he scarcely talks to me. And if I ask why, he is impatient and evasive. I don't understand what is wrong, but I cannot bear it any longer." A tear spilled and ran down her cheek.

This was too much for Miranda. She didn't care what Philip thought best; this was her own sister. "It's smugglers," she blurted out.

"What?"

"A gang of smugglers. With leaders from outside the village. Terrible men."

Rosalind digested this. Miranda watched a whole train of thought pass across her face. "Philip told you of this?" she asked finally.

"Oh no. I learned by accident. I overheard a...conversation."

"Ah." Rosalind mused further. "I suppose these men must be very dangerous."

"They lo..." Miranda stopped and merely nodded. She did not intend to reveal the extent of her activities. Rosalind would never approve. The disguise would remain her secret.

"And Philip thinks he is protecting me. While I go nearly mad wondering what is wrong." Rosalind took a deep breath. "I suppose they have some plan. Why not simply inform the authorities?"

"I don't know. I heard only what I told you."

Rosalind's face showed mainly relief now. "Well, no doubt Philip and Alan will know what is best to do."

Miranda didn't think the matter could be dismissed so easily, but she couldn't say so to Rosalind. It would only distress and frighten her. Thus, when her sister turned to lighter topics, she responded, and they said no more about the threat to Clairvon's peace.

At midmorning, the trip began to grow wearisome. To Miranda, it seemed more like her journey north than a pleasant outing. She was tired of the swaying of the carriage and the jolting of the ruts, and the scenery hardly varied. When they stopped for luncheon in Morpeth, Rosalind looked pale, and Miranda began to worry about her. "Are you all right?" she murmured as they walked together into the small inn.

"Only tired," was the quiet reply. "Don't speak of it." And indeed, over cold ham and salad, Rosalind positively sparkled with gaiety. She seemed more like her old self than Miranda had seen her in Northumberland. Philip smiled foolishly at her through the meal, and Alan seemed surprised and charmed. Everyone was in far better spirits when they resumed their journey, and it seemed no time at all until they reached the outskirts of Newcastle and turned west to find the wall.

"We'll stay the night in Newcastle," Rosalind told Miranda. "There will be a good inn there. So you must see all you want of the wall this afternoon. It will be light till nearly ten."

"Do you really want to see it?" asked Miranda.

Rosalind looked self-conscious. "I'm sure it will be very interesting."

"But you only proposed it to tease Philip," added her sister.

Rosalind flushed, then smiled sheepishly. "Well, yes."

"There it is," called Philip from beside the carriage. "An impressive construction."

Miranda stuck her head out. Before them was a tall, thick fortification of ancient gray stone, overgrown with moss and lichen and broken in some places, but still massive. The road ran along it, and they pulled up in the wall's shadow and got down. "A solid job," said Alan, laying his hand on the stone. "Ditched there, too, I think. They had good engineers."

"None better," replied Philip. "The legions pushed back the native tribes this far, then built the wall to hold them. There were forts all along here."

"Must have taken a good number of men," commented Alan.

"It was the border of the empire," said Philip.

Alan laughed. "Then I suppose being sent here was like a posting to Australia. Must have gotten all the men who made a slip of some kind in Rome."

Philip looked nonplussed.

"Would you like to walk a little?" Alan asked Miranda. "Or are you too tired?"

"Oh no. I am so cramped from sitting." She took his arm, and they strolled along the wall, leaving Philip and Rosalind together. For a while they walked in silence. Miranda was surprised that she found this so comfortable. A month ago, she would not have imagined such ease with a man outside her family. But at last her curiosity became too strong. "What did Fitch say?" she asked him.

Alan glanced down at her, disconcerted.

"About the shooting," she prompted. "Did he see anyone?"

Alan hesitated a moment more, then replied, "He said not."

"Really? Or you just do not wish to tell me?"

Again, he examined her face. She was somehow different today, he thought. Her questions held not petulance and childish resentment, but calm inquiry. She seemed older in some way, more steady. He had a sudden desire to confide everything in her, to enjoy her sympathy and to discover her opinion of his plans. But at once he saw this as selfishness. Why should she be burdened with a worry she could do nothing to remedy? For his conviction remained that Miranda should have no contact with the smugglers. "That is what he said," Alan repeated.

Miranda believed him, butshe also believed that there was

more to it than that. Alan's tone implied that he doubted Fitch's story, which meant that Fitch was in league with the gang. He was not among the servants they had brought today, she noted, and she was certain they were present as guards. She wondered how many of the local men were involved. She had not noticed any being particularly friendly with the outsiders at the wedding. "Another mystery, then," she said lightly, almost teasingly. Now that she knew the truth, through her own efforts, she felt much more in charity with Alan.

"Yes." He watched her uncertainly.

"Some sort of silly accident, I suppose?"

"Perhaps."

Miranda laughed, enjoying her small triumph in making him uneasy. He deserved it, for not telling her. She imagined a scene where Philip and Alan at last came to explain, with the smugglers perhaps arrested and the whole matter resolved. Miranda decided she would take it all very coolly. "Oh, yes," she would say. "Taken, are they? That *is* good. Shall we go riding tomorrow?" She would get Rosalind to do the same. That would show them.

"What are you thinking of?" wondered Alan. "You looked frightfully pleased with yourself."

Miranda just shook her head. "Tell me more about the wall," she said.

"I know nothing more. Philip is the scholar." He watched her face, intrigued by this more complex person he now saw. He had admired Miranda's spirit and forthrightness and found her pleasing to look at, but he had not until this moment seen her as a woman. Today, he was charmed by intimations, at least, of the woman she would be.

Miranda was gazing about. A breeze blew wisps of blond hair about her face, under a straw hat tied with pink ribbons. Her gown was pink also, and lent her skin a pretty glow. She looked vibrantly alive as she reached out to touch the great stones of Hadrian's Wall.

"You know," he said, "when you go up to London for the Season, I shall have to go as well."

Miranda turned to stare at him.

"I should like to see you among the fashionables. I think you will make a great hit."

"You do?" Miranda was immensely pleased, and startled.

"Yes. You will be thought most refreshing. And a wit, I daresay."

Miranda's cheeks burned. She had secretly dreamed this might be true, but it was quite different to hear it said aloud, and by a man who had seen something of the world. She nearly clasped her hands before her breast, only drawing back at the last moment. She reached for the kind of sophistication a London wit might have. "You are very kind to say so."

Alan threw back his head and laughed. "Oh yes. You'll do very well indeed. Far better than I did."

"But perhaps you didn't try," Miranda suggested.

He looked surprised. How had she guessed that?

"I'm sure if you wished it, you could be a great success in London." Just in time, she bit off the word *also*. She was not, she reminded herself, the toast of Almack's *yet*.

Alan was thoughtful. "A creditable performance, perhaps," he agreed.

"Will you ask me to stand up with you for the quadrille?" said Miranda.

"No. A country dance, or even a waltz, but I always mistake the figures in a quadrille."

She laughed. "I don't know how to waltz. Mama says I must learn."

"It is simple. Your feet move in a sort of box." He demonstrated, then put one hand at her waist and grasped her fingers with the other. "Like this." But when he looked up from his feet, he met her green eyes just inches away and stopped in embarrassment. Miranda was even more flustered. She had never been so close to a man, so *embraced* by one. And though the sensation was not unpleasant, it was certainly unsettling. Alan was astonished by a sudden desire to gather Miranda even closer and kiss her. The delicate curve of her lips held his gaze transfixed.

He dropped her hand and stepped hastily back. "Well," he said, "you will have better teachers than I."

Miranda took a deep breath, her confusion lessened by his. "But you *will* ask me to dance," she said.

"Of course." His tone was over hearty. "And to go riding in the park at the fashionable hour, where I am a bit more at home."

"It will be so pleasant to know someone in London. Do you *promise* to come?"

Meeting her eyes once again, Alan was filled with a burning desire to reserve all Miranda's dances. "Yes," he replied quite seriously.

"Good." She took his arm again, and they walked on. The sun was moving down the western sky, and the light shone warm and orange. A lark trilled high above.

"I do prefer the country to London, though," said Alan after a time. "You cannot smell new grass or walk under a whole sky in London."

"Do you live in the country?"

"I have a house in Hertfordshire. My parents' house. I haven't been there since…the funeral. The servants are seeing to it."

"It reminds you of them," said Miranda softly.

He nodded, pain in his face. "I knew it would be mine—one day. But not so soon, without warning." He choked a little. He had not had time three years ago to mourn his parents' sudden death. The war had consumed him. And in the last year he had turned away from all feeling.

"What is it like?" said Miranda.

Alan realized that he wanted to tell her, needed to talk about the place. "Not as grand as Philip's castle. It's a Queen Anne house, low and gabled, rambling in all directions. Red brick. There's a splendid rose garden in back. My mother loved roses."

He lost himself in the past. Miranda saw his eyes go far away and slackened her pace to match his lagging step. She imagined losing her parents in a sudden accident, in Rome, and shivered.

Alan started. "I beg your pardon."

"No," she said. "I was just thinking how awful it must have been. I wouldn't go home either." Her eyes burned with suppressed tears.

"Not for a while," he agreed. "But I believe I shall soon. I wish you could see the house."

"I should like to."

He saw the rooms and corridors vividly, and himself escorting a smiling, eager Miranda through them. Longing filled him, and he turned to her, took her hands, and started to speak.

"We'd better go," called Philip from the carriage, and when Alan turned it was as if a spell shattered. What was he thinking of, he wondered as they walked back. This was a girl not yet out. He was the only man she had ever known well, and a guest of her family. He could not take advantage of that. He must keep a greater distance. When they were both in London—and he was more determined than ever to go—that would be the time to think of going further.

Miranda drifted back to the carriage in a happy daze. She had recognized the look in Alan Creighton's eyes, though she had never seen it before, and it had temporarily banished all thoughts of smugglers from her mind. The future suddenly offered new and fascinating possibilities. She was entranced by them all the way back to Newcastle.

NINETEEN

THE RETURN JOURNEY FROM NEWCASTLE WAS UNEVENTFUL. The Clairvon party reached home again at three in the afternoon, and dispersed. Miranda ran upstairs at once and burst into her room, flinging her shawl and bonnet onto the bed. She was opening her writing desk when Jane Jenkins appeared around the open wardrobe, frowning at her over a pile of fresh ironing. "You're back then," said the maid.

Miranda jumped, quickly shut her journal, and replaced it in the desk. "Yes."

"The laundress got the tea stain out of your pink muslin." Jenkins disappeared behind the wardrobe door again to put away the clean clothes.

"Oh. Oh, good," said Miranda. She fidgeted a little, waiting for the woman to finish and leave.

"No way to treat your hat," the maid added, reappearing and picking up Miranda's things from the bed. "It'll be crushed, likely as not, lying there. Neatness is next to godliness, you know."

"I thought it was cleanliness," Miranda couldn't help replying.

"One and the same," was the confident answer. "Shall I lay out your blue for dinner, miss?"

"No. Never mind. I can do it." Miranda nearly stammered in her eagerness to be left alone.

Jane Jenkins's long, dour face grew even longer. "Not at all, miss. It's my job to help you, as her ladyship asked. The blue?"

"Yes, all right."

"And then, perhaps, I'll do your hair? It's a bit…untidy from your traveling." The maid looked at Miranda's efforts with her hair as if they were the work of the devil.

"No!"

Jenkins stared at her.

"I mean, I want to...to lie down for a while. I'm tired."

"All this driving about from one end of the county to the other." Jenkins nodded as if she had predicted it. "And the Lord knows how her ladyship will be feeling. But there's no time for me to come back before I go to her." She picked up the hair brush and gazed at Miranda with implacable purpose.

Exasperated, Miranda darted around her, snatched her shawl from the bed, and fled. She was at the end of the corridor before Jenkins called after her, and she ignored the maid's scandalized exclamation and ran down the stairs and through the hall, throwing her shawl around her shoulders as she pulled the great front door open.

Miranda had longed to be alone for the last day, since her walk with Alan had been ended by their return to Newcastle. In the close confines of the inn and the carriage, she couldn't think properly about what had happened. She had most wanted to set it all down in her journal, but denied that, she was happy to walk along the gravel drive in solitude and muse on this new thing that had come into her life.

She had often imagined, of course, the meeting between herself and her future mate. She had seen it as rather like the scenes in her favorite novels. She would be in some desperate strait, and he would appear just as her fate seemed sealed and carry her away. She knew, naturally, that she was not likely to be pursued by mad monks or homicidal uncles. Her only uncle was a very quiet gentleman who farmed a small estate in Lincolnshire. But there were other perils open even to a modern miss with no madness in the family.

Yet it had not been that way at all. She had been introduced to Alan in the most conventional way and not realized for the longest time that he would be more than an ordinary acquaintance. And then, yesterday... Miranda sighed as she remembered the look in his eyes when he spoke of dancing together in London. In that instant, she understood that love had little to do with fleeing on horseback through haunted marshes or forcing oneself to walk through a chamber lined with skulls. It had a quiet, undramatic power that made it more thrilling than any of those things. And it was capable, in unmarked silence, of turning one's life upside down.

When she once again noticed her surroundings, Miranda was outside the park on the cliffs north of the abbey. She had been walking quite fast, and she was a good way along the path. It had been a dreary, gray day, with short spatterings of rain as they drove home, and now, in late afternoon, there was a mist rising from the sea to catch in the clefts and hollows of the coast. Miranda pulled her shawl tighter about her shoulders and started to turn back. She might have half an hour before dinner to write in her journal, she thought. Surely Jane would be gone by now.

But as she turned, a low dark shape in the shadowed ravine ahead caught her eye. It was the abandoned house she had found on her first walk near Clairvon, and it was deathly quiet. The dog that had guarded the door was gone, or at least invisible from this distance.

Miranda hesitated. She didn't want to go down there, really. The place looked sinister and threatening, and she certainly did not want to meet any of the smugglers. On the other hand, if she could find out anything more about their plans by examining the house when it was empty, she could not throw away the opportunity. It was even more important now that nothing befall Alan. She intended to tell him all she knew tonight, as soon as they could be apart from the others—omitting only the disguise she had used to find it out. But perhaps the house held some vital clue?

Slowly, reluctantly, Miranda moved down the slope toward the house. The path was screened by bushes, and she stopped frequently to listen for signs that the place was inhabited after all. But there was nothing, only the hiss of the surf and the soughing of the light wind that drove the clouds.

At last she reached the edge of the open area around the house. Here, she strained her ears for several minutes, almost hoping to hear something that would send her scurrying home. The air was murky in the shadow of the cliffs, but she could not see anything suspicious. Finally, she stepped out of the bushes and stared at the tumble-down walls. Nothing.

Her heart pounding, fists clenched at her sides, she strode forward, around the corner of the building and straight up to the sagging door. If anything was going to happen, she told herself, she wanted to know right away.

But nothing did. The ancient cottage remained silent. No mastiff surged forward to attack her. No rough voice asked her business. Taking a deep breath, Miranda went inside.

It was even darker within the walls. She paused a moment, blinking, trying to see. There was the dog's collar and rope. He had been untied and taken away. Beyond, the house was one large room whose peaked ceiling was the roof. A hole in the slates in one corner let in more light, and she could see that the place was filled with large wooden packing crates. This must be the smugglers' spoils.

She went to the nearest and tried to open it, but it was nailed securely shut. So were the second and third she examined, but the fourth yielded to her tugging and revealed rows of bottles packed in straw. She was struggling to open a fifth when she heard voices outside.

Miranda froze. They were coming closer, and they were male. It was unlikely to be anyone but the smugglers. She gazed frantically around the room. There was nowhere to hide, and only one way out. If she fled through the door she would be seen and questioned. Miranda considered trying to brazen it out, telling them she had just wandered in on a walk, curious about the place. But then she remembered the shots. Men who would risk that would not let her simply walk away. She looked around again.

At the back of the room was a crate with the lid half off. She ran to it and found that it was empty. The voices were nearly at the door. Panicked, Miranda gathered up her skirts and climbed into the crate, easing the lid into place over her head. As it dropped silently down, cutting off even the dim light of the house, she heard heavy footsteps enter.

"See," said a gravelly contemptuous voice. "All's well."

Another man merely growled in reply.

"Stow it," said the first. "We've had our drink, and no harm. Let's finish up so's I can get moving."

"And *I'm* stuck here for the night," complained the other. "If you hadn't done for the dog…"

"How was I to know the cursed thing would die from a kick? It was a surly, dirty creature any road."

"Bill's not got over…"

"The devil take Bill, and you, too! Where'd you leave that hammer?"

Miranda listened in terror as they stumbled about the room and then began to hammer at something. It took her a few minutes to realize that they were securing the lids of the crates not yet nailed down. It was all she could do not to cry out then. But she was too afraid to burst out of the crate and try for the door.

After a time, they came to her hiding place. Their legs brushed the wood on either side, inches from her shoulders, and she had to press her hands over her lips when they shook the lid to settle it more firmly. Then came the pounding and vibration of the nails, two on each side, trapping her completely.

"That's got it," said the second man then. "They're ready for the ship. I suppose as much will be coming off it, too. It's all loading and unloading, and then loading again, this crib."

"And money. Don't forget that, Dick Townshend. More money than you'd see in a year in London."

"Maybe. I had a job coming up that…"

"Ahh, don't give me that." Footsteps retreated. "I'm off, then."

"What's your hurry? I've got a bit left in that bottle. Come to that, we might slip open one of these boxes and pull out some good Scotch whiskey."

"Jem'll skin you alive for that," replied the first man. "And I ain't sitting here in the damp. You got the watch, fair and square." The only response was a growl. One set of footsteps retreated and were soon lost in the sound of the surf.

Miranda heard the remaining man moving around for a while, and then a sigh as he settled near the door and uncorked his bottle. "Bloody Jem," she heard him mutter. She crouched in the crate, her knees drawn up nearly to her chin and her head bent. She could rest her head on her knees; otherwise she could not change position. But this discomfort seemed negligible beside what she had heard. These crates were to be shipped out. If she could not escape, she would be sent across the channel without any means of getting home. Yet if she began pounding on the wood and demanded to be let out, she might well be killed. Tears welled in her eyes, and she clenched her teeth and blinked to banish them.

There must be something she could do, if she could only think of it.

TWENTY

ROSALIND CAME DOWN TO DINNER A LITTLE LATE THAT EVENING, for she had fallen asleep on their return from Newcastle, worn out from traveling. She found Philip and Alan waiting for her, leaning on the mantel side by side and talking earnestly together. They fell silent when she entered, but Rosalind merely smiled. "Where is Miranda?" she asked them.

"We thought, perhaps, she was coming down with you," answered Alan.

"I haven't seen her since we returned." Rosalind went to the bell rope and rang. When Forbes appeared, ready to announce dinner, she said, "Would you send someone to fetch Miss Miranda, please?" He went out again. Rosalind smiled. "It is not like Miranda to be late to dinner. Perhaps she fell asleep, too."

But Forbes returned to say that Miranda was not in her room, and had not been seen by any of the servants since midafternoon.

"That's odd," said Rosalind. "She told me she wanted to sit in her room. She was very eager to be alone."

Philip and Alan exchanged a concerned glance. "Perhaps she is exploring the house?" said Philip.

"Or has gone for a walk?" added Alan. "I'll look in the park."

"We will search the house, my lord," said Forbes.

Rosalind looked from one grim face to another, puzzled. Then she remembered the news Miranda had given her. "You don't think something has happened to her?" she cried. What, she thought, would smugglers want with Miranda?

"No, no," replied Philip hastily. "Come along, Forbes."

The three men went out together. "Have you heard something?" said Philip to Forbes then, his voice harsh.

"No, sir. But they tell me nothing now. I am not trusted."

"Do they suspect our plan?" snapped Alan, his fear making him sharp. "Could they have taken her as hostage?"

"I have no reason to believe so, sir," was Forbes's reply. "Everything seems much as usual except that I am no longer told anything important, since I objected to their plans some time ago."

"She might have gone walking," offered Philip. "She often does."

"I'll look outdoors," said Alan curtly, turning on his heel.

"Dinner—" began Forbes, and Alan cut him off.

"Blast dinner!"

There was a silence as Alan walked away.

"I was only going to say, my lord, that dinner can be held for as long as necessary."

Philip nodded. "We'd best check the house."

Rosalind sat in the drawing room twisting her hands in her lap. She could not really believe that something had happened to her sister, and yet Philip and the others had been so worried. And they knew far more about the situation than she, or Miranda. Perhaps there was more, much worse, that she had no idea of? Rosalind frowned, then rose and went to the door. There was no one about, and she could not hear voices. She didn't wish to ring and perhaps interrupt the search, but at least she could join it. She started for the stairs to the third floor.

An hour later, Philip, Rosalind, and Alan again stood in the drawing room. "If she is in the park, she is unconscious," said Alan. "I shouted everywhere."

"She is not in the house," added Philip. "Not even the cellars."

"Or the attics," agreed Rosalind. Her voice rose. "Where can she be?"

"We'll find her," insisted Alan, but his face was as pale as hers.

"Do you think the smugglers might have taken her for some reason?" Rosalind raised her chin when the two men turned to stare at her. "Miranda told me about them. We are not idiots, you know."

"Miranda told you!" Alan Creighton put a hand to his forehead.

"What has she been up to? God knows where she might have gone to 'investigate.'"

"Do we call it off tonight?" asked Philip, his shock at his wife's revelation lost in the greater worry. "I'll have to send word soon."

"Wait. Let me think." Alan began to pace. His forehead creased with the effort of thinking logically when he wanted only to rush out with his saber and attack the villains. "If they were holding her," he said slowly, "they would have sent word—some threat or demand."

"They wouldn't just…" Philip stopped, unable to voice *that* fear. Rosalind went even whiter.

"I don't think so. Why take such a risk? It is one thing to shoot from concealment, and well over your target's heads. It is quite another to…" His knuckles whitened as he clenched his fists. "No."

"But then where is she?" wailed Rosalind.

"She might have had an accident," Alan replied. "Perhaps she did go walking and fell. Or she may be poking about on her own. I hope to God she isn't!"

"Do we call it off?" repeated Philip.

Alan hesitated. "No," he said. "Not unless we get some message from them. Conditions are right tonight. We don't know when we will have another opportunity."

"What are you going to do?" asked Rosalind apprehensively.

"Take the smugglers," said Philip. "When they are all together and actually breaking the law. We got a few of them on our side and discovered there is a ship tonight. Alan spoke to the soldiers at Lindisfarne, and they communicated with the excisemen. They will start to gather secretly nearby in an hour. We'll have a good-sized band at our backs."

"And Miranda?" Rosalind looked from her husband to Alan.

"We will search for her until the time of the raid," said Alan. "If they have her, they will surely tell us, and we will call it off, of course." He gritted his teeth at the idea of Miranda in their hands. "If she is carrying out some plan of her own…"

"She wouldn't be late for dinner unless something was wrong," said Rosalind, "She wouldn't want us to know if it was some prank; she would come home."

This was too obviously true to be debated. An unhappy silence fell on the group.

"We'll search," said Philip finally, and laid a hand on Alan's arm. The latter nodded. "I'll fetch the stablemen," added Philip. "You get Forbes and Jenkins."

"Can't I help?" asked Rosalind, but her husband shook his head. She watched them go out. This was intolerable. They couldn't actually expect her to sit here and simply wait. She knew Miranda better than any of them. Indeed, it was this latter fact that caused her the most worry. She *did* know Miranda, and she was certain she was in trouble. Miranda was agile as a goat. She didn't trip and hit her head on a sedate country walk. And when she did fall, she was up again in a moment. She had given their mother heart palpitations more than once with her antics. Moreover, she was relentlessly inquisitive and supremely confident of her own powers. She *would* spy on smugglers and think herself quite clever to do so. Hadn't she found out things Rosalind had never even suspected? But unless she was in trouble, she wouldn't let her escapades keep her from home when she was expected. Thus, Rosalind had to conclude, she *was* in trouble.

Rosalind reexamined Alan Creighton's assumption that if the smugglers had captured Miranda, they would try to use her to their advantage. It still seemed likely. They must know that Philip would be working against them. Miranda would be a perfect weapon to guarantee that he would stop.

So—Rosalind breathed a deep sigh—they would not just kill her if she stumbled into their way. There was a chance. But what could she do? She sat down, trying to compose her mind. Surely her knowledge of Miranda could help somehow? The clock on the mantel chimed eight. A candle fluttered in a sudden draft.

Rosalind's head came up, and she stared at the opposite wall for a long moment, then rose and hurried out of the room.

In the kitchen, she found Cook, Alice, and Jane Jenkins in solemn colloquy over the oven. They didn't see her at first, and she had to clear her throat to get their attention. All three jumped. "Oh, my lady!" said Alice. "You scared me half to death, you did."

"I'm sorry," said Rosalind. "I wanted to speak to you."

The cook spoke. As usual, Rosalind could make nothing of her heavy accent, except that she was not pleased.

"Mrs. MacCrory says the chicken is spoilt," translated Alice. "It's all dried out. She says you can only keep a chicken warm for so long."

"It doesn't matter," replied Rosalind. "I don't think anyone is going to eat tonight."

Cook spoke again.

"She says you should have a bite yourself, my lady. To keep your strength up," said Alice.

"In a moment, perhaps. I wanted..." But her words overlapped Mrs. MacCrory's more vehement pronouncement.

"She says you can't neglect yourself at a time like this," continued Alice with relish. "Eating for two, and all."

"Very well! Fix me a plate. But I want to speak to you, Alice."

"Me?" The kitchenmaid gazed at her apprehensively. It was one thing to convey the cook's decided remarks—she rather enjoyed that—it was quite another to have to speak on her own.

"Yes. You know that my sister Miranda is missing?"

Grimacing, Alice nodded.

"They are out searching for her now, but I thought you might be able to help."

"Me?" repeated Alice, in an even more worried tone. She started to twist her hands in her apron.

"You. Miranda talked with you now and then, didn't she? Perhaps she said something, or asked you questions, that might tell us where she went tonight."

"No, my lady," answered Alice. "I don't know nothing about it." But the guilty expression on her face made Rosalind doubt her.

"About where she is now, you mean?"

"Yes, my lady."

"But you do know something, Alice. That is plain. And you must tell me."

"I...I don't," the maid protested. But her eyes shifted like a cornered rabbit's.

Rosalind waited.

"She made me promise never to tell!" wailed Alice at last. "I swore I wouldn't."

Rosalind nodded. "You should keep your word," she agreed. "Unless there is an emergency, as there is now. Miranda may be hurt, you know, or in trouble. You might know something that would allow us to find her. So you can't keep that to yourself, can you?"

"N-no, my lady." Alice looked utterly woebegone. "But it weren't my fault, what she did. I just saw her, and then, when I realized it was Miss Miranda, I couldn't keep still, and she made me promise..."

"Yes, Alice. It's all right. I won't blame you. Just tell me the whole story, from the beginning."

The kitchenmaid gulped, and said, "I was coming home from my mother's, on my day out, and I saw this boy running around the corner. Leastways, I *thought* it was a boy, and then he came closer, and it was Miss Miranda."

"What do you mean?"

"She was wearing some of the master's old clothes, my lady, so as to look like a boy. I knew her right away, but nobody else in the village did, on account of not seeing her before."

Jane Jenkins gasped and clasped her hands as if in prayer. The cook looked mildly scandalized and deeply interested. Rosalind wished she had taken Alice upstairs to question her. "The master's clothes," she repeated faintly.

"Old ones," Alice assured her, "from when he was a boy. She had a cap, too, and she looked ever so different. I couldn't believe my eyes at first."

"I daresay." Rosalind took a breath. "Did she...say why she was dressed so?"

Alice looked doubtful. "Well, she *said* it was a joke, but I didn't see how it could be." She looked self-conscious. "I didn't think it was my place to ask questions."

"The devil's work," murmured Jane, shaking her head.

"Did she go out that way more than once?" wondered Rosalind.

"Oh, yes, my lady. She went to Corrie Phelps's wedding with me."

"Did she indeed?" Rosalind sat down in one of the kitchen chairs. If Miranda were wandering the countryside dressed as a boy, the smugglers might have her without knowing her identity. And they might do anything. Rosalind looked up. "What do you know about the smugglers, any of you?"

Alice's face went stony. Mrs. MacCrory pursed her lips. Only Jane Jenkins spoke. "Smugglers, my lady?" she said. "You don't mean that idiot Rob Hartley has started his nonsense again? I thought he learned his lesson twenty years ago."

"It isn't..." began Alice angrily, then stopped.

"I see that you do know," said Rosalind. She looked from one face to another. "Perhaps too well. Perhaps some of your family is involved, Alice? Friends of yours, Mrs. MacCrory?"

"None of mine," declared Jane.

"You don't have any friends," declared Alice. "Not with the way you're always threatening them with hellfire."

"I pass on the Lord's word. Those that don't like..."

"Never mind," interrupted Rosalind, with uncharacteristic heat. "Listen to me, Alice. There will be trouble tonight for the smugglers. I know that. Help me find Miranda, and I will do what I can for your friends."

Alice's struggle showed in her face. "I can't," she said finally. "I can't tell, my lady."

Rosalind understood. This was her family now. She nodded, and threw caution to the winds. "There will be a raid tonight," she told them. "All the smugglers will be caught and sent to jail. Your friends, too."

Alice turned white. Mrs. MacCrory sat down heavily in the rocking chair beside the hearth.

"Serve them right, too," declared Jane Jenkins.

Alice started to leap at her, and Rosalind stepped between. "I've got to go," said Alice, and turned the other way.

Rosalind gripped her arm. "I can't let you go, Alice."

"My brother!"

The two women stared at each other, eyes only four inches apart. Rosalind held on, and, after a while, Alice slumped and collapsed. "I can't let him go to jail," she said, sniffing back tears. "You can't make me."

"Are many of the village men smuggling?" asked Rosalind quietly. Alice didn't answer, but Mrs. MacCrory nodded. When she added a sentence, Rosalind looked to Alice.

The girl seemed broken, but she translated. "It's not them leading. There's some outsiders. Two of them came in the spring, full of ideas and promises of gold. People listened. And then more came, and more. I don't know how many there are now, but they're running things. And if anybody tries to quit, they threaten him. Eddie Forbes tried." Alice looked desolate. "And now it's too late."

"Perhaps not," said Rosalind. The others turned to stare at her. "Couldn't we warn just *some* of them? Your brother. Forbes's nephew."

"They'd all hear," said Alice. "You couldn't help it." She frowned. "I'd like to see that Jem in jail, I would! He's a pig."

Rosalind thought. "If we could think of some warning that only your friends would understand," she said. "Because those villains must be caught." She had a momentary flash of guilt as she thought of Philip. He would be furious if he could hear her now.

Alice was shaking her head. "Anything we say, they'll…" Then she stopped as if surprised by something, and turned slowly to look at Mrs. MacCrory.

"What is it, Alice?" said Rosalind.

"Those Londoners don't believe Mrs. MacCrory has the Sight," replied Alice slowly. "That Jem, he laughs at me whenever he sees me since I told him about it. Asks if I've seen any ghosts lately, and the like." She looked as if she might spit. "Pig."

"How does that help?" Rosalind gazed at her.

"Well, what if we told them Mrs. MacCrory had a vision?" Alice chewed her lower lip. "Of disaster, like, on the run tonight?" She warmed to the subject. "Maybe one of them tie-foons. Or a sea serpent! The village men'd listen, most of them, and they'd hang back. But those high-and-mighty Londoners wouldn't."

"But wouldn't they force our men to go?" wondered Rosalind.

Alice scoffed. "They'd *try*. But it's harder to bully folks in the dark, on the moors." She frowned. "You're sure they'll be taken? Because if they come back, and…"

"I'm sure," said Rosalind, and said a brief prayer that Philip's plan was successful.

"Well, then." Alice looked hopefully at her.

"Are you willing, Mrs. MacCrory?" asked Rosalind. The cook simply smiled a broad, delighted smile, and Rosalind smiled back. "It will certainly increase your reputation," she added. The cook threw back her head and laughed.

"We'll go right away," said Alice, untying her apron. "It'll be nearly time."

"I'm going with you," Rosalind told her.

All three servants looked aghast. "My lady!" cried Jane Jenkins. "You cannot expose yourself to these…"

"Either I go," said Rosalind, "or no one does." Before they could object again, she added, "I shall be disguised, of course. I'll wear one of your old dresses, Mrs. MacCrory. And a bonnet to hide my face." Alice gaped, openmouthed. "We are still looking for Miranda, you know." Rosalind was adamant. "Indeed, I am mainly looking for Miranda. And you must help me, as I have helped you."

"I'll have no part of this sinful game," insisted Jenkins.

"No, Jane, of course not. You will stay here and do what is necessary to make it appear we are here, too."

Jane opened her mouth to protest again, but Rosalind silenced her with a look.

Alice started to laugh, a bit hysterically. "It's plain you're sisters, is all I can say. My lady."

"Of course we are." Rosalind smiled. "Shall we get ready?"

TWENTY-ONE

MIRANDA WAS FEELING SICK. THE CRATE IN WHICH SHE WAS trapped was swaying in the grip of two men who occasionally tripped or jostled it in a way that made her stomach lurch and her head crack painfully against the wood. She longed to cry out in fear and frustration and beat her fists on the sides of the crate, but she couldn't make the slightest sound. She was deathly afraid she was about to be put on a ship to France, yet she was even more afraid of her captors and what they would do if they discovered her.

"They're all stinking heavy," said one of the men who carried her.

"This is the last. We can get some dinner before the boat comes."

"Aye. Let bloody Jem and his lads guard their precious boxes till then. I'm for a pint, myself."

"I'm with you."

They lowered the crate to the earth, dropping it the last four inches so that Miranda cracked her elbow agonizingly. She managed not to cry out, but one of the men said, "What was that? Do you think we broke a bottle?"

"Who cares?" said the other.

"Jem will, and that Frog captain, when they check the merchandise."

"Blast 'em both. They'll have no way of knowing who carried this box."

"Eh. That's right, I guess."

"Let's get out of here."

Miranda heard their footsteps retreat. She rubbed her elbow as she contemplated a new danger. The smugglers would check their cargo. She hadn't thought of that. So she would not be going to France, at least. But she would be caught soon unless she could do something.

She retrieved the small piece of wood she had found in the bottom of the crate after she was nailed inside. It was narrow enough to fit between the lid and the wall, but not strong enough to pry them apart without breaking. She had been carefully working with it throughout her captivity, loosening the lid a tiny bit in one place, and then another. One corner was showing promising signs of giving.

Lantern light shone through the narrow cracks in the sides of the crate, and Miranda froze.

"They're all here?" asked a rough voice she almost recognized.

"Every one. How long?"

"An hour, mebbe. Longer. Where are all our fine village lads?"

It was the man from the cellar, the one who had threatened Forbes, Miranda realized. Alice had told her at the wedding that his name was Jem Peters, and what she had heard since made her think he was the leader of the smugglers.

"Getting supper, likely," replied the second man.

"Likely," echoed Jem with contempt. "Whining numbskulls."

"What's that noise?"

Miranda listened, but heard nothing through the crate.

"Douse the lantern, idiot!" hissed Jem, and the light disappeared. "Down." There was a rustling in the bushes as the two men hid.

And then Miranda heard it. It was a voice calling her name—Henry Jenkins's voice, she thought. She pressed her forehead against the side of the crate and bit her lower lip. Tears of frustration gathered in her eyes. If only she could answer him! But his calls were faint and far off. He might not hear, and Jem and his friend certainly *would*. She would be found and silenced long before Jenkins could do anything. His voice faded in the distance.

"What's up?" muttered Jem savagely.

"A girl lost from the abbey. Baron's sister."

Jem swore. "On this night, of all nights," he said, then paused. "Still, it'll keep him busy, won't it? And that army friend of his, too. Won't be up to no tricks if they're hunting a girl. Just keep them away from here."

They moved away, and Miranda strained to catch even an echo of her name. But there was nothing. After a while, she started working with her small board again. It really did seem to be doing some good. As long as she was very careful, she might actually be able to pry off the lid. If, she thought, she had enough time. Time would be her main problem from here. She pushed the wood into the widest crack and worked it back and forth, then moved it three inches to the left and wiggled it again; then three inches to the right. A nail creaked, and she stopped, but there was no response. No light showed through the crate. She went back to work.

TWENTY-TWO

PHILIP MET ALAN AT THE GATES OF CLAIRVON ABBEY AT NINE thirty. "Any sign?" he asked.

Alan shook his head. He looked years older than he had just days ago walking along the road beside Hadrian's Wall. "She seems to have disappeared into thin air."

"The men have begun to arrive. Are you sure you want to go ahead?"

Wearily, Alan nodded. "There's no reason we know of not to. If it turns out they do have her, we'll draw back. But they *can't*, Philip. I know this kind of man, this Jem. He'd use her against us."

Philip simply nodded. There was nothing more he could say. "Will you speak to the men?"

"Yes."

They walked together out onto the moor until they came to a shed with a broken-backed roof well away from the road. It was one of the estate's outbuildings, but it had not been used for years, even by the smugglers, and they had chosen it as a meeting place for their raid tonight. Inside, by the meager light of a half-closed dark lantern, stood six soldiers and three excisemen. All of them drew to attention when they saw Alan and Philip.

"The rest will be here within half an hour," the lieutenant in charge of the Lindisfarne garrison told them. "We've been coming in over the moor by two and threes, well wrapped up so no one will notice the uniforms."

"Good. We're nearly ready, then. The gang will be loading in a cove just north of here. There's a small half-ruined house in it. You can recognize the place by that, should you get separated from the group. But try not to. We need to attack these ruffians in force. The leaders are the worst kind of villain."

The men nodded. "Half down one side of the valley, half down the other?" said the lieutenant.

"That's right. And everyone quiet until you hear the signal. We want to get as many as we can. Go slowly. Make no noise. We'll have time."

"Ay," said one of the excisemen, rubbing his hands together. "We'll get them this time. Think they're so clever."

Philip looked at him with distaste, then turned back to Alan. "The villagers," he whispered. "Isn't there any way...?"

"Not to separate them without alerting the others," murmured Alan in reply. "I'm sorry."

Philip sighed. He wanted the smuggling stopped, but he hated the thought of villagers he knew going to jail. They had tried to come up with a plan that might spare them, but there was always the chance that word would get to the leaders, and that would be fatal. Most of all, he did not want those men loose and eager for revenge on him and his family.

Two more men slipped in and pushed back cloaks to reveal army uniforms. "Anyone see you?" asked the lieutenant sharply.

"No, sir. We came cross the moor, like you said."

"Right."

They waited. A group of three men entered, and, five minutes later, two more. "That's it," the lieutenant informed them, and Philip nodded.

"You're all armed?" asked Alan, and received nods and indications of weapons in return. "Shoot only if you must," he said. "We don't want unnecessary killing."

The eager exciseman laughed, and Alan turned to glare at him. "I mean it."

The man's grin faded.

"Let's go," Alan added.

"What about Miranda?" Philip whispered to him. "Shouldn't you mention her?" He drew back at the sight of Alan's face, so grim and stony he hardly knew him.

But Alan nodded. "There's a girl missing," he told the men. "Lady Highdene's sister. We don't think the smugglers have her, because they've sent no message. But keep an eye out."

"What's she look like?" asked the lieutenant practically.

Alan nearly choked.

"Blond," put in Philip. "Above medium height. Slender. Wearing a sprig muslin gown, we believe."

They all took this in. Alan, recovered, signaled with a gesture that they should move, and they filed out in silence to melt into the misty evening.

TWENTY-THREE

"How do I look?" asked Rosalind, turning once around. When she faced them again, two of her servants were trying not to laugh at her, and the other was glaring disapprovingly, arms crossed on her thin chest. "Do you think I'll be recognized?"

"No, my lady," Alice choked out. Mrs. MacCrory's eyes twinkled almost maniacally.

Rosalind wore the cook's second-best black dress, an old-fashioned gown with long sleeves and a high neck trimmed with black velvet. The fit was poor, but not disastrous, as Mrs. MacCrory had gained in girth since the dress was made and Rosalind was increasing. With it she wore a black hat that even the cook had put aside. Its straw was disintegrating, and the black feathers on the crown were dusty and shedding. But it boasted a veil that hid Rosalind's features and bright hair, and she was not interested tonight in looking smart.

Mrs. MacCrory spoke, and Alice giggled before she translated. "She says we won't introduce you at all. Everyone will think you're the very spirit of death and disaster standing at her shoulder." She giggled again.

Rosalind smiled behind her veil. "A splendid idea. Shall we go?"

"No good will come of this blasphemous masquerade," declared Jane Jenkins. "My lady, it's not my place to say so, but you should be ashamed. Dressed like a…"

"Just make it appear that all is as usual here," said Rosalind. "We will be back before long." And gathering Alice and the cook with a gesture, she led them out the kitchen door and into the stableyard. The pony trap was awaiting them there, harnessed at Rosalind's orders before she changed.

"Where are we going?" asked Rosalind when they had all squeezed in. She took up the reins and got the vehicle moving.

"They'll be at the alehouse," said Alice. "Most of them, anyway. We'd best hurry. They'll be leaving for…they'll be going soon."

Rosalind urged the horse to a trot. As they drove, she thought of something. "Alice."

"Yes, my lady?"

She wasn't sure how to ask her question. "Will everyone be able to…will they know what Mrs. MacCrory is saying?"

Both the other women laughed. "Most of us here have a little Gaelic, my lady," responded Alice. "We have relatives in Scotland, and all. It's only the southerners who can't understand."

"Then the ringleaders won't know what you're saying," concluded Rosalind happily.

Alice shrugged. "Someone'll tell them. But it won't matter. They think countrymen are all fools." She sniffed.

"Which is the alehouse?" They were approaching the village, a huddle of dark shapes against the curve of the moor.

"Turn there. We'd better hide the trap first."

Alice guided her into a narrow lane between two houses, and Rosalind took her direction gratefully. She wouldn't have thought of hiding the carriage, she realized.

"If someone saw us, I'll tell them I ordered the trap myself, on account of the emergency," added Alice as they climbed down. "They might have watchers out, though I expect they'd be nearer the…the sea." She helped Mrs. MacCrory down, and the three of them set off along the village street.

There was a dim light filtering through thin curtains outside the house that served as tavern and meeting place. A murmur of voices could be heard through the wooden door, but this did not prepare Rosalind for the smoke and noise when Alice swung it open. The small room was filled with village men and a few outsiders, lit by smoky lamps and a sullen fire. In the ruddy light, the men's faces gleamed, and the tankards they held shone copper bright. When the door opened, they fell silent and stared in a way that made Rosalind want to step back. Tonight, at least, there was not a woman in the place.

"Alice!" said a young man not much older than the kitchen-maid. As he strode forward, Rosalind saw that they looked very much alike. "What are you doing here, girl?"

"I had to speak to you, Tom." Alice stepped quickly inside, drawing the others with her. She took Tom's arm and pulled him into a corner.

"Not now," he hissed. "Alice, you know tonight's…" He broke off, glancing sidelong at her companions.

"That's why I had to come. You remember Mrs. MacCrory." Alice looked at Cook. "My brother Tom, ma'am."

Both of them nodded, Tom impatiently. Rosalind noticed that several of the men nearby were listening without seeming to. She bent her head in the dim corner and left things to Alice.

"This is no time…" Tom was beginning, when his sister interrupted him.

"Mrs. MacCrory has had a *vision*," she said, in a voice that seemed a whisper but carried well beyond their little circle. "About tonight!"

Tom fell silent. He looked doubtful but uneasy. Other men were giving up the pretense of not listening and leaning forward.

"She *saw*," added Alice portentously. "I had to come and warn you."

Mrs. MacCrory nodded, her expression serious, her blue eyes bright. They had decided it would be more effective if Alice told their tale while she looked on.

"Saw?" echoed Tom. Other men exchanged glances.

"Something terrible is going to happen tonight," Alice intoned. "An awful disaster." She shook her head, and Rosalind had to hide a smile. Alice should have gone on the stage. "Death," Alice added. "She smells death in the air."

A hush fell over their corner of the room.

"Death and destruction," continued Alice. "Homes without their fathers and brothers. Weeping and wailing." She clutched Tom's sleeve again. "Oh, Tom. I had to come and tell you."

Her brother looked bewildered, and uneasy. "But what's it about? What's going to happen?"

Mrs. MacCrory spoke at last, briefly.

"Of course the Sight's not like that," Alice agreed. "It doesn't show you everything. If it did, Cook would win all the pools."

This drew a few smiles.

"But it does give warning," Alice went on. "You can't go out tonight, Tom. Stay home!" She clung to his arm, gazing up into his face with real fear and pleading.

The latter impressed Tom as much as the story, but he shook her off and stepped back. "I can't do that, Alice," he whispered fiercely. "You know what they'd do."

"But, Tom, something's going to go awfully wrong." The raw emotion in her voice caused a stir. Men exchanged worried looks and moved from foot to foot. And then the group parted to let a larger man through.

"What's this, then?" He shoved the last of the group aside and stood before Alice. "The little girl from the abbey, eh? The baron's little kitchen drudge. What're you doing here, girl? You and the two crows. The magpie and her crows, eh?" He laughed, and a few of the others joined him.

"I had to speak to my brother," replied Alice, standing very straight, her cheeks burning.

"Did you now? About what, then?"

Alice was silent. Tom moved to stand beside her. "The old lady had a vision, Jem," said a short, squint-eyed man in the crowd. "Says there's going to be a disaster tonight."

"Eh?" Jem leaned forward and peered at them. "Which old lady?" he asked. "Which old crow?"

Rosalind longed to throw back her veil and command him to

hold his tongue. But she knew that impulse was both foolish and, perhaps, dangerous. She shrank back a little.

Mrs. MacCrory stiffened as his liquor-soaked breath engulfed her. She raised her chin, fixed him with a piercing blue eye, and began to speak.

Her voice was compelling and musical. It rose and fell so lilt-ingly Rosalind found her head nodding with the cadence. Though she couldn't understand a word, she got emotions—warning, sadness, fear, hope. Watching the faces around her, she saw the village men, and Alice too, enthralled. Those men from outside the village were silenced, but uncomprehending. Rosalind caught a movement in the corner of her eye, and saw two village men slip out of the house and into the night.

"Enough!" roared Jem at last. "Enough of this gabble. What the hell is she saying? Is she some kind of frenchie or eyetalian?"

"Scots," said the squint-eyed man, who looked much less smug than before. Indeed, he had gone quite pale, as had many of the villagers.

Jem glared at him. "Scotsmen speak our lingo as well as you rabble. Had a Scot in my regiment. Is this some kind of trick?" He gazed around the room, and men quailed before him· No one dared answer. "Well?"

The silence was broken by the entrance of another Londoner. "What's up?" he said. "It's time to get moving."

The tension stretched a moment longer, then broke as Jem growled and pushed his way toward the door. "Get back to your kitchens," he said to Alice over his shoulder. "And stay out of things that ain't your business."

There was a collective sigh when he went out. A few others followed, but most of the men milled about nervously, talking in whispers together.

"You won't go, Tom," murmured Alice. "Please."

Her brother's face was creased in thought. "I have to go," he concluded finally. "They'll be after any as doesn't. But I can hang back, ready to run for it." He looked at Mrs. MacCrory, then at Alice. "We can all of us stay back."

There were nods all about the room, and relieved expressions.

"Be careful," said Alice. "And will you...tell Eddie, too?"

Tom grinned. "Aye. I'll tell him. If he shows up." Tom looked at another man. "Maybe there's a reason Eddie and George took sick just tonight." The other nodded.

Rosalind leaned forward and whispered in Alice's ear.

"Oh, Tom," she said as he started out. "Have you seen the young lady from the abbey? Her ladyship's sister? She's gone missing."

Rosalind watched the men's faces from behind her veil. They all looked simply startled, and perhaps a little concerned. There were no guilty glances or triumphant grins.

Tom shook his head, looked around for confirmation, and shook it again. "Missing is she?" he repeated.

"What about...what about Mrs. MacCrory's cousin? The one who came to the wedding? Have you seen him?"

Tom eyed her. "We still haven't settled that little puzzle, my girl."

"He gone missing, too?" asked a man behind Tom. "Mebbe they've run off together."

This raised a laugh. Another added, "Eddie Forbes'll be glad to hear it," and got a chuckle. Tom frowned. But a low call from outside put a stop to conversation, and one by one the men filed silently out, grins gone from their faces. In five minutes, the women were alone in an empty room.

Alice let out a huge sigh and sank into a chair. Mrs. MacCrory took another. She looked tired.

"Do you think we convinced them?" Rosalind asked quietly.

"Some of them," replied Alice. "Did you see Nat Wetherall and Sam Green go out? They won't be on the beach tonight."

Mrs. MacCrory said something.

"Maybe," answered Alice. "I hope so. But how can all the village men stay off the beach? Jem and his dirty friends will make them go down." She shook her head.

The cook spoke again, and Alice brightened. "That's true."

"What?" asked Rosalind.

"Cook says that our men know how to hide on the moor, my lady," Alice said. "Better than any Londoner or any soldier, either. If they're on their guard, which they *will* be, no doubt of that, they may get away."

"I hope so," said Rosalind. Having seen the group, and its leaders, she was convinced that the village men were not chiefly at fault. Mistaken, yes, but not deserving of prison, as Jem and his friends certainly were. "I suppose we should be getting back," she added.

The others rose, and they walked together back to the trap. The first part of the short journey passed in silence, then Alice said, "I'm sorry we couldn't find out about Miss Miranda, my lady. Maybe she'll be back at the abbey by this time."

Rosalind nodded, but she didn't think it likely. Her fears, which had been pushed back by action, rushed up again. Somewhere in the darkness around them was Miranda. Rosalind couldn't even imagine her position. But she had the sense suddenly that the night was full of moving shapes and tense whispers. The smugglers, the men poised to attack them, Philip and Alan. All of the people she loved were out there; anything might happen to them. Rosalind shivered.

"Are you cold, my lady?" asked Alice. "We're nearly there."

Mrs. MacCrory added something.

"Cook says she'll make a nice pot of tea, and that you must have some supper, even though the chicken will probably taste like old leather by now."

Rosalind laughed a little despite her fears. "We'll all have some, unless Jane has eaten it. And then we will try to think if there is anything else we can do."

"Yes, my lady." Alice didn't sound hopeful, and Rosalind didn't blame her. She was afraid herself that there was nothing they could do now but wait.

TWENTY-FOUR

AT ALMOST EXACTLY THAT MOMENT, MIRANDA MANAGED TO free the lid of her crate. What had seemed like eons of painstaking work with her small piece of wood at last paid off as the top and side parted a good inch. Wiggling around in the crate, Miranda got her back against the lid and pushed with her legs. With a heart-stopping creak, it came loose and lifted.

But before she could jump out and run, voices and lantern light emerged from the darkness, and she had to crouch again and lower the lid into place. Miranda nearly shrieked in frustration as she recognized Jem's voice again. She had missed by moments! A few seconds sooner, and she would have been racing up the hill now and back to the house. It was almost more than she could bear.

Cautiously, she put her eye to the crack left between the side and top of the crate—and nearly gasped aloud when she found an expanse of blue cloth inches away. "This one's not closed proper," said a man directly above her, and rattled the lid of her crate. "Shall I nail it again?"

Miranda held her breath. It seemed to her the man must hear her heart pounding; it was like a bass drum in her ears.

"Don't bother," called someone further off. "We'll have to open them for the frogs."

There was a grunt of acceptance and a slight crunch of foot-steps. Miranda waited a moment, then dared to look out again.

No one was so near this time, but the beach—she could see now that she was on the edge of the beach—was filled with crates and men, dimly lit by several lanterns. One man, Jem she thought, was standing at the edge of the water waving a lantern back and forth above his head. The smuggling ship must be about to arrive.

She eased up the lid very slightly, and was nearly caught when a man she hadn't seen before peered out of the low bushes behind her. There were men all through the brush, she saw when she looked more closely. They seemed to be hiding, which was odd, but they certainly cut off her escape. Miranda leaned her head against the wood. Perhaps if she waited until the ship actually arrived, they would be distracted and she could escape.

"Did you see the pony trap?" Alan Creighton whispered to Philip on the hill above the smugglers' beach.

"Yes. I don't understand it." They could not see each other's faces in the darkness, but Alan could hear the worry in his cousin's voice. "You don't suppose there's something wrong at home?"

"They wouldn't go into the village tonight. Who was it? Could you see?"

"It looked like some of the servants. The cook."

Alan gripped his arm painfully. "Warning them?"

"They knew nothing about it. I would wager anything that Forbes is trustworthy. He might have told them any time this past week."

"But if they overheard?"

"We have been so careful," objected Philip.

There was a silence. "I don't like it," said Alan then, "but we can't call it off. If they're ready for us, we shall just have to fight the harder. Waiting might let them escape altogether."

"If they're there at all," replied Philip with sudden pessimism.

"They have to signal their ship, one way or another." Alan gripped his arm again. "Time," he said. "We'll meet below."

Philip returned his grip, and they separated to lead the two prongs of the attack on the beach.

Two lines of men crept through the darkness, cupping the narrow beach at the end of the small valley between them. They moved slowly, sliding each foot to keep from making noise, pausing on signal when their leaders hit a rough patch. Below, a small coasting vessel approached the shore, a swinging lantern answering the one Jem held, and lowered a boat over the side. Stealthily, two crew members rowed it into the surf. Three landsmen went into the water to meet it and help pull it in. Others moved toward the crates.

When Alan reached his position on the hill just above the beach, he gave the man directly behind him the prearranged hand signal and waited while it was passed along the whole line. His side was in place. He would give Philip another few minutes, then go in. He watched as a group of men unloaded several boxes from the long boat, then went to bend over the first crate below and examine its contents. After a moment, they stepped back and refastened the cover. It was heaved into the boat as they moved to a second. Alan shifted slightly. He wanted to hit before too much had been loaded. Philip must be ready.

Alan took a breath and raised his pistol. Pointing it straight up in the air, he cocked and fired. The report boomed from one side of the narrow canyon to the other, freezing the smugglers for an instant while Alan's group cast themselves, shouting and firing once in the air, down the slope. He heard similar sounds from the opposite side, and grinned with relief.

The men on the beach dropped behind the crates there, and two or three pulled pistols from their coats. They fired, not in the air. "Take cover," cried Alan in his battlefield voice. "We have them. Close in slowly." He crouched behind a bush and crawled from it to another further ahead.

The two men from the ship broke from cover and ran to shove their long boat into the water. A shot rang out and hit one of them, but then they were out of the circle of lantern light and safely hidden by the waves. The boat moved slowly out to sea and out of range. At the same moment, someone on shore recovered his wits and all the lanterns were doused.

"Don't move," called Alan. "Let your eyes grow used to the darkness. They can't see any better than we can."

He gave them a moment, then shouted again. "Identify the man next to you. Keep close, and move forward."

A shot whined past his ear, and he ducked and moved left. "Bill?" he whispered.

"Yes, sir," murmured the man next in line.

"Is Dick behind you?"

"Yes, sir."

"Good. Let's go."

They moved. There was a half-moon obscured by racing clouds, and they could see well enough to stay together and make certain no one ran past them. They worked their way slowly down the valley, an occasional shot passing harmlessly over their heads. Once, Alan thought he heard someone move in a thicket to the right· But then a moor bird cried a sleepy protest, and he went on.

Soon, his men formed a half circle centering on the beach. They could see only a scattering of shadows where the crates rested, but they could hear the smugglers arguing with one another, though not the precise words they used.

Miranda, from her closer vantage, didn't miss a word. "Sniveling cowards," Jem was saying. "Bloody deserters. Where are they?"

"Slipped off into the bushes," answered one of his mates. "Reckon they got away."

"I'll kill them," promised Jem. "Every blasted one."

"Don't look like you'll get the chance," was the response. "Huh. That old woman was right."

"Shut your trap," ordered Jem savagely. "She set us up. Any fool can see that. I'll kill her, too. I'll kill them all!"

"You'll have to get through these fellers first," said the other. "And they don't seem inclined to give way."

Jem roared with rage and stood up. "Come on out, ye cowards. Sodding 'cisers. Boot lickers. Step out here and fight like men!"

A shot whizzed past his ear, and he ducked again.

"Hold your fire," Alan cried from the other side. Miranda, in her crate, felt a thrill of hope and excitement. She had heard only voices before, and seen the smugglers take cover. Now she understood.

"Drop your weapons and come out," continued Alan, "and you won't be harmed."

"No, only transported," muttered a man near Miranda.

"We don't wish to fire on you," called Alan. "But you are outnumbered, and under arrest. Throw down your guns."

Jem cursed, and shot his pistol in the direction of the voice. For a long moment, Miranda held her breath in fear.

"It's no good," Alan called then from a slightly different position, and she breathed again. "We have you. You can't escape."

"I'll kill *you* anyway," shouted Jem, and fired again. The men around him on the beach murmured and shifted about. They had no heart for a pitched battle.

"Most unlikely," replied Alan, from much closer, Miranda thought. She heard Jem move from behind one crate, along the sand, to crouch behind hers, the closest to the bushes. When he cocked his pistol again, it was inches from her ear. She thought she could hear him breathing, and she froze to utter stillness.

Two of the smugglers broke from cover and ran toward the brush at the other end of the beach. Dark figures rose to grapple with them and bring them down. For a moment, there were stifled cries, then silence again.

"Give it up, Jem," called Alan. Miranda thought he must be within arm's length.

Miranda felt Jem shift against the side of the crate. And to her horror, she heard movements in the bushes on the other side. Alan was *there*. He did not realize Jem had come so close; he was trying to circle around and surprise him. Alan moved again, closer, and it was obvious Jem heard as well, for he shifted upward, ready to stand and spring. If Alan spoke again, the smuggler's aim would be assured.

Another man lost his nerve and ran. He was captured by those on the right side of the beach.

"Another down," said Alan. His voice was just on the far side of the crate. "You're losing…"

As Jem moved, so did Miranda. The buttons of his coat clattered on the crate as he sprang erect, and the wooden lid rattled as Miranda shoved it straight up as hard as she could.

The lid hit something with a crack, and Jem's pistol went off. In the next moment Jem and Alan Creighton were wrestling across the now-open box.

Miranda crouched again, heart pounding, and her hand encountered the small piece of wood she had used to pry off the lid. Without pausing to think, she picked it up and jammed it with all her strength into Jem's dark waistcoat.

Jem cried out, and twisted to try to see his new attacker. Alan quickly landed a blow to the temple that knocked the smuggler out cold.

The beach erupted in chaos. The men Alan had gathered rushed to support his effort, and those remaining on the beach scattered in hopes of escape. The two factions met at the verge of the bushes and dissolved into struggling knots. But the smugglers were far outnumbered, and within minutes, they were all taken.

Alan took no part in this. As soon as Jem had fallen, he had swept Miranda into his arms, lifting her from the crate and holding her close against his chest. He did not even notice when Philip began directing the consolidation of the prisoners. "Are you all right?" he demanded. "Have they hurt you?" He kissed her brow, her cheeks, then her lips, hard.

It was some time before she could answer, breathlessly, "They didn't know I was there. I hid."

Two men came for Jem, dragging him over to the other bound smugglers. Neither Alan nor Miranda noticed.

"Hid?" echoed Alan, and she explained what had happened. His grip about her waist tightened as she spoke. He felt he could never let her go. "You are never *ever* to do such a thing again," he commanded when she had finished.

"But I didn't *do* anything," she replied. "It was the merest accident that I…"

"Never," he repeated. "I shan't permit it."

Miranda looked up at him, quite comfortable in the tight grip of his arms. "You won't always be there to prevent me," she suggested saucily.

"Yes, I will," he assured her. "Always!" And he bent to kiss her again.

Behind them, Philip observed for a doubtful moment, then started the transport of the prisoners to the wagon they had waiting.

TWENTY-FIVE

AND SO, AT LAST, I COME TO THE FINAL CHAPTER OF MY VERY own adventure, just as I have set it down here. My journal is nearly as long as a novel now, but it is not at all like the one I expected to write. I have the ruined towers and the wild cliffs, but they are peopled by characters who now seem far more sensible and likable than any I encountered in *The Black Abbott* or the other tales I read. Funnier, too. How I wish I might have seen Rosalind in Mrs. MacCrory's old hat, helping her prophesy in the village alehouse. Of course, *she* is desolate she didn't see me dancing with Alice at the wedding. Alan and Philip think us half demented when we look at one another and suddenly begin to giggle. We are not telling them about our penchant for disguise. At least, not yet.

Everything is settled between Alan and me. He left today to look over his house and decide what work must be done before he is married. I miss him dreadfully, but we will meet again in London soon, where I shall have my Season and all the parties and plays I have always longed for. Shakespeare, too! Alan has promised to show me whatever I want to see! I have not finished the list I am making. What will he say when he receives it, I wonder?

And then, at the end of the Season, we shall be married and go to live in Hertfordshire. Rosalind approves, and she is writing Mama. Just think, if I *had* gone to Rome, I never would have met Alan or helped capture a band of smugglers. I shall never complain again when I cannot go just where I please, for I see now that adventures are not found where you expect them. Just the opposite. And they are much more nasty and unpleasant than I realized, and far more wonderful.

Alan is the sort of man who has adventures. Perhaps that is what I love most about him. He says he will *never* have another, but

I don't believe him. It's not so easy to change. Besides, how very flat life would be without an adventure—just a small one!—now and then. I'm sure Alan will come to agree, once he has recovered a little from seeing the lid pop off that crate.

ONE

THREE DAYS AFTER HE INHERITED THE TITLE DUKE OF Tereford, James Cantrell set off to visit the ducal townhouse just off London's Berkeley Square. He walked from his rooms, as the distance was short and the April day pleasant. He hoped to make this first encounter cordially brief and be off riding before the sunlight faded.

He had just entered the square when a shouted greeting turned his head. Henry Deeping was approaching, an unknown young man beside him.

"Have you met my friend Cantrell?" Henry asked his companion when they reached James. "Sorry—Tereford, I should say. He's just become a duke. Stephan Kandler, meet the newest peer of the realm as well as the handsomest man in London."

As they exchanged bows, James silently cursed whatever idiot had saddled him with that label. He'd inherited his powerful frame, black hair, and blue eyes from his father. It was nothing to do with him. "That's nonsense," he said.

"Yes, your grace." Henry's teasing tone had changed recently. It held the slightest trace of envy.

James had heard it from others since he'd come into his inheritance. His cronies were young men who shared his interest in

sport, met while boxing or fencing, on the hunting field, or perhaps clipping a wafer at Manton's shooting gallery, where Henry
Deeping had an uncanny ability. They were generally not plump
in the pocket. Some lived on allowances from their fathers and
would inherit as James had; others would have a moderate income
all their lives. All of them preferred vigorous activity to smoky
gaming hells or drunken revels.

They'd been more or less equals. But now circumstances had
pulled James away, into the peerage and wealth, and he was feeling
the distance. One old man's death, and his life was changed. Which
was particularly hard with Henry. They'd known each since they
were uneasy twelve-year-olds arriving at school.

"We're headed over to Manton's if you'd care to come," Henry
said. He sounded repentant.

"I can't just now," James replied. He didn't want to mention
that he was headed for Tereford House. It was just another measure of the distance from Henry. He saw that Henry noticed the
vagueness of his reply.

"Another time perhaps," said Henry's companion in a Germanic
accent.

James gave a noncommittal reply, wondering where Henry had
met the fellow. His friend was considering the diplomatic corps as
a means to make his way in the world. Perhaps this Kandler had
something to do with that.

They separated. James walked across the square and into the
narrow street containing Tereford House.

The massive stone building, of no particular architectural
distinction, loomed over the cobbles. Its walls showed signs of
neglect, and the windows on the upper floors were all shuttered.
There was no funerary hatchment above the door. Owing to
the eccentricities of his great uncle, the recently deceased sixth
duke, James had never been inside. His every approach had been
rebuffed.

He walked up to the door and plied the tarnished knocker. When that brought no response, he rapped on the door with the knob of his cane. He had sent word ahead, of course, and had expected a better reception than this. At last the door opened, and he strolled inside—to be immediately assailed by a wave of stale mustiness. The odor was heavy rather than sharp, but it insinuated itself into the nostrils like an unwanted guest. James suspected that it would swiftly permeate his clothes and hair. His dark brows drew together. The atmosphere in the dim entryway, with closed doors on each side and at the back next to a curving stair, was oppressive. It seemed almost threatening.

One older female servant stood before him. She dropped a curtsy. "Your grace," she said, as if the phrase was unfamiliar.

"Where is the rest of the staff?" They really ought to have lined up to receive him. He had given them a time for his visit.

"There's only me. Your grace."

"What?"

"Keys is there." She pointed to a small side table. A ring of old-fashioned keys lay on it.

James noticed a small portmanteau sitting at her feet.

She followed his eyes. "I'll be going then. Your grace." Before James could reply, she picked up the case and marched through the still open front door.

Her footsteps faded, leaving behind a dismal silence. The smell seemed to crowd closer, pressing on him. The light dimmed briefly as a carriage passed outside. James suppressed a desire to flee. He had a pleasant set of rooms in Hill Street where he had, for some years, been living a life that suited him quite well. He might own this house now, but that didn't mean he had to live here. Or perhaps he did. A duke had duties. It occurred to him that the servant might have walked off with some valuable items. He shrugged. Her bag had been too small to contain much.

He walked over to the closed door on the right and turned

the knob. The door opened a few inches and then hit some sort of obstacle. He pushed harder. It remained stuck. James had to put his shoulder to the panels and shove with the strength developed in Gentleman Jackson's boxing saloon before it gave way, with a crash of some largish object falling inside. He forced his way through but managed only one step before he was brought up short, his jaw dropping. The chamber—a well-proportioned parlor with high ceilings and elaborate moldings—was stuffed to bursting with a mad jumble of objects. Furniture of varying eras teetered in haphazard stacks—sofas, chairs, tables, cabinets. Paintings and other ornaments were pushed into every available crevice. Folds and swathes of fabric that might have been draperies or bedclothes drooped over the mass, which towered far above his head. There was no room to move. "Good God!" The stale odor was much worse here, and a scurrying sound did not bode well.

James backed out hastily. He thought of the shuttered rooms on the upper floors. Were they all…? But perhaps only this one was a mare's nest. He walked across the entryway and tried the door on the left. It concealed a larger room in the same wretched condition. His heart, which had not been precisely singing, sank. He'd assumed that his new position would require a good deal of tedious effort, but he hadn't expected chaos.

The click of footsteps approached from outside. The front door was still open, and now a fashionably dressed young lady walked through it. She was accompanied by a maid and a footman. The latter started to shut the door behind them. "Don't," commanded James. The young servant shied like a nervous horse.

"What is that smell?" the lady inquired, putting a gloved hand to her nose.

"What are you doing here?" James asked the bane of his existence.

"You mentioned that you were going to look over the house today."

"And in what way is this your concern?"

"I was so curious. There are all sorts of rumors about this place. No one has been inside for years." She went over to one of the parlor doors and peered around it. "Oh!" She crossed to look into the other side. "Good heavens!"

"Indeed."

"Well, this is going to be a great deal of work." She smiled. "You won't like that."

"You have no idea what I…" James had to stop, because he knew that she had a very good idea.

"I know more about your affairs than you do," she added.

It was nearly true. Once, it certainly had been. That admission took him back thirteen years to his first meeting with Cecelia Vainsmede. He'd been just fifteen, recently orphaned, and in the midst of a blazing row with his new trustee. Blazing on his side, at any rate. Nigel Vainsmede had been pained and evasive and clearly just wishing he'd go away. They'd fallen into one of their infuriating bouts of pushing in and fending off, insisting and eluding. James had understood by that time that his trustee might agree to a point simply to be rid of him, but he would never carry through with any action. Vainsmede would forget—willfully, it seemed to James. Insultingly.

And then a small blonde girl had marched into her father's library and ordered them to stop at once. Even at nine years old, Cecelia had been a determined character with a glare far beyond her years. James had been surprised into silence. Vainsmede had actually looked grateful. And on that day they had established the routine that allowed them to function for the next ten years—speaking to each other only through Cecelia. James would approach her with, "Please tell your father." And she would manage the matter, whatever it was. James didn't have to plead, which he hated, and Nigel Vainsmede didn't have to do anything at all, which was his main hope in life as far as James could tell.

James and Cecelia had worked together all through their youth. Cecelia was not a friend, and not family, but some indefinable other sort of close connection. And she did know a great deal about him. More than he knew about her. Although he had observed, along with the rest of the *haut ton*, that she had grown up to be a very pretty young lady. Today, in a walking dress of sprig muslin and a straw bonnet decorated with matching blue ribbons, she was lithely lovely. Her hair was less golden than it had been at nine but far better cut. She had the face of a renaissance Madonna except for the rather too lush lips. And her luminous blue eyes missed very little, as he had cause to know. Not that any of this was relevant at the moment. "Your father has not been my trustee for three years," James pointed out.

"And you have done nothing much since then."

He would have denied it, but what did it matter? Instead he said, "I never could understand why my father appointed *your* father as my trustee."

"It was odd," she agreed.

"They were just barely friends, I would say."

"Hardly that," she replied. "Papa was astonished when he heard."

"As was I." James remembered the bewildered outrage of his fifteen-year-old self when told that he would be under the thumb of a stranger until he reached the age of twenty-five. "And, begging your pardon, but your father is hardly a pattern card of wisdom."

"No. He is indolent and self-centered. Almost as much as you are."

"Why Miss Vainsmede!" He rarely called her that. They had dropped formalities and begun using first names when she was twelve. "I am not the least indolent."

She hid a smile. "Only if you count various forms of sport. Which I do not. I have thought about the trusteeship, however. From what I've learned of your father—I did not know him of course—I think he preferred to be in charge."

A crack of laughter escaped James. "Preferred! An extreme understatement. He had the soul of an autocrat and the temper of a frustrated tyrant."

She frowned at him. "Yes. Well. Having heard something of that, I came to the conclusion that your father chose mine because he was confident Papa would do nothing in particular."

"What?"

"I think that your father disliked the idea of not being…present to oversee your upbringing, and he couldn't bear the idea of anyone *doing* anything about that."

James frowned as he worked through this convoluted sentence.

"And so he chose my father because he was confident Papa wouldn't…bestir himself and try to make changes in the arrangements."

Surprise kept him silent for a long moment. "You know, that is the best theory I have heard. It might even be right."

"You needn't sound so astonished," Cecelia replied. "I often have quite good ideas."

"What a crack-brained notion!"

"I beg your pardon?"

"My father's, not yours." James shook his head. "You think he drove me nearly to distraction just to fend off change?"

"If he had lived…" she began.

"Oh, that would have been far worse. A never-ending battle of wills."

"You don't know that. I was often annoyed with my father when I was younger, but we get along well now."

"Because he lets you be as scandalous as you please, Cecilia."

"Oh, nonsense."

James raised one dark brow.

"I *wish* I could learn to do that," exclaimed his pretty visitor. "You are said to have the most killing sneer in the *ton*, you know."

He was not going to tell her that he had spent much of a summer before the mirror when he was sixteen perfecting the gesture.

"And it was *not* scandalous for me to attend one ball without a chaperone. I was surrounded by friends and acquaintances. What could happen to me in such a crowd?" She shook her head. "At any rate, I am quite on the shelf at twenty-two. So it doesn't matter."

"Don't be stupid." James knew, from the laments of young gentlemen acquaintances, that Cecelia had refused several offers. She was anything but "on the shelf."

"I am never stupid," she replied coldly.

He was about to make an acid retort when he recalled that Cecelia was a positive glutton for work. She'd also learned a great deal about estate management and business as her father pushed tasks off on her, his only offspring. She'd come to manage much of Vainsmede's affairs as well as the trust. Indeed, she'd taken to it as James never had. He thought of the challenge confronting him. Could he cajole her into taking some of it on?

She'd gone to open the door at the rear of the entryway. "There is just barely room to edge along the hall here," she said. "Why would anyone keep all these newspapers? There must be years of them. Do you suppose the whole house is like this?"

"I have a sinking feeling that it may be worse. The sole servant ran off as if she was conscious of her failure."

"One servant couldn't care for such a large house even if it hadn't been…"

"A rubbish collection? I think Uncle Percival must have actually been mad. People called him eccentric, but this is…" James peered down the cluttered hallway. "No wonder he refused all my visits."

"Did you try to visit him?" Cecelia asked.

"Of course."

"Huh."

"Is that so surprising?" asked James.

"Well, yes, because you don't care for anyone but yourself."

"Don't start up this old refrain."

"It's the truth."

"More a matter of opinion and definition," James replied.

She waved this aside. "You will have to do better now that you are the head of your family."

"A meaningless label. I shall have to bring some order." He grimaced at the stacks of newspapers. "But no more than that."

"A great deal more," said Cecelia. "You have a duty…"

"As Uncle Percival did?" James gestured at their surroundings.

"His failure is all the more reason for you to shoulder your responsibilities."

"I don't think so."

Cecelia put her hands on her hips, just as she had done at nine years old. "Under our system the bulk of the money and all of the property in the great families passes to one man, in this case you. You are obliged to manage it for good of the whole." She suddenly looked doubtful. "If there is any money."

"There is," he replied. This had been a continual sore point during the years of the trust. And after, in fact. His father had not left a fortune. "Quite a bit of it, seemingly. I had a visit from a rather sour banker. Uncle Percival was a miser as well as a…" James gestured at the mess. "A connoisseur of detritus. But if you think I will tolerate the whining of indigent relatives, you are deluded." He had made do when he was far from wealthy. Others could follow suit.

"You must take care of your people."

She was interrupted by a rustle of newsprint. "I daresay there are rats," James said.

"Do you think to frighten me? You never could."

This was true. And he had really tried a few times in his youth.

"I am consumed by morbid curiosity," Cecelia added as she slipped down the hall. James followed. Her attendants came straggling after, the maid looking uneasy at the thought of rodents.

They found other rooms as jumbled as the first two. Indeed, the muddle seemed to worsen toward the rear of the house. "Is that a spinning wheel?" Cecelia exclaimed at one point. "Why would a duke want such a thing?"

"It appears he was unable to resist acquiring any object that he came across," replied James.

"But where would he come across a spinning wheel?"

"In a tenant's cottage?"

"Do you suppose he bought it from them?"

"I have no idea." James pushed aside a hanging swag of cloth. Dust billowed out and set them all coughing. He stifled a curse.

At last they came into what might have been a library. James thought he could see bookshelves behind the piles of refuse. There was a desk, he realized, with a chair pulled up to it. He hadn't noticed at first because it was buried under mountains of documents. At one side sat a large wicker basket brimming with correspondence.

Cecelia picked up a sheaf of pages from the desk, glanced over it, and set it down again. She rummaged in the basket. "These are all letters," she said.

"Wonderful."

"May I?"

James gestured his permission, and she opened one from the top. "Oh, this is bad. Your cousin Elvira needs help."

"I have no knowledge of a cousin Elvira."

"Oh, I suppose she must have been your Uncle Percival's cousin. She sounds rather desperate."

"Well, that is the point of a begging letter, is it not? The effect is diminished if one doesn't sound desperate."

"Yes, but James…"

"My God, do you suppose they're all like that?" The basket was as long as his arm and nearly as deep. It was mounded with correspondence.

Cecelia dug deeper. "They all seem to be personal letters. Just thrown in here. I suppose they go back for months."

"Years," James guessed. Dust lay over them, as it did everything here.

"You must read them."

"I don't think so. For once I approve of Uncle Percival's methods. I would say throw them in the fire, if lighting a fire in this place wasn't an act of madness."

"Have you no family feeling?"

"None. You read them, if you're so interested."

She shuffled through the upper layer. "Here's one from your grandmother."

"Which one?"

"Lady Wilton."

"Oh no."

Cecelia opened the sheet and read. "She seems to have misplaced an earl."

"What?"

"A long lost heir has gone missing."

"Who? No, never mind. I don't care." The enormity of the task facing him descended on James, looming like the piles of objects leaning over his head. He looked up. One wrong move, and all that would fall about his ears. He wanted none of it.

A flicker of movement diverted him. A rat had emerged from a crevice between a gilded chair leg and a hideous outsized vase. The creature stared at him, insolent, seeming to know that it was well out of reach. "Wonderful," murmured James.

Cecelia looked up. "What?"

He started to point out the animal, to make her jump, then bit back the words as an idea recurred. He, and her father, had taken advantage of her energetic capabilities over the years. He knew it. He was fairly certain she knew it. Her father had probably never noticed. But Cecelia hadn't minded. She'd said once that the things she'd learned and done had given her a more interesting life than most young ladies were allowed. Might his current plight not intrigue her? So instead of mentioning the rodent, he offered his most charming smile. "Perhaps you would like to have that basket," he suggested. "It must be full of compelling stories."

Her blue eyes glinted as if she understood exactly what he was up to. "No, James. This mare's nest is all yours. I think, actually, that you deserve it."

"How can you say so?"

"It is like those old Greek stories, where the thing one tries hardest to avoid fatefully descends."

"Thing?" said James, gazing at the looming piles of *things*.

"You loathe organizational tasks. And this one is monumental."

"You have always been the most annoying girl," said James.

"Oh, I shall enjoy watching you dig out." Cecelia turned away. "My curiosity is satisfied. I'll be on my way."

"It isn't like you to avoid work."

She looked over her shoulder at him. "*Your* work. And as you've pointed out our...collaboration ended three years ago. We will call this visit a final farewell to those days."

She edged her way out, leaving James in his wreck of an inheritance. He was conscious of a sharp pang of regret. He put it down to resentment over her refusal to help him.

ABOUT THE AUTHOR

Jane Ashford discovered Georgette Heyer in junior high school and was captivated by the glittering world and witty language of Regency England. That delight was part of what led her to study English literature and travel widely. Her books have been published all over Europe as well as in the United States. Jane was nominated for a Career Achievement Award by *RT Book Reviews*. Born in Ohio, she is now somewhat nomadic. Find her on the web at janeashford.com and on Facebook at facebook.com/JaneAshfordWriter, where you can sign up for her monthly newsletter.